GUNSLINGER

Connie Mason

LEISURE BOOKS   NEW YORK CITY

A LEISURE BOOK®

June 1999

Published by

Dorchester Publishing Co., Inc.
276 Fifth Avenue
New York, NY 10001

ISBN 0-8439-4532-X

GUNSLINGER

Chapter One

He blew into Trouble Creek on a raw April wind, beneath a sky that had a sullen, almost bruised look. The tails of his gray duster flapped behind him in the breeze like giant bat wings, revealing long, muscled legs clad in buckskin trousers mellowed to the color of butternut. A fine layer of trail dust covered his hat and coated his face, making the deeply grooved squint lines around his eyes more pronounced. The man rode tall in the saddle; one could see his tension in the set of his broad shoulders and the stiffness of his spine.

He reined his mustang down Trouble Creek's main street, his dark eyes narrowed into wary slits. Though he looked neither right nor left, his inscrutable gaze remained watchful. Nothing escaped his notice. Not the ragtag collection of buildings he remembered from his youth nor the two new saloons that hadn't been there eight years ago when he'd returned to make peace with his father.

A rueful smile touched his full lips when he noted that Miss Milly's whorehouse was still the grandest place on the town's main street. A deep dimple appeared in his right cheek with his smile. It was totally unexpected in his rough-hewn dark face, which spoke eloquently of his Indian heritage.

The rider drew rein in front of the Devil's Den saloon, dismounted, looped his reins around the hitching post and stretched his weary muscles. His throat felt dry as a desert and he was in desperate need of something potent enough to cut the dust clogging his throat.

"Desperado Jones!"

The stranger spit out a curse. Was there nowhere in this part of the world he could travel without being recognized? But what did he expect? His reputation as a fast gun had spread throughout Texas and the West like wildfire. Few suspected that his reputation alone was usually enough to deter all but the most determined men from challenging him. His mean-as-hell reputation had kept him from being killed. His reluctance to kill in cold blood had kept him out of jail, except for minor infringements, throughout his illustrious career as a hired gun. As long as he continued to walk that thin line between legal and illegal, the law couldn't touch him.

But every now and then, like today, a trigger-happy young fool challenged him, forcing him to defend himself. Desperado Jones had the reputation of a lightning draw, so fast, in fact, that no man had ever outdrawn him. But unlike most gunslingers, Desperado Jones rarely shot to kill.

"Desperado Jones! Turn around."

Desperado glanced over his shoulder, sighing in resignation when he saw a cocky young cowboy standing several yards behind him, his legs splayed wide, the fingers of his right hand twitching over the butt of his gun, clearly eager to prove himself to his friends.

Desperado turned slowly, moving aside his duster to reveal a pair of twin Colt .45 six-shooters riding low on either hip and tied down gunman style around each thigh with a leather thong. "I hear you," he answered in a low, hoarse rasp that made the onlookers gathered on the wooden sidewalks step backward.

"I know who you are and I'm gonna prove I'm a faster draw than you," the young man boasted. "Draw whenever you're ready."

"You don't have to do this," Desperado said in a creepy whisper he'd affected to frighten his challengers.

The young man blanched but held his ground, sending Desperado a narrow-eyed look that reminded him of a shifty rattlesnake he'd once encountered. "Tate Talbot doesn't back down."

Desperado pegged Tate Talbot for a smart-ass young fool who thought himself invincible. He needed a lesson and Desperado decided he was just the man to give it to him.

"Go ahead, Talbot, draw," Desperado rasped as he assumed the stance of a seasoned gunfighter. Immediately a dozen or more people flattened themselves against the weatherbeaten businesses lining the street.

Talbot looked uncertain for a moment, then his fingers unflexed and dove for his gun. He was fast, but Desperado was faster. His six-shooter appeared in his hand as if by magic, already belching smoke before Talbot's gun had cleared his holster. The shot reverberated loudly in the unnatural silence, followed by a scream as Talbot's gun flew out of his hand.

"You broke my hand!" Talbot cried, cradling his injured hand against his chest. "That's my gun hand. You'll pay for this, Desperado Jones. Mark my words."

Desperado watched dispassionately as Talbot's friends led him away, presumably to the doctor's office. He shook his head in disgust. It was times like this that made him regret taking up the profession that had earned him the reputation of a fast gun. To Desperado's knowledge, he *was* the fastest gun in Texas, and maybe in the entire West. Most of the time his reputation alone made the jobs he undertook simple. But squaring off for a shootout every time some overzealous kid with a fast gun and a mean streak challenged him was becoming monotonous. There were too many saddle bums and would-be gunmen out there hoping to make a name for themselves by outdrawing Desperado Jones.

Desperado started toward the saloon, needing that drink more than ever after the gunplay just now. He shouldn't have come to Trouble Creek in the first place, he grumbled to himself. He hadn't been back in eight years and had no reason to return now. When a twist of fate had brought him close to Trouble Creek, he'd decided to satisfy his curiosity and visit the town he hadn't seen since he'd returned to make peace with his father and attended his funeral instead. Cursing his damn curiosity, Desperado vowed that this was the last time he'd ever set foot in Trouble Creek.

"Mr. Desperado Jones?"

Tired of messing around with young fools bent on making a name for themselves, Desperado crouched low and whipped around, his gun appearing in his hand faster than a snake can strike. The breath went out of him in a loud whoosh and he slapped his gun back in his holster when he realized his name had come from the lips of a female.

And what a female! She was tall, blonde and slim; her long legs were encased in skin-tight Levi's that cupped her bottom like loving hands. Her Stetson wasn't nearly as battered as his and did little to hide her startling green eyes and flawless complexion.

His eyes settled on her unfettered breasts, their fullness clearly visible beneath her buckskin jacket and silk shirt. His eyes narrowed in surprise when he noted that she was packing guns and looked as if she knew how to use them. He heard her take in a noisy breath, then expel it with a loud sigh, and he suspected he had frightened her. It would serve her right, he thought. She shouldn't have come up on him like that without warning. She could have gotten herself killed.

"Yeah, I'm Desperado Jones. What can I do for

you?" He knew what he'd like to do and wondered if the lady would object. He knew instinctively that she would. Half-breed Apache Indians weren't all that popular in these parts.

"I wondered if you knew you'd just made an enemy," the woman said. "The man you just shot is Tate Talbot. His father is Calvin Talbot, a land speculator and mayor of Trouble Creek. He's also a land-grabbing, money-hungry scoundrel who uses underhanded, often illegal, methods to purchase valuable land holdings from unsuspecting ranchers. And his son," she said bitterly, "is a despicable bas . . . Well, let's just leave it at that."

"You don't say," Desperado muttered, more interested in the woman's attributes than her words. "Why are you telling me this, Miss . . ."

"Sommers, Chloe Sommers. I own the Ralston spread north of town."

Desperado went still. His face took on a hard-edged remoteness and his dark eyes glittered dangerously. Those were the only outward signs that he recognized the name. His mind went back in time to the day his widowed father brought home a new wife. Norie Sommers had hated twelve-year-old Logan Ralston on sight. Not only did she despise his dark skin but she hated it that he was Ted Ralston's son from his union with Dancing Star, an Apache woman Ted had married despite the disapproval of his friends and neighbors.

Desperado remembered his mother as a gentle, loving woman who adored her husband and lavished special attention upon her son. Her death had been a terrible blow to both young Logan and his father. For a time they had managed alone, until Ted Ralston grew lonely and began courting a widow visiting from another city. They had married after a brief courtship.

Young Logan had always known his stepmother didn't want him around. But it wasn't until Norie became pregnant that he learned the depth of her hatred.

Chloe Sommers tipped her head up and searched Desperado's face, puzzled by his sudden stillness. His fierce expression and dark features betrayed his Indian heritage. His face was all sharp angles, jutting cheekbones and black, slanting eyebrows. His mouth was wide, with a generous lower lip. His face was set in cold, sardonic lines that destroyed any hint of gentleness. There was an innate pride in his bearing, handed down, she supposed, from his proud forebears, there for all to see . . . and to fear. But it was Desperado's eyes that intrigued Chloe. A person could fall into those fathomless black depths and become lost. She bit her lip, wondering where that thought had come from. But Chloe wasn't about to let this formidable gunslinger frighten her. She needed him too badly.

Desperado said something, bringing Chloe's wandering attention back. "What did you say?"

"I said I'm not afraid of the Talbots."

"I didn't think you were," Chloe said, eyeing him with renewed interest. "Would you happen to be looking for a job, Mr. Jones? I'm looking to hire a gunman. I'm taking my herd to the railhead at Dodge soon and I need a gunman to make sure my beeves arrive safely. If I fail, my ranch will be sold

15

to pay the back taxes, leaving the way open for Calvin Talbot to gobble up my holdings, and I can't let that happen."

One eyebrow arched sardonically as he studied her with unabashed sexual speculation. "Are you running the ranch by yourself?"

Chloe's chin lifted. "For the past two years, I have. My stepfather left the ranch to my mother. We ran it together until she died." She searched his face, as if looking for something familiar. "Are you from around here, Mr. Jones?"

"Just passing through," Desperado rasped. His next sentence came unbidden to his tongue. "Did your stepfather die without heirs?"

Chloe stared into the distance, as if trying to recall something from her memory. "There was a son, Logan Ralston, but he died a long time ago. I never knew him because I didn't arrive at the ranch until after he'd left. All I recall is that my stepfather was sad a very long time after his death." She blinked away the memory. "Let's get back to the question at hand. About that job, Mr. Jones. I need your gun and I'm willing to pay for it."

Desperado knew he had acquired the reputation of being a ruthless killer. He had worked hard to achieve that reputation; it was the way he wanted to be seen by the world. He'd been hired countless times to do exactly what Chloe Sommers had asked of him, but never by a woman. Having a woman boss didn't appeal to him. Never had, never would.

"Sorry, Miss Sommers," Desperado drawled. "I don't work for women. They're too flighty and unpredictable."

"You're turning me down? I can pay, if that's what you're worried about."

"I'm not interested in your money."

"Why you . . . you gunslinging half-breed!" Chloe spit out. "I don't need you anyway. There must be dozens of men in Trouble Creek willing to work for a woman." With a toss of her head that nearly dislodged her hat, she whirled on her heel and strode off.

Desperado watched her walk away, his first genuine smile in a long time curving his lips. There was something deliciously tempting about the way a woman filled out a pair of Levi's and a silk shirt, especially a tall, slim woman with swaying hips and unfettered breasts. He stared at her bottom, thinking he had never seen one he liked as much. It was narrow, high and round, exactly the way he liked women's bottoms. He licked his lips.

As he walked to the saloon, Desperado's thoughts turned inward, traveling back many years in time, to those days before he'd been sent away. He hadn't known Chloe then for she hadn't arrived to join her mother at the ranch until after his departure. But whether she knew it or not, Chloe was as much to blame as her mother for his being sent away from the only home he'd ever known and a father he loved. And all because Norie Sommers Ralston was pregnant and couldn't abide the sight of her half-breed stepson. Norie had convinced Ted that having a savage around during her pregnancy would likely cause her to miscarry, so twelve-year-old Logan had been sent to stay with an elderly aunt in San Antonio until after Norie's child was born.

Young as he was, Logan knew Norie hated him because his father loved him, and that she wanted him out of her life forever. He also knew that Ted wouldn't have sent him away had he known his son would never return.

Desperado had vowed to forget the three years of banishment forced upon him by Norie, but he'd never quite succeeded. After Norie lost the child she carried, Logan waited expectantly for his father to send for him. But all he'd gotten was a visit from Ted Ralston. His father had explained that Norie had conceived again and that he had to stay with his aunt indefinitely because of his wife's frail health.

He also explained that Norie's small daughter from her previous marriage had arrived to live at the ranch and that Norie feared Logan would be a bad influence on the child. All this his father had told him in a sad voice that clearly expressed his grief over the situation. He'd promised Logan that his banishment wouldn't last forever. Famous last words, Desperado thought as he pushed open the swinging doors of the saloon and stepped inside.

Conversation came to a halt as Desperado ambled through the swinging doors of the Devil's Den. He paid little heed to the sudden quiet as he bellied up to the bar and ordered a bottle of whiskey. The bartender set a bottle and glass in front of him and scooted away, as if he expected Desperado to shoot him instead of paying him. Cocking one foot on the railing, Desperado gazed into the mirror behind the bar. It was a habit he'd established long ago. It allowed him to watch his back at all times. He either sat with his back to the wall and faced the door or stood in front of a mirror. The practice had kept him alive.

Desperado poured himself a whiskey, tossed it down, grimaced and poured another. It burned all the way down, unclogging his throat and slipping smoothly down his gullet to settle warmly in his stomach.

Conversation had resumed, but Desperado knew what everyone was thinking. They were wondering what he was doing in town and who had hired him. They'd be surprised to know that he didn't know himself why he'd returned to Trouble Creek. It wasn't a town one visited on a whim, or yearned to return to after one left. Yet something deep, dark and unresolved had drawn him here. And that was before he had met the gun-toting, entrancing Miss Chloe Sommers, the woman who now owned the land that by rights should be his.

He chugged down another whiskey, recalling the day he'd run away from his aunt's house. He knew the way home and intended to inform his father when he arrived that he was going to stay no matter what his stepmother said. Unfortunately he'd never reached home. His horse had stumbled into a hole and broken a leg, pinning Logan beneath him. Logan's leg had also been broken and he feared he was going to die out there on the desert. He drifted in and out of consciousness for two days before an Apache hunting party stumbled upon him.

Desperado dragged his thoughts away from that

fateful day and tossed back another whiskey, staring glumly into the mirror. Suddenly the swinging doors slammed inward and Desperado squinted against the glare of sunlight reflecting back to him in the mirror. He blinked, then blinked again, stunned to see the curvy, trouser-clad Miss Chloe Sommers push through the swinging doors. Time hung suspended as every man in the saloon ogled the feminine curves so blatantly displayed in tight, definitely unfeminine clothing. With his back to her, Desperado watched through the mirror as Chloe's long-legged stride brought her to the center of the saloon, where she paused uncertainly as if to gather her thoughts.

Chloe had never been inside a saloon before but desperation made her dare anything. After being curtly rejected by the despicable gunslinger known as Desperado Jones, she had no other choice. If she failed to get her herd to the railhead, Calvin Talbot would buy her ranch for the back taxes. And without a hired gun along on the trail drive, she hadn't a snowball's chance in hell of reaching the railhead with enough cattle left to sell.

Curling her lip in what she hoped was a mean-as-hell expression, she scanned the room and its occupants. A few of the men she knew, most she didn't. All looked disreputable. Then her gaze lit on Desperado Jones and she no longer had to pretend the mean-as-hell look; suddenly it was very real. He had his back to her, nonchalantly sipping his whiskey. Chloe knew he watched her in the mirror, and that made her even angrier.

When she had the undivided attention of everyone in the saloon, with possibly the exception of Desperado Jones, she cleared her throat and said, "I'm hiring on a gunslinger. Do any of you polecats have the guts to apply for the job?"

No one stepped forward to volunteer. Undaunted, Chloe said, "The job pays well."

Like puppets on a string, the men turned their heads to stare at Desperado, who pretended not to have heard. Boldly Chloe approached the gunslinger, intending to shame him into accepting.

"What about you, Mr. Jones? Are you interested in the job?"

With studied indifference, Desperado calmly sipped his whiskey. Chloe felt like a fool when the saloon customers, following Desperado's example, resumed their conversation and returned to the activities she had interrupted. Her face flaming, Chloe brazenly tapped Desperado on the shoulder.

Desperado turned slowly, his dark eyes kindling with desire as they slid over her curves with blatant speculation.

"I haven't changed my mind, lady. I don't work for females," he drawled in that raspy voice of his that sent shivers down her spine. "But," he added, stunning her with a dimpled smile, "I'll gladly accommodate you in any other way."

Someone in the room tittered. Then another. Until the entire room echoed with laughter. Seething with outrage and embarrassed by Desperado's brazen suggestion, Chloe flung her arm back and let it fly straight toward Desperado's bristly cheek. Desperado must have read her mind for he caught her wrist in a viselike grip before her blow connected.

"Don't ever raise your hand to me," he said in his creepy whisper.

"Or what?" Chloe challenged with false bravado. There were too many eyes upon her to back down before the ornery half-breed.

He smiled again, displaying that damnable dimple. "Or you won't like the consequences."

"Go to hell!" she shouted, wresting her wrist from his grasp and whirling on her heel.

Desperado watched her strut from the room, her sweet little bottom all taut and hard beneath her Levi's. Her bottom wasn't the only thing all taut and hard, he thought ruefully. His own trousers barely contained the rigid length of his sex and he thought about what he'd like to do to the long-legged, gun-toting little hellion who'd had the audacity to think she could slap Desperado Jones and get away with it. His stern frown was softened by the dimple in his cheek as he stifled a grin. The female wildcat didn't know with whom she was dealing, but he sure as hell would like the opportunity to show her.

Desperado picked up his bottle and glass and moved to an empty table facing the door. Jones was a realist. He knew that someday a man would come along with a gun faster than his and blow him away. But until that day arrived he was taking no chances. His mind alert for unexpected danger, Desperado allowed his thoughts to drift back to the past again.

The day the Indian hunting party had found young Logan Ralston would have probably been his last on this earth had they not stumbled upon him when they did. When one fierce brave raised his gun to end his life, Logan had closed his eyes and awaited death. The medicine bag given to him by his Indian grandfather had saved his life. One of the braves had spotted it and stopped the other from shooting. After crudely setting his broken leg, they had carried him to their village.

"Desperado Jones?"

Desperado cursed beneath his breath when he heard his name spoken, expecting another challenge. His gun appeared in his hand with lightning speed. He might have let his mind wander but his senses were well honed after years of living dangerously, of walking a thin line between life and death. The man who had addressed him didn't look dangerous, but experience had taught him that appearances could be deceiving.

"Whoa, put the gun down, Mr. Jones," the man said. He held his coat open. "As you can see, I'm unarmed."

Desperado's dark, penetrating gaze studied the man standing before him. He looked like a prosperous businessman in his dark suit, vest and pristine white shirt. There wasn't a speck of dust on either his brand-new Stetson or shiny boots. The man was neither young nor old, but somewhere in between. Desperado was slightly repelled by his nearly colorless blue eyes and guileless smile. Instinctively he knew that this man would make a formidable enemy.

"What can I do for you, mister?" Desperado asked as he shoved his six-shooter back into his holster.

"The question is, what I can do for you? My name is Calvin Talbot."

When Desperado merely stared at him, Talbot cleared his throat and said, "The man who challenged you to a shoot-out is my son."

Desperado calmly took a slim cigar from his duster pocket, lit it and blew a puff of smoke into Talbot's face. "You don't say." The way he said it, raspy and mean, usually scared all but the most determined challengers away. Which was exactly Desperado's intention. He'd avoided more than his share of gunfights that way.

"You got me all wrong, Jones," Talbot said, surprising Desperado. "The young whippersnapper deserved his comeuppance. He was getting too cocky for his own good. He'll heal and maybe learn something from the experience." He held out his hand. "No hard feelings?"

Desperado stared at the soft white hand, flicked the ash from his cigar on Talbot's shiny boots and said, "State your business, Talbot. I'm thinking of moving on. Trouble Creek has nothing to offer me."

Talbot stared at his own outstretched hand and hastily withdrew it. Desperado had no idea why he'd developed such an intense dislike for Talbot without even knowing the man, but something about Talbot rubbed him the wrong way. He thought about Chloe Sommers and what she'd said about the unscrupulous land speculator and liked him even less.

"Perhaps Trouble Creek has nothing to offer you, Jones, but I do," Talbot said. "May I sit down? I think you'll be interested in what I have to say."

Desperado took his time mulling over Talbot's words before dragging out a chair with his foot and shoving it in Talbot's direction. "Make it fast, Talbot."

Talbot sat down, scooted the chair closer to the table and leaned forward. "I need someone like you, Jones, and I'm willing to pay top dollar." He let that sink in before continuing. "When you hear my offer, you won't be able to turn it down."

Desperado studied him through eyes as cold and dark as death. People often wondered how it would feel to stare into those cold eyes over the barrel of a gun and know it was the last sight they'd ever see. "Who do I have to kill?"

"That's the beauty of it," Talbot said, warming to the subject. "You don't have to kill anyone. Unless you want to," he added hastily. "I'll leave that up to you. But we can't talk here. Come to my office later, where we can discuss my offer in private." He scraped his chair back. "Enjoy your drink, Jones. I'll see you in . . . say, an hour?"

"Maybe," Desperado returned, not really anxious to take any job Talbot had to offer but still curious enough to ask, "Can you give me a hint? I want to make sure it's worth my time."

Talbot cast a furtive glance around, as if to satisfy himself that no one was listening, and sat back down. He leaned toward Desperado and said, "There's a piece of land I want. It's standing in the way of progress. I'm willing to do anything to own it. That's where you come in. I want you to help me get it. The job pays five hundred dollars."

Desperado whistled softly. "That's a helluva lot of money, Talbot."

Just then a waitress came along and the conversation skidded to an abrupt halt. "I'll tell you more later," Talbot said as he doffed his hat and made a hasty exit.

"More whiskey, Mr. Jones?" the waitress asked as she sidled up beside him.

He shook his head.

"Anything else I can do for you? Anything at all?"

She smelled of cheap whiskey, cheaper perfume and sex, and Desperado grimaced in distaste. He wasn't that hard up yet, although he hadn't had a woman in some time.

"Thanks for the offer, honey," Desperado drawled, "but I got business elsewhere in an hour. Maybe some other time, when I don't have to rush."

That seemed to placate the woman and she strutted off, hips swaying provocatively. Desperado nursed his drink for another hour, trying to decide whether or not his curiosity was strong enough to warrant a visit to Calvin Talbot's office. His curiosity might not be strong enough but the money sure was a powerful inducement.

He'd hired out his gun for a helluva lot less in the past, to men who expected more of him than Talbot. He usually turned down jobs involving outright killings. A gunslinger had to set his own rules, and Desperado refused to do cold-blooded murder. His high principles had kept him out of jail, except for short stints for minor infringements, and he wasn't going to change his policy now.

Desperado was still thinking when he saw a man

wearing a badge enter the saloon. The man spotted Desperado immediately and wended his way around tables until he stood beside Desperado's table.

"I'm Marshal Townsend," he said. "It's my duty to keep peace in this town."

"Have I done anything to cause trouble?" Desperado rasped in his mean-as-hell voice. In his opinion Townsend had coward written all over him.

Townsend stepped back a pace. "There was that shoot-out in the street," the marshal began. "We don't cotton to shoot-outs in Trouble Creek."

"You're talking to the wrong person. I was merely defending myself." He inched his hand toward his gun butt and wondered how long Townsend would flaunt his authority before turning tail and running. Silently he started counting to ten.

On the count of three, Townsend backed away, saying, "This is just a warning, Jones, no harm done. But it's my duty to tell you that if you intend to remain in town you'd best keep your nose clean." Before Desperado could answer, Townsend backed all the way to the door, then made a hasty exit.

Desperado chuckled to himself. Whoever had hired Townsend should have found someone with backbone.

A short time later Desperado left the saloon and ambled down the street to Calvin Talbot's office. Despite his misgivings about the land speculator, curiosity had won out. Engrossed in thought, he unintentionally bumped into Chloe Sommers coming out of the general store, her arms loaded with packages. The packages went flying and his arms went around her to steady her. He'd expected to be poked by sharp angles and bony joints and was startled to discover that the body molded against his was softly rounded and as femininely endowed as any woman he'd ever held.

"Watch where you're going," Chloe admonished. A moment later she realized just whose hard body was pressed so intimately against hers and jerked out of his embrace. She tipped up her head to stare into his dark face. Her next thought came unbidden. Desperado's eyes were beautiful. Impenetrable black and thickly lashed, they looked as though they could see into one's soul. He was also pleasing to look at, though not classically handsome, Chloe thought, surprised by this new discovery. His features were too bold, too dark, too . . . Indian. She shuddered and looked away.

"Sorry," Desperado said, grinning unrepentantly. He bent to help her retrieve her packages.

"You haven't changed your mind, have you, Mr. Jones?" Chloe asked hopefully. "I really could use a hired gun, and your reputation in that area is unsurpassed. As you learned earlier, even a small town like Trouble Creek has heard of you. I'm a little surprised you didn't kill Tate Talbot."

Desperado frowned. "You sound almost sorry I didn't."

Chloe's green eyes hardened. "I hate the bastard! Killing him would be no loss to anyone, including his father."

"The wildcat has sharp claws," Desperado remarked. "I'll have to remember not to rile you if I

stay around long enough to encounter you again."
He tipped his hat. "Good day, Miss Sommers."

"Wait! About that job—"

"I haven't changed my mind. I don't work for females. Never have, never will."

Chloe bristled angrily. "Why are you so preju-
diced against women? There's nothing a man can
do that I can't."

He gave her a slow grin, granting her a glimpse
of his deliciously wicked dimple. "You'd be surprised by what a man can do that you can't." A
predatory gleam darkened his eyes. "Then again,
maybe you already know. If not, I'd be more than
happy to show you."

"Why you . . . you unprincipled rattlesnake!
There's nothing you can teach me."

She whirled on her heel, her angry steps carrying
her away from him. Though she couldn't see him
smiling, she knew without a single doubt that were
she to turn around she'd see that damn dimple.

Chapter Two

Desperado blew a ring of cigar smoke into the air and regarded Calvin Talbot through the gray mist as he considered the land baron's surprising proposition. Blowing smoke rings was a ploy he used whenever he needed extra time to compose his thoughts.

"Let me get this straight," Desperado drawled, flicking a cigar ash on Talbot's shiny wooden desk. "You want me to accept the job the Sommers woman offered me."

Talbot eyed the fallen ash with distaste. "Exactly. But you'll be in my employ the whole time."

"Perhaps you should explain what you expect of me before I accept the job. I draw the line at killing women."

Talbot grimaced. "Killing won't be necessary. Tate wanted to handle it but he's too hotheaded for his own good. Besides, he's made no secret of the fact that he wants Chloe Sommers. Your job will be to sabotage the trail drive. I don't want those cattle reaching the railhead."

Desperado sat back in the chair, stretching his long legs out in front of him and blowing a trail of smoke into the air as he digested Talbot's words. "Any particular reason you don't want Chloe Sommers to sell her herd?"

"My reasons are my own," Talbot said shortly.

"Not good enough, Talbot. Give me more than that."

Talbot slanted Desperado a measuring glance, as if trying to make up his mind. At length, he said, "The Ralston property is a valuable piece of land. I want it for reasons I can't disclose at this time. If Chloe doesn't sell her herd, she can't pay her taxes. That's all you need to know."

"So I'm to hire on as a gunslinger and do whatever is necessary to prevent the herd from reaching the railhead," Desperado summarized.

"That's the general idea," Talbot said. "You're to turn your head when 'accidents' occur. Tate and his friends will provide the actual mishaps. You're to do nothing to prevent them, and aid Tate when you can. Make Chloe Sommers believe you're working for her. Make yourself indispensable to her, but do nothing to stop my men. If she can't be persuaded to abandon the trail drive, your job is to make sure the herd never reaches its destination."

"That's a helluva lot to ask for a paltry five hundred dollars," Desperado rasped. "The Ralston land must be worth a helluva lot to you or you wouldn't go to all this trouble to seize it."

"Seven hundred and fifty dollars, that's as high as I go."

"Half now and the rest when the job is completed."

"Does that mean you'll take the job?" Talbot asked, apparently thrilled to have hired a man of Desperado's reputation with so little effort.

Suddenly the door to Talbot's office flew open and Tate Talbot barged inside. "What the hell is *he* doing here?" Tate barked, sending Desperado a daunting look that made little impression on the gunslinger.

"I've just offered Mr. Jones a job," Talbot said expansively.

"A job!" Tate exploded. "After what he did to me?" He held up his bandaged hand. "I won't be able to use my gun hand for weeks."

"That's why I hired Mr. Jones," Calvin explained. "You know how badly I want the Ralston land. You had the opportunity to get it legally, but you went and ruined your chances of marrying the gal by getting drunk and playing rough."

Tate hung his head. "It wasn't my fault, Pa. The bitch asked for it."

"I'm sure she did," Calvin said dryly. "But that's water under the bridge. I need someone to sabotage that trail drive. Having Mr. Jones turn up in town when he did was a stroke of luck."

Tate shot Desperado a venomous look. "Don't expect me to take orders from a gunslinger."

"You'll take orders from me," Calvin said tersely.

"You're not levelheaded enough to do what needs to be done. Challenging Mr. Jones was stupid. I can't afford stupid. Get out of here, son. Mr. Jones and I have unfinished business."

Tate glared at Desperado, his uninjured fist clenching and unclenching at his side. Desperado knew he'd made another enemy but didn't much care. Making enemies had become a way of life; dimly he wondered what his life would have been like had his father not married Norie Sommers.

For one thing he wouldn't have been adopted by Black Bear and Prairie Moon, the Apache couple who had cared for him after he'd been brought more dead than alive to the Indian village after his accident. He wouldn't have spent nearly seven years living with the Apache, learning the special skills and fighting tactics of his mother's people. He had proved an apt pupil and had taken off on his own at the age of twenty-one. For the next eight years he had worked hard to earn his reputation as a gunslinger, and he'd succeeded.

Desperado's ruminations came to a halt when Calvin repeated, "Do we have a deal, Mr. Jones?"

Desperado looked up, surprised to see that Tate had left and he and Calvin were alone again.

"I need time to think it over," Desperado hedged. He had no idea what made him hesitate. Talbot's offer was more than generous.

Calvin rose abruptly. "Very well. I have business elsewhere. Meet me back here in two hours. Does that suit you?"

"Yeah." He uncoiled his long length from the chair and strode out the door. Once outside he ambled over to the local cafe and found an empty table against the wall. When the waitress came to take his order he asked for steak, roasted potatoes, green beans, apple pie and plenty of hot, black coffee. Then he sat back and considered the various reasons why he should or shouldn't work for Calvin Talbot.

By rights the Ralston spread belonged to him, or to the man he used to be. Unfortunately, he'd given up the right to inherit when he'd let his family believe he was dead. At the time he'd thought he was punishing his father by remaining dead to him. As he gained in maturity and wisdom he began to realize that he had wronged his father. He had left the Indian village to return home and make peace with Ted Ralston. To his regret he'd arrived too late to see his father alive. He had attended the funeral incognito. That was eight years ago.

He'd watched dispassionately as two females, both heavily veiled and draped in black, wept beside the grave. Desperado lingered long enough to learn that Ted Ralston, still under the impression that his only son was dead, had left all his worldly goods, including the Ralston spread, to his wife, Norie Sommers Ralston.

Losing the ranch had been a bitter blow, but at the time Desperado had had no use for roots and responsibility, so he'd left town as stealthily as he'd entered. Rather than stir up a hornet's nest, Desperado decided to keep his identity a secret and let everyone go on believing that Logan Ralston had died on the prairie all those years ago.

But as the years passed, Desperado began to realize how wrong he'd been to let everyone believe him dead. His stubbornness had cost him his home and his inheritance. His resentment of the Sommers women was deeply ingrained. It wasn't right that Chloe now owned *his* land. It would be ironic should Chloe lose the land that was never really hers to claim.

But isn't it your fault that your father believed you dead and left his land to Norie and her daughter? a saner voice inside him prodded. *You wanted to punish him for abandoning you and ended up losing everything.* Desperado shook his head to clear it of those disturbing thoughts.

His face hardened. He had a profession now and was damn good at it. He owed Chloe Sommers nothing . . . not a damn thing. Seven hundred and fifty dollars was a helluva lot of money to turn down. Not only did he resent the sexy-as-hell, trouser-wearing little wildcat for stealing his birthright, but he had a living to make.

Not that he actually cared who owned the Ralston spread, he tried to convince himself. It no longer mattered. He'd given up the right to his inheritance when he failed to speak up at his father's funeral. So what the hell? Why not take the job Talbot offered? He wouldn't mind seeing more of the delectable Miss Sommers. Maybe he could even coax her into his bed before he moved on.

By the time Desperado's meal arrived, he had made up his mind to accept Talbot's offer. He even made a wager with himself as to how quickly he would get Chloe Sommers into his bed.

*   *   *

Desperado found Talbot pacing his office when he returned two hours later.

"Well? Have you made up your mind?" Talbot asked anxiously. "I took the liberty of withdrawing three hundred and seventy-five dollars from my safe. It's yours right now if you agree to work for me."

"I reckon I can handle the job," Desperado rasped. He held out his hand and Talbot placed a wad of bills in his palm.

"It's all there, but you can count it if you want."

Desperado tested the weight in his palm. "It's all there." The money disappeared in his vest pocket. "What if Miss Sommers has changed her mind about hiring me?"

"I'm sure you can persuade her. Maybe I'll send Tate and the boys around to stir up a little mischief. That ought to convince her she needs a hired gun. Just make sure that herd never reaches the railhead. Do we understand one another?"

"Perfectly," Desperado said. "I'll ride out there after I've visited the bathhouse and barbershop."

"Do you need directions to the ranch?"

Desperado almost laughed in Talbot's face. "No need. I know where to find it."

"Rider coming, Miss Chloe!"

Chloe turned up her collar to protect her neck from the raw wind howling across the prairie and stared at the sullen gray horizon. She spotted the rider but he was too far away to identify. She hoped it was one of the men from the saloon who had thought over her offer and decided to hire on as gunslinger. There was still a lot of preparation necessary before the trail drive could begin. The cattle had already been rounded up but still had to be branded before the trek to the railhead could commence, and all kinds of mishaps could occur without an experienced gunman on hand to keep predators at bay. Unfortunately, only inexperienced young cowboys with little or no knowledge of trail drives had signed on as drovers, and she'd had to settle for what she could get. Desperado Jones wasn't the only man in Trouble Creek unwilling to work for a woman.

Desperado Jones had been a perfect choice to join her crew, but the ornery sidewinder had refused her offer. She still fumed at his sexual innuendos and blatant disrespect. Did he think she was a loose woman? Truthfully, Chloe didn't know how to take Desperado Jones. He was like no man she knew. She'd gone all shivery inside when he spoke in that raspy voice of his. And those black eyes . . . When he looked at her she imagined all kinds of wicked things she had no business thinking about.

Chloe noted that the rider wore a gray duster and sat tall in the saddle, and a prickling sensation began at the back of her neck. His battered hat rode low over his brow; the turned-down brim obscured his face, but Chloe had no difficulty identifying Desperado Jones. She could pick him out of a hundred men just by the way he sat his horse and the confident manner in which he rode.

Chloe waited on the porch for Desperado to draw rein and tell her what had brought him to the Ralston ranch. She didn't harbor any false hopes that he might have changed his mind; he didn't appear to be the kind to back down. Not that she would hire him after the disrespectful way in which he had treated her. Nevertheless, a thrill of anticipation sped down her spine as he rode toward her.

The first thing she noticed was that he wore clean clothing and his face was free of the trail dust she'd noted earlier. He had shaved, too. "What can I do for you, Mr. Jones?" Chloe asked coolly as he dismounted and joined her on the porch.

"I've been thinking about that job you offered," Desperado drawled. "Is it still open?"

"To the right man," she answered curtly. "I'm inclined to believe that every able-bodied man in Trouble Creek is a coward. Either that or they all fear Calvin Talbot and the town marshal, who happens to be Talbot's man."

"I've reconsidered, Miss Sommers. I'll take the job. Where can I bed down?"

"Just wait a darn minute," Chloe sputtered. "What makes you think I'll have you? You made your views clear back in town. Am I supposed to believe you suddenly had a change of heart? What made you decide to hire on?"

Chloe shivered beneath the probing heat of his black eyes. It seemed to cut clear through to all her vital spots. His next words did nothing to diminish her distrust of the handsome half-breed.

"I decided to stick around town for a while and I got to thinking it wouldn't be half bad having a beautiful boss," he said in that sexy rasp that set her heart to pounding.

"Why? Trouble Creek is hardly the kind of town a man of your reputation would enjoy."

"How do you know what I enjoy?" Desperado asked, giving her the full benefit of his dimple.

Flustered, Chloe searched for an answer and failed to find one. "I don't know what you enjoy, Mr. Jones, nor am I interested enough to find out." There, that ought to put him in his place, she thought smugly.

It did nothing of the sort. Instead, he moved so close to her, she caught an intoxicating whiff of cigar smoke and musk. Her gaze was drawn to his, but she couldn't stand the tension and quickly looked away.

"I'm *very* interested in learning what you enjoy, Miss Sommers," Desperado said in a voice so full of promise Chloe found it difficult to breathe. Instinctively she knew this man was dangerous. In more ways than the obvious.

"You never said where I'm to bed down," Desperado went on when Chloe continued to stare at him with a combination of fascination and fear.

Finally finding her tongue, Chloe said, "I never said you were hired, Mr. Jones. Perhaps I no longer need a hired gun."

Desperado's knowing gaze made a slow sweep of the area, lingering a telling moment on a group of cowboys engaged in various chores. When his inspection was complete he turned back to Chloe, his expression far too smug for her liking.

"What did you do, empty out the schoolroom?" he asked, jerking his head toward the cowboys, who had stopped working to stare at him and Chloe.

Chloe's mouth thinned. She wasn't about to tell him they were the only ones willing to hire on. She suspected Talbot had scared off all the experienced men, hoping that her herd would never reach the railhead. "They're old enough to drive cattle, that's all I care about."

"Those two over by the barn look to be about sixteen," Desperado observed. "And those two walking across the yard can't even be that old. How many drovers have you hired?"

"Twelve. Do you have a problem with that?"

"Are any over sixteen?" Desperado probed relentlessly.

"A few."

"One . . . two?"

"Dammit, what business is it of yours? I'm doing the best I can."

"I'm just trying to prove that you *do* need me, Miss Sommers. These young pups are incapable of defending your herd. You offered me a job today and I've decided to accept. How much does it pay?"

"Fifty dollars a month and found."

Desperado nearly laughed in her face. The pay was chicken feed compared to what Talbot was paying him. "This should be a prosperous ranch. Why is everything in disrepair?" Desperado knew his father hadn't been a wealthy man, but neither had he been a poor one. Their taxes had always been paid on time, with money left over to make repairs when needed.

"The drought a few years back was hard on us.

The water dried up and we lost most of our herd. And Mama never was good with money. Somehow the inheritance my stepfather left her slipped through her fingers. I'm trying to turn the last disastrous years around and make a profit this year. My hard work will have paid off once I sell my herd and pay the taxes. I'm not going to lose my land," she said fiercely.

Desperado's dark brows slanted downward. Hearing Chloe speak so possessively of *his* inheritance gave him a hollow feeling in the pit of his stomach. And learning how Norie had dribbled away his father's money gave him another reason to hold a grudge against the Sommers women. Nothing was going to give him back his inheritance, but he could make damn sure Norie's daughter wasn't the one to enjoy the fruits of his father's labors.

"Fifty dollars will do just fine," he said, "but I'll expect fringe benefits." His eyes glinted with a predatory light.

Chloe went still, but the wary look in her green eyes gave mute testimony to her confusion. "F-f-fringe benefits? I don't know what you're talking about."

Desperado's grin was anything but comforting as he cupped her cheek in his callused palm. "Think about it," he said in a raspy whisper most women found hard to resist. He dropped his hand and his smile faded. What in the hell was wrong with him? When he was around the enticing Miss Chloe Sommers, all he could think about was sex and how he'd like to peel those trousers down her long legs and

41

awaken the woman hiding within her masculine attire. Unfortunately, lusting after the woman he'd been paid to ruin wasn't a good idea.

Then again, what could it hurt?

Her full red lips lured him. Seduced him. He leaned in for a stolen kiss and felt the cold barrel of a gun poking him in a place so vital he blanched. His brows shot upward and he slowly backed away, his hands flung upward in surrender.

"Whoa, lady, take it easy. Point that gun elsewhere. I'm kinda fond of the family jewels."

"Ours is strictly a business arrangement, Mr. Jones. I do not like to be touched, is that clear? Keep that in mind and we'll deal well with one another. You can take your gear to the bunkhouse. If you're hungry, go to the cookhouse. Randy will rustle you up some grub to hold you over till supper."

Desperado heard little beyond her remark about not wanting to be touched. Had he mistaken the interest in her eyes when she gazed at him?

"I'm not hungry. I'll take my gear to the bunkhouse and have a look around, talk to some of the drovers, see what's going on." He started to walk away, then whirled around to face her. "By the way, just so you'll be prepared, I'll be touching you again. Only the next time I'll make sure your guns are lying on the ground beside your clothes. And the only thing primed and loaded will be me."

The battle Chloe waged to keep herself from raising her gun and shooting the smirk off Desperado's face was a fierce one. She feared she'd made a terrible mistake. She had troubles enough without butting heads with a half-breed gunslinger with a hankering for her body. Men were all alike. They were base creatures driven by the appendage that hung between their legs. They took what they wanted from a woman without so much as a by-your-leave and didn't care who they hurt to satisfy their needs.

It wasn't Desperado she saw when she'd pulled her gun. It was Tate Talbot, despoiler of innocent women. At one time she had been enamored of Tate. He'd come calling on her, and her mother had approved of the courtship. But she'd learned the hard way that Tate wasn't the man she thought he was. He could be cruel and vicious when he wanted something he couldn't have. It galled her to think she had fallen for his line of bull. One night Tate had taken her to a dance in town. He started to drink, and when he drove her home he—

"Miss Chloe, is that the gunslinger everyone in town is talking about?"

Chloe slapped her gun back in her holster and discarded her painful recollections long enough to answer the young towheaded cowboy who had trotted up to join her.

"His name is Desperado Jones, Cory," Chloe said. "I hired him to guard the herd during the trail drive."

Cory's young face took on a belligerent look. "Don't know why we need a hired gunslinger. Me and the boys can take care of trouble."

"You and the boys will be busy tending to the herd. Hiring Mr. Jones was a precautionary measure. I need to get those cattle to the railhead safely, and you all know the dangers involved. I explained about Calvin Talbot before you hired on. He'll do anything to keep me from selling the herd."

"I reckon," Cory said sullenly. "But there's some who won't like having a hired gun around. Take Rowdy for example, he's hotheaded and rattle-snake mean when riled. I hope Jones don't think because we're young we ain't capable."

Chloe had had no idea her drovers felt like that. She'd thought they'd be pleased as punch to have an experienced gunman along on the trail drive. Not only would she have to keep Desperado Jones under control, but now it looked as if she had to keep peace between the cowboys and the gun-slinger.

Desperado Jones walked into the empty bunk-house, chose a bottom bunk next to the door and dropped his saddlebags. The bunkhouse was neat and cleaner than most, he thought as he cast a jaded glance around the room. Various articles of clothing were draped over chairs to dry in front of the potbellied stove. A guitar was propped against a bunk and a harmonica lay on the table where someone had abandoned it.

Desperado was about to wander outside and get acquainted with some of the hands when he heard the door slam and the jangle of spurs. Years of liv-ing dangerously made him whirl and reach for his gun. He relaxed when he recalled that he had noth-ing to fear here. He soon discovered his mistake.

The cowboy who swaggered up to him was more lad than man, but Desperado didn't like the ornery look on his boyish features.

"You Desperado Jones?" the boy asked.

Desperado nodded. "Who are you?"

"Rowdy. That's my bunk you just claimed for yourself."

Desperado's face hardened. If the kid wanted mean, Desperado would give him mean. Best to get these things out of the way before settling in. It was time this cocky youngster learned not to mess with Desperado Jones.

"It's my bunk now, kid," he said in a raspy whisper that turned most men's legs to jelly. Unfortunately, Rowdy was too young and cocky to know real fear.

"I don't care if you *are* a gunslinger," Rowdy claimed, eyeing Desperado warily. "The only reason you're here is because Miss Chloe decided she needed an experienced gunhand. I coulda told her she didn't need you, but she didn't ask me. I can shoot a gun as well as any cowboy and rope better than most. We don't need a gunslinger on the trail drive."

"I'm here to stay, Rowdy," Desperado said, "so get used to it. You got an argument with that? We can always settle it outside."

He flexed his hand over his gun, hoping to frighten the boy enough to back him down before real trouble started. The last thing he wanted was to draw against another cocky kid with an itchy trigger finger.

Desperado held his breath, waiting for Rowdy to make up his mind. Prudence must have won out, for Rowdy shrugged and took a cautious step backward. His expression wasn't so ornery anymore, just belligerent.

"Take the damn bunk if it means that much to you," Rowdy muttered, backing away toward the door. "I can't stand here jawing with you when there's work to be done. If the herd don't get branded in time, the trail drive will be delayed. And I know Miss Chloe won't like that."

Desperado merely smiled as Rowdy beat a hasty retreat. He sighed, wondering if he would have to intimidate every one of the hired hands before they accepted him.

"What are you trying to do, alienate all my hands?" Chloe asked from the doorway. "You're supposed to get along with them, not scare the stuffing out of them."

Desperado bit out a curse when he saw Chloe's trouser-clad figure poised in the doorway, long legs splayed, hands on curvy hips. It was all he could do to keep his eyes from popping out and rolling on the floor. She looked so damn sexy his hands itched to fill themselves with her. His eyes kindled with desire as she crossed the room to confront him.

"That was nothing, just a small misunderstanding," Desperado said. " 'Pears like the hands resent me. Rowdy is a troublemaker. He needed to be put down. It's best the hands know right off that I'm a bad-ass gunslinger who won't take sass from anyone."

"Just as long as you know I'm the boss," Chloe huffed. "Everyone here takes orders from me."

Desperado had the unaccountable urge to laugh. It was just like a woman to think she was in charge.

Chloe's mother had been like that. But he was a stronger man than his father. No woman was going to tie Desperado Jones in knots like his stepmother did to his father. If he ever had a child, which was highly unlikely, he wouldn't let some woman talk him into sending him or her away.

"Is that why you dress like a man?" Desperado challenged. "So the hired hands will take you seriously?" He thumbed his hat back and let his heated gaze slowly roam over her curves. "Let me tell you, lady, it ain't working. You're too damn provocative in those tight trousers to be mistaken for anything but a beautiful woman. I'm surprised a man hasn't put you in your place."

"And just where is that place, Mr. Jones?" Chloe challenged. "Are you deliberately goading me?"

"Why, ma'am," Desperado drawled, letting his gaze linger on her heaving breasts, "why would I goad you? Everyone knows a woman's place is in the home, taking care of her man and raising his children. A real woman doesn't prance around in tight trousers, trying to run a ranch like a man."

"Why you despicable . . . half-breed!" Chloe flung out. "How dare you ridicule my mode of dress or the way I live my life! You're a hired gun, a man who kills for a living. You have no business finding fault with me. For your information, I don't need a man. I'm perfectly content with my life. Having someone telling me how to dress and what to do doesn't appeal to me."

"What does appeal to you?" Desperado whispered in a sexy-as-sin voice. "Doesn't *anything* about men please you?"

"Very little," Chloe retorted. The look she gave him dared him to prove otherwise.

Desperado was just the man to answer her unspoken challenge. Before she realized what he intended, before she could reach for her gun, he tugged her into his arms and held her captive against him. He heard her gasp as her breasts came into heated contact with the hard wall of his chest, but that was the last sound she made.

Chloe stared into his face, stunned by what she saw. His eyes were narrowed, his lips full and soft. His nostrils were flared as if he was aroused by the scent of her. Awareness slammed through her as she sensed his sharp desire, and the knowledge that he wanted her sent heat surging through her veins. He enthralled her. Mesmerized her with his animal magnetism. His dark face was stark with hunger and sexual arousal, and she suddenly knew what being prey for the hunter felt like. She realized what was coming the moment his head lowered toward hers, but the strength of his arms prevented her from reaching for her gun.

No! This can't be happening, her mind cried out. No man had touched her since . . . And that had been such a horrible experience, she'd vowed she'd let no man touch her again. Yet here she was, caught in a web of seduction so powerful she felt like a female for the first time in over three years. She made a feeble effort to shove him away, but her strength had suddenly deserted her.

Then his mouth was gliding smoothly over hers, prodding her lips open with his tongue, tasting her and letting her taste him. His taste was intoxicating. Delicious. Manly. Without realizing it, she stopped fighting him and gave herself up to the kiss. She wasn't aware of what his hands were doing until she felt them slide beneath her jacket to cup her breasts.

Determined to put the gunslinger in his place once and for all, Chloe broke off the kiss and managed to shove him away. "Don't you ever do that again!"

Desperado stepped back and stared at her. Her eyes glowed beneath her mask of fury. Her breasts rose and fell with her ragged breathing. He gave her a slow, dimpled smile. "I don't need to. I just proved that you do need a man." His smile grew wider. "I knew there had to be *something* you liked about men."

Enraged beyond speech, Chloe hauled off and slapped him. Then she whirled on her heel and stomped away, her hips swaying in time to her jangling spurs.

Chapter Three

During the following days Desperado reacquainted himself with the ranch and land that should have been his. The more he saw, the deeper his resentment grew against Norie Sommers and her daughter. He began to understand just how much he'd been deprived of and felt comfortable with his decision to work for Talbot. If he couldn't have the ranch, then neither should Chloe, who was unrelated to Ted Ralston by blood.

Desperado's attempts to befriend the cowboys were met with suspicion and outright hostility. Time and again he was rebuffed by the resentful hands when he offered to lend a hand with the branding or join in the preparations for the trail drive. After a while he stopped offering and spent long hours riding out alone, pretending to search the property for trespassers. After all, wasn't that what Chloe Sommers was paying him for?

So far neither of the Talbots had caused any mischief, and Desperado wondered when and where they would strike. If nothing happened in the next day or two, he was going to have to ride into town and find out what in the hell was going on. If they had something devious in mind, he wanted to know about it.

Desperado rather enjoyed riding the perimeters of the Ralston spread. Even if the land belonged to another, he took possessive pride in the acres of rolling hills, flat plains and abundant grass that supported a sizable herd of prime longhorn cattle. If the land were his, he knew he could make it prosper, just as his father had done. He could spit nails whenever he thought about how his stepmother had neglected the land and spent his father's life savings. But when his thoughts turned to Chloe, the hatred he felt for Norie dissipated somewhat, turning to something of a more intimate nature.

Chloe, with her taut bottom, firm breasts and long legs, made him ache every time he saw her strutting around the ranch. Despite the painful memories her name evoked, Desperado found himself yearning to thrust himself inside her and hear her call out his name while he stroked her to shuddering completion. He recalled that she was only four or so years younger than he, and he seriously doubted that the gun-toting miss was still a virgin.

He wondered where Chloe was now. He'd seen her ride out this morning, and Cory had told him she'd gone to look for strays the hands might have missed. She could be anywhere. He didn't know why he should worry about her; she was perfectly capable of taking care of herself. On that thought Desperado decided to return to the ranch house. His stomach was growling, and Randy was a fairly decent cook.

Desperado was galloping past a stand of cotton-wood trees that followed a meandering stream when he heard a shot. He drew rein and listened. The sound of voices echoed through the trees, and a prickling began at the base of his skull. He wheeled his mustang into the woods.

Chloe had spied a calf stuck in the mud beside the stream and had dismounted to rescue it. Ankle-deep in mud, she'd pushed and pulled until the maverick bawled out a loud cry and sprang free. Wiping her hands on her trousers, she walked back to where she'd left her horse and stopped dead in her tracks when she saw Tate Talbot and two of his rowdy friends converging upon her. She made a mad dash for her horse but was stopped cold in her tracks when the three horsemen surrounded her.

Undaunted, Chloe reached for her gun, but she wasn't fast enough. Tate's two pals had their guns cocked and trained on her.

"Aw, you wouldn't shoot me, would you, Chloe, honey?" Tate taunted in that charming voice he'd used on her when they were courting. It was a voice she'd come to hate with an abiding passion.

"Would a starving man beg for food?" Chloe shot back. "What do you want, Tate?"

"Just a few words with you."

Chloe's blood chilled and she swung her gun up,

pulled the hammer back and aimed at Tate despite the six-shooters pointed straight at her middle.

"I wouldn't if I were you," Tate warned as he dismounted and walked toward her. "My friends have itchy trigger fingers. Drop the weapon, honey."

Her finger tightened on the trigger. Tate must have divined her intention for he dove for her gun hand and deflected it upward just as the gun fired. Tate spit out a curse as he wrested the gun from her hand and tossed it to the ground.

"You weren't this ornery when we were courting," Tate complained.

Chloe's chin rose in open defiance. "I've learned a great deal since then," she hissed. "I learned to shoot straight and distrust bastards like you."

"And you learned to wear trousers and flaunt yourself like a cheap whore," he taunted.

"Men learned to keep their distance," Chloe said with pride. "Go away and take your friends with you."

"I thought you and me could renew our 'friendship,'" he purred into her ear. "I'll send the boys away. No one need know what we're doing out here. Maybe this time you'll appreciate what I can do for you. I'm the only man who has ever mastered you, Chloe Sommers."

Chloe laughed in his face. "The only way I'll ever appreciate you is dead. I was your victim once but never again. Mr. Jones is in my employ now." Her gaze fell on Tate's injured hand. "You have reason to know he's a dangerous man. Leave now or you'll find yourself at the business end of his gun. This time he won't be so lenient with you."

"Desperado Jones won't do a damn thing to me," Tate bragged loudly.

"Tate," one of his pals warned, "keep your mouth shut. Your pa will have your hide if you spill the beans."

Chloe wondered what that was all about but didn't have time to pursue the subject as Tate grabbed her with his left hand and pulled her against him. "If I wanted to I could take you right here, with the boys watching, but I'm gonna let you worry and wonder when I'm gonna catch you alone again. I'm just gonna give you a little taste of what you're gonna get next time we meet."

Chloe felt bile rising in her throat as Tate's mouth slammed down on hers. At one time she hadn't minded his kisses. She'd even considered spending a lifetime with him, until he'd shown his true colors. She'd been naive and foolish then, blinded by his blond good looks and boyish charm. Then in one night of pure hell he'd exposed his black soul and mean spirit.

In a move that caught Tate by surprise, Chloe grabbed his broken hand and gave it a vicious twist. Tate screamed and spun away, nursing his injured hand against his chest.

His face contorted with fury and pain. "You vicious bitch! You're gonna be sorry you did that."

He started toward her and she backed away, abruptly stopping at the edge of the water. "You're gonna get it now," he warned. "Grab her, boys," he bellowed to his friends. "She needs to be taught a lesson."

"Drop your guns. All of you. One false move and

you're dead men. Move away from her, Talbot. Real slow like."

Chloe let out a ragged cry. Never had she been so happy to hear that raspy, mean-as-hell voice. Desperado sat rigid in the saddle, his face, what she could see of it in the shadows beneath the brim of his hat, made even her shiver with fear.

Tate backed away from Chloe, his hands raised in the air. "Now see here, Jones, Pa ain't gonna like this."

"Somehow I don't think he'd approve of what you intended to do to Miss Sommers."

"She wants it," Tate said sullenly. "That sweet little body of hers is just crying for it. Hell, her and me—"

Chloe exploded in outrage when she realized what Tate was about to reveal. She spied her gun lying at her feet, swept it up into her hand, and before Tate had finished speaking she cocked back the hammer and shot his hat off.

Tate picked up his hat and stared at the hole. "Now what did you go and do that for?"

"Guess," Chloe bit out. "I aimed for your head. Be grateful I was too angry to shoot straight. Get out of here and don't come back. If you or your friends set foot on my property again, I'll consider you trespassing and shoot to kill."

Tate gave her a knowing smirk. "This ain't gonna be your land for long. You gotta get those cows to the railhead before you can pay your taxes. I'm betting you don't make it."

Chloe saw red. She raised her gun, so angry she

would have plugged him through the heart if Desperado hadn't stopped her.

"He's not worth it, Chloe. Put the gun down. If there's any killing to be done, I'll do it." He turned to Tate and his pals. "Go on. Get out of here before I let the lady have her way."

Tate mounted with difficulty, somewhat handicapped without the use of his right hand. "I'm going." He cast Desperado a meaningful look. "I'll talk to you, later."

Chloe was too relieved to pay much heed to Tate's words. She kept her gun trained on him until he and his men rode out of sight. Then she let her arm fall and collapsed against a tree. Desperado was out of the saddle immediately.

"Are you all right? Did they . . . they didn't hurt you, did they?"

"The worst that bastard did was kiss me," she said, scrubbing her lips with the back of her hand. "How did you know where to find me?"

"I was in the vicinity and heard the gunshot." He stared at her, his thoughts running amok. A gut feeling told him there was more than met the eye between Chloe and Tate Talbot. Tate's words hinted at shared intimacy, and that puzzled him. Especially in light of Chloe's palpable hatred for the young fool.

"Thank God," Chloe said on a sigh.

"I don't think it's a good idea for you to ride out alone. Next time, take one of the hands. Or tell me and I'll accompany you. That's what you're paying me for. Can you ride?"

"I'm perfectly fine." She stepped away from the

tree and staggered forward two steps before Desperado swept her up into his arms.

"You're not as tough as you look, are you?" he rasped into her ear. "You can dress and act like a man but underneath you're all woman, soft and sweet smelling. Just like a kitten. Shall I make you purr for me, honey?"

Chloe stiffened in his arms. "Don't call me honey. I'm Miss Sommers to you. And you can put me down now. I'm perfectly capable of standing on my own two feet."

Desperado wanted to kick himself for speaking aloud his thoughts. Chloe made him do and say things he wouldn't have done or said under any other circumstances. He had a reputation to uphold, and displaying softness toward a woman wasn't the kind of image a gunslinger needed. With a gruffness more in keeping with his image, he tossed Chloe into her saddle and swiftly mounted his own horse.

"Are you ready, boss?" he mocked.

"Whenever you are, Mr. Jones," she said haughtily.

He let her lead the way, deliberately remaining behind in order to watch for intruders, or so he told himself. But if he wanted to be perfectly honest, he ate her dust so he could watch her taut little rump bouncing in the saddle.

Everyone was sleeping that night when Desperado rose stealthily from his bunk and slipped outside with his boots in one hand and gunbelt in the other. He had gone to bed fully dressed, and by the time he cut his horse out from the remuda and rode bareback into the night, his gunbelt was firmly in place and his boots were on his feet where they belonged. He wasn't certain where Tate would be waiting, but he figured it wouldn't be too far from the house. And the only place nearby where horsemen could hide was in a shallow ravine a short distance behind the house.

He rode to the edge of the ravine and drew rein. His hunch paid off when he saw a lone horseman making his way up from the ravine. Brilliant moonlight made it easy to identify Tate Talbot. He was alone.

"About time you showed up," Tate complained.

"I wasn't sure where to find you."

"Yeah, well, I couldn't come right out and name the place with Chloe Sommers listening, now could I?"

"I'm here now, what is it?"

"Pa wanted me to tell you we're gonna make our move tonight."

"I thought you made it earlier when you accosted Miss Sommers."

"Naw, that wasn't part of it. That was between me and Chloe. That's another ax I got to grind with you, Jones. You stopped something that was none of your business. Chloe and me go a long way back. Don't interfere, you might not like the consequences."

"Are you hankering to get your other hand shot up?" Desperado drawled.

Tate reached for his gun with his left hand but must have thought better of it, for he let it drop at his side. "Pa is calling the shots now, but my time will come."

"Is that all, Talbot?" There were many things Desperado didn't like about Tate Talbot. One of them was the way his lip curled when he talked about Chloe. What in the hell was between them anyway?

"Look behind you. Even as I speak the barn is going up in flames."

Desperado looked over his shoulder and cursed viciously when he saw a bright red glow lighting up the night sky. "Was that necessary?"

"Pa says it is. He wants to scare Chloe so she'll think twice about driving her cattle to Dodge. If she sells them in Texas, she'll get only five dollars a head, not enough to pay her taxes. That's why she's so anxious to take them to the railhead, you know. She can get twelve dollars a head there."

Desperado stared at the angry glow turning the night sky red and thought about the various animals kept in the barn: three mares due to foal and two prize stallions his father had bred. He felt like a lowdown skunk.

Suddenly Desperado felt a terrible need to return to the ranch. He touched his spurs to his mustang and the powerful animal took flight.

"Wait!" Tate called after him. "We're not finished yet. Pa said you're to do whatever is necessary to change Chloe's mind about the trail drive."

Desperado returned to a scene straight from hell. The barn roof was ablaze and the fire was spreading fast. The terrified screams of trapped animals pierced the air. Everything was chaos as the cowboys ran around without direction. He looked for Chloe but didn't see her. First things first, he decided as he firmly and deftly organized a bucket brigade. The brigade was in place when he saw Chloe stumble from the barn, leading one of the stallions.

He sprinted forward, barking to one of the men to take the horse while he led Chloe away from the inferno.

"There's a mare still in there," Chloe gasped between bouts of coughing. "I have to go back."

"I'll get her," Desperado volunteered before he realized what he was saying. For a moment he'd forgotten who was paying him. But he couldn't stand aside and let a helpless animal perish in the fire.

"Be careful," Chloe called as he dashed inside the burning barn.

Desperado immediately dropped to the floor where the air was less polluted and crawled on his belly toward the screaming horse. Apparently the fire had been set in the loft and was quickly spreading throughout the entire barn. The air was so thick with smoke he couldn't see two feet in front of him. He felt sparks burn through to his skin as part of the loft dropped down, missing him by mere inches. Undaunted, he crept forward, inch by slow inch. The heat was nearly unbearable. Flames licked at him, searing his eyebrows and hair, and he came close to giving up. Then he saw the badly frightened mare thrashing around in a stall and he reached up to unlatch the gate. The mare reared, pawed the fetid air and leaped over Desperado in a desperate lunge toward the door.

Suddenly a beam fell behind Desperado, sending a flurry of sparks in all directions, and he knew he was a dead man. His escape route had been blocked. Desperado had faced death many times during his professional career and he'd always assumed he'd die with a gun in his hand. Somehow burning to death seemed an ignominious end for a gunslinger of his illustrious reputation. Then he thought of Chloe and realized he didn't want to die. He hadn't even bedded the tempting spitfire yet.

Piles of straw blazed all around him and Desperado realized he must think of something soon or perish. He glanced upward and realized that the entire roof was about to cave in on top of him. Then, out of the blue, he recalled something from his childhood. He was about twelve years old when a fractious stallion, having caught the scent of a mare in heat, had kicked out the side of a stall. His father had nailed a couple of boards over the hole. If he could remember the right stall, he knew he could easily kick the boards out.

Desperado let his mind wander backward in time, then he laughed aloud when he remembered which stall his father had hastily repaired. Damned if he wasn't going to beat the devil of his due yet! He just hoped his father had never made permanent repairs to that hole.

Inch by grueling inch he elbowed his way toward the next to last stall at the far end of the barn. Flames were licking at his heels. His lungs were burning and his throat clogged with choking smoke as he crawled into the stall and ran his hands over the rough boards, frantically searching for the hole. Just when he feared he'd entered the wrong stall, he found the hole, still crudely patched, just as he remembered.

He rose unsteadily to his feet. He was dizzy and slightly disoriented but determined to escape this burning hell. He kicked with all his might against the boards nailed across the hole. All he got for his effort was a jarring that rattled his teeth. He tried again, dismayed when he realized that inhaling large quantities of smoke had sapped his strength. Then he saw a pitchfork sticking out of the hay and thanked his lucky stars.

Using the handle of the pitchfork as a lever, he was able to pry off both the boards. And just in time. He squeezed through the hole seconds before the roof caved in. He rolled over and over until he was clear of the shooting flames and flying sparks. He lay sprawled on the ground, unable to move, his lungs burning, sucking in huge gulps of air.

He lay there for a long time. Then he surged to his feet and staggered to where Chloe and the cowboys milled helplessly around, watching the barn disappear in a solid wall of flame. He spied Chloe standing beside Cory, her head buried in her hands while the cowboy clumsily patted her quaking shoulders. As he walked over to join them he heard Cory say, "Crying ain't gonna bring that gunslinger back, Miss Chloe."

Chloe was crying? Over him? No one had ever cried over him. He felt something stir inside him, but couldn't put a name to it. The thought that someone cared enough about him to mourn his passing was a new and thrilling concept.

Suddenly one of the cowboys saw him and let out a yelp of surprise. "He ain't dead! Damned if the gunslinger don't have more lives than a cat. Only a wizard could escape that inferno."

Chloe raised her head and stared at Desperado. He read disbelief in those expressive green eyes, and something else. Joy? He stood rooted to the spot, staring at her and she at him. Then his legs started to buckle and he heard her cry out.

"Help him!"

Immediately two cowboys sprinted forward to support him until he felt strong enough to stand on his own.

"How did you escape the fire?" Chloe asked, dashing away her tears. Her gaze slid over him, as if to reassure herself that he had indeed escaped unscathed.

Desperado gave in to a fit of coughing. When he'd cleared the smoke from his lungs, he said in that sandpaper voice of his, "I found a patched place in one of the stalls and kicked out the boards."

Chloe stared at him. He could almost see the wheels turning in her head. "*I* didn't even know about the patch."

"I was lucky." One side of his mouth kicked up into a smile. "I couldn't die before I collected my first paycheck."

Chloe gave him an exasperated look. "There's nothing more anyone can do here. There's still time before sunup to catch a few hours' sleep. I suggest that everyone go back to bed. We'll clean up this mess in the morning."

The cowboys must have agreed for they began drifting back to their beds. Desperado hung back, hoping for a private word with Chloe.

"That goes for you, too, Mr. Jones," Chloe said crisply.

"There's something I want to discuss with you."

"Tomorrow. Rest is what we need right now. Good night, Mr. Jones."

Desperado watched her walk away, thinking he'd never known a more stubborn woman in his life. Or a more determined one. After tonight's fire Desperado realized that Talbot would stop at nothing to own this land, and he wondered why. "Accidents" like this could turn ugly and lead to the loss of lives. He had no idea why that bothered him but it did.

Chloe could become an innocent victim to Talbot's greed, and Desperado knew he couldn't let that happen, no matter how much he resented the fact that she called herself owner of his property. Somehow he had to convince her to give up the trail drive and sell her herd in Texas for less money.

After the hands had gone about their chores the next morning, Desperado heated water in the cookhouse and took a bath in the big wooden tub kept there for that purpose. The stink of smoke had saturated his hair, his body and his clothing, and he soaped and scrubbed until the odor no longer offended him. Then he washed his dirty clothes in the bath water, hung them to dry over chairs and donned the clean shirt and trousers he had carried along with him.

Feeling more like himself now, Desperado headed toward the house to try to talk Chloe out of undertaking a demanding trail drive that hadn't a snowball's chance in hell of succeeding. Not with a man like Talbot determined to stop her.

Chloe answered his knock and invited him into the kitchen for a cup of coffee. It was the first time he'd been inside his childhood home since he was twelve years old, and he was immediately assailed by painful memories. He looked at the wood-burning stove and pictured his mother standing beside it, stirring a pot of something delicious. He saw his father entering the kitchen and giving his mother a hug.

Desperado knew his parents had been happy and he could never understand why Ted Ralston had married a self-centered woman like Norie Sommers after having had a loving relationship with Dancing Star. Desperado had heard the story many times of how Ted Ralston had met and then married his Indian mother despite outraged citizens of the community who had advised against it. But he couldn't think about that now. He had a mission to accomplish this morning and he wasn't going to let anything deter him.

"Sugar and cream, Mr. Jones?"

Desperado jerked his thoughts back to the present, to the woman whose mother had been instrumental in turning him into a gunfighter with nothing to look forward to but an ignominious death at the hands of some trigger-happy young punk with a fast draw.

"Black," he answered. He watched with avid interest as she bent to pour cream in her own coffee. Her silk shirt gaped open at the neckline, revealing a wedge of creamy flesh with just a hint of cleavage. He had to force himself to look away. Instead he stared at her curvy hips, enticingly encased in tight trousers, which did damn little to restore his sanity or ease the throbbing between his legs.

Chloe set the cream pitcher down and searched his face. "Your eyebrows are singed."

"They'll grow back."

"Your hair is singed, too."

He brushed his long fingers through his thick, dark locks and felt the charred ends against his fingertips. "I'll trim them off later." He sipped his coffee, watching Chloe from beneath eyes fringed with indecently long black lashes.

Chloe flushed beneath Desperado's intense perusal. She wondered what he wanted to say and why he didn't just spit it out. When he looked at her like that, she wanted to dive into those fathomless black eyes and forget to come up for air. Danger lurked in his eyes, in the proud thrust of his chin, in the implied power of his honed muscles. Something about Desperado Jones disturbed her deeply. He was too much. Too much pure animal magnetism and too much sexual awareness.

"What did you wish to talk to me about?" Chloe asked while she still had the presence of mind to form the words.

"I think you should give up your plans for the trail drive," Desperado said.

Chloe's mouth gaped open in surprise. "What? Give up the trail drive? Never! What in blazes made you suggest a ridiculous thing like that?"

"For one thing, the fire last night. We both know who started it and why."

Chloe did know but it made little difference. She wasn't going to give up, not for anything. "I meant to ask you about your whereabouts last night," she said, cocking a golden brow at him. "Where were you when the fire was being set? Rowdy told me you weren't in your bed. If you recall, I'm paying you to stop this kind of harassment."

Desperado gave her a searing look. "Are you accusing me of something? For your information, I heard a noise outside and went to investigate. I saw someone riding away and gave chase. I lost him near the ravine behind the house. I didn't know the barn was on fire until I started back and saw the red sky. I got back as fast as I could."

Chloe was in a quandary. Desperado sounded and looked sincere, but she knew how untrustworthy men could be. This time she decided to trust him. She needed Desperado too much to let him go. Not only was Calvin Talbot determined to get her land but Tate Talbot was stalking her. Because of that terrible night two years ago, he thought he owned her. "I want patrols out every night until the trail drive."

"I'll see to it," Desperado acknowledged. "But I think you should listen to my advice. Sell your herd in Texas and save yourself the heartache of losing them on the drive."

"I can't get enough money for them in Texas."

"You might lose your land to Calvin Talbot, but you'll still have your life and enough money to live on until you find a husband."

"I'll never marry," Chloe gritted out. "Nor will I sit meekly by and let Talbot claim my land."

"Don't say I didn't warn you."

"You're not going back on your word, are you?" Chloe charged. "We had an agreement."

Desperado took a long time to answer, and Chloe feared he was going to quit, leaving her without the protection she so desperately needed. Anger built inside her until she thought she'd explode from it. Did he want more money? She decided to find out.

"Every gunfighter has a price, Mr. Jones. Name yours."

Chapter Four

Desperado sent Chloe a smile charged with sexual innuendo. He seriously doubted she'd want to know his price. She'd run screaming if she knew he wanted her naked beneath him with her legs spread and his name on her lips.

"What makes you think my price is anything other than what we've already agreed upon?" he rasped in a low, provocative voice meant to tease the senses.

"Why else would you try to talk me out of undertaking this trail drive?" Chloe charged. "You want more money, it's as simple as that. I'll go sixty dollars a month, but that's all I can afford."

"What if more money isn't what I had in mind?" he taunted.

Chloe stared at him. "What else could you . . ." Comprehension suddenly dawned. "Oh. You mean . . ." A telltale red crept up her neck. Her voice hardened. "Money is all you're going to get, Mr. Jones. Take it or leave it."

"Keep your money," Desperado rasped. He didn't know what in the hell got into him every time he was around the trouser-clad temptress. He wasn't here to play games with the gun-toting beauty. He was being paid handsomely by Calvin Talbot to sabotage a trail drive.

"You're leaving?" Chloe asked, clearly stunned.

"No, I'm staying. If you have any sense you'd take my advice and sell your cows in Texas."

"Are you afraid of the Talbots?" Chloe challenged.

He gave a derisive snort. "Me? Not on your life. But you should be."

"I'm not afraid of them," Chloe said defiantly. "Besides, I'm paying you to see that my herd reaches the railhead safely."

Desperado said nothing. What could he say when he and Chloe were on opposite sides, working against one another?

"Is that all you wanted, Mr. Jones?"

"Are you dismissing me?"

She rose and so did he. "I'm sure you have better things to do than to try to convince me to sell my herd in Texas for the ridiculous price of five dollars a head. Shouldn't you be patrolling the area or something?"

She moved toward the door and he trailed behind, his gaze following the enticing sway of her hips with avid appreciation. Few women could wear trousers and carry it off the way she did. She opened the door, but he was so engrossed in tracing the curves of her sweet little body that he plowed into her. His arms came around her and his body reacted so violently he couldn't suppress the groan that slipped past his lips.

Turning in his arms, Chloe brought her hands up to push against his chest. "Remove your arms, Mr. Jones."

Her face was so close to his that the urgent need to taste those luscious red lips became a physical ache. His head dipped and his mouth closed over hers. She whimpered a protest, moaned a denial, but Desperado was too aroused by her taste and scent to stop now. His tongue gently prodded the seam of her lips, and to his astonishment she opened her mouth. He was unaware that her intention had been to scream a protest. His tongue swept inside. His passion was so quick to ignite that he scarcely felt her struggle.

He belatedly realized she wasn't a willing participant when he felt cold steel digging into his belly. With great reluctance he broke off the kiss and backed away.

Chloe looked into Desperado's fierce gaze and saw within his eyes the feral heat of an animal deprived of its right to mate. Anger warred with desire inside her. Fury with pleasure. She'd never felt desire before, and no man had ever given her pleasure. It was humiliating to know that a half-breed gunslinger could spark these incendiary emotions in her.

Her first instinct had been to melt into his arms. Her second had been to draw her gun and stop this sidewinder from working his wiles on her. Her second instinct had won out. Though her body wanted his kisses to go on forever, her mind knew better than to allow a man, any man, to manipulate her through seduction.

"You pulled a gun on me," Desperado rasped, pushing her away as if she had bitten him. "I warned you once about that."

"And I warned you about taking liberties with my body. I hired you for one purpose, Mr. Jones. All I require of you is that you perform the job you're being paid for. If I suddenly find myself in need of a man, I'll find someone whose reputation isn't quite so unsavory."

The sound Desperado made was more of a growl than a word as he grasped her wrist and removed the gun from her hand with so little effort she wondered why she had bothered to threaten him with it. She had known he was strong, but the ease with which he had disarmed her utterly dismayed her. She was still gaping at him when he thrust her gun back in her holster.

"I strongly advise you to keep your gun in the holster where it belongs, Miss Sommers," he drawled, "and leave the shooting to me. Keep that in mind the next time I kiss you."

"There won't be a next time!" Chloe called after him as he turned and strode through the door.

Desperado smiled to himself as he walked to the still-smoldering barn to see what could be salvaged. Chloe Sommers didn't know it, but she was ripe for bedding. Desperado strongly suspected that Tate Talbot had bedded Chloe. Maybe he still did. But

Desperado was experienced enough to know that Talbot must have been a terrible kisser, if Chloe's reaction to his kiss was any indication. Most men feared her temper and her guns, he supposed, but she was exactly the kind of woman that appealed to him. Spunky and full of vinegar. Bedding her was bound to give him one helluva ride.

Desperado soon learned that Chloe wasn't going to let the loss of a barn or Calvin Talbot's threats stop her from driving her herd from northern Texas to the railhead at Dodge City. The branding continued. A chuck wagon was outfitted and stocked for the drive, which would take from a month to six weeks, barring inclement weather and accidents.

Still determined to stop Chloe from putting her life in danger, Desperado began to explore ways to sabotage the trail drive without endangering lives. Though he was on Talbot's payroll, he didn't want to see Chloe hurt.

Two days later a gate was found open on a pen holding cows still needing to be branded, and about a hundred head had wandered off. Naturally Chloe was livid. Work had to be stopped while the cattle were rounded up. Three days after that, all the branding irons had mysteriously disappeared and a run had to be made to town to order new ones from the blacksmith. It took two weeks for replacements to be made.

Desperado grew desperate as the target date to begin the trail drive approached. Nothing seemed to faze Chloe. Most women would be a nervous wreck after a series of "accidents" like those she'd had to endure. Desperado's admiration for the little spitfire grew by leaps and bounds. And it lasted about as long as it took him to remember that Chloe now claimed the land that should have been his. How could he admire a woman spawned by Norie Sommers? It was almost too much to ask. He could desire her. Want her in his bed even, but that didn't mean he had to like her. But dammit, that was just what was happening.

Liking the various women he'd bedded had never been a priority for Desperado. He took his pleasure where and when he found the time and thought little about the women whose names and faces he forgot soon afterward. However, there was something about Chloe Sommers that caught his fancy. For one thing she wasn't like those other women he'd bedded. She was strong, vital and independent . . . and too damn stubborn for her own good.

The days passed with alarming speed. Little by little the cowboys were coming to trust him. Almost losing his life in that burning barn had made him one of them. With the exception of Rowdy, who still had a chip on his shoulder where Desperado was concerned, the young cowhands had come to respect him. Desperado felt guilty for pulling the wool over their eyes and suspected they would hate him as much as Rowdy did when they learned he'd been paid to sabotage the trail drive.

Desperado had never experienced guilt before and it bothered him. Hell, Chloe felt no guilt for taking land that didn't belong to her, so why should he feel bad about sabotaging her operation?

Desperado heard someone calling his name and

waited up for Cory to join him. Desperado liked the young cowboy. He liked Rusty and Duke and Randy the cook, too. Though he knew forming attachments could be dangerous to a gunslinger, he felt a grudging admiration for these hardworking boys. He made a silent vow to do all he could to protect these youngsters from becoming Talbot's victims. He didn't consider saving lives a betrayal of his promise to Talbot. In his long career as a hired gunman Desperado had never deliberately taken a life. He'd scared the hell out of a lot of men; he had that down to a science. But actually shooting someone in cold blood wasn't his style.

"Miss Chloe wants to see you," Cory said as he sprinted up to join him.

"Do you know what she wants?"

"She didn't say. You'll find her in the chuck wagon, checking supplies."

"Thanks, Cory."

"We're branding the last of the cows today," Cory said in parting. "We sure could use your help if you aren't busy with something else."

Desperado couldn't stop the smile kicking up the corner of his mouth. Not long ago these same cowboys would barely speak to him. For the first time in his adult life he felt as if he was appreciated for something other than his skill with a gun.

"It all depends on Miss Sommers. She might have some chore for me. If not, I'll be happy to lend you a hand."

Cory answered Desperado's smile with one of his own and hurried off as Desperado headed over to the chuck wagon parked beneath a shade tree.

"You wanted to see me?" he asked as he poked his head inside the chuck wagon.

"Yes," Chloe said crisply. "Thank you for coming so promptly."

It was obvious to Desperado that Chloe wanted to keep their association as businesslike as possible. He wondered whom she trusted less, him or herself.

"I don't want the others to hear our conversation. That's why I asked you to meet me here."

"Is there something you want to say to me that you don't want the others to hear? Maybe you'd like another kiss."

She ignored him. He laughed. She stared at his dimple, then cleared her throat. "I want your advice about something," she said crisply. "I don't want the hands to think I don't know what I'm doing."

Desperado sobered immediately. It must be serious if a proud, stubborn woman like Chloe wanted *his* advice. "I'm all ears. What do you want to know?"

Chloe stared off into space, as if reluctant to ask for advice, especially from someone like Desperado Jones. Suddenly her gaze drifted back, clashing with his, and he felt as if he'd been gut shot. Her eyes were so intensely green he felt hypnotized by them. He shook his head, cursing himself for harboring foolish thoughts about a woman who considered him dirt under her feet. A woman he had every reason to hate.

A woman he'd been hired to ruin.

Chloe stepped down from the chuck wagon and faced him squarely. "I've never been on a trail drive before." Desperado knew how much it cost her to admit her lack and felt grudging admiration. "Neither have any of my drovers. I wonder if you would look over the provisions and tell me if anything is missing. And perhaps you can advise the others about the gear they'll be needing."

"You're still determined, aren't you? Talbot hasn't frightened you at all, has he? Why do you insist on placing your life in danger?"

"My life is my own to do with as I please," Chloe returned. "All I need from you is a little advice, and of course, your gun. I don't intend to fail, no matter what Talbot does to stop me. Now, will you look at the supplies or shall I find someone in town to come out to advise me?"

"If I can't discourage you, the least I can do is make sure the boys eat well," Desperado grumbled sourly. Damn, what an onerous chore this was becoming. He'd had no idea when he'd taken this job that he'd have to deal with such a headstrong little fool.

Desperado had been on trail drives a time or two and knew what insufficient food and inadequate clothing could do for the drovers' morale. He was also aware of how long certain foods lasted and which were depleted before others.

With that in mind he made a thorough inspection of the contents of the chuck wagon, making mental notes as he tallied the supplies in his head. When he finished he had a pretty fair idea of the additional supplies needed to keep the drovers happy.

"You need at least one more sack of flour and

another of cornmeal," he enumerated. "And another rasher of bacon. Plan on cutting two or three cows from your herd to provide fresh meat for the drive, and include some spices to pep up the stews Randy will be making." He poked into a large covered tin. "There are plenty of beans, but I'd include some dried apples for pies and cobblers. The pots you've included seem adequate for your needs, but I'd recommend another barrel of water. Some tins of canned fruit would make your hands mighty happy."

"Is that all?"

"I'm partial to peppermint sticks."

"I'll see what I can do," Chloe said dryly. "Thank you."

"Anything else you want to know?"

Chloe regarded him warily. Oh, yes, there were many things she wanted to know about the mysterious Desperado Jones. Curiosity bubbled up inside her and she blurted out, "What is your real name?"

"Among the Apache I am known as Fast Hand."

Chloe smiled despite herself. The name fit him. "I mean your real name. Is it something you're ashamed of?"

He gave her a withering look but Chloe remained undaunted. "Are you wanted by the law under your real name?"

"I'm not a wanted man by any name," Desperado rasped.

"Then why won't you tell me?"

"Why are you interested?" he shot back.

"Curiosity. Why did you decide to become a gun-slinger?"

"Nosy today, aren't you? Very well, I'll tell you that much. I decided to hire out my gun because it was what I did best. I'd just left the Apache village, with nothing to my name but my horse and my guns. I'd learned many useful skills from the Apache and decided to use them to earn my keep. I kind of fell into my first job, and the others came easy once my reputation as a fast gun grew. There, are you satisfied?"

"Was your mother or father Indian?" Chloe asked, eager to know more about the mysterious Desperado Jones. Her appetite for information had just been whetted.

"My mother. She died when I was nine."

"Are you originally from this area? What is your real—"

"I've said all I'm going to," Desperado rasped, putting an end to her questions but not to her curiosity. There was so much more she wanted to know.

"If you're finished with me, I promised the boys I'd help with the branding. With any luck, the branding will be completed today."

For some reason Chloe couldn't turn her gaze away from his lips. She remember his kiss and how hard his lips had felt and how they had softened as he deepened the kiss. She licked her own lips, as if his taste still lingered. She had no idea she was staring until she heard Desperado chuckle.

"See anything you like, honey?" His sexy whisper sent chills racing down her spine. No man had ever caused that kind of reaction in her before. Flushing, she looked away, embarrassed to be caught staring at him.

His question still hung in the air between them, heavy and potent. She chose to ignore it. "I'm sorry, I just thought of something I have to do. Thanks, you've answered all my questions." She whirled on her heel and strode away, all too aware of Desperado's dark gaze following her.

Later that day she happened to walk by the branding pen and saw Desperado wielding the branding iron with amazing dexterity. June had burst upon the land, bringing sunshine and hot weather with it. Due to the heat, she supposed, Desperado had stripped to the waist. His skin was shiny with sweat, and Chloe stopped in her tracks, struck dumb by the sight of smooth dark skin stretched taut over sleek muscles. He was so blatantly male she had to turn her eyes away.

"That's the last of them, Miss Chloe," Cory called as the last cow in the pen bawled out his displeasure.

"Good work," Chloe returned, carefully averting her eyes from Desperado's glistening bare flesh. "I'm going to town now to buy extra provisions for the drive. Check your gear with Mr. Jones. If you're lacking anything, you can purchase whatever you need in town tomorrow."

"Does that mean we'll be leaving soon?" Rowdy asked excitedly. "Hot damn, I can hardly wait!"

"About a week into the drive you'll be wishing you were back here tucked safely in your bunk," Desperado said dryly. "It's damn hard work."

"Thank you for your words of encouragement," Chloe said with asperity. "We'll be heading out day after tomorrow," she continued. "There's not much left to be done, so the lot of you may as well go into town tonight. It will be your last opportunity to have fun for a long time. And you'll have all day tomorrow to nurse your hangovers. But I'll expect every one of you to be bright-eyed and bushy-tailed come sunup day after tomorrow."

"You can depend on us," red-headed Rusty said as he gave a whoop and a holler and hightailed it to the bunkhouse to get ready for a night of carousing. The others followed, leaving Desperado and Chloe alone.

"Was that wise?" Desperado asked. "Shouldn't you have kept a couple of boys behind to guard the herd?"

"That's what I'm paying you for," Chloe said, trying not to sound smug.

Desperado sent her a disgruntled look. "What if I wanted to go to town and raise hell with the boys? Or seek . . . uh . . . female companionship. As you say, it will be a long time before we see a town again."

"Men!" Chloe spat disgustedly. "Is gratification all you males think about?"

Desperado grinned. "Pretty much."

That damned dimple was going to be her undoing, Chloe thought as she tried to think of a fitting reply. "Sorry, Mr. Jones, you're going to have to disappoint the soiled doves in Trouble Creek this time. As long as you're on my payroll you'll follow orders. You're needed tonight to guard the herd.

Your gun is important to me. If trouble looks for us tonight, I'm sure you can handle it."

"You're expecting a helluva lot from me, lady," Desperado grumbled.

"That's why I'm paying you double what I'm paying the drovers."

Desperado regarded her thoughtfully. "Are you sure you're not envious of those soiled doves you accused me of wanting to visit in town? Does the thought of me romping in bed with one or more of them turn you green with jealousy?"

Chloe felt hot color rising from her neck to the roots of her hair. How dare Desperado Jones accuse her of being jealous? He could sport with every whore in Trouble Creek, for all she cared.

Isn't that lying just a little? a tiny voice in her head whispered. *Wasn't there an ulterior motive behind your decision to keep Desperado on the ranch tonight?* No! she silently admonished herself. She had no reason to be jealous of a sidewinder like Desperado Jones. So what if his kisses drove her to distraction and made her wonder what it would be like to be loved by a man who cared for her feelings? She didn't actually *know* Desperado would be a caring, unselfish lover, but she had plenty of reason to believe he would be skilled. Unlike crude, brutish Tate Talbot, who took what he wanted no matter who he had to hurt to get it.

"You're conceited as well as arrogant, Mr. Jones," Chloe snapped. "I'll let the soiled doves fight over you, and may the best woman win. But not tonight. Tonight you'll be protecting my herd."

"Talk about arrogant," Desperado mumbled to

himself as he watched Chloe stride away. He remembered now why he'd steered clear of working for a female. Women were bossy, impossibly demanding, and foolishly irresponsible. Chloe had an abundance of all three of those shortcomings.

Not to mention the fact that she was the daughter of the woman who had ruined his life. Norie and Chloe had taken his ranch and made a shambles of it after his father's death. But Desperado knew that even had he stepped forward and identified himself at his father's funeral, the terms of Ted Ralston's will wouldn't have changed. Desperado had heard in town that his father had left all his worldly goods to Norie. Identifying himself would have done nothing but cause a scandal.

Chloe watched Desperado ride out after supper to relieve Cory and Rowdy so they could go into town. For some inexplicable reason she felt restless tonight. Anticipation, she supposed. That and the fact that she'd let all the cowboys go for the night. She hated to admit it, but Desperado had been right. She shouldn't have acted without thinking it over. Too late now, she thought as she washed, dried and put away the supper dishes.

Eating supper by herself was the worst part of being alone, Chloe decided as she mounted the stairs to her bedroom. She smiled ruefully. There *was* one other thing lonelier than eating alone and that was sleeping alone, but *that* had never occurred to her until Desperado Jones came along.

She entered her room and lit a lamp. She stared at the long shadows dancing on the walls and felt a sudden chill. She quickly crossed to the window and slammed it shut, but her action did little to dispel the prickles that ran down her spine.

"Foolish girl," she said aloud as she removed her gunbelt, draped it over the bedpost and sat down to remove her boots.

Alerted by a noise, she whipped her head around in the direction of the sound. When Tate Talbot stepped from the deep shadows in the far corner of the room, Chloe glanced at her gunbelt hanging from the bedpost.

"I wouldn't if I were you," Tate warned as he snatched the gunbelt away and tossed it into the corner.

"What do you want? How did you get in?"

"Through the window," Tate said smugly.

"I could shoot you for breaking and entering and no one would fault me."

"Not without a gun, you can't. I've come to give you one last chance to sell your land to Pa before something real bad happens to you and your drovers."

"Your father will never get my land," Chloe bit out. "There is other land available. Why does he want mine?"

"Pa's got his reasons. He says to tell you he'll pay the back taxes and give you five hundred dollars free and clear for the deed to the land. He doesn't have to give you anything, you understand. He could have it for the taxes alone, but I talked him into offering you something because I still have feelings for you." He stepped closer. "I still want you, Chloe. You were set to marry me once."

"That was before you showed your true colors,"

Chloe hissed. "I wouldn't have you now on a silver platter."

"That's too bad," Tate said with mock regret. "It would make things so much easier for everyone. If you married me, the land would be mine and you wouldn't have to undertake a trail drive that could prove disastrous to everyone involved."

"Are you threatening me?" Chloe charged.

Tate shrugged. "Take it any way you want." He stared at her; his gaze traveled up her long legs, then settled disconcertingly on her breasts. "It's not too late, you know. We can take up where we left off. You're the best I ever had, you know."

"Go to hell!" Chloe shouted, shaking with anger. She'd had just about all she could take from the rapacious bastard.

"Someone's coming," Chloe said, hoping to distract Tate long enough for her to dive under the bed for the shotgun she kept there for emergencies. It worked. When Tate glanced toward the door, Chloe dove to the floor, reached beneath the bed ruffle and retrieved the shotgun. She swung it up at Tate before he could reach for his own weapon.

"What the hell?" Tate said, his mouth hanging open in surprise. "Where did that come from? Is it loaded?"

"You're going to find out if you're not out of here by the time I count to three."

"You're just ornery enough to do it," Tate complained as he stared down the gun barrel.

"One."

"I wasn't gonna hurt you."

"Two."

85

"Shit!" He headed toward the door.

"The way you came in," Chloe ordered.

He scrambled toward the window, threw it open and stepped over the ledge onto the spindly limb of a young oak tree growing outside her window.

"You ain't no woman, you're a damn she-wolf," Tate called as he clung to the branch. "Me and Pa know how to treat fractious women. You're gonna be sorry, Chloe Sommers."

Chloe heard a loud crack and suddenly Tate disappeared from sight. She ran to the window in time to hear a loud thump as Tate hit the ground, followed by a string of curses.

"I'm already sorry I didn't shoot you," she called down to him. "Now get off my property before Mr. Jones finds you. He won't be as lenient with you as I am."

Tate hobbled off, holding his rump and shaking his fist at her. Chloe didn't know she was trembling until she set the shotgun down and felt her legs quaking beneath her. Damn that Tate Talbot, she thought. Would she never be free of him? For two years he'd been a thorn in her side, ever since he'd given her cause to hate him.

Chloe slammed and locked the window and pulled down the shade. She knew all the downstairs doors and windows were locked but she still couldn't relax enough to undress and go to bed. She'd feel a whole lot safer if Desperado were here. That thought spawned another. She couldn't sleep anyway, so why not ride out and lend a hand with the cows?

Chloe strapped her gunbelt around her slim hips,

pulled on her boots and spared a moment to run a brush through her long blonde hair. Leaving her hat behind, she made her way downstairs and headed out the back door. She smelled the smoke the moment she stepped out on the porch. Then she saw the fire. It was licking at the corner of the house. As she ran for a bucket she realized she couldn't fight this alone. The fire hadn't done much damage yet and could be easily controlled with another pair of hands helping her.

Chloe hesitated but a moment before she drew her gun and fired into the air.

Desperado heard the shot, realized it was coming from the house and dug his heels into the mustang's sides. The shot had been too far off to spook the herd, and he hoped nothing would disturb them while he investigated. He knew he shouldn't feel that way—he'd been paid by Talbot to prevent the trail drive—but somewhere along the line he'd begun to take his job as Chloe's protector seriously.

Desperado kneed his mount around the corner of the house, and a great weight seemed to lift from him when he spied Chloe, her trim figure outlined in the moonlight, furiously pumping water from the well into a bucket.

Then he saw the flames licking at the corner of the house.

Chapter Five

The fire was quickly extinguished. Chloe had discovered it too quickly for it to do serious damage. The paint was peeled from one corner of the house and the wood was scorched, but apparently the fire had been hastily set, without much thought or planning.

"Who did this?" Desperado asked as he squatted down to inspect the charred wood.

"Tate Talbot," Chloe replied.

He rose slowly. "Did you see him? How did you discover the fire so quickly? I shudder to think what might have happened if you were asleep. Don't say I didn't warn you."

"Tate was in my bedroom tonight," Chloe mumbled.

Desperado went still, then he gripped her arms

so hard he knew he must be bruising her. "What did you say?"

"Mr. Jones, you're hurting me."

"Sorry," he muttered, releasing her so suddenly she stumbled backward. "Would you care to explain what Talbot was doing in your bedroom?"

"He wasn't there at my invitation," Chloe declared, rubbing her arms where Desperado's grip had left red marks on her skin. "He climbed the tree beside my window and let himself in. He was waiting for me when I went up to bed."

"What happened?" His voice was taut with anger, though he had no idea why. It shouldn't matter to him whom Chloe chose to entertain in her bedroom.

"He came to warn me not to undertake the trail drive. He carried a message from his father that I took exception to."

Desperado's gaze went to her gunbelt and he recalled the shot that had summoned him. "Did you shoot him?"

Chloe wrinkled her nose. "I should have. He snatched away my gunbelt and put it where I couldn't reach it, but fortunately I keep a shotgun under the bed. I made him leave the same way he came." She grinned. "Evidently the tree limb wasn't sturdy enough to hold his weight, for he fell most of the way to the ground. Serves the arrogant jackass right. He thought I would—" She paused, as if suddenly aware of what she was about to reveal. "Never mind, it's not important."

Desperado thought different but didn't press the

issue. "So Talbot started the fire because he was angry with you. How did you discover it so fast?"

"After the fight with Tate I couldn't sleep and decided to ride out and lend a hand with the herd. I smelled the smoke the second my feet hit the back steps. I fired a shot into the air, hoping you'd hear it. I didn't know if I could fight it on my own."

"You did right," Desperado said. "Fortunately, the fire did little damage. Will you be all right now? I should get back to the herd. There's lightning off in the distance; it wouldn't take much to spook five hundred head of prime beef on the hoof."

"I'll be fine," Chloe assured him. "Once again I'm in your debt."

"I'm only doing my job," Desperado rasped.

"Good night, Mr. Jones. I'll send Cory and Rowdy out to relieve you in the morning."

Desperado watched her walk into the house, wondering when he had begun to take his responsibility to Chloe and the Ralston spread seriously. He wasn't supposed to give a damn about Chloe, or whether or not she kept the ranch. He had every right to resent the curvy beauty for taking what should have been his. But suddenly the money Talbot had offered him didn't look as attractive as it had before he'd come to know Miss Chloe Sommers.

Desperado shook his head. A gunfighter couldn't afford to have a conscience. Hiring his gun out was a dangerous profession, and he didn't belong in it if he couldn't keep his mind on business and his hands off of Chloe's sweet little body.

Satisfied that his mind was once more on track,

Desperado returned to the herd. It occurred to him that tonight would be a perfect time to stampede the herd. He was all alone, the cows were edgy, and it would take little effort to spook them. It would be days before they could be rounded up again. A stampede might be exactly the kind of shock Chloe needed to persuade her to give up this foolish endeavor. He had half convinced himself to follow through with his plan when he heard a rider approaching.

Desperado's hand hovered over his gun. He relaxed when he recognized Chloe's blonde head glowing in the moonlight as she rode toward him.

"What's wrong?" he asked as she drew rein next to him.

"Nothing. I couldn't sleep so I decided to give you a hand with the herd. They seem a mite edgy."

"There's a storm brewing," Desperado said. He wondered if fate had had a hand in sending Chloe out here. It sure as hell put an end to any plan he might have concocted for stampeding the herd. It shocked him to realize he was more relieved than upset. What in the hell kind of gunslinger was he if he couldn't stomach the thought of bringing Chloe to financial ruin?

The trail drive began on a somber note. Sheets of rain soaked the ground as jagged lightning cut a brilliant swath across angry gray skies. The drovers had rolled out of bed at four that morning, noted the threatening weather and grumbled among themselves about whether or not it was an ominous sign. The speculation continued throughout breakfast.

Chloe was already waiting when they appeared at the gathering site. The chuck wagon, with Randy on the driver's bench, was ready to roll. The supply wagon had lined up behind it, with Cory handling the reins. Everyone was decked out in slickers and hats with brims turned down to deflect the rain. The cows were edgy and sluggish this morning, but somehow the drovers got them moving.

Since Desperado hadn't been hired on as a drover, he rode ahead, his thoughts drifting aimlessly. He wondered when and where Talbot would strike next and how he would handle it. He was getting paid to look the other way when "accidents" occurred, and he wondered how long he could sit back and watch danger stalk Chloe. Calvin Talbot's money guaranteed his compliance, but he was beginning to think he'd made a mistake.

Rain plagued them all day, yet they moved the herd about ten miles before Chloe called a stop for the night. The herd spread out on a level plain, seemingly content to munch sweet grass. Chloe had worked out a night schedule that allowed three men at a time to stay with the herd in two-hour shifts.

The rain stopped just as the chuck wagon pulled up. Randy built a cook fire and started the evening meal of stew and biscuits he'd planned for the first night, and before long the savory odor of cooked meat and vegetables permeated the air. The drovers had lunched in the saddle on jerky and hardtack they carried in their saddlebags and they were looking forward to a hot meal and dry clothing.

Desperado studied Chloe from beneath his hat brim while he ate. She looked bedraggled and tired, and this was just the first day of many. A month of this grueling pace was going to be too much for her, he reflected, noting her drooping eyelids. It seemed to take all of her effort to get the fork from her plate to her mouth. Before he realized what he was doing, he set down his own plate and walked over to join her.

"Why don't you turn in? I'll see to everything tonight."

Chloe's head shot up. "I'm not tired."

"The hell you aren't. Look around you. You aren't the only one nearly asleep. This is new to the drovers, too. But they'll harden. After a few days they'll be pros."

"Perhaps you're right," Chloe observed.

"Spread out your bedroll under the supply wagon. If it rains again you'll be dry. But I'd get out of those wet clothes if I were you."

Chloe nodded, only too glad to comply.

Desperado watched Chloe climb into the supply wagon to change her clothing and had to restrain himself to keep from following. When she came out and ambled off toward a wooded hillside, he shot to his feet and followed.

"Where do you think you're going?" Chloe challenged.

"I'm only doing what you paid me to do," Desperado returned. "Do you think Talbot gave up on you? You can bet your sweet little butt his men are out there somewhere just waiting to catch you alone, or cause mischief."

"I need privacy," Chloe persisted.

He gave her a cocky grin. "I won't look."

Expelling an angry puff of air, Chloe turned on her heel and proceeded into the woods. "You can stop right there," Chloe ordered as she disappeared behind a wall of thick shrubbery. "I still don't think this is necessary. You're just trying to annoy me."

Desperado plucked a blade of grass and stuck it between his teeth as he lounged against a tree and waited for Chloe to finish her business. "If I wanted to annoy you, I'd find a more pleasurable way to do it."

He heard the rustle of cloth and closed his eyes, groaning when he imagined Chloe skinning her Levi's over her hips and down her long sleek legs. Damn! What was wrong with him? He couldn't recall ever getting an erection just thinking about a woman's legs.

Just then Chloe stepped from behind the shrubbery, buckling her gunbelt over her slim hips. She gave him a disgruntled look and brushed past him. Unfortunately, she didn't look where she was going and tripped, landing right into Desperado's arms. He spit out the blade of grass and grinned at her.

"Unhand me," she ordered brusquely. "Why must you always touch me?" She was pressed against his hard body, so close she could feel his hot breath fan her cheek.

"You feel good," Desperado rasped against her ear. "You're not as hard-bitten as you pretend.

You're soft in all the right places, honey. What man wouldn't want to touch you?"

Chloe knew he was speaking but she was distracted by his full lips and didn't hear a word. They looked so soft and inviting she wanted to touch them with her fingertip.

"Go ahead, touch them," Desperado whispered in that sexy-as-sin voice. Chloe sucked in a startled breath. Could he read her mind? "Go ahead," he taunted. "I won't bite you."

She laced her fingers together to keep them from creeping up to his lips. "Why would I want to touch you?"

He chuckled, a surprisingly lighthearted sound for a notorious desperado. "The same reason I want to touch you. Admit it. I attract you. You're curious about me. You're wondering if I'm as good in the sack as your other lovers."

Now he really was ticking her off. Had he heard some gossip in town about her? "You're being absurd," Chloe charged, pushing against his arms.

Chloe blanched when Desperado refused to release her. Being alone with the handsome gunslinger was becoming too dangerous for her peace of mind. She felt overwhelmed by him. Unable to form a coherent thought. Submerged in a thick fog of sensuality. The feeling was so new and overpowering it frightened her. It didn't take a prophet to know he wanted her sexually. Every look held sensual promise. And if she didn't control her response, she feared she'd succumb to the pure animal magnetism of Desperado Jones.

"You want to kiss me, Chloe," Desperado whispered. "Go ahead, I won't stop you."

"Conceited ass," Chloe hissed. "Why, I wouldn't kiss you if you were the last—" He swallowed the rest of her sentence when his mouth closed forcibly over hers. She beat against his chest, but it was like batting her fists against a solid brick wall. He didn't even feel it.

His lips were like velvet, Chloe thought distractedly as he deepened the kiss. When he prodded her lips apart with his tongue, she was so caught up in the taste and scent of him that she opened to him, allowing his tongue to plunder at will. She had no idea how it happened, but suddenly her arms were around his neck, holding onto him as if he were the only stable thing in her life. She didn't come to her senses until he started lowering her to the ground.

"No! I don't want this!" she gasped, shoving him away. "I'm your employer. We can't do this."

"We can if we want to."

"You're a gunslinger and a—"

Desperado stiffened. "A half-breed. Say it."

"I wasn't going to say that," Chloe protested. "We should get back to the campsite. The others will begin to wonder where we disappeared to."

"They're all sleeping like babies right now. Except for the drovers on first watch. But you're right. I wouldn't want to sully your 'unblemished' reputation. Go to bed, Miss Sommers."

Chloe stared at him. What did he mean by that remark? Did he know about Tate? Did he think she took lovers to her bed? She tried to tell herself it didn't matter what he thought. She wasn't paying him to think. She was paying him to see that the herd arrived in Dodge City safely.

She whirled away from him. "Good night, Mr. Jones. Look after my herd. I can take care of myself."

After that first rainy day the weather gave way to warm days and plenty of sunshine. They lost two cows in a swollen creek a week into the drive. Rusty almost lost his own life trying to rescue them. They lost a day after the crossing when Chloe called a halt to rest the herd and to give the drovers time to recuperate from their difficult day.

Desperado managed to steer clear of Chloe those first hectic days. He made a habit of riding ahead to scout the area and to keep an eye out for rustlers. He knew the Talbots would strike soon and supposed they would contact him first.

They reached the Canadian River a week later and found it overflowing its banks. Spring rains had made for lush grazing but played havoc with streams and rivers. Desperado tried to find a less dangerous crossing, but no matter how far he followed the bank, the river still remained dangerously turbulent.

"We'll have to cross here," Chloe decided when Desperado reported his findings. "I was told that this is the best place to cross, that under normal conditions the river is shallow enough to cross without getting our stirrups wet. Obviously this has been an unusual spring. We'll camp here tonight and herd them across first thing tomorrow morning."

Desperado slept fitfully that night. River crossings were dangerous and this one promised to be a killer. He wished he had tried harder to stop Chloe from undertaking so dangerous a trek, but perhaps the Talbots would make their move soon and end the drive once and for all.

That night someone tried to stampede the herd, but the drovers on duty managed to stop it before it really started. The next morning the drovers started the cattle moving across the swollen river. The current was swift, but the first one hundred made it across safely. The water reached the drovers' thighs before the ground started to rise again. Chloe went across with the next hundred, and Desperado didn't realize he was holding his breath while she crossed until he felt his head spin from lack of air. When she reached the opposite bank safely, he let out his breath in a great whoosh and took in another.

Desperado waited until the last hundred cows were being herded across before following them into the cold water. From the corner of his eye he saw that Chloe had started back into the water and he wondered what in God's name she was doing. Then he saw the calf struggling in deep water and let out a curse.

"Chloe, go back!" he shouted. "I'll get the calf."

His voice didn't carry over the noise of rushing water and bellowing cows. Abruptly changing course, he urged his mustang toward the floundering calf. Suddenly he saw something that knocked the breath from him. A fallen tree carrying a ton of debris was barreling downstream straight at Chloe.

He shouted a warning. She didn't hear him. He wasn't going to reach her in time. Acting out of fear and pure instinct, Desperado unwound his rope from his saddlehorn and swung it high in the air, forming a large loop.

Desperado realized that if he missed he wouldn't have another chance. He offered up a brief prayer to the God he hadn't acknowledged in years and sent the rope flying. He let out a roar of approval when the rope settled around Chloe's slim waist. Then he gave a vicious yank, pulling her off her horse with scant seconds to spare. An ungodly bellow rent the air as both the calf and Chloe's hapless horse were carried downstream, snagged within the knot of debris.

Slowly he reeled Chloe in, like a fish on a line. Then he reached down and plucked her out of the water. "You little fool!" he scolded. "What made you do a damn fool thing like that? I ought to . . ." What? What did he really want to do to her? Shake some sense into her? Kiss her? Beat her black and blue? Undress her and make slow love to her? Yes, he decided. All of the above. And more.

"I didn't see the logjam," Chloe sputtered, clinging to his saddle. "I wanted to save the calf."

"Now both the calf and your horse are lost." His horse had found solid ground and he hauled her up, settling her between his thighs as he headed toward shore where the drovers anxiously awaited them.

Chloe slid from the saddle and sat on the ground to catch her breath while the drovers crowded around Desperado, patting his back and congratulating him for his heroic feat.

"Here come the chuck wagon and supply wagon!" Chloe cried, drawing attention to the dark, swirling water again. "They won't make it across!"

Spitting out a curse, Desperado mounted his horse and urged him back into the water. The chuck wagon had just rolled down to the water's edge when Desperado reached the opposite shore.

"I'll lead the team across," he told Randy as he grasped the lead reins and led the protesting animals into the water. "Wait here until I return," he called back to Rowdy, who was driving the supply wagon.

The chuck wagon had reached the middle when Desperado realized that Rowdy had started across in deliberate defiance of his warning. When the chuck wagon hit high ground, Desperado left Randy on his own to go back for the supply wagon. Rowdy wasn't having the same kind of luck as Randy had had crossing the river. His team was frightened and pulling in opposite directions beneath Rowdy's inept handling. The heavy covered wagon was floundering and in danger of overturning when Desperado grasped the reins from Rowdy's fingers and struggled to bring the team under control. Then he led them safely across.

"I coulda handled it," Rowdy complained when they pulled onto a grassy area on the opposite shore.

Desperado gave him one of his mean-as-hell looks and promptly ignored him. He was so exhausted he could barely move. He slid from the saddle and collapsed on the ground, his breath coming in short, uneven spurts. Not even exhaustion, however, could dim his sense of awareness when Chloe sat down beside him.

"Are you all right?" she asked. "You more than earned your pay today."

He searched her face, surprised at her concern; then he gave her a weary smile. "That's quite a compliment coming from you."

"Don't let it go to your head, Mr. Jones," she said saucily, returning his smile. "We'll camp here a night or two to rest the men and cows. This is the last river we'll have to cross in Texas. That leaves the Beaver River in the Oklahoma panhandle and the Cimarron in Kansas. With any luck, they will have already crested by the time we reach them."

"How do you know so much about the trail between here and Dodge City?" Desperado wondered aloud.

"From Ted Ralston, my stepfather. He'd undertaken many a trail drive in his time and enjoyed talking about them. He also kept meticulous records about every hardship he'd encountered during various drives throughout the years. I know every river and every stream and creek along the route. I've never seen them, of course. Ted would never allow me to accompany him. But I feel as if I know every danger the trail has to offer."

Desperado's admiration for the scrappy beauty rose considerably. She might be a tenderfoot but she hadn't undertaken this drive without first learning everything she could about the trail. He could fault Chloe for many things but stupidity wasn't one of them.

The next day Desperado rode ahead to scout the area. He had a gut feeling they were being trailed and expected to find Tate Talbot and his cronies out there somewhere. His hunch paid off when he ran into Tate a few miles north of the campsite. He came from behind a boulder and rode out to meet Desperado.

"What are you doing here?" Desperado wanted to know when he reined in beside Tate.

"Keeping an eye on you," Tate snarled. "The drive would be over if you hadn't gone and acted the hero. Was pulling Chloe out of the water necessary? I told Pa I could handle this for him, but he didn't trust me. He had to go and hire a gunslinger." He shoved his injured right hand under Desperado's nose. "It's almost healed. I've been practicing. One day I'll call you out and I won't lose."

"Is that a fact?" Desperado drawled.

"Yeah, that's a fact. There's something else I don't like. It's the way you're handling your job. Things got to start happening soon. Pa will have a fit if those cows reach Dodge City. I got a plan. My pals and I will do the work, all we need is your cooperation."

"Spit it out, Tate," Desperado rasped. "Who do you plan to kill this time? That last fire you started fizzled out. You could have killed Miss Sommers if she hadn't outsmarted you."

"Ha! The day hasn't come when Chloe can outsmart me. Has she told you about her and me?"

Tate taunted. "She's a hot little piece, Jones." He sent Desperado a narrow-eyed look. "Or have you already found that out for yourself? I'm warning you, don't touch her. She's mine."

Desperado merely stared at him.

"Never mind. I was the first but I knew I wouldn't be the last. Have you found that sweet little mole on the inside of her left thigh yet? She likes it when you—"

Desperado leaped at Tate from his horse's back, taking Tate down with him. They rolled on the ground, exchanging punches, but Tate didn't have a chance. When Desperado deemed the young fool had had enough, he hauled him to his feet.

"You're a liar and a braggart, Talbot. Chloe hates your guts. If you so much as looked cross-eyed at her she'd shoot your balls off and feed them to the pigs."

Desperado released Tate so fast he landed on his rump. He rose quickly and dusted himself off. "Chloe doesn't really hate me," he said with sly innuendo. "It's all pretense. Ask anyone. We were gonna get hitched. Her mother gave us her blessing."

"Yeah? What happened to break you up?"

"A misunderstanding," Tate muttered, refusing to look Desperado in the eye. "Then she took it into her head to run the ranch herself after her ma died. Damn shame. She was the best I ever had. She had a tight little—"

"Don't say it," Desperado warned. A muscle jumped in his jaw. Tate must have sensed that he had goaded Desperado too far, for he abruptly fell silent, staring at Desperado's gun as if he expected it to jump out of the holster and bite him.

"If you're through damaging a lady's reputation, I'll hear your plan now," Desperado rasped.

Tate's manner changed when he realized Desperado wasn't going to kill him. "That's more like it," he said with considerably more confidence. "I've been scouting ahead. There's a deep ravine about ten or fifteen miles from where you're camped. My friends and I will camp nearby. There is plenty of good grazing land a mile or so from the ravine. I know you scout ahead. You're to conveniently forget to mention the ravine. I'll leave it to you to convince Chloe to camp somewhere nearby that night."

"What then?" Desperado asked. He knew what was coming but wanted to hear it from Talbot.

"We'll take it from there. See that you make yourself scarce while we stampede the herd into the ravine. Half or more of the herd will be lost before they can be stopped. Even at twelve dollars a head there won't be enough money to pay the taxes and Pa will get what he wants."

Desperado was torn. He still had the money Calvin Talbot had paid him to sabotage the drive and it seemed to weigh him down. To whom did he owe loyalty? A man who had paid him seven hundred and fifty dollars or a woman who'd offered him fifty dollars a month? In truth he owed Chloe nothing. Whether or not she lost the ranch was immaterial to him, he tried to convince himself. The ranch was lost to him anyway and had been for a very long time.

"What's the matter, Jones, are you having second thoughts?" Tate taunted. "Are you a hired gun or has Chloe's taut little body made you soft in the head?" He sent Desperado a challenging look. "Chloe must be hard up to bed a half-breed gunslinger."

Hearing the truth about himself had a sobering effect on Desperado. He should know better than to think Chloe would look favorably upon a man with an unsavory reputation and Indian blood flowing through his veins. He belonged to a breed of restless men who hired out their guns and disappeared into the sunset when someone faster came along. His future was uncertain. A gunslinger had no guarantee of long life and happiness. Had he become a rancher like his father, he could have earned respectability and eventually married and fathered children.

But his life had taken a far different course from what his father had envisioned for him. Because Norie Sommers had hated him, he had found refuge with his mother's people and lost his right to become the rancher he was meant to be. He was a gunslinger and a damn good one. He'd taken Calvin Talbot's money and now his reputation was at stake. He had no choice but the obvious one.

"One more word about Chloe and you're a dead man," Desperado hissed. "My reputation speaks for itself, but I draw the line at slandering a lady. I was hired by your father to do a job and I intend to fulfill my obligation. Therefore I won't be around when you stampede the cattle into the ravine."

"Now you're talking," Tate said, gloating. "We

may not see eye to eye on a lot of things but we can still work together to get a job done. Pa would see you in hell if you double-crossed him."

"I'm already there," Desperado muttered as he turned his horse back toward camp.

Chapter Six

Indecision rode Desperado mercilessly. He knew what was going to happen and didn't like it. Though he went to bed and tried to sleep, sleep eluded him. His body was tense, his mind alert, waiting, waiting for the sound that would signal the stampede. He knew what was coming, yet he couldn't bring himself to accept the inevitable.

He wondered why he'd suddenly found a conscience when he hadn't had one in years. Cursing his misplaced morals, Desperado decided to ride out to the herd and do what he could to prevent senseless loss of lives. He hated the thought of any of the young cowboys getting hurt in the stampede. He rose from his bedroll, strapped on his guns and picked his way around the sleeping men to his horse. He happened to glance under the supply wagon where Chloe had made up her bed and froze in mid-stride, gaping at Chloe's empty bedroll. He spit out a curse. If trouble didn't find Chloe, she went out looking for it.

Raw panic kicked him in the gut. There was only one place Chloe could be. With the herd. He didn't bother saddling his horse as he leaped upon the mustang's back and booted him in the ribs. Then he heard the unmistakable sound of gunfire, followed by the thunder of pounding hooves. Shouting an Indian whoop into his horse's ear, he rode hell for leather toward the stampeding herd.

Chloe had felt edgy all evening. And this time she couldn't fault Desperado Jones and those dark, sexy eyes of his, which seemed to follow her with an intensity that turned her blood to liquid fire. No, this time her nervousness was the result of a vaguely disturbing premonition. But without solid proof of trouble, she had no reason to alert Desperado or the drovers. Since sleep was out of the question, she decided to ride out to the herd and make sure all was well.

Nothing seemed amiss when she reached the herd. The three men on night duty were crooning softly to keep the herd calm. Chloe rode over to join them.

"What are you doing here, Miss Chloe?" a young man named Sonny asked.

"Couldn't sleep," Chloe mumbled, ashamed to admit her lack of faith in her own men's ability. "Everything all right?"

"Everything is fine," Sonny said. "Me, Pete and

Lucky haven't had a speck of trouble with the herd tonight."

"Good. Things have gone smoothly thus far and I want to keep it that way. Keep your eyes—"

Suddenly all hell broke loose. Three men came riding out of the darkness, whooping and hollering like banshees and firing into the air. Complete chaos followed in short order. The cows, spooked by the unexpected noise, stampeded toward the ravine, just as Talbot had planned.

Unprepared for disaster, the three inexperienced drovers didn't react fast enough to head them off.

"Head them off before they scatter!" Chloe shouted as she took off after the frightened herd. Had she known that the herd was headed toward tragedy, she would have been horrified.

Chloe and the drovers tried unsuccessfully to stop the stampede. More men are needed, Chloe thought distractedly as she rode ahead of the drovers. She prayed that the rest of the drovers had heard the commotion and would arrive in time to lend a hand. She needed Desperado. She needed him now more than ever.

The earth shook beneath him as Desperado plunged into the midst of five hundred head of stampeding cattle. He searched frantically for Chloe but the cloud of dust blinded him. His heart nearly stopped when he finally spied her. She was racing alongside the herd, heading directly for the ravine, unaware of the peril awaiting her. Panic accelerated his heartbeat. Unless he could stop Chloe, she would ride straight into the ravine and sure death.

He felt a spark of hope when he saw that the drovers from camp had arrived. But he had eyes only for Chloe and the imminent danger. She had reached the front of the stampeding herd now and began firing her pistol into the air in an attempt to turn the leaders. Desperado held his breath. If she succeeded in turning the herd back into themselves, the stampeding cows could be stopped before they reached the ravine. Unfortunately, the ploy didn't work, and the drovers were too far away to help Chloe. Within minutes she would be swept over the ravine and buried beneath tons of dying cattle.

Digging his heels in, Desperado used skills learned from the Indians as he leaned low over his mustang's neck and whispered encouraging words. "There's a ravine ahead!" he shouted as he passed each of the drovers. "Turn the herd away from it."

The drovers began shooting into the air, trying to head the herd in another direction. Slowly but surely the herd turned from the ravine. Desperado's relief was short-lived. He saw at a glance that the tactic had come too late to save Chloe. If he didn't do something fast she'd be swept into the ravine by the turning edge of the herd. After a quick assessment of the situation, he came to but one conclusion. The only way to reach Chloe in time was to cut through the herd. It was perilous. Foolhardy. Stupid. But he was willing to take the risk to save Chloe's life.

*　　*　　*

Chloe realized that the rest of her crew had arrived and felt enormous relief. She'd been unable to turn the herd on her own and knew that every available hand was needed to stop them. She saw Sonny fighting his way to her and motioned for him to stay where he was, but he seemed determined to reach her. Then she saw Desperado plunge into the middle of the stampeding herd and her breath nearly stopped. What did he think he was doing?

Her gelding shied beneath her and it took all her strength to control the frightened animal. But she couldn't blame him. The stampeding herd was crowding her mount. She saw Sonny signaling her but couldn't make out what he was trying to convey. He cupped his mouth and shouted something, then he pointed behind her. This time she understood, and the blood froze in her veins.

Ravine? There was a ravine behind her? She turned in her saddle and saw what she hadn't seen before. Less than twenty yards ahead of her the earth fell sharply away. She tried to angle around the herd, but they charging animals were still crowding her toward the edge. Then she saw Desperado, fighting his way through the herd toward her. He wasn't going to make it! He was going to be swept beneath the cutting hooves of five hundred head of cattle.

Abruptly her attention was diverted when the herd made a slight deviation, pushing her even closer to the ravine. There was no hope for her now. She was a goner. She'd be swept over the cliff. Her gelding shied, pawing the air as the cattle brushed against it, edging it toward the ravine. Chloe squeezed her eyes shut and awaited death. She hadn't counted on Desperado's determination to save her.

Instead of plunging down the ravine as she expected, she felt herself being lifted from the saddle. When she opened her eyes, she was resting between Desperado's hard thighs, his strong arms holding her firmly against his chest.

"They're turning!" Desperado called to Sonny and Lucky as he fought his way to the edge of the herd. "I'll take care of Chloe. You and the others can handle it from here."

"My horse . . ." Chloe began.

Desperado rode to the edge of the ravine and looked down. The sky had turned from inky black to pearly gray, allowing Chloe a glimpse of her horse at the bottom of the ravine. He was stomping the ground and shaking his mane, but obviously unhurt. She saw the skid marks where he had slid down, and she shuddered. She knew she wouldn't have been as lucky as her mount.

"Someone will bring him back," Desperado said as he reined his mustang toward the campsite.

His arms felt like heaven, Chloe mused as they closed strongly around her. So safe, so comforting. She had no idea how he had reached her in time, but she thanked God that he had. She clung to him like a lifeline as they rode into camp.

The camp was deserted. Every able-bodied man was with the herd and probably would be for some time. Desperado dismounted and reached for Chloe. She slid down his body until her feet touched the ground.

"Can you stand?" he asked gruffly, as if speech was difficult.

She nodded and he slowly withdrew his arms. Without his support, her legs began to buckle. Her brush with death had frightened her more than she cared to admit. She had almost lost her life, and Desperado had saved her at great risk to his own. His hands returned to her waist, supporting her while she gained her balance.

She licked her lips, staring at him with more than simple gratitude. His eyes were wary as he returned her regard, but she saw something so sweet in their dark depths it fired her blood and set her pulses to racing. She heard him groan moments before his mouth came down hard on hers. She tasted raw desperation on his lips, and something wild and primitive.

Desperado knew he had lost control the moment his lips touched Chloe's. He'd never felt this kind of wildness for a woman. His body strained against hers as he pulled her roughly into his arms. He felt but a momentary resistance, then she melted against him. He wanted this woman, even though he knew she was the last woman he should want.

Even though he knew that once wouldn't be enough.

Pulling back, he stared at her. Her eyes widened as if in acknowledgment of the need they shared. Her chest rose and fell with her ragged breathing, and his nostrils flared at the scent of her arousal. He watched her eyes flutter, listened to the soft moan escaping her lips, and he knew that nothing short of death would stop him from taking this

113

woman whose seductive green eyes and lush red lips were more temptation than a man should have to bear. Chloe Sommers had driven him beyond the bounds of sanity.

"Not here," he rasped gruffly.

"What?"

"I'll find a place where we won't be disturbed. You want the same thing I want, don't you?"

"I . . . I . . ."

"Don't worry. Leave everything to me. No woman could look at me like that and not want the same thing I do."

He snatched a blanket from his bedroll, scooped her into his arms and carried her to a deserted spot behind a rust-colored butte beyond the campsite.

"Mr. Jones, what—"

His lips effectively halted her words. He couldn't seem to get enough of her mouth. Her taste, her scent, everything about her was unique. He couldn't wait to get her naked, to explore her sweet curves and discover the secrets of her slim body. Would she hold him snugly within her? Did she know how to drive a man mad by using those tiny inner muscles on his rod when it was buried deep inside her? He didn't care about the men who had been before him: he'd make her forget all of them.

He stopped beneath a concealing overhang and tossed down the blanket. Then he lowered her to the ground and followed her down.

"Where are we?" Chloe gasped as she glanced around in confusion.

"Where we can be alone." His fingers touched her breast. He felt Chloe's heart thump beneath his fingertips and fought the almost savage urge to tear off her clothes and thrust himself deep inside her. With shaking hands he unbuckled her gunbelt and pulled it free.

"This is what we both want, Chloe. We've been heading toward this moment since we first met. Lift your hips, honey, so I can undress you."

The doubt in her eyes did nothing to deter him as he worked the buttons on the flap of her trousers free and began to skim them down her long legs. When she grasped his wrists, he said, "Look at me, honey."

She tipped her head back and stared at him. "Take your hands away. I want to see all of you. Then you can see all of me. Don't worry about the drovers. They'll be occupied with the herd for hours."

Her hands dropped away, and he didn't give her a chance to change her mind as he deftly removed her boots and stockings. He kept her gaze from straying from his by sheer dint of will as he skimmed her denims and drawers down her long legs and tossed them aside. Then he sat back on his heels and looked his fill. Her body was peaches and cream and golden where it had been kissed by the sun.

Her legs were every bit as long and shapely as he'd imagined. He followed the enticing turn of her ankles past a pair of dimpled knees, his gaze coming to rest on the inner softness of her white thighs. He tried to stifle a groan and failed as his gaze homed in on the curly blonde thatch of hair crowning her woman's mound. He lowered his head and kissed her there, eliciting a shocked gasp from Chloe. She tried to bring her legs together but he wouldn't allow it as he gently spread her thighs and touched her there. The moment he touched her silken flesh, a great shudder passed through him.

"Desperado!"

"I love it when you say my name like that," he groaned.

Reluctantly he let her legs fall together so he could concentrate on removing the rest of her clothing. "Lift your shoulders," he rasped. Need rode him hard. If he didn't put himself inside her soon he was going to explode.

With surprising dexterity he removed her jacket, blouse and camisole, grinning to himself when he realized he'd been right. She wore nothing to fetter those glorious feminine mounds. High and proud, her creamy breasts were crowned with pointed coral nipples already puckered with arousal.

"I knew you'd be perfect," Desperado groaned as he raised one tempting breast and sucked a nipple into his mouth. His rod jerked violently against the rough material of his trousers, and he raised his hips so he could unfasten the buttons and relieve the pressure without removing his mouth from her breast.

Chloe arched into him, melting under his touch like warm butter. She was still dazed after her near brush with death and unable to think past the way her body was responding to Desperado's touch. She'd known back at the campsite, when she'd looked into Desperado's dark eyes, that it would end like this. There could be no other conclusion to the attraction between them . . . this taking and giving in the most intimate of acts.

Despite her painful experience with Tate Talbot, Chloe knew instinctively that this man would not hurt her. Desperado Jones might be a gunslinger with a reputation for violence, but she felt no fear when he touched her. She felt desire. She wanted him. She yearned for the pleasure his mysterious dark eyes and dimpled smile promised.

Suddenly Desperado surged to his feet and began stripping off his clothes. She closed her eyes, but something profound and urgent compelled her to open them again.

"That's it, honey, look at me. Touch and sight are a big part of the pleasure we're going to share."

Chloe sucked in a startled breath when his trousers dropped, revealing him in all his naked glory. He was huge! All solid muscle and bone and magnificent bronze flesh. She dragged her gaze upward along his body to his face. His skin was drawn taut over high, sharp cheekbones, his expression stark with hunger. His Indian heritage was apparent in every line and angle of his proud face. He was all savage need and hard, turgid flesh.

His teeth were bared in a feral smile as he lowered himself beside her on the blanket. "I've dreamt about this since the moment I saw you, honey. Soon I'm going to be inside you, just as full and hard and deep as I can."

His erotic words were like an aphrodisiac. Chloe knew she should stop this before it was too late, but her aroused body refused to cooperate. She could do nothing but moan when his hands began a slow exploration of her body. Her breasts felt swollen and her nipples ached as he caressed and teased and rolled the pouting buds between his thumb and forefinger. The ability to form a coherent thought vanished when his mouth replaced his fingers and he began to suckle her.

Intense pleasure settled where his mouth worked so diligently, and lower, pooling between her legs. She tried to tighten her knees to stop the fire from spreading, but Desperado settled between her legs, spreading them even wider. She felt no shame. What she felt was a growing need to experience more of the pleasure Desperado was offering.

His mouth left her breasts and he grinned down at her. "You're wet and ready for me," he rasped. "I can smell your sweet arousal."

Embarrassment flooded her and she tried to dislodge him from the cradle of her thighs, but he wouldn't allow it.

She shivered as he regarded her through hooded eyes. Cool air touched her aroused nipples, and she desperately wanted his mouth to return to her breasts. Her fingers wound through his thick dark hair, dragging his head back to that aching place.

"Do you like my mouth and hands on you?" His voice was rough with wanting.

She nodded.

"I like to be touched, too. Touch me, honey. Put your arms around my neck, run your hands over my body. Do whatever you like."

Her mouth went dry. She couldn't count the times she'd wanted to touch the gunslinger and denied herself that pleasure. The thought of touching a man intimately had never occurred to her until Desperado came along with his sexy voice, handsome bronze face and dark, probing eyes that melted her bones. She knew that what she was dong was wrong, that the gunslinger would ride off into the sunset after he got what he wanted from her, but for the first time, and maybe the last time, she wanted to taste passion. And she wanted it from Desperado.

Tentatively she touched his chest. The soft mat of hair felt like silk beneath her fingertips. Emboldened, she explored further. His shoulders, his back . . . then she dared to touch the hard mounds of his buttocks. When she heard him moan, her hands fell away and she stared into the stark features of a man too far gone with passion to turn back.

"I can't wait," he gasped in a voice tense with pain. "Feel how much I want you."

He dragged her hand between them, placing it on his rod. Velvet on steel, she thought dimly as she curled her hand around him and squeezed gently. He hissed out a breath. She squeezed again and he roared his approval.

Suddenly he flung her hand away. "No more! You're killing me, woman." His hand cupped her mound and he eased a finger inside her. "You're ready for me and I'm sure as hell ready for you."

He drew back a little and Chloe felt his erection prod against her opening. She stiffened, recalling what had happened the last time a man had torn into her unprepared body. She'd bled for a week and couldn't sit a horse for longer than that. And the pain. She couldn't go through that again.

"No!" The word was torn from her throat.

Desperado went still. "I won't hurt you. I'm not a monster. Nor am I an inexperienced lover. I know what women like and I'll make it good for you."

She had heard those words before. "I . . . I can't do this. I . . . ohhhh . . ."

He found her mouth and thrust deep with his tongue, just as his sex had found her center. He was inside her. Not all the way, but almost. Stretching her but not hurting her.

"That wasn't so bad, was it?" he rasped into her ear. "Can you take more of me?"

Chloe couldn't think. She couldn't relax. She wanted to move. She did. It was all the invitation he needed as he slid all the way in. She sighed and relaxed when she felt herself stretching to accommodate his heavy sex. There was no pain. He thrust in and out and she held her breath, waiting for something hurtful that never came.

Suddenly she needed more. She twisted, writhed. Trying to get away? No. Trying to get closer . . . to get more. A massive upsurge of pleasure blocked out her inhibitions, her fear, overwhelming her with the need to search for something . . . something that had no name. What Desperado was doing to her wasn't hurtful, or despicable, or obscene. What she felt was pure, unbridled rapture.

She wasn't a virgin but Desperado hadn't expected her to be one. She had come to him hot, sweet and needy. Then all thought ceased when he felt her muscles tighten and her sheath pulsate around him, cradling him in wet, torrid heat. The bliss was so overwhelming he thought he'd died and gone to heaven.

Groaning out his pleasure, he began a rhythm of thrust and withdraw calculated to bring both of them the most pleasure. He heard her sobbing his name, felt her nails scoring his shoulders, and all his long-suppressed passion exploded in a wild frenzy of need as he thrust again and again, until he felt her sheath convulse in hard, rhythmic spasms. His own climax burst upon him suddenly. He bared his teeth, threw his head back and roared. Then he rode with the pleasure, letting it carry them to uncharted territory.

Blood pounded in his head in the aftermath of the most fulfilling sex he'd ever experienced. He heard Chloe murmur against his neck where her head rested, and he realized he was too heavy for her, but for some reason he wasn't ready yet to leave her body. He levered himself onto his elbows and stared down at her.

"Are you all right?"

"I . . . you didn't hurt me." She sounded surprised.

He scowled. "Why would I hurt you? Is it because of my reputation? Making love to a woman has nothing to do with my profession. I think I just proved that."

"We should return to the campsite," Chloe said. "This was a mistake. I don't know what got into me."

He gave her a crooked grin. "I got into you."

A trail of red crept up her neck. "This never

should have happened and will never happen again." She tried to shove him away. "There is no excuse for my wanton behavior."

Heaving a reluctant sigh, Desperado pulled himself out of her tight passage and sat back on his heels. "No need to make excuses. We wanted one another. It's as simple as that." He searched her face, not liking what he saw. "Are you embarrassed?"

She nodded. "You're a . . ."

Desperado's face hardened. "A gunslinger? Halfbreed? Which do you like least? No, let me guess. You hate the idea of being intimate with a halfbreed. Am I the first Indian you've bedded? Did you learn something about savages just now? We're not as repulsive as some people make us out to be. My Indian blood didn't seem to matter when you took me into your body, or when you urged me on, or called my name at the peak of your pleasure. My back will bear the marks of your nails for a long time to come."

"Stop!" Chloe cried, placing her hands over her ears to block out his taunting words. "You don't know anything about me."

His smile did not reach his eyes. "I know you weren't a virgin. There were others before me. Perhaps Tate Talbot is more to your liking."

"How dare you!" She scooted out from beneath him and began to jerk on her clothes. "You're finished with this outfit, Mr. Jones. When we return to camp, collect your pay and get out."

"I'm not going anywhere, Miss Sommers," Desperado drawled. "You need me whether you know it or not. Go ahead and forget what just happened here if you think you can, but I will remember with pleasure the way you gave yourself to a half-breed gunslinger."

"Get out of here! Just get the hell away from me! I don't want to remember anything about you or what we just did. I found the act repulsive."

"Repulsive?" he repeated. "I don't think so, lady. You were hot and wet for me and I gave you what you asked for." Suddenly he smiled at her, a genuine smile that revealed those intriguing dimples. "That was the best ride I've ever had, honey. I can't recall when I've enjoyed anything more. There's a heap of passion inside that curvy little body of yours. I know I wasn't the first to have you, but was I the first to tap into that passion?"

Chloe buckled on her gunbelt and whirled to confront him. The fury blazing from the turbulent depths of her green eyes all but incinerated him. "Whatever you're thinking about me is wrong. I know you've already reached your own conclusion, but for your information I am not a loose woman."

Desperado's dark brows drew together. "I never said you were. I reckon you're picky when it comes to men. That's why you're so riled about letting a half-breed make love to you."

She placed her hands on her hips and glared at him. She looked so adorable Desperado had a hard time remembering what they were arguing about.

"If you weren't so hardheaded you'd know your Indian blood has nothing to do with my anger. Once a man ra—" She turned away, unable to continue. "Never mind, you wouldn't be interested.

Just get on your horse and ride. You're no longer working for me."

"Like hell!" Desperado hissed. "You hired me to do a job and I'm going to do it whether you like it or not. I think I can control myself around you from now on. Just don't ever look at me again like you did back there at camp. I'm a man, Chloe. I know when a woman wants me, and you, boss lady, were damn hot for me."

Hearing the truth sent color rushing to Chloe's cheeks. She *had* wanted him. She'd never wanted anything more in her life. But he was . . . a gunslinger. The half-breed part didn't bother her as much as the knowledge that she'd let herself be seduced by a man with a violent past and no future. She'd promised herself after Tate's brutal attack that she'd never be taken advantage of again.

Yet she knew in her heart that Desperado hadn't taken advantage of her. It made her angry to think she could desire the gunslinger sexually. She'd thought Tate's brutal attack had killed desire in her forever. She was not the helpless female she'd been then. Hadn't been since she'd learned to ride and shoot. But her guns were useless against a man like Desperado Jones, who used seduction instead of force to get what he wanted.

"What we just did is best forgotten, Mr. Jones," Chloe said crisply. "I'm going back to camp now. Pick up your pay before you leave."

"I told you, I'm not going anywhere," Desperado rasped in a voice that brooked no argument. "Go on back. I'll follow in a few minutes."

"I'm not paying you beyond today," Chloe declared as she turned on her heel and strode away.

Desperado hissed out an angry breath. Never would he understand women. He knew when a woman wanted him, and Chloe Sommers had damn sure wanted him. She was hot and willing in his arms, and had enjoyed him as much as he had enjoyed her. Chloe Sommers was a liar. Had she been a virgin, he could understand her anger, but he'd found no obstruction impeding his entrance. She'd been tight, damn tight, but others had been there before him.

Suddenly the thought of other men possessing Chloe's sweet body made him see red. Then he remembered that Chloe had seemed frightened moments before he'd entered her, and dimly he wondered if one or all of her lovers had been rough or forced her. Or . . . God, he'd drive himself mad with that kind of conjecture.

One glaring truth remained after considering everything that had led him to this moment. He would never allow the Talbots to hurt Chloe.

Chapter Seven

The drovers had started to drift back to camp by the time Chloe returned. Randy had a fire started and was slicing bacon for the men's breakfast. He looked up when Chloe stopped by the chuck wagon to pour herself a cup of strong black coffee.

Randy gave her a searching look. "Are you all right, Miss Chloe? That stampede was pretty darn scary. Do you know who started it?"

"I think we can blame the stampede on the Talbots."

"That was a brave thing Desperado did. We all thought you were a goner for sure."

Chloe didn't want to hear about Desperado's bravery. She didn't want to think about him at all. She was so angry at herself for letting passion carry her away, and at Desperado for taking advantage of her lapse, that she wanted to climb into her bedroll, pull the blanket over her head and forget every blissful moment she'd spent in the arms of the smooth-talking gunslinger.

A few more men staggered back to camp, tired, hungry and grumpy at being roused out of bed. Rowdy ambled over to join her, helping himself to a cup of coffee.

"There's something mighty strange going on around here," Rowdy observed. "Desperado always rides ahead to scout. How did he happen to miss that ravine when it lay less than a mile from our campsite?"

Chloe recalled thinking the same thing, but Desperado's lovemaking had completely blanked the thought from her mind. "I don't know but I certainly intend to find out."

"Where is the gunslinger?" Rowdy asked. "I thought he'd be here basking in the limelight. Most of the boys think he's a hero. I think he's a traitor."

"Desperado's mustang is in the remuda with the others," Randy said. "He's bound to be around here somewhere."

Chloe didn't want to face Desperado so soon after making a fool of herself in his arms. Guilt and shame rode her mercilessly. "I'm going to scout ahead," she said. "You're right, Rowdy, we can no longer trust Mr. Jones. From now on I'll do the scouting." She finished her coffee and handed the empty cup to Randy.

"Don't you want some breakfast, Miss Chloe?" Randy asked. "The bacon and biscuits are ready."

Chloe snatched a biscuit from the tray Randy held, split it in half, forked bacon onto one of the halves and slapped it together. "This will do. Get the herd moving as soon as everyone has eaten, Rowdy. I'll join you later, after I've made sure there are no more surprises along the route. We crossed the Oklahoma border some miles back and will be in Kansas before long. I can't depend on Mr. Jones, so I'm counting on you and the rest of the drovers to get the herd to Dodge for me."

Rowdy's chest puffed up. "You can depend on me, Miss Chloe. I told you, you don't need no gunslinger."

Chloe started toward the remuda. Cory jumped to his feet. "I'll saddle a horse for you, Miss Chloe. Your gelding needs a rest after his ordeal. How about that mare with a star on her forehead?"

"She'll do just fine."

Moments later Chloe rode out to the herd and saw that they were peacefully chomping grass after their exhausting stampede. She spotted Sonny and rode up to him. Lucky and Pete came up to join them. "I want the herd moving within the hour," Chloe said. "I'm riding ahead to scout."

"Alone?" Sonny asked. "What about Desperado?"

"He's on his own from now on," Chloe said tersely.

"But . . ."

Chloe didn't wait around to find out what Lucky was about to say as she spurred her mount north toward the Kansas border. She rode a good ten miles before deciding that no more surprises lay in store for them. Their next obstacle would be the Cimarron River just over the Kansas border.

Chloe stopped to rest and water her mare in a

shallow creek before starting back. She sat down on a flat rock beside the creek, and before she knew it her eyelids began to droop. She couldn't resist the urge to lie down and take a catnap before starting back. She'd gotten no sleep the night before and within a few minutes she was sound asleep. A short time later she must have sensed danger for she awoke abruptly. A shadow blocked out the sun and she stared up into Tate Talbot's grinning face.

"I saw you leave camp," Tate said. "Where is your watchdog?"

Still groggy, Chloe sat up and looked around to get her bearings. Suddenly she remembered where she was, and that once again she had placed herself in a potentially dangerous situation. Instinct made her reach for her gun. It wasn't in her gunbelt. She glanced at Tate and saw it dangling from his fingertips.

"I took the liberty of removing it from your gunbelt while you slept. You're too damn trigger happy for your own good."

"What do you want?"

"I want to know why we can't take up where we left off two years ago. I know I can work a deal with Pa to let you and me live at the ranch. He don't want the house anyway; it's the land he wants."

"Why?" Chloe asked curiously. "Why is your father so interested in my land?"

Tate shrugged. "I don't question Pa. He knows what he's doing."

"No deal, Tate," Chloe retorted. "You showed your true colors two years ago. I want nothing more to do with you."

"You're giving it to that half-breed, ain't you?" Tate charged. "You little slut! I was the one who broke you in. You owe me."

Chloe couldn't believe her ears. "I owe you?" she all but shouted. "You conceited jackass! Don't you know I hated what you did to me? And I hated you for doing it. Why don't you leave me alone? I know you started the stampede. You knew about the ravine. You knew I'd lose half my herd if they stampeded and couldn't be stopped before reaching the ravine. It didn't work, Tate Talbot. My crew may be young but they pulled together and stopped the herd before any damage was done."

"You got yourself in a tight spot, didn't you, Chloe? That ought to teach you not to mess with the Talbots. If that gunslinger hadn't snatched you away in time, you would have plunged into the ravine." He touched her cheek. "That's not what I intended, little honey. I don't want you hurt. I want you for myself."

She slapped his hand away. "Don't touch me!"

Tate's face hardened. "I'll bet you let that half-breed do more than touch you."

Chloe's expression must have betrayed her for Tate reached for her, a nasty snarl curling his lips. "If you're going to give it to a savage, you damn well can give it to me."

"Step away from her, Talbot."

Tate spun around, paling when he found himself looking down the barrel of Desperado's gun. "What are you, some kind of magician?" Tate gasped. "Do you make a habit of turning up when you're least

130

wanted? Get lost. Me and Chloe have unfinished business."

"Is that true, Chloe?" His question was directed at Chloe but he never took his eyes off of Tate.

"No! I want nothing to do with Tate Talbot."

"Return Chloe's weapon," Desperado ordered.

Tate's eyes promised revenge as he tossed the gun at Chloe. She caught it handily and tucked it into her gunbelt.

"You won't be so cocky when my boys arrive. They probably saw you riding up and have their sights on you."

Desperado gave him a contemptuous grin. "You'll find your friends tied up down the trail a ways."

"Have you forgotten whose side you're on, Jones?" Tate taunted.

Chloe gave Desperado a sharp look. "What does he mean, Mr. Jones? Have you gained a new employer since I fired you this morning?"

Talbot gave a roar of laughter. "That's rich. You can't fire Jones, he's working for my father, always has been."

Chloe darted a shocked glance at Desperado, saw his fingers flex at his sides, and felt a suffocating weight settle over her. It couldn't be true! Yet in her heart she knew it was. She'd allowed a traitorous viper to seduce her. How the gunslinger must be laughing at her.

"Shut up, Talbot," Desperado rasped.

"Hell no, I won't shut up," Talbot roared, ignoring the dangerous glint in Desperado's eyes. "It's time Chloe learned exactly where you stand."

131

The pain of his betrayal was like a kick in the gut, squeezing out her breath. "Is that true, Mr. Jones?"

The look Desperado sent Tate should have scared the hell out of him, but if it did, Tate showed no sign of it. Apparently he felt confident that his father's money paid for his safety.

"Of course it's true. Why in the hell do you suppose Jones didn't tell you about the ravine? Who do you think caused all those minor 'accidents' back at the ranch? They were delaying tactics meant to frighten you into selling your cows in Texas instead of taking them to Dodge."

Flayed by Chloe's contemptuous gaze, Desperado experienced emotions that were new to him. Shame. Guilt. And others equally foreign he couldn't identify.

"Did you fire the barn?" Chloe asked point blank.

"No."

"Liar! Did you set fire to my house?"

"No."

"Liar. Did you scatter the herd before the drive began?"

"Yes. But no harm was done."

"What about the branding irons? Their loss set us back two weeks."

"I . . . yes, I took them."

"How much did Calvin Talbot pay you?" Chloe demanded.

Desperado said nothing, feeling lower than a skunk.

"I can tell you that," Tate said, barging into the void. "Pa paid him seven hundred and fifty dollars to make sure your herd never reaches Dodge. He's already collected the first half of the money. He'll collect the rest when the job is done." He sent Desperado an accusatory glance. "To my knowledge, the gunslinger hasn't earned a plug nickel. I've done most of the work myself."

"You've said enough, Talbot," Desperado warned. "I've got a message for you to take back to your father." Pinning Tate with his hard gaze, he dug into his vest pocket, removed a wad of bills and tossed them at Tate's feet. "Tell your father the deal's off. The money is all there," he said as Tate scrambled to gather up the bills. "I'm cutting all ties with the Talbots. From now on I'm working for Chloe."

"Like hell!" Chloe shouted. "I'll take my chances without you. I don't hire men I can't trust."

Desperado smarted beneath Chloe's well-deserved censure. If he was wise he'd get on his horse and ride hell for leather away from anything and everything connected with his past. No one knew he was Logan Ralston, and he meant to keep it that way. Unfortunately, his newly discovered conscience wouldn't let him abandon a woman who desperately needed him, whether or not she chose to acknowledge that need.

"You heard the little lady, Jones," Tate taunted. "We don't need you. Me and Chloe are about to strike a deal on our own. Pa gets the land and Chloe and me are gonna get hitched and live at the ranch."

Chloe sent him a quelling look. "You're no better than Desperado, Tate Talbot! I'm going to take my herd to Dodge, sell to the highest bidder and pay my taxes with the proceeds from the sale. I don't need Desperado Jones, and I sure as hell don't need you."

"You do need me, Chloe," Tate boasted. "Have you told Jones about you and me? Does he know I was your first lover? No matter how many lovers you've taken after me, you'll always remember that first time. I'm told women remember things like that."

Chloe blanched. "That's something I've tried hard to forget. Both of you get out of my sight. I'm the head of this outfit and I have every confidence that my drovers will get my herd to Dodge safely."

"Your cows will never reach Dodge," Tate said with complete confidence.

"Would you like to place a bet on that?" Desperado rasped. "You have me to contend with now, Talbot."

For the first time, Tate looked uncertain. "You thinking about double-crossing Pa?" he asked with obvious surprise.

"Damn right. From now on Chloe is my responsibility. You and your father can go to hell. No one is going to take Chloe's land from her."

Tate gave him a twisted grin. "So that's the way the wind blows. You're poking her, just like I suspected. Was she as hot for you as she was for me?"

Desperado's eyes went murky and his lips flattened. Tate must have seen his hand inching toward his gun for he retreated a step. "You wouldn't shoot a man who can't defend himself, would you?" He held out his right hand. "It still ain't healed. I've been practicing with my left hand, but I'm no match for a crack shot like you."

"You're not worth shooting, Talbot. But I intend to leave you with a reminder of what I'm capable of."

The only indication of what he intended was the muscle that jumped along his rigid jawline. Clenching his right hand into a fist, he let fly with a hook that caught Tate on the chin. Tate staggered backward but couldn't escape Desperado's left jab. That blow felled him. He lay on the ground, stunned and unable to rise as Desperado placed a booted foot atop his chest.

"Now that we understand one another," Desperado drawled, "you can go. Don't forget to rescue your friends."

"You ain't heard the last from me, Jones," Tate gasped beneath the weight of Desperado's foot. "Mark my words, those cows will never reach Dodge." Desperado lifted his foot. Tate's heated gaze lingered a moment on Chloe before he lifted himself off the ground and slunk off.

"Let's get the hell back to camp," Desperado said gruffly.

"How did you find me?"

"Same way Talbot did. I tracked you. When I returned to camp and learned you were scouting ahead, I decided to follow."

"I meant what I said," Chloe asserted. "You're no longer working for me."

He grasped her waist and tossed her into the saddle. "I don't give a hoot in hell what you want, Chloe. I'm not going to stand by and let the Talbots steal Ralston land out from under you. I don't care what you and Tate once were to one another." *Liar*. "You can even forget what happened between us today if it will ease your conscience."

"I don't understand. Why should you care about me or my land?" Chloe challenged. "You're a gunslinger. You go where fate takes you and use your gun to flout the law."

"I'm not an outlaw," he retorted. "There is one thing I do well, and people pay for my services."

"Have you no conscience? What you intended to do to me has 'illegal' written all over it."

Desperado had the grace to look away. "I had my reasons. Reasons you don't know about."

"You seduced me," Chloe charged.

"You wanted it as much as I did. The way you looked at me was . . . well, let's just say no woman could have expressed her needs more thoroughly than you did by simply looking at me. I gave us what we both wanted."

Now it was Chloe's turn to flush. "I . . . I must have lost my mind."

"It certainly wasn't your virginity you lost," Desperado taunted, and could have bit his tongue afterward. He wasn't being fair. But it rankled to think that Tate Talbot had been the first with Chloe.

Desperado wasn't prepared for Chloe's rage. She launched herself at him from her mare's back. Not expecting the attack, Desperado fell backward to the ground, taking Chloe with him. They rolled on the ground as she pounded him with her fists. It was all Desperado could do to keep from hurting her as he defended himself as best he could. When she began to tire, he grasped her wrists and rolled her beneath him.

"Are you through?" he drawled.

She writhed beneath him, trying to escape, but his hard body gave not an inch. "You don't know me at all. How dare you judge me?"

"You're right," Desperado agreed. "I have no right to judge you. I'm sorry."

"That's not good enough, Mr. Jones."

"Will this do?" he asked as he covered her mouth with his.

He tasted the sweet puff of air that left her lungs and he deepened the kiss. She tried to keep her lips closed against his invading tongue, but he probed until her mouth grudgingly opened, allowing his tongue to sweep inside. He kissed her until he felt her body relax, until she arched against him and moaned. Until her arms came around his neck. He touched her intimately between her legs before he broke off the kiss.

"Now do you accept my apology?"

No longer driven mad by his warm mouth, hot kisses and talented hands, Chloe was finally able to think clearly again. What was she doing? She didn't want a repeat of what had happened this morning. Nor did she want this treacherous half-breed anywhere near her. His kisses stole her mind and left her body aching with need. It was intolerable. No half-breed gunslinger was going to turn her life upside down.

"I accept your apology," Chloe said before he had a chance to kiss her senseless again.

137

He grinned at her. She had the unaccountable urge to kiss the dimple in his cheek but restrained herself. "Now, where were we?" he asked.

"You were going to let me up. It's time I returned to camp. No telling what Tate has planned, and I want to warn the drovers."

"That's not what I had in mind." Desperado sighed as he rose slowly to his feet. So slowly Chloe knew he was reluctant to let her go. She scooted out from beneath him. When he moved to help her mount, she sprang up into her saddle before he could touch her. She didn't know if she could resist his hands upon her again, in places where she still ached from his fevered caresses.

Touching her heels to her mount, she rode off. "Don't bother to follow," Chloe called over her shoulder. "I fired you, remember?"

The only thing Desperado remembered was how warm her sweetly curved body felt in his arms. And how arousing her kisses were. He wondered how long it would be before his erection subsided.

Desperado made himself scarce during the following days. But he wasn't idle. Far from it. He rarely slept during the following days of the drive. Three times he'd stopped Tate and his friends from stampeding the herd. He patrolled at night, making the drovers aware of his presence while cautioning them not to tell Chloe about his activities on their behalf.

He watched Chloe like a hawk. When she rode out alone, he was right behind her. An expert tracker, he followed her everywhere. Twice he'd stopped Tate from accosting her. He still laughed when he recalled how frightened Tate's friends were of him. They feared his gun, and with good reason. His reputation as a lightning draw was no exaggeration. He'd worked hard to make the world see him as a dangerous desperado with an itchy trigger finger.

It was the way things had to be, he tried to convince himself. He was a man with no past, no future, no place to call home. Then he'd met Chloe Sommers, the daughter of a woman he had every reason to despise, and suddenly he'd found a conscience. He hoped to hell he hadn't found more than a conscience, for he didn't know if he could handle a deeper emotion. He convinced himself that what he felt for Chloe was simply lust. Just looking at her made him hot and hard and primed to go off.

Thanks to Desperado's intervention, the herd crossed the Kansas border and the Cimarron River without mishap. Another few days would see them in Dodge. One night he became careless and rode straight into Chloe when she came to check on the herd before retiring.

Chloe reined in sharply. "What are you doing here? I thought I told you to leave."

"No one tells Desperado Jones what to do."

Just then Cory rode up to join them. "Something wrong, Miss Chloe?"

Chloe gritted her teeth in frustration. Obviously the drovers knew about Desperado and had chosen not to tell her. Even Rowdy had remained silent, and Rowdy didn't like the gunslinger any more than she did. "How long has this traitor been riding with the herd?"

Cory shrugged. "I . . . don't recall. Seems like he's always here. If you don't mind my saying, Miss Chloe, all us drovers appreciate having Desperado around. Even Rowdy thinks he's a necessary evil."

"I do mind your saying, Cory," Chloe maintained. "This is my drive. You work for me. I fired Mr. Jones, he has no business being here."

"Whatever you say, Miss Chloe," Cory said. "We're almost to Dodge anyway."

"So we are," Chloe snapped. "Go back to camp, I'll take over for you here."

Cory didn't argue as he turned his horse and rode back to camp, leaving Chloe and Desperado alone but for two drovers patrolling the outer perimeter of the herd.

Chloe turned back to confront Desperado, her green eyes blazing furiously. "What do I have to do to get rid of you, Mr. Jones?"

"Nothing, I reckon. Once my mind is made up, nothing is going to change it. I intend to protect you, Chloe, whether you like it or not."

Chloe went still. "Why?"

"Damned if I know. Maybe I feel guilty about deceiving you."

Chloe gave a shout of laughter. "Who are you trying to kid? You don't have a guilty bone in your body. And I doubt you ever had a conscience. You had your fun, now get out of here."

"I don't think so."

Her gun was out of the holster before Desperado

had a chance to react. He grinned at her. "You're fast for a woman."

Chloe caught her breath. That dimple was distracting as hell. She looked elsewhere. "If I ever see you within shouting distance of me, my men, or my herd, I'm going to shoot to kill."

"You're serious, aren't you?" Desperado rasped.

"Deadly serious. Now turn around and ride."

Desperado made as if to wheel his mustang away from her. He surprised her instead by bringing his horse beside hers. Fast as a whip, he reached out, twisted her gun from her hand and shoved it back in her holster. Then he pulled her head forward and kissed her. Hard. Full on the lips. A stunningly tempestuous kiss meant to remind her, she was sure, of the passion they had once shared.

Desperado left the trail drive after that last confrontation with Chloe, but he didn't go far. Dodge lay but two days away and he didn't dare relax his vigilance now. Once he was certain the herd was safe from Talbot's machinations and Chloe's land was secure, he intended to ride as far away from Trouble Creek as he could get.

Desperado trailed Tate Talbot and his friends throughout the remaining days of the drive. He made sure he was seen from time to time so that the trio knew they were being followed. Cowards that they were, he doubted they'd do anything more to sabotage the drive as long as they knew Desperado Jones was watching them.

When Talbot and his friends rode into Dodge hours ahead of the herd, Desperado was close behind. He didn't relax his guard until they took rooms at the hotel. Only then did he follow their example and engage a room for himself. In the several hours before the herd reached town, Desperado got a haircut, soaked in a hot tub and bought himself the biggest steak the Dodge House had to offer.

He was standing in front of the Longbranch Saloon, smoking a long black cigar, when Chloe and her drovers herded the cattle down the main street to the holding pens near the railroad. When Chloe happened to glance in his direction, he tipped his hat and smiled. He laughed when she lifted her chin and looked through him.

Later that day Desperado watched from a distance as Chloe's herd was auctioned to the highest bidder. Beef was at a premium back East, and she received the unheard-of price of thirteen dollars a head. The buyer paid her in cash, and Desperado felt a glimmer of admiration for the plucky wildcat. Now that she had more than enough money to pay her taxes, Desperado considered leaving the next day for parts unknown. It wasn't healthy for him to stick around in one place too long.

After the auction, Desperado saw Chloe enter the hotel and take a room. He wondered how long she would stay in Dodge, then chided himself for caring. He'd thought he'd lost the ability to care when he'd lost his conscience. Obviously he hadn't, for something deep and disturbing stirred inside him when he thought of riding away and never seeing Chloe again. Having no patience for maudlin sentiments, Desperado pulled his hat down over his forehead and walked away.

At loose ends after a late supper that night, Desperado felt restless and decided to visit the Longbranch Saloon and maybe sample one of the local women. At this point he was willing to try anything to banish thoughts of Chloe from his mind. He strode through the swinging doors and saw Tate and his friends standing at the bar, drinking and talking with a man he recognized as the day clerk at the hotel. They were so engrossed in their conversation they failed to see Desperado slide out a chair and sit down at a table close to the bar. Desperado watched with growing rage as the clerk accepted money from Tate and handed him a key. Then he heard Tate say, "Keep your mouth shut about this. I'm going to surprise my girlfriend and I don't want anyone to know."

Chloe.

Unwinding his long, lean length from the chair, Desperado hurried after Tate, his face set in hard lines. Outside the saloon, Tate had disappeared. He couldn't have had too great a head start but he had a key and room number, which Desperado didn't. He stormed into the hotel, startling the night clerk and two men checking in. He must have appeared menacing to them for the two men immediately made for the door and the clerk backed up against the wall, away from Desperado.

"C-c-can I help you, sir? Did you lose your key?"

"Quick!" Desperado rasped, "I need Miss Sommers' room number."

"I'm sorry, sir, rules, you know. We aren't allowed to—"

Desperado reached across the counter and dragged the quaking clerk forward until they were nose to nose. "I don't give a shit about rules. Do you know who I am?"

The clerk shook his head, unable to speak beyond a squeak.

"My name is Desperado Jones. Ever hear of me?"

"Y-y-yes, sir," he stammered. "Who hasn't? You'll find Miss Sommers in room 215. Second floor, on the right."

Desperado released the clerk so fast the poor man hit the floor with a thud. Seconds later Desperado was bounding up the narrow staircase to the second floor, thinking he must be either crazy in the head or under the spell of the full moon.

Chloe had gone directly up to her room after placing her money in the hotel safe. She'd seen both Tate and Desperado in town and was taking no chances. That money was her assurance that she would keep the land she'd grown to love. She owed it to Ted Ralston to fight for the ranch he'd built. Then she'd ordered a bath and dinner and gone to bed, falling asleep immediately.

She slept so soundly she didn't hear the key she'd left in the door fall to the floor, or the scraping of a second key turning in the lock. Or the click of a door opening and closing. She was aware of nothing until she felt a heavy body smelling strongly of sweat and alcohol fall upon her.

She opened her mouth to scream.

144

Immediately a hand covered her mouth.

"Don't fight it, baby. This time Desperado ain't around to interfere. Spread those white thighs for me, I can't wait to push myself inside you. It'll be like old times."

He removed his hand to kiss her, and Chloe promptly bit his lower lip, drawing blood. He cursed and slapped her hard. "Bitch! Lie still. I'll show you what a real man is like. I'm a better man than Desperado Jones any day."

He shoved her nightdress up past her knees and slid between her legs. She kicked him and he slapped her again. "You're forcing me to hurt you."

"I'll kill you," Chloe warned.

The scrape of an opening door caught Chloe's attention as a sliver of light spilled into the room and a low, angry hiss pierced the silence. "Not if I kill him first! Get away from her, Talbot."

Desperado's menacing form was silhouetted in the open doorway, feet planted wide apart, fists clenched at his sides.

Tate reared up, finally realizing they weren't alone. "This is none of your business, Jones," he grated as he wiped blood from his lip.

"I'm making it my business. Move away from Chloe. I'm not going to use my guns on you. I'll give you a sporting chance. Then I'm going to beat the shit out of you."

Chapter Eight

Chloe turned her face to the wall, listening to the sound of Desperado's fists thudding into Tate's body. Not that Tate didn't deserve everything Desperado dished out. Tate Talbot was an animal without a redeeming bone in his body. Rape was an ugly act, yet that was exactly what Tate had done to her. And tonight he'd tried to do it again. He seemed to think she belonged to him and whatever he did was all right.

She heard Tate cursing, heard him whimpering, heard him begging, and it did her heart good. Had she the strength, she would have beaten him herself. The knowledge that Tate didn't stand a chance against a man like Desperado brought a smile to her lips. Her smile died when she heard the door slam and the key turn in the lock. She dared a glance over her shoulder and saw Desperado strike a match to the lamp. When the light flared, he turned to regard her. His face remained half in shadows but she could tell by his rigid stance that he was angry. His jaw was clenched so tightly she thought it a miracle his teeth didn't crack.

His voice grated harshly in the charged silence. "You can turn around now. I tossed the bastard out on his ass. It will take a while for his friends to pick up the pieces."

"You didn't kill him, did you?" Though she hated Tate, she didn't want his death on her conscience.

"He'll live." He searched her face, his expression grim. "Did he hurt you?"

She shook her head. "A little. Not badly. How did he get in? How did you know you'd find him in my room?"

"I saw Talbot in the Longbranch with the day clerk from the hotel. When the clerk exchanged a key for Talbot's money, I put two and two together and realized Talbot intended to pay you an un-scheduled visit. I hope I didn't interrupt something you and your former lover had planned."

"Damn you, Desperado Jones! You know how I feel about the Talbots. And Tate is the worst of them. If you call him my former lover again, I'll make you sorry. And don't think I can't do it!"

"Women have needs, just like men," he said bluntly. "It's your choice of lovers I'm questioning."

"Tate Talbot was never my lover!" she spat from between clenched teeth.

Desperado shrugged. "He said . . . Well, hell, you weren't a virgin and I just assumed—"

"Why do men always jump to conclusions?"

Chloe blasted. "Do they value a woman's virginity more than they value the woman herself?"

Desperado appeared to mull over that question before answering. "I reckon most men do. I have no room to talk. I'm no angel myself. If you wanted Tate Talbot . . ." His words trailed off, as if completing his sentence was painful.

Chloe shuddered at the memory of that terrible night she'd lost her virginity. "I thank God I found out what Tate was like before I agreed to marry him."

She touched his arm. "You showed me the difference between loving and the obscenity Tate forced upon me."

Desperado looked confused. "Forced? He wasn't your lover?" The look on his face was so fierce she felt an unaccountable urge to run, though she knew his fury wasn't directed at her. "Tell me what happened," he said quietly, too quietly.

Chloe shook her head and looked away, plucking nervously at the blanket. "I . . . can't. I don't want to think about it."

Desperado perched on the bed beside her and lifted her chin. "Tate Talbot hurt you, didn't he?"

Rage built inside her. Rage she'd buried deep within her for too long. She'd told no one about her humiliation after it had happened. But she'd changed after that. She had quietly gone about making certain she'd never be taken advantage of again. Now the horror of that night returned, bringing with it all the pent-up resentment and emotions she'd kept under strict control for the last two years. The hurt had been a part of her too long, and suddenly she felt as if she'd been offered a chance to unburden herself.

She dragged in a sustaining breath and whispered the words she'd never breathed to a living soul. "Tate Talbot raped me. He was courting me at the time. Mama encouraged me to accept his proposal. She thought him a perfect man for me."

Desperado said nothing; he didn't need to. His fathomless black eyes spoke eloquently of his rage.

She closed her eyes, her mind wandering back to that dreadful night. She winced as if in pain but somehow managed to continue. "Tate took me to a dance in town one night. He'd had too much to drink but I never thought he'd—" She swallowed with difficulty. "He wanted me to . . . to make love with him. I said no. He insisted. I got angry and told him I never wanted to see him again. Tate Talbot is an ugly drunk. He stopped the carriage, threw me to the ground and . . . r . . . raped me. I was an innocent."

She turned her face away, unable to look Desperado in the eye. "I wanted to die." Did he believe her? Or did he still think Tate had been her lover? She didn't know why, but it mattered that he believe her. "Somehow I found the courage to go on. I never told anyone. Afterward I learned how to defend myself against scum like Tate Talbot. No man has ever gotten close to me again. Until you."

Grasping her chin between thumb and forefinger, Desperado lifted her face to his. She raised her eyes and saw something she'd never seen there before. Compassion. Regret. And something that mystified her.

"You've told me enough," he rasped. The words sounded as if they had come from the deepest depths of his soul. "I've done a lot of rotten things in my life but I've never raped a woman." He rose abruptly. "Get some sleep."

"Where are you going?" Had her confession disgusted him?

"To finish what I started with Tate Talbot."

He was going to kill Tate! Chloe thought, seized by a terrible fear. He could end up in jail, or dead at the hands of Tate's friends, and she didn't want that for him.

She wanted . . . "Don't go!"

He turned back to her. His face was set in harsh lines and his dark eyes promised terrible retribution to the man who had caused her suffering. Never had she seen a man more bent on mayhem than Desperado Jones. She wasn't even sure he'd heard her until he enunciated very slowly, "You don't want me to go?"

"Please," she heard herself saying. "I don't want you to leave." She remembered what had almost happened in this room tonight, and there was no pretense in her shudder of revulsion. "I need you. Stay with me."

He looked overwhelmed, and more than a little wary. "Do you know what you're asking me?"

"I know exactly what I'm asking. I don't want to be alone tonight."

A subtle change came over his harsh features. The corners of his mouth kicked up into a crooked smile and his eyes seemed to glow from within. "If I stay with you in this room tonight, I want you to know exactly what will happen," he rasped. "I'm going to climb into that bed with you and love you in all the ways possible for a man to love a woman. What we're going to have if I stay is primitive, basic sex. We're going to get hot and sweaty, and it will be so good you'll think you've died and gone to heaven. I'm going to make you want it as badly as I do. What we do *won't* be rape. Now," he said, his voice so low she could barely hear him, "ask me again."

Chloe swallowed past the lump in her throat as she vividly recalled the morning Desperado had made love to her. She'd never known such pleasure existed until Desperado had shown her how wonderfully fulfilling sex could be between a man and a woman.

She took so long to answer, Desperado must have thought she'd changed her mind for he turned abruptly and walked toward the door. His jangling spurs roused her from her reverie and she cried out his name.

"Don't go! Stay with me. Love me."

His answer was a long, drawn-out groan. She heard the key turn in the lock and then he was standing beside the bed, his gaze hot and hungry as he shed his gunbelt and shrugged out of his shirt and vest. Chloe felt the bed dip as he sat down to remove his boots and pants. When he was naked he reached over to turn down the lamp.

"No! I want to see all of you. Stand up."

"Chloe . . ." His voice was taut with warning as

his body reacted violently to her words. But he obeyed despite his misgivings.

Chloe dragged in a startled breath as she stared at his rigid sex. Without volition her fingers closed around his erection. She watched him closely as she stroked him, her eyes widening as he grew even larger and harder. His tormented groan gave hint of the turbulence that lay just beneath the surface, and she reluctantly released him. Her gaze slid down his strong, muscular legs, then back up to his massive chest and shoulders, carefully avoiding his sex this time. His skin was the color of warm honey and she wanted to touch him all over. She noticed a small bag attached to a string around his neck and curiosity made her ask, "What's in that bag around your neck? I've noticed it before."

Desperado touched the rawhide pouch. "It's my medicine bag. It carries my good fortune and small mementos of my life. It was given to me by my Indian grandfather. I only saw him once, and he wanted me to have it so I wouldn't forget him."

"I see," Chloe said, too engrossed in other parts of his anatomy to waste time wondering about the medicine bag. "Turn around."

"Chloe . . ." His voice shook from the restraint he was imposing upon himself.

When she touched the velvet smooth roundness of his buttocks he jerked as if gut shot. He turned abruptly, his night-dark eyes savage bright with implied violence. And something else. Promise. "No more!" he growled as he flung himself down on the bed beside her.

The breath slammed from her chest as he

dragged her against him and covered her mouth with his. It was as if she had unleashed a sleeping beast within him as his mouth moved sensuously over hers, driving all thought from her mind but for this moment, this man, and the longing deep within her that only he could assuage.

A cry of protest escaped her throat when the warmth of his lips left hers, but the cry turned into a purr of pleasure when his lips slid over her cheek, tracing a burning path down her neck to her breast. When he found his way barred by her shift, he ripped it down the middle and shoved it aside. He did nothing for a long moment but look at her breasts.

"They're beautiful," he said, cupping a full, rose-tipped mound in his hand. "A perfect fit for my hand." He bent his head and licked a puckered nipple with his tongue. Then he drew the rosy bud into his mouth and sucked upon it. When the tip grew hard he abandoned it for the other tasty morsel, and Chloe got a glimpse of what torture was like.

"Now, please," she gasped, letting her legs fall apart in blatant invitation.

"Not yet," Desperado growled as he tore away the remnants of her shift and tossed them on the floor. Then he returned his attention to her mouth, pressing hot, humid kisses against her open lips, driving his tongue in then out just as his loins jerked against hers in imitation of the sex act.

Her breath came in jagged gasps. She wanted him inside her so badly she felt she would die if he didn't end this soon. She groaned in frustration and grasped his hair when his mouth left hers and started a slow descent down her trembling body.

"Damn you! What are you doing to me?"

He kissed her navel and grinned up at her. "Giving you what we both want, honey. I swear you won't be sorry. Now let loose of my hair and lie back so I can love you."

Short on patience and aroused beyond human endurance, Chloe tried to pull him inside her. Laughing, he grasped her legs and spread them wide. Then he lowered his head and touched her heated center with his tongue. Briefly. She gave a muted shriek and tried to close her legs.

He laughed again, raised her hips up to his mouth and buried his face in the sweet scent of her arousal. He licked at her, sucked at her. She went wild beneath him; never in her wildest dreams did she think such wickedness existed. But what wonderful, glorious wickedness! She felt wet pleasure flowing from her and should have been embarrassed, but Desperado seemed unconcerned as he lapped up the liquid essence of her desire with obvious relish. Then his tongue slid inside her, deep, sending her to oblivion. She cried out and undulated beneath him, unable to contain the overwhelming sensations roiling through her.

"Desperado! I can't . . . Please. It's too much."

Desperado didn't answer. Didn't even lift his head as his mouth and tongue pushed her over the edge. Lights flashed before her closed eyes as her body flew upward to touch the stars.

Desperado gazed rapturously into Chloe's passion-glazed face as she slowly tumbled back to reality. His distended sex throbbed with the need to thrust into that warm, wet place he so desperately craved, but he deliberately denied himself his own pleasure until Chloe was fully aware of what he was doing. He wanted to take her to paradise again, but with her full knowledge of what was happening.

Her eyelids fluttered open and she raised her hand to her head, as if confused by what had just happened. She released a shaky breath. "I . . . I thought I died and went to heaven."

"I told you so," he rasped smugly. "Did you like that?"

"It was terribly wicked."

"Not when it brings us both pleasure. I'm going to come inside you now, Chloe. Are you ready for me?"

He touched her between her legs and felt her trembling response. "You're more than ready," he said in a voice harsh with need. "Damnation, I'm going to die if I have to wait much longer. Shall I arouse you again, honey?" He didn't know how he'd survive if she said yes but he'd give it a damn good shot.

"Come inside me now, Desperado."

Her words unleashed a powerful force inside him. Before she could change her mind, he flexed his hips and pierced her cleanly, thrusting himself into the sweetest, tightest, hottest place he'd ever had the pleasure to visit. He grasped her buttocks and pounded into her; his eyes were narrowed and his face was rigid with concentration as he thrust and withdrew, again and again, wringing moans from her that set him aflame.

He felt her nails digging into his shoulders and welcomed the sting, secure in the knowledge that he was giving her the same kind of pleasure he was receiving. Her wordless cries made his heart feel newborn, bringing a dimension to his life that had been lacking before Chloe Sommers strutted into it. He felt needy and uncertain, but happier than he could ever recall.

Then his thoughts scattered as blood rushed to his loins in anticipation of his climax. Before he disintegrated he glanced down at Chloe. She was breathing hard, her lips parted, her eyes tightly closed. Her body was rigid as she strained against him, reaching for that elusive goal. He licked her lips and whispered, "Hurry, honey. I don't want to leave you behind."

He knew she heard him for her fingers tightened on his shoulders and she pushed up against him, as if struggling to catch up. Fearing he'd go off without her, he worked a hand between them and massaged the rigid bud he found nestled in a fold of sensitive flesh. He heard Chloe scream out his name, felt the contractions squeezing his sex and let himself fly. He soared further and higher than he ever had in his life.

Chloe awoke to the sounds of chirping birds and street noises. She stretched, overwhelmed by a contentment she'd never dreamed was possible. She'd never felt more satisfied or complete in her entire life. The soreness between her legs reminded her of last night's activity, and she smiled. Making love with Desperado had been an inspiring experience. *He* was inspiring.

She smiled when she recalled how Desperado had wanted her again last night after a brief rest. Then he had given her free reign to do as she wished to him. First she had explored his body, murmuring over the scars from old wounds that marred his smooth bronze flesh. She had kissed and caressed and satisfied her curiosity as Desperado writhed and moaned and promised dire consequences if she didn't end it soon.

Of course she had ignored him. She tittered to herself when she recalled how he'd nearly jerked off the bed when she'd decided to see what he tasted like. Unfortunately, he hadn't allowed her to do more than run her tongue down his length a time or two before he let out a roar, pulled her over him and thrust himself inside her. She had thoroughly enjoyed being in the dominant position, controlling him with the pressure of her legs. When he tried to thrust them both to completion, she had deliberately slowed him down, making it last until she felt him trembling beneath her and knew he could bear no more. Then she had let him have his way, until the pressure grew unbearable and she climaxed violently.

Afterward they had slept. And judging by the thick wedge of sunlight shining through the window, it appeared as if they had overslept. She glanced over at Desperado. In sleep his features were not so tautly drawn or stern. He looked younger, less damaged by life. She wondered what his childhood had been like, and if he'd been loved by his parents. She wanted to know everything about him. Had he been raised by Indians? What happened to his white parent? She smiled when she thought of the child Desperado must have been. She had a vivid picture of his naked bronze body, playing beneath the baking sun.

"Is that smile for me?"

Chloe flushed guiltily. "I was just thinking."

"About what?"

"About your childhood. Were you happy? Were your parents good to you?"

His face hardened, and she chided herself for prying. If Desperado wanted her to know about his childhood he'd tell her. "I'm sorry. You don't have to tell me anything."

"There are other things I'd rather do than talk right now."

"Are you evading my questions?"

"Probably. Turn around. Slide your back against my chest."

Chloe stared at him for a long moment, then did what he asked. She fit perfectly in the cradle of his body and snuggled against him. Her eyes widened and she let out a yelp of surprise when she felt his hard sex prodding her from behind.

"Again? I didn't think . . ." She bit her lip in consternation. "That is . . . Doesn't a man need to regain his strength?"

"I did. And I've never felt stronger. Lift your leg a little so I can slide inside you."

"But this isn't the way . . ."

Chloe soon learned that Desperado knew exactly what he wanted and how to go about getting it. He pulled her bottom into the cradle of his thighs, found her opening and thrust inside. Then he moved, in and out, rapidly, with sure deep strokes, quickly taking Chloe on a spiraling journey to bliss.

"Where did you learn so much about . . . about . . . this?" Chloe asked when her breathing returned to normal.

"Here and there," Desperado said dryly. "Did you think all Indians were savages?"

Chloe had the grace to flush. That was exactly what she had thought when she'd thought about it at all. "How did you come by your name? Jones isn't your real name, is it?"

"It's as good as any," Desperado said with a shrug. "Names meant little to me when I left the Apache village and struck out on my own. Someone called me a desperado after my first job and the name stuck. Jones was my own idea."

"Why didn't you use your white father's name?"

His lips thinned. "I cut all ties with my white family many years ago," he said tersely. "Why all the questions?"

"I was just remembering," Chloe mused. "My stepfather had a son by an Indian woman. Mama mentioned him a time or two. His name was Logan."

"What happened to him?" Desperado asked in a hushed voice.

"Mama said he was attacked and killed by wild animals. He was returning from San Antonio, where he had been visiting relatives." She shuddered. "I recall hearing the story and feeling so sorry for that poor boy. His horse was found dead on the prairie, and everyone assumed his body had been carried off by wild animals.

"Ted was sad for a long time. I think he blamed himself and Mama for Logan's death, but I never found out why."

"I'm tired of this subject," Desperado said, swinging his legs from the bed. "I'm famished. Shall we go down to the hotel dining room for breakfast?"

Chloe wrinkled her nose as if sniffing something offensive. "I'm not going anywhere until I've had a bath."

Desperado gave her a wicked grin. "What you smell is spent pleasure, honey. But I know what you mean. I'll order you up a bath and mosey over to the bathhouse for mine. I'll meet you in the dining room in an hour."

Desperado was waiting for Chloe when she entered the dining room. He waved and she waved back as she quickly wended her way through the maze of tables. He seated her and picked up the menu. Moments later the waitress appeared to take their order.

"See anything you like?" Desperado asked.

"I'm starved," Chloe admitted, giving him a sheepish grin. Then she ordered black coffee and enough food to satisfy the most voracious of appetites.

"I like a woman with a healthy appetite," Desperado rasped, sending her a wicked look that conveyed exactly which of her appetites he liked best. Then he proceeded to order nearly every breakfast item on the menu.

Desperado watched through hooded lids as Chloe sipped her coffee, a half-smile on his face when he recalled everything that had transpired between them last night and this morning. He tried hard not to give a name to what he felt for Chloe. He told himself it was a primitive and purely physical response to a sexy woman he'd taken a shine to. Unfortunately, his mind refused to accept that explanation. Though he tried to deny it, he found something profoundly stirring about Chloe Sommers.

Perhaps it was the way she made him feel, as though he could conquer the world with her beside him. She made him long for something he'd never had. A home and family. But casting off an old life and forging a new one was easier said than done. A man with his reputation and skill couldn't decide to change the course of his life overnight. But if he could . . . He shook his head to clear it of insane ideas. Even if he decided to pursue a new life, he'd be chasing rainbows to think that Chloe would want him. Chloe was a lady. She wasn't for the likes of him.

Granted, he had given her pleasure, but that didn't mean she wanted to spend the rest of her life with a half-breed gunslinger. No, the best thing he could do for Chloe was to get on with his life so she could get on with hers.

"What are you thinking?" Chloe asked, interrupting his morbid thoughts. "You look so solemn."

"I was just wondering where my next job will take me," he lied.

She set her cup down carefully. Desperado

couldn't help noticing that her hand shook. "Have you had another job offer already?"

"Not yet, but I reckon one will come along."

She cleared her throat. "You could always stay on at the Ralston ranch. The boys seem to get along with you, and I could use a good foreman."

His dark brows arched upward. "I thought you fired me."

"A woman is entitled to change her mind." She fidgeted a moment, then said, "Forget I asked. Men like you never light in one place for long."

The conversation was going in a direction he found discomfiting. "Tate Talbot and his friends left town," he said, abruptly changing the subject. "The desk clerk told me they checked out early this morning, and the hostler said they collected their horses and rode out of town shortly after dawn."

"Thank God," Chloe breathed.

"Don't count on being rid of them yet," Desperado warned. "You won't be safe from the Talbots until your taxes are paid."

"Do you think they'll try to steal my money?"

"I wouldn't put it past them. The Talbots aren't the kind to give up."

Desperado's words got him to thinking. He couldn't leave Chloe now. She still needed him. Not until the taxes were marked paid in full would he relax his vigilance.

Their breakfast came then and they dug in, each determined to maintain the tenuous harmony that existed between them. Neither spoke again until their plates were clean and the waitress had refilled their coffee cups. Chloe was the first to break the charged silence, "I paid the men last night. They've probably spent most of it in bars and brothels, but they've more than earned their night's entertainment."

Desperado wondered where all this was leading. He didn't have long to wait.

"I suppose you want your pay so you can move on. It's in the hotel safe."

"My job's not done yet, Chloe."

Chloe looked confused. "What? What did you say?"

"I reckon I'll hang around to make sure you get back to the ranch safely. I've nothing better to do right now. When do you plan to leave Dodge?"

"First thing tomorrow morning," Chloe said, staring at Desperado as if he'd lost his mind. "Are you sure about this?"

"Yeah, real sure. I'll round up the hands and meet you at daybreak in front of the hotel."

"Desperado . . ."

God, when she looked at him like that, he wanted to take her in his arms and kiss her silly. Then he wanted to . . . "Chloe, don't . . ."

She looked away. "I just wanted to thank you. For . . . everything. In case I don't get around to it before you leave."

She shot to her feet. "I've got to buy supplies for our trip back."

Desperado watched her walk away, admiring the long, lean line of her legs and slim hips. He wondered how in the hell he was going to keep his hands off of the trouser-clad wildcat for the next ten days or so. He smiled inwardly. Perhaps he didn't have to. Maybe Chloe wouldn't object to continuing their affair. She certainly had wanted him last night.

Suddenly the conscience he'd recently discovered poked at him. He tried to tell it to leave him alone, but it wouldn't listen. *Tell Chloe who you are*, that voice in his head prodded relentlessly. *Tell her you're Logan Ralston*. But his need to conceal his true identity was so deeply ingrained that he cast that thought aside. Besides, Chloe's first reaction upon learning his true identity would be to question his reason for returning to Trouble Creek. She would undoubtedly think he'd come to claim her land.

But she'd be wrong, Desperado thought. He wanted neither the land nor the responsibility that went along with it. His father had made his wishes known in his will, and Desperado had abided by them. He hadn't liked it but he had accepted it. Had he arrived at Trouble Creek before his father had died instead of the day of his father's funeral, things might have been different. The ranch, the land, everything Ted Ralston owned would have been his.

Back then he wasn't the hardened gunslinger he was now, and Desperado knew the ranch would have prospered under his care. But fate had intervened and his father had died before they'd made their peace.

Desperado no longer resented Chloe. Nor did he blame his father. The woman he held responsible for the estrangement between him and his father was dead now, and he'd lost whatever right he might have had to his inheritance. Would Chloe believe that he hadn't returned to Trouble Creek to take her land? Hell no! Not after he'd hired on with Talbot, even though he'd changed horses in midstream and come over to Chloe's side.

After long and careful thought, Desperado decided to keep his identity a secret. Nothing, except maybe the family Bible he'd stolen from the house after his father's funeral and carried in his saddlebag and the miniature of his mother in his medicine bag, linked him to the lad named Logan Ralston.

Chapter Nine

It was apparent that each of the Ralston drovers suffered from overindulgence of one kind or another, but all were present and accounted for bright and early the following morning as Chloe and Desperado emerged from the hotel together.

Chloe felt no guilt over the past two nights spent in Desperado's arms. When he had knocked on her hotel room door the night before, she did not question his right to be there. She had opened the door and welcomed him into her bed as if he belonged there. When he disappeared from her life, at least she'd have the memories. Men like Desperado Jones never hung around in one place long. They were loners. They shunned permanent attachments and kept a tight hold upon their emotions. Desperado Jones would never allow himself to fall in love.

"Mount up," Desperado rasped to the men as he helped Chloe into her saddle. Moments later he leaped onto his mustang and led the hung-over drovers out of town.

Chloe followed close behind Desperado, admiring the way he sat a horse. So tall and straight, like a proud Indian warrior, at one with the elements and the world around him. But was he at peace? Chloe wondered. His profession was not an easy one, nor a safe one. She sensed within him a turbulence that had nothing to do with his dangerous profession. Desperado Jones was a complex man plagued by demons. Chloe was no fool. She could tell a tormented man when she saw one.

The first day and night on the trail passed uneventfully. Chloe had sold the lumbering chuck wagon in Dodge and replaced it with faster pack-horses to carry their supplies. They all ate the meal Randy had prepared and the hands bedded down shortly afterward, since most were still suffering from the previous night's revelry. Chloe chose a spot beneath a tree a short distance away from the sleeping drovers.

Desperado looked longingly at Chloe, then placed his own bedroll where he could keep an eye on her. He felt a strong responsibility to protect Chloe, though he seriously doubted that any of the Ralston hands would treat her with anything but respect. But Tate Talbot and his cronies were still out there somewhere, and Desperado couldn't afford to relax his vigilance. He tried not to think about Chloe's future after he left Trouble Creek.

Chloe would be alone then and vulnerable to the Talbots' underhanded dealings.

Unexpected rain showers followed them most of the next day. The men broke out their slickers and hunkered down in their saddles as rain ran down the brims of their hats and pelted down their backs. Desperado rode beside Chloe, aware that she was as miserable as he. But unlike Chloe, he was an old hand at coping with inclement weather and uncomfortable situations.

"Are you all right?" he asked solicitously. "Maybe we should head for the next town and get a hotel room for the night."

Chloe shook her head, sending drops of water spinning around her. "No, I want to get home. If Tate reaches town first, he and his father might decide to burn down the ranch house out of spite. You beat Tate up pretty good and he's not likely to forget it."

Desperado's dark eyes glinted with malice. "I would have killed him had I known what he did to you."

Chloe sighed. "That's over and done with. I'd go crazy if I dwelled on the past. I've gone on with my life even though Tate won't let me forget."

"Tate still wants you and we both know it," Desperado rasped. "You should marry, Chloe. A husband could protect you."

Chloe gave a snort of disgust. "You've seen the men in Trouble Creek. Who among them would you suggest?"

Desperado thought about that and decided no one in Trouble Creek was worthy of Chloe. She was nothing like her mean-spirited, self-centered mother. If he tried hard enough he could imagine himself settling down with a woman like Chloe. Having children with Chloe. That thought startled him and he kneed his horse, sending him sprinting away from Chloe and the disturbing thoughts that gave him no rest.

"I'm riding ahead to find a good camping spot," he called over his shoulder. "Keep the men moving."

Desperado located a deserted mine entrance large enough to shelter both men and horses from the rain, which was now pounding down upon them with unrelenting vehemence. It was a wet, bedraggled group that bedded down that night on the dry sandy floor of the cave-like mine entrance. Tired from their long ride, the men soon were snoring peacefully in their bedrolls. But Desperado couldn't sleep. The closer they got to the ranch, the more confused he became. Riding away and leaving Chloe behind was going to be damn difficult.

Rising stealthily, Desperado stepped over the sleeping men, picked up a lantern and headed down the main tunnel. He'd always been fascinated with mines, and since he couldn't sleep, he decided to explore. The tunnel twisted and turned and ended abruptly where a cave-in blocked the path.

"What are you doing?" The voice came from behind him.

Desperado spun and reached for his gun, then relaxed when he saw Chloe in the lantern's glare.

"I couldn't sleep. Thought I'd explore a little."

She walked into the circle of light. "Neither could

I. I saw you leave and decided to follow."

"That wasn't wise," Desperado rasped in that sexy-as-sin voice as he reached for her. "I've missed you."

She came into his arms without protest. "I didn't follow you for this," she said, resting her hands against his chest.

"Why did you follow me?"

"I . . . we need to talk."

His mouth hovered inches above hers. "I'm a man of action. Talking bores me."

To prove his words, his mouth came down on hers, his kiss as violent as it was needy. He kissed her with all the pent-up hunger that had been grinding inside him during the past two days. He wanted her. His fingers were already working the buttons on her blouse as he eased her down onto the hard-packed earth beneath their feet.

"No! We can't do this!" Chloe gasped when she finally found her mouth free. "The men—"

"They're sleeping," Desperado whispered against her ear. "I want you, Chloe. These past two days have been torture for me."

"Me, too," Chloe admitted shyly, "but that doesn't mean we have to give in to our . . . mutual attraction."

"It's more than mutual attraction and you know it," Desperado growled as he pulled her beneath him.

Chloe's heart began to pound. "What would you call it if not mutual attraction?"

"Damned if I know," Desperado said, too aroused even to consider his confused feelings. "Let's call it lust, for lack of anything better." He stripped off her blouse and stared at her breasts. Then he lowered his head and sucked a plump nipple into his mouth.

"Wait!" Chloe said, pushing against his shoulders. "There is something I need to say."

He lifted his head, his expression stark with unrelenting need. "Spit it out, sweetheart. We might not get another chance to be alone like this, and talking is a waste of time."

"I just wanted to know if you had changed your mind about staying on at the ranch. The job offer still stands."

"Does it matter so much whether or not I stay?"

Chloe flushed and looked away. "Yes, dammit, it does matter."

Desperado eased away from her, his expression guarded. "You deserve better than me, Chloe. I'm a loner, always have been. You don't need a half-breed gunslinger complicating your life. I don't know where my next job will take me. A man in my line of work knows there's a bullet out there somewhere with his name on it. I'm hard, ruthless, and good at what I do. Is that the kind of man you want?"

"You could change," Chloe whispered hopefully. "Nothing is written in stone."

He gave her a hard, humorless smile. "I'm too old to change. Men looking to make a name for themselves will always find me. Beating Desperado Jones at the draw would be a feather in any man's cap. I couldn't drag you into that kind of life."

"If any man is capable of changing, it's you. I

don't care about your past. It's your future I'm concerned about."

"You don't know a damn thing about me," Desperado said harshly. "I don't want you to care about me."

"I'll always care about you," Chloe said with feeling. "I don't know how to explain what I feel, but I do know I'll miss you when you walk out of my life."

"If you knew . . ."

"What? What were you going to say?"

"Nothing. God, Chloe, I can't think with you in my arms. Can't we just forget about tomorrow and concentrate on here and now? You can't begin to know how desperately I want you." His lips touched hers, a gentle promise of more to come.

"I think I can," she whispered against his mouth as her arms went around him.

With sudden insight she realized that Desperado was right. Tomorrow could take care of itself. All that mattered was here and now and the man who set her body afire with a simple touch. There were still several days remaining for him to change his mind. His hands were on her breasts, his mouth claiming hers, and her thoughts skidded to a halt. She had no idea how he'd removed her trousers and underwear, or his own clothing, but her body was singing with joy as naked skin brushed against naked skin. This might be the last time they'd be together like this, and she intended to make the most of it.

"Love me, Desperado. Please love me," she moaned against his lips.

"Aw, sweetheart, that's what I've been trying to do but you've been talking too much."

His kisses were wild and hot, falling like scalding rain on her face, her neck, her shoulders. Then her thoughts scattered as he suckled her nipples into hard peaks, and aimed his mouth downward, to forbidden territory. When he buried his head between her legs, she cried out and arched upward into the heat of his mouth. She was so ready she climaxed almost immediately. Her whole body was still pulsating when he scrambled upward and plunged into her tight passage, intensifying her contractions. Desperado growled low in his throat, grasped her hips and pumped his loins against hers in a wild frenzy of thrust and withdrawal. She felt a second climax begin, and her eyes widened, surprised that she had summoned the strength to respond again.

"Go for it, sweetheart," Desperado urged on a tormented gasp. "You're one helluva woman."

That was the last thing Chloe heard as she shattered into a million pieces. When next she opened her eyes she saw Desperado bending over her, his lips kicked upward into a smile, his dimple firmly in place. God, she loved his smile! Before she realized what she was doing, she kissed the dimple in his cheek.

"I've wanted to do that for a long time," she said without apology.

His dark eyes glowed with sudden warmth. "That damn dimple has gotten me into a lot of trouble."

"Woman trouble?"

"It's time to go back and get some rest," he said,

adroitly changing the subject. He didn't want to discuss all those nameless, faceless women he'd bedded in his lifetime. "Can I help you dress?"

"I can manage. Will you think about my job offer?"

"We've already been through this. I'm not the kind to settle down."

They finished dressing in silence. Desperado picked up the lantern. "Are you ready?" Chloe nodded and they retraced their steps back to their bedrolls. Their gazes met and clung for a tense moment before parting.

The journey home resumed the following morning. The weather turned clear and blistering hot and they took their time so as not to tire their horses. Summer was ending when they finally reached the ranch. That night in the mine had been the last opportunity for Desperado and Chloe to be alone, and Desperado felt the lack keenly, even though he knew it was only a matter of time before he would ride out of Chloe's life forever.

Desperado was happy to see that the house was still standing when they arrived. Nothing seemed to have been disturbed during their absence. The two men left behind to look after things reported nothing amiss, but Desperado didn't trust the Talbots. He knew it wouldn't be long before they started harassing Chloe again to sell the land. In his brief association with the Talbots he'd learned that they would stop at nothing to gain what they wanted. Why they wanted the Ralston ranch was a mystery Desperado hoped to solve before he left

Trouble Creek for good. He owed Chloe that much.

"Everything seems as it was," Chloe said on a note of relief. "Perhaps the Talbots have given up on me."

"Don't count on it," Desperado muttered beneath his breath.

"I can't wait to have a bath and a decent meal," Chloe said enthusiastically. "Will you stay on for a few days?"

Desperado was torn. He wanted to stay with Chloe but knew he was only fooling himself by thinking he could change. Even if he wanted to change, circumstances wouldn't let him. Dimly he wondered how Chloe would react should she somehow find out that he was Logan Ralston. And she was bound to find out if he hung around long enough. One day someone would remember him; things were bound to change between them after that.

"I think it best for both of us if I get a room in town. I intend to stay just long enough to make sure the Talbots aren't going to bother you again."

Chloe felt the crushing weight of disappointment. She'd been alone for a long time and had taken care of herself and her mother since Ted's death, but never had she felt such an overwhelming sense of loss. She couldn't imagine what was wrong with her. She wasn't in love with Desperado so why . . . ?

Good Lord! *Was* she in love with Desperado Jones? Though she had tried to hide her sexuality by wearing trousers and toting a gun, Desperado had exposed her femininity. His loving had shown

175

her that mating with a man needn't be repulsive or feared. It could be wonderfully fulfilling and pleasurable beyond imagination.

She wanted it to last forever.

But Desperado wanted no restraints or commitments. He was a free spirit. He didn't need her.

"If you change your mind, there's always a place for you in the bunkhouse."

"I'll try to remember."

Chloe watched him ride away, biting her lip to keep from calling him back.

Tate Talbot had reached town the previous day, still bearing bruises from Desperado's beating. He faced his father across the expanse of his desk.

"Damn him, Pa! Jones turned on us," Tate railed. "He threw your money at me and said to tell you he no longer worked for you. I warned you about him. I told you you should have let me handle things. If not for Jones, Chloe would be in my bed now and her land ours. That half-breed gunslinger is a double-crossing snake."

Calvin's lips thinned into a grimace when he noted the fading bruises on Tate's face. "Did Jones do that?"

"Yeah," Tate said sheepishly, "but he caught me unaware."

"He probably caught you with your pants down around your ankles," Calvin said with disgust. "If you hadn't gone and ruined everything by forcing yourself on the girl, she'd be your wife now and none of this would have been necessary."

"See here, Pa, that wasn't entirely my fault. I admit I had a little too much to drink that night but I thought she was willing. She never told anyone about what I done, so she couldn't have been too angry."

"That's neither here nor there," Calvin said dismissively. "Our problem now is getting rid of Desperado Jones. If he's taken up Chloe's cause, I'll never get the land, and time is running out. When the railroad starts buying up land for the spur, I intend to own every parcel it passes through. I'll stand to make a fortune, since I purchased most of the land for a pittance."

"Are you sure the railroad is coming through here, Pa?" Tate asked.

"As sure as I can be. My contacts in Washington assured me that a spur line will be built to connect Dodge City with Amarillo, and Trouble Creek is a likely spot for it to pass through. Once I have the Ralston spread, I'll own all the land lying between Trouble Creek and Amarillo."

"What are we gonna do about Jones?" Tate asked. "I saw him checking into the hotel a short time ago. Maybe he means to stick around town until he tires of Chloe. The little she-devil must find him more attractive than me," Tate said sourly.

"We're going to get even," Calvin snarled. "No one betrays the Talbots and gets away with it."

"I could challenge him again," Tate suggested.

"You'd lose," Calvin said flatly. "The man cannot be outdrawn. I'd like to know more about Jones before I lay my plans. No one seems to know a thing about his background."

"Leave it to me, Pa," Tate bragged. "I'll dig up

something. Every man has a past, especially a man like Jones. Maybe the Texas Rangers have something on him."

"Already checked that out," Calvin revealed. "Oddly enough, the man isn't wanted by the law. Oh, they know about him and keep tabs on him, but there is nothing they can pin on him."

"Sonofabitch!" Tate cursed. "How can a renowned gunslinger not be wanted by the law? Never mind, I'll not let you down this time, Pa."

"Big words considering you always come out the loser where Jones is concerned. Get me some information on Jones and I'll overlook your failures. The Sommers girl has the money to pay her taxes, thanks to your bungling and Jones's defection. Our only hope now is to get rid of Jones and convince Chloe to marry you. Try to keep your hands off of her until she's your wife."

Tate was glad he hadn't told his father what he had done to earn a beating. Damn Chloe Sommers, he cursed beneath his breath. He was convinced that she was playing hard to get with him. She wanted to make him jealous by bedding Jones. Well, he had news for her. As soon as he and Pa got rid of Jones, he was going to take what he wanted. Once Chloe was his wife he'd make her toe the line or suffer the consequences.

Stationed behind a pillar holding up the balcony of Miss Milly's brothel, Tate watched Desperado leave the hotel and amble across the street to the Devil's Den. He waited a moment to make sure Desperado was going to stay put before darting into the hotel.

At first the clerk was reluctant to give Tate the spare key to Desperado's room, but the color of Tate's money and a few threatening words soon convinced him to hand over the key. Tate had no idea what he was looking for, but he'd seen Desperado carry in his saddlebags earlier today and he reckoned it couldn't hurt to look through them.

The hallway was empty when he let himself into Desperado's room. He spotted the saddlebags immediately. They were lying on the floor where Desperado had dropped them. Fearing Desperado's vengeance should he be caught rifling through the gunslinger's belongings, Tate wasted little time as he unlatched the bags and rummaged inside. He cursed softly to himself when he found little beyond the normal personal items men usually carried. Then his questing hand touched upon a book and he tugged it free, wondering what kind of book a man like Desperado would read.

To Tate's surprise, the book appeared to be a family Bible. Intrigued by his find, Tate opened the cover and chuckled gleefully when names he recognized were inscribed inside. He sat back on his heels, wondering why Desperado Jones would carry a Bible belonging to the Ralston family. Had he stolen it? Was he somehow connected to the Ralston family?

The Talbots had arrived in town about five years ago, after Calvin had heard about the railroad spur. He'd come to buy up land, expecting to make a fortune from his inside information. Ted Ralston was already dead and his wife Norie was in ill health.

Tate stared thoughtfully at one of the names inscribed in the Bible. It registered the birth of Logan Ralston and then his death fifteen years later. Tate didn't know exactly what it meant, but he made careful note of the dates and put the Bible back where he had found it. After making sure nothing was out of place, he left the room, returned the key to the clerk and hightailed it back to his father's office.

"What do you make of it, Pa?" Tate asked after he'd informed his father of his find. "Why would Jones carry a Bible belonging to the Ralston family?"

"Beats me," Calvin muttered. "Maybe I'll go over to the newspaper office later and see what I can find out. Meanwhile, keep your eyes and ears open."

Desperado left the saloon and headed over to Talbot's office. He relished the thought of telling Talbot to leave Chloe alone. Tate had already left when Desperado barged into Calvin's office.

"What the hell—" Calvin blustered when he saw Desperado looming in the doorway. "I don't cotton to double-crossers, Jones. I thought we had a deal. You took my money, but obviously you preferred sexual favors to greenbacks," he said dryly. "I never thought you'd let sex interfere with a job. I hope she was worth it."

"One more word about Chloe and you'll eat lead, Talbot," Desperado growled. "Didn't Tate return your money to you? I gave it to him with a message. I quit working for you the day Chloe nearly got herself killed."

"What's one more death to a man like you?" Calvin said with derision. "Never mind answering that. I didn't want Chloe dead either. All I want is her land."

"Just why is the Ralston spread so damn important to you?"

"That's none of your business. Why are you sticking around town anyway? Haven't you had your fill of Chloe yet?"

A strong will was all that kept Desperado from knocking the smirk off Talbot's face. "I'm leaving as soon as I receive your word that you'll stop harassing Chloe Sommers."

"That good, is she?" Calvin remarked. "No wonder Tate is so eager to have her again. Obviously once wasn't enough for him either."

Desperado reached over the desk and hauled Calvin across the hard surface until they were nose to nose. His face was as hard as a slab of granite.

"If Tate so much as touches Chloe, I'll kill him. Tell him that. As for you, I suggest you concentrate on the land you already cheated ranchers out of and leave the Ralston spread alone."

"See here, Jones," Calvin sputtered as he wrested free of Desperado's bruising grip. "Tate's intentions toward Chloe are honorable. He wants to make her his wife."

"She doesn't want him. She deserves better than an abuser of women."

"Did Chloe tell you that? She's lying, Jones. Chloe led Tate on until he was unable to control himself. A man can take only so much."

Desperado knew if he didn't leave now he wouldn't be responsible for his actions. Only a fool would believe that Chloe had led Tate on. Tate had turned on an innocent young woman and used her cruelly.

"I've said all I'm going to on the subject, Talbot. Once Chloe pays her taxes, you can't touch her land. And you can tell Tate he hasn't a snowball's chance in hell of marrying her."

"We'll just see about that, won't we, Jones?"

"If I were you I would think twice about doing anything to hurt Chloe," Desperado warned. "My influence is far-reaching. I'll know if you've disregarded my warning." He tipped his hat. "Good day, Mr. Talbot."

Chloe missed Desperado already and he'd only been gone a day. The man was infuriating and arrogant but she sensed in him an innate goodness despite his violent profession. She'd forgiven him long ago for working for Talbot. How could she not? He'd saved her life and had gotten her herd to Dodge without serious mishap. How could she let him ride out of her life and never see him again?

But Desperado Jones wasn't the kind of man to settle down. For the rest of her life she would remember how sweetly he had made love to her, how easily he had banished her preconceived ideas of what lovemaking was like. He had shown her a side of himself that few people were allowed to see. She knew there was more to Desperado Jones than met the eye.

Chloe's bed seemed cold and empty that first night home. She wondered if Desperado's bed was as empty as hers and decided that it probably wasn't. There wasn't a woman in town who wouldn't give her eyeteeth to share a bed with dark, dangerous Desperado Jones.

Chloe rose bright and early the next morning. Today she was going into town to pay her taxes. And there would be plenty of money left over to replace the barn that had burned down. After a hasty breakfast, Chloe placed the money in her saddlebags and carried them to the corral. As she rounded the corner she saw Desperado's mustang tied to a fence post next to her mare. Then she saw Desperado striding in her direction from the bunkhouse.

"Morning," he drawled. His warm perusal sent hot color to her cheeks.

"What are you doing here? I thought you spent the night in town."

"I did. Thought I'd ride out this morning and escort you to town. You don't want to take unnecessary chances with that money."

"Thank you."

"I saddled your horse," he said, taking her saddlebags and throwing them over her horse's withers.

"Thank you again. I suppose you'll leave after you see me safely to the tax office," she ventured.

"I suppose," Desperado rasped. The thought of leaving Chloe and never seeing her again made his gut clench painfully. If only . . . But no, better to leave without revealing his identity, he decided. He'd learned the hard way that one can never go back, one can only go forward.

The ride to town was uneventful. Desperado waited outside with the horses while Chloe paid her taxes to the town clerk. Then he escorted her to the bank to deposit the surplus. They parted company shortly afterward.

"Will I see you again?" Chloe asked.

"Probably," Desperado rasped. "I'll be out to see the boys before I leave."

"Desperado, I . . ."

God, he didn't want to hear it. Leaving Chloe was the hardest thing he'd ever had to do. He placed a finger across her lips. "No, don't say anything you'll regret. You know what I am, Chloe. I can't change."

Then he whirled on his heel and strode away. Neither of them noticed Calvin Talbot exiting the newspaper office, but he saw them. A cunning smile curved his lips as he walked toward Chloe.

"Ah, just the person I wanted to see," Talbot said exuberantly when he reached her.

"What do you want, Mr. Talbot?" Chloe asked crossly. She'd had all she could take from the Talbots.

"I spent the morning in the newspaper office and thought I'd share my findings with you."

A chill crept down Chloe's spine. "Nothing I want to hear, I'm sure." She turned away.

"But I insist," Talbot said, grasping her elbow in a bruising grip. "I'm certain you'll be interested in what I have to say."

"Let go of me," she bit out.

"Miss Sommers, hear me out. I learned something today that could change your entire life. Did you know that Desperado Jones came to Trouble Creek with an agenda? I think you'd be interested to hear why he showed up when he did."

Chloe's eyes narrowed suspiciously. "An agenda? I don't understand."

"Of course you don't understand, my dear. I'll be happy to explain. The man we know as Desperado Jones is really Logan Ralston, Ted Ralston's long-lost son. Obviously he came here to claim the Ralston land you've thought of as your own all these years."

Chapter Ten

Chloe's gaze settled on Calvin Talbot as she tried to make sense out of his words. It wasn't possible. Talbot was lying. Desperado would have said something if he was Logan Ralston.

"I don't believe you!"

Talbot gave her a pitying look. "Would a man like Jones show up in a town like Trouble Creek if he didn't have an agenda? Think about it, my dear." He tipped his hat and ambled off down the street, chuckling to himself.

Chloe's mind whirled in confusion as she rode back to the ranch. Talbot's words kept returning to haunt her. Why indeed had Desperado come to Trouble Creek? Normally the town was quiet and unremarkable, nearly indistinguishable from any other small Texas cattle town. Desperado had arrived unannounced and unexpected. No one had summoned him. He'd had no job awaiting him in Trouble Creek. Was he really Logan Ralston, Ted's missing son? Had he come to claim his father's property?

According to Ted's will, her mother had inherited all Ted's worldly goods, which in turn had come to her through her mother's will. She hadn't been at the reading of Ted's will so she didn't know the particulars, but she vaguely recalled her mother mentioning a codicil. Her mother hadn't seemed too worried about the codicil, so Chloe had promptly forgotten it.

A cowboy sprinted up to take her horse when Chloe drew rein in front of the house. She nodded distractedly, dismounted and went inside. Her heart told her that Talbot was lying. Desperado would not have lied about something so important, would he? They had been as intimate as two people could be; he wouldn't have kept that bit of knowledge from her. Unless . . . No, she wouldn't believe it of Desperado. If there was a way to either prove or disprove that Desperado was Logan Ralston, she reflected, the answer lay somewhere in this house.

Suddenly Chloe recalled the several crates of personal items belonging to Ted that Norie had stored in a shed behind the house. The proof she needed might very well lie within those musty crates.

Chloe located three wooden crates in the shed with Ted's name scrawled across the top and promptly pried opened the first with a crowbar she found nearby. There was nothing inside but neatly folded clothing. The second yielded letters and papers and ranch records from years gone by. Sighing in disappointment, she turned to the last crate. It was filled with personal mementos and odd pieces of jewelry. At the bottom of the crate she found several framed paintings. She picked one up, stared at it hard and nearly lost the ability to speak.

The painting was of a beautiful Indian woman and a little boy about ten years old. The boy was darkly handsome with twinkling black eyes and a deep dimple in his right cheek. Young Logan Ralston was a youthful version of Desperado Jones. Though hardened by his choice of profession, Desperado's features had changed little over the years. Talbot had been right. Desperado Jones and Logan Ralston were one and the same. That thought led to another. Had Desperado come to Trouble Creek to seize the land she'd considered hers? Could he actually do it?

The lawyer who had drawn up Ted's will still practiced in town. Though elderly and failing in health, Thadeous Baker still kept an office above the newspaper. Chloe intended to call upon Lawyer Baker bright and early the following morning. She had to know if there was any legal way Desperado could claim her land before she confronted the gunslinger with her knowledge.

Chloe had countless questions that needed answering, but first she had to arm herself with information that only Lawyer Baker could provide. Desperado had told her he was leaving town soon. Had everything he'd told her been a pack of lies? Why had he helped her defeat the Talbots if he meant to claim her land? Why had he agreed to work for the Talbots in the first place? Nothing made sense. But first things first. She'd give Desperado a chance to answer all her questions after she'd seen Ted's lawyer.

Chloe leaned forward in her chair and said, "I want to know about the codicil to Ted's will. I distinctly recall Mama mentioning it. But since she didn't seem overly concerned about it, I promptly dismissed it."

A battered desk separated Chloe from the elderly Thadeous Baker. She'd been waiting for him when he opened his office at eight that morning. Baker appeared somewhat startled when Chloe asked him about the codicil to Ted Ralston's will but seemed willing enough to talk about it.

"I have a copy of the will on file," Baker said.

Chloe glanced about the cluttered room and seriously doubted the lawyer could find anything, much less a will dating back several years. But to her surprise Baker went to a bulging filing cabinet, pulled open a drawer and withdrew a folder bearing Ted Ralston's name.

"Ah, here it is," Baker said, returning to his seat behind his desk. He opened the folder and quickly scanned the contents to refresh his memory. "According to Ted's will, all his worldly goods were left to your mother, with one small provision. Should his son Logan turn up alive, the land and everything on it would automatically revert to his son. Now you'd better tell me what this is all about."

"I have reason to believe that Desperado Jones and Logan Ralston are the same man."

Baker's eyebrows rose so high they nearly disappeared into his receding hairline as he peered at Chloe over his rimless glasses. "What a preposterous idea! If Desperado Jones really is Logan Ralston, which in my opinion is highly unlikely, then he could claim the land, the ranch, and all Ted's worldly goods, or what's left of them," he added. "But mind you, I'd have to have solid proof before he could claim anything."

Chloe rose. "Thank you, Mr. Baker, I reckon you've answered my question."

"You realize I'm going to have to pursue this, Miss Sommers," Baker called after her. "I owe it to Ted Ralston to follow the provisions of his will."

His words went right over Chloe. She'd learned what she had come for and now it was time to confront Desperado. She had to know. She'd given herself to a gunslinger; had she given herself to Ted Ralston's son as well?

Desperado was about to walk over to the cafe for breakfast when he heard a frantic knocking on the door. "Coming," he called, wondering who could be visiting this early in the morning. He checked his gun out of habit, then flung open the door.

"Chloe! Is something wrong?" His first thought was that there was trouble at the Ralston ranch.

"Everything is wrong, Desperado," Chloe bit out. "May I come in?"

"Of course." Desperado stepped aside and Chloe brushed past him. His brow furrowed. He could tell by the expression on Chloe's face that something terrible had happened. If one of the Talbots had given her grief, he'd personally take care of it.

Chloe walked over to the window, then whirled to confront him. "Who are you? I want to know the truth. Who are you, *really*?"

"You know who I am," Desperado said after a tense pause. "What is this all about?"

"What were you doing in Trouble Creek the day I asked you to work for me?"

"Just riding through."

"Liar!" Chloe shouted. "What else have you lied to me about?" Her hands were clenched at her sides, her face flushed, and Desperado felt something lurch in the pit of his belly.

What did Chloe know? he wondered. He reached her in three long strides and dragged her against him. He muttered a curse when he felt her stiffen in his arms.

"Tell me what's bothering you."

"What's bothering me is you, Logan Ralston!" Chloe all but shouted.

"What? What did you call me?"

"I called you Logan Ralston. That's your name, isn't it?"

"Who told you?"

"Does it matter? Is it true? Or are you going to deny it?"

Desperado shrugged and looked away. "Maybe."

"Maybe, hell! You know it's true. Why did you pretend to be dead? Ted mourned you every day of his life. How could you be so heartless?"

Chloe's accusations set off a firestorm within him. Grasping her arms, he gave her a rough shake. "Heartless! I'll tell you about heartless. Heartless was the way your mother convinced my father to send me away so she wouldn't have to look upon my dark, Indian face. For three years Norie found excuses to keep me from returning home. She was jealous of my father's love and wanted him all to herself. Yes, dammit, I'm Logan Ralston!"

He saw tears gathering in the corners of her eyes and relaxed his grip.

"You let Ted believe you were dead," she accused.

"I thought it was better that way."

Chloe rubbed her arms where his fingers had left bruises. "Better for whom? Surely not Ted."

Desperado had the decency to flush. "I was a kid, banished from my home at a woman's whim. I begged my father to let me return home, but Norie always came up with a reason why I should remain in San Antonio. After three years I decided I'd had enough and left my aunt's house without permission. I was determined to convince Father to let me stay home once I arrived. I had an accident along the way. Fortunately, I was found by Indians, nursed back to health and adopted by an Indian family."

"You were held captive!" Chloe cried. "I knew there was an explanation."

"No, I wasn't held captive. I stayed with the Indians because they treated me like one of their own. Unlike my father, they wanted me. I grew to love them. From my foster father I learned how to take care of myself, how to survive in a hostile environment. I struck out on my own when I felt there was nothing more they could teach me."

"Why didn't you let Ted know you were alive?"

"I did set out one day to make peace with my

father. I'd grown mature enough by then to want to end the estrangement. Unfortunately, I arrived too late. I stood on the sidelines at Father's funeral. Rumor had it that he'd left his entire estate to his wife, and I didn't bother to stick around after that. The only reason I'd returned to Trouble Creek in the first place was to see my father. Father's will contained his final wishes, and I figured I didn't have the right to reveal my identity and challenge his will."

"Are you telling me you didn't know about the codicil to the will?"

Desperado's brow furrowed. "What codicil?"

"Don't lie to me! You returned to Trouble Creek to claim your inheritance."

"I don't know what you're talking about. There is no inheritance."

"Why *did* you return?"

"I'm not sure."

"I don't believe you. You came to claim the ranch, didn't you?"

Desperado pondered his answer. "That hadn't been my intention. Not at first, anyway."

"So you admit—"

"No, hear me out. Don't condemn me out of hand. I admit I wanted to see you lose your land when I agreed to work for Talbot. I thought it would give me some kind of satisfaction after all the heartache your mother caused me. I didn't want the ranch for myself, mind you. Shouldering that kind of responsibility didn't appeal to me. I just didn't want Norie's daughter to have something that should have been mine. I know it doesn't make sense, but my feelings were confused."

"Oh, God, I can't bear this. Did you intend to seduce me all along?"

"I . . . Dammit, Chloe. I . . . aw, shit! I just couldn't help myself. I wanted you from the moment I laid eyes on you. I made love to you simply because it was something I had to do. I could no more stop myself than I could stop breathing."

Chloe pushed past him. He blocked her path. "Where are you going?"

"I have to get out of here. I can't listen to this. I thought you were beginning to care for me. I refused to believe you were going to walk out of my life. I hoped to convince you to stay. I was wrong, dead wrong. Only a desperate spinster like myself would believe a man like you could care for someone."

He caught her arm, swinging her around to face him. "You're not going anywhere. I do care for you. I'm leaving because you deserve better than me."

Chloe laughed without mirth. "Were you really going to leave? Or were you getting ready to spring your little surprise on me? How soon do you want me to vacate the ranch?"

"I have no legal claim on the ranch, Chloe, and you know it."

"I suggest you visit Mr. Baker. He was your father's lawyer. His practice is located above the newspaper office. It will be most enlightening, I assure you." She gazed pointedly at his hand where it clasped her arm. "Please let me go."

"No, you're not going anywhere in the frame of mind you're in. I don't want the damn ranch."

She glared at him. "What *do* you want, Logan Ralston?"

He looked deeply into eyes that reminded him of green fire and knew exactly what he wanted. He wanted something he'd never had before. He wanted a home, a wife, children. He wanted Chloe Sommers. He tried to convey his emotions without words, but she refused to heed his silent plea. Unaccustomed to the strange feelings assailing him, and lacking the words to voice them, Desperado sought another way to make her understand.

Sweeping her into his arms, he carried her to the bed and followed her down onto the colorful but somewhat tattered quilt. She remained stiff, but unresisting as she stared up at him.

"I don't want you," she said without conviction. "Everything has changed."

"Nothing has changed," Desperado rasped into her ear. He pushed his loins against her softness, making her aware of his rock-hard erection. "I want you, Chloe Sommers."

"That might have worked yesterday," Chloe asserted.

He stroked her breast. "It will still work. Forget who I am. Just remember how good we are together."

"How can I forget your reason for being in Trouble Creek? You want—"

Her words died in her throat as his mouth came down hard on hers. His need for her was raw and consuming. It throbbed inside him as he fought the natural inclination to take what he wanted. Chloe was the first woman whose feelings he'd truly cared about. He had deliberately denied his own feelings, fearing that he wasn't good enough for her. He'd fought the urge to tell her the truth about himself, aware of the rift it would cause. But now that the truth was out, he had to use whatever means at his disposal to convince her he wasn't out to claim her land. Didn't she realize it was legally hers, that he could do nothing to take it from her?

He pressed himself closer, his face stark with determination. He felt her hand creep between them and he smiled inwardly. She wanted him as badly as he wanted her. His smile faded as he felt cold steel against his belly.

He sucked in his breath. "What the hell!"

"Get off of me, Desperado," Chloe warned as she pushed the barrel of her gun into his gut. "I can't think straight with you kissing me."

"Don't think, sweetheart, just feel."

"No. I have to think. I've got to decide what to do. Will you move, or are you going to make me shoot?"

Desperado was fairly certain she wouldn't shoot him but he could see she was in no mood to make love. Slowly, reluctantly, he pushed himself to his feet and watched through narrowed lids as she leaped off the bed, her gun still steady in her hand.

"What are you going to do?" Desperado asked.

"I'm going home to pack. You'll be wanting to move into your house." She moved toward the door.

"Dammit, Chloe, I don't want your land!"

"Nevertheless, it's yours. Talk to Mr. Baker if you don't believe me."

Chloe opened the door and stepped into the hall.

Desperado didn't stop her. The only way to clear up this misunderstanding was to pay a visit to Lawyer Baker. Moments later Desperado left the hotel and headed over to the lawyer's office. He climbed the flight of stairs, rapped sharply on the door and entered.

Baker looked up from the journal he was perusing and invited Desperado inside. "You look familiar. Can I help you, sir?" he asked.

"I sure as hell hope so," Desperado rasped. He recognized Baker from his childhood, though his memory of his father's lawyer was hazy.

"Ah, now I know who you are. Everyone in town is talking about the gunslinger who rode into Trouble Creek and went to work for Chloe Sommers out at the Ralston spread. You're Desperado Jones." He paused, peering closely into Desperado's dark features. "I've been intending to call on you ever since Miss Sommers came to my office and told me an extraordinary story."

"That's exactly what I want to talk to you about," Desperado confided.

"First, answer my question, young man. Are you Logan Ralston, Ted Ralston's son?"

"I had hoped to keep that knowledge private," Desperado said. "There was no sense in giving out that information when I never intended to stay in town."

"Why are you here?" Baker inquired. "Trouble Creek doesn't have much to offer a hired gun."

"Curiosity, I suppose. I happened to be in the vicinity and thought I'd ride through and see if the town had changed since I left."

Baker frowned. "What kind of man would allow his own father to believe him dead all these years?"

"The kind of man Logan Ralston became," Desperado rasped. "I returned several years ago to make peace with my father, but instead I arrived in time to attend his funeral. I'd heard he left everything to his wife and I decided to move on."

"Obviously you didn't know about the codicil."

There it was again. Chloe had mentioned a codicil to his father's will, too. "Tell me about the codicil."

"Your body was never found," Baker began, "and your father never gave up hope that you would be found alive somewhere. Before he died he added a codicil to his will. The codicil left the door open for Logan Ralston to claim his inheritance should he turn up alive one day."

"Damnation!" Desperado spat. "Chloe was right. I don't want the ranch, Mr. Baker."

"Nevertheless, it's yours," Baker said. "All you have to do to make it legal is to prove your identity and sign a few papers."

Sudden inspiration struck Desperado. "What if I sign the ranch over to Chloe? Can I do that?"

"First things first," Baker cautioned. "Do you have identification of some kind? You have the look of young Logan, from what I recall of him, but I need solid proof."

Desperado removed the medicine bag he wore on a string around his neck and dumped the contents into his palm. From among a collection of bear teeth and relics given to him by his Indian grandfather, Desperado plucked out a small miniature of a woman and a young boy. He presented it to Baker. "Father had this painting done of Mother and me when I was about ten years old. There is a larger one just like it out at the ranch. It hung in Father's bedroom before he married Norie."

Baker studied the miniature, then Desperado's dark features. "Kinda looks like the boy I remember. But you could have stolen it."

"I don't steal," Desperado rasped in that mean-as-hell voice. "But if you need more proof, I have the family Bible I took from the house after Father's funeral. It belonged to family, not to Norie Sommers. Would you like to see it? It's in my saddlebags."

"No," Baker said, holding up his hand. "I'm convinced, though I don't understand why a young man who had everything would give it all up to become a gunslinger."

"I reckon you wouldn't understand," Desperado said. "But that's all water under the bridge. At the time I had my reasons. Suddenly they no longer seem important."

"Well, Mr. Ralston, come back day after tomorrow and I'll have the papers ready for your signature."

"How long will it take to give it all back to Chloe?"

"Let's get the legalities settled first, then we'll talk about the transfer, if you're still of that mind." He gazed at Desperado over the wire rims of his glasses. "Have you ever thought of marrying and settling down? You couldn't find a better woman than Chloe Sommers. She's had a rough time of it since Ted died. I hope you realize that she won't be able to hang onto the ranch for long after you sign it over to her. It's something you should think about."

"I've already thought about it and discarded the notion," Desperado contended. "I'm not the marrying kind."

"Just a thought," Baker said. "When you return I should have all the papers ready for your signature. Meanwhile, think hard about signing away your inheritance. I don't know the circumstances that kept you away from home all the years prior to your father's death, and I don't want to know. That is between you and your conscience. But I do know that Ted Ralston wanted you to inherit. That's why he put the codicil in his will. It's something to consider."

Desperado nodded and took his leave. The contents of his father's will had stunned him. He cursed himself roundly for being such a stubborn fool where his father was concerned. But he'd been just a kid at the time, and rejection was a bitter pill to swallow. He'd let his hatred for his father's wife keep him from returning home and was sickened to realize that Norie must have been ecstatic when she'd learned of his "death." Belatedly he realized how much his father must have suffered, the hell he'd put the poor man through, and all because of a woman who couldn't stand the sight of her half-breed stepson.

Desperado needed a drink . . . bad. He turned into the saloon, bellied up to the bar and ordered whiskey straight. Three shots later he left, while his mind was still able to function. His stomach was growling, so he walked over to the cafe and ordered a meal and lots of strong black coffee. He was just finishing his coffee when Calvin Talbot entered the cafe, saw Desperado and ambled over to his table.

"Mind if I join you?" Talbot asked, not waiting for an answer as he pulled out a chair.

"Suit yourself. Is there anything particular you want to talk about?"

"I understand you paid a visit to Thadeous Baker?"

Desperado gave him a sour look. "News travels fast."

"This is a small town. Care to tell me what your visit was all about?"

"Go to hell, Talbot. You'll find out soon enough without me telling you." He rose abruptly. "Excuse me, I have business to conduct."

Talbot smiled, apparently unfazed by Desperado's rudeness. "You're right, I have ways of finding out what I want to know. I assume your visit had to do with the fact that you're Logan Ralston."

"Assume what you want," Desperado said in parting.

"I'll be talking to you soon," Talbot called after him.

Desperado was aware that he garnered more attention than usual as he strode back to his hotel. Did the whole town know of his visit to the lawyer? he wondered distractedly. He supposed if the townspeople knew that much, they also knew he was Logan Ralston, Ted Ralston's long-lost son. He didn't give a damn what everyone thought. Once he turned everything over to Chloe, he'd shake the dust from his feet and leave for parts unknown. He'd hung around in one place too long as it was.

After leaving Desperado's room, Chloe rode back to the ranch as if the hounds of hell were after her. She'd come too close to letting Desperado make love to her, and that realization angered her. She'd been duped into believing he cared for her when all he'd really wanted was her ranch. He wasn't protecting her cattle for her, he was protecting them for himself. She'd worked her butt off to pay the taxes, and now she was going to lose everything to a man who didn't give a damn about the land she'd come to love.

What was she going to do now? Move into town and get a job, she supposed. Desperado had told her he didn't want the ranch, but she didn't believe him, not after he'd lied to her about so many things. He'd already admitted he'd taken the job with Talbot because he harbored ill will toward her and her mother. Despite his denial, somehow he had learned about the codicil to Ted's will and had come over to her side because he intended to claim the land for himself.

What would he do with it? Chloe wondered. Then the shocking thought occurred to her that Desperado might sell lock, stock and barrel to Calvin Talbot. He'd always insisted he wasn't the settling-down kind. Chloe was sorry now that she hadn't pulled the trigger when she'd had her gun pressed against Desperado's belly. But she discarded that thought seconds later. She could never shoot the man who had taught her that making love could bring pleasure, not pain.

Desperado awoke late the following morning with a hangover. He'd sat in the saloon until the wee hours of the morning, contemplating the hard decisions he'd made in life and the consequences of those decisions. He arose slowly, holding his head to keep it from splitting apart. Keeping his motions steady and even, he washed and dressed and left the hotel. He needed black coffee and plenty of it. The stronger the better.

He had just stepped out onto the wooden sidewalk when he collided with Chloe. She stumbled against him and his arms went around her to steady her. She felt so good he didn't want to let her go. "Were you coming to see me?" he asked hopefully.

Chloe pulled away and glared at him. "Not a chance. I'm checking into the hotel."

For the first time he noted the carpetbag she carried in one hand. "Why in the hell would you do a thing like that?"

"I don't want to impose upon your hospitality."

"Chloe, I don't want the ranch."

"Did I hear you right?" Calvin Talbot said as he joined them. "I was on my way to your hotel room to discuss your willingness to sell the Ralston spread," he told Desperado. "Rumor has it that Ted Ralston left a codicil to his will making you the new owner of his property. Obviously you have satisfactorily proven your identity to the lawyer. I'm elated

203

to hear you say that you aren't interested in keeping the ranch."

"What makes you think I want to sell the ranch, Talbot?"

"You wouldn't!" Chloe gasped.

"You have nothing to say about this, Miss Sommers," Talbot said dismissively. "You had your chance. Since the ranch no longer belongs to you, my future dealings will be with Logan Ralston."

Being referred to as Logan Ralston sounded strange to Desperado's ears. It had been years since anyone had called him by that name.

"Your father worked a lifetime for that land," Chloe said, ignoring Talbot. "He wanted you to have it. He even left a codicil in his will to that effect. You simply can't sell it and walk away as if it means nothing to you."

Talbot sent Chloe a quelling look. "Is there someplace we can talk in private, Ralston?"

Desperado's head was pounding so painfully he could barely think. "I was on my way to the cafe for breakfast. You can join me if you like."

"Excellent," Talbot said, rubbing his hands in gleeful anticipation.

They walked off together, leaving Chloe behind, fuming in impotent rage.

Desperado refused to talk until he'd gulped down three cups of coffee. Then he settled back and indicated his readiness.

"You know what I want, Jones, or Ralston, or whatever you want to call yourself."

"Jones will do," Desperado said, not yet ready to assume his real identity.

"Very well, Jones. Let's get down to business. We both know you're a loner. You have no intention of turning into a rancher, or settling down for good. Your kind has itchy feet and a nervous trigger finger. You like what you do and aren't about to change. I'm willing to take the land off your hands at a decent price."

"Do you intend to live out there?" Desperado queried.

"I have no intention of moving that far from town. I promised Tate he could live on the ranch after he and Chloe are married. All I want is the land."

Tate marry Chloe? Over my dead body, he thought. "Why do you want the Ralston spread? You already own half the county."

"Nearly every parcel north of town except for yours," Talbot boasted. "Well, what do you say? Shall we discuss price?"

"Don't bother. My answer is no, Talbot," Desperado rasped. "I wouldn't sell the ranch to you if you were the last person on earth and I was starving." He rose abruptly and tipped his hat. "Good day, Talbot."

Chapter Eleven

Desperado walked out of the cafe with one purpose in mind. He was determined to find out why Calvin Talbot was gobbling up land north of town. If he didn't intend to ranch or live on one of his properties, what did he intend to do with all the land?

He ducked into the telegraph office, composed a telegram and paid to have it sent to Atchison, Topeka and Santa Fe headquarters in Topeka. Now all he had to do was wait for an answer. If what he suspected was true, Talbot stood to make a small fortune from his recent land buys.

Desperado's next project was to convince Chloe to return to the ranch. With grim purpose he headed over to the hotel and obtained Chloe's room number from the clerk. Chloe's room was on the first floor, at the end of a long hallway. Desperado stopped before her door and rapped sharply.

There was a long pause before Chloe answered. "Who is it?"

"It's Jones, let me in."

"Go away. I have nothing more to say to you except I hope you struck a lucrative deal with Calvin Talbot."

"I didn't sell the ranch. Open up, Chloe."

He heard the key scrape in the lock and then the door was flung open. "You didn't sell the ranch?" she asked, clearly skeptical.

Desperado pushed his way inside and closed the door behind him. "No, I have no intention of selling the ranch, not to Talbot or anyone else."

Hope flared in Chloe's heart. "Are you going to settle down and become a rancher?"

"I . . . that remains to be seen. All that aside, I want you back where you belong. You're as much a part of the ranch as I am. Will you come? Or do I have to carry you home."

Chloe turned away. "The ranch is no longer my home."

"It is if I say it is."

Chloe gazed into his eyes, startled by the depth of desire burning within them. Her blood heated, sending liquid fire surging through her veins. All he had to do was look at her from beneath those long black lashes and she literally melted. He must have read her mind for suddenly his arms went around her, dragging her against him. Chloe wanted to resist, but Desperado's sensual appeal kept pulling her in another direction. Toward incredible pleasure . . . and eternal damnation.

"Oh God, sweetheart, I want you," Desperado whispered against her mouth. "Nothing is ever going to change the attraction we have for one another. Can you feel it? It's like a magnet pulling us together." He tilted her chin up so he could look into her eyes. "Tell me it's the same for you."

Chloe shook her head, but she was irresistibly drawn into his glittering gaze. How could she love a man who had lied to her? A man who would love her and leave her? Desperado Jones wasn't the forever kind of man she needed. But despite her inner warnings, he was the man she wanted. The only man she needed.

"Tell me, sweetheart, tell me you want me," Desperado urged in that sexy-as-sin voice she couldn't resist.

"Yes, I want you!" Chloe cried. "Are you happy now?"

He grinned, and that compelling dimple appeared as if by magic. "Happy as a puppy with his face in a bowl of food."

She nervously rimmed her lips with the tip of her tongue. His dark, probing gaze seemed to pierce through to her soul. She was startled when he reached down and removed her gunbelt. "I'm not taking any chances this time," he said as he tossed the gunbelt into the far corner of the room. "Shall I help you undress?"

"I don't want—"

"Yes, you do, you just admitted it." His hand moved to the first button on her blouse, slipping it through its buttonhole. A tantalizing glimpse of cleavage fired his blood and he loosened another button. His touch seemed to mesmerize her and he continued unbuttoning until her blouse gaped open to where it was tucked into her trousers.

His fingers began to work the buttons on her trousers, fumbling clumsily in his eagerness. Suddenly she flung his hands aside and stepped away. "I can't let you do this. What if you get me with child? When you leave, as you're bound to do, I'll be left alone with a child to support."

Before he could stop himself, Desperado said something that came as close to a commitment as he was capable of giving. "What if I don't leave? What if I stayed on at the ranch with you?"

Chloe's eyebrows shot upward. "Are you offering marriage?"

Desperado shifted uncomfortably. Finally he said, "I'm a half-breed, Chloe. You know my reputation. You wouldn't want a permanent arrangement with a man like me."

"Why don't you let me decide that?"

Desperado found it difficult to believe that a beautiful, desirable woman like Chloe wanted to marry him. Unless . . . His face hardened. "Rest assured I won't turn you out of your home, if that's your reason for wanting to marry me."

"Damn you!" Chloe hissed. "You don't know me at all if you think I'd use my body to influence you."

Their gazes clashed, held, locked. Desperado wouldn't allow himself to believe that Chloe wanted to marry him. His next thought nearly brought him to his knees. Did she love him? No, he scolded himself; how could she love a scoundrel like him?

Did he love her? Desperado knew that what he felt for Chloe went deeper than simple lust. But love? He didn't trust his heart where women were concerned. He'd never had anything but sexual relationships with women, and he needed more time to explore these new emotions churning inside him.

"What are you thinking?" Chloe asked when the tense silence dragged on.

His dimpled smile banished her good sense. "I'm thinking you talk too much." His hands returned to her waist as he deftly popped the buttons free on the fly of her trousers. "I want to love you, sweetheart."

Chloe couldn't fight the clamoring of her own body. Nor could she deny the growing love she felt for Desperado Jones.

"Have me, then, Desperado. But don't expect me to live in your home as your whore."

Desperado flinched at her bald statement. "Whore" wasn't a word he'd ever apply to Chloe. She could be hard, brusque and argumentive. Her wariness where men were concerned had been the result of Tate Talbot's brutal attack. She was sweet when she wanted to be, and soft and womanly in all the right places. He'd never known a woman like Chloe Sommers, and the truth of the matter was he'd never expected to meet someone who captured his heart and his imagination the way Chloe did. If it was the last thing he ever did, he'd change her mind about living on the ranch. Once he signed it over to her, she'd have no reason to live elsewhere.

Sweeping her from her feet, he carried her to the bed and finished undressing her. He pulled off her boots, then skimmed her skin-tight trousers and drawers over her hips and down her slender legs. Seconds later he stripped off her blouse and camisole. Then he stood above her, his eyes dark with passion.

"My God, you're beautiful." With shaking hands he reached out and brushed a stray blonde curl from her brow. "It's a damn shame to cover up that glorious hair with a man's hat."

His eyes made glowing love to her as they slid over her breasts, glided past her navel, finally stopping at the thatch of hair shielding her womanhood. The pale skin of her body contrasted delightfully with the golden tan of her face, the vee formed by the open collar of her blouse, and her arms where the sun was allowed to touch. "You're perfect," he rasped harshly.

"Take off your clothes," Chloe whispered, apparently resigned to making love with the sexiest man she'd ever known. A man she desperately wanted despite her misgivings.

Desperado grinned. "Your wish is my command."

He undressed swiftly, flinging his clothing away with careless disregard. Then he stood before her, unflinching as her gaze devoured him. His sex rose majestically in response, growing so hard and stiff he feared he'd explode and embarrass himself.

"Lie down beside me," Chloe invited. He obliged instantly. When he started to take her into his arms, she pushed him back down, staring at the head of his sex and the pearly drop of semen glistening at its tip. "No, lie back. You've had it your way every time, now it's my turn."

Desperado's sex leaped at her words. She could have asked anything of him and he would have agreed.

Chloe got to her knees and leaned over him. Desperado groaned as she began to explore his body, nuzzling and kissing a path that ultimately led to his aroused sex. Her hands and mouth on his flesh combined to drive him to the brink of madness. Sweat beaded his brow, and his jaw clenched when her hair brushed between his legs.

Beneath her hand his rod, already stiff and distended, grew even larger . . . harder. Then her tongue flicked out and licked at the tip. His body arched off the bed and his hoarse cry pierced the silence of the room. "Chloe! You're killing me."

She lifted her head and grinned at him. "Good." Then her lips closed over him.

Desperado fought for control as the blinding need to spend himself drew his body into a taut bow. He reined in his galloping passion and concentrated on breathing deeply while she had her way with his willing body.

Maintaining control was no easy task. The consuming heat of her mouth scorched him, sending him spiraling toward a level of pleasure he'd never achieved before. He softly groaned her name, urging her on with endearments and words he wasn't even aware of. His fists balled in her hair, moving her head up and down on him to increase his pleasure.

Chloe knew he was enjoying what she was doing to him and gloried in the power she held over him. Why did the man always have to be the aggressor? It felt good to be the one calling the shots. She increased the pressure of her lips, moving up and down along the length of his velvety staff. She was his master now. Her tough-as-nails lover was completely at her mercy.

"Chloe," he gritted from between clenched teeth, "I'm warning you. I'm going to . . . If you don't want me to . . ."

Chloe knew what he was telling her, but she wanted to bring this to completion. Desperado had other ideas; he rolled over and pinned her beneath him. "Let's see who's the master now," he growled.

Chloe gasped as he teased her nipples between his thumb and forefinger. The dimple flashed in his cheek when she arched up against him, offering more of herself; then he placed his mouth where his fingers had been. Chloe groaned as he suckled her breasts.

"Now, Desperado. Come inside me now."

"Turnabout is fair play," Desperado rasped.

Her heart leaped into her throat when she felt him spread her legs and place them over his shoulders. Then his lips traveled slowly downward, to the moist folds between her thighs. His mouth found the sensitive nub at the entrance of her sex and he lapped at it with delicate strokes of his tongue. Suddenly his tongue dipped inside her, not deeply, but enough to drive her wild.

213

His shoulders were wedged solidly between her thighs. She felt his tongue thrust deeply and cried out as her body reacted violently. She shuddered and edged closer to climax. She sobbed his name as he reared up over her and thrust his engorged shaft into her quivering body. He gave her no respite, but set up a rhythm that flung her quickly over the edge. She screamed, convulsing around him in hard, pulsing spasms. She was barely conscious when he threw back his head and surrendered to pleasure.

She was lying on her back, one arm covering her eyes. He was lying beside her, breathing deeply in an effort to control his pounding heart. He had never gotten so far out of control before with a woman. He didn't know what it all meant, but he did know Chloe was someone special. Someone he'd never tire of. Was that love?

"What are you thinking?" Chloe asked, turning to face him.

"That I could do this every night for the rest of my life."

Chloe's brows arched upward. "With me?"

For a moment he was thunderstruck. There was so much hope in her voice. He wanted to tell her that there was no other woman he'd ever want in his bed but he wasn't certain he was ready for that kind of commitment. Damn, why couldn't he say the words she wanted to hear?

Because you're afraid you'll disappoint her, his conscience replied. *She'll find out you're not the kind of man she needs and she'll spend the rest of her life regretting it.*

"Of course with you," Desperado said teasingly. "There isn't a man alive who wouldn't want you in his bed every night for the rest of his life."

His answer was lightly given, and he could tell by Chloe's expression that it wasn't exactly the answer she wanted. He stroked her breast, pleased at the way her nipple puckered, as if begging for his touch. He took a nipple into his mouth and felt her arch against him. He lifted his head and stared into her expressive, passion-glazed eyes.

"Maybe I can't be the forever kind of man you want, honey, but I can certainly make you happy for as long as you can tolerate me."

She gazed up at him, her eyes misty. "I don't think we're talking about the same kind of happiness. But if that's all you're capable of giving, I reckon I can settle for that. You'd be surprised at how long I can tolerate certain things, Desperado Jones."

"Is that an invitation, Miss Sommers?" he asked as he lowered his head and kissed her. After that she forgot what they had been talking about as their passion flared into white-hot desire and they made love again.

While Chloe and Desperado made love, Tate Talbot and his father were holed up in Calvin's office. Tate paced while Calvin sat in contemplative silence, his fingers steepled before him.

"Are you just going to sit there and do nothing, Pa?" Tate demanded.

"I'm thinking, son, I'm thinking. You'd be better off if you'd do more of it."

"Shit! Are you still blaming me for letting Chloe's cattle get through to Dodge?"

"You have to admit you bungled the job," Calvin charged.

"Yeah, well, I can't help it if Chloe twitched her tail at Desperado and got him to change sides. Hell, I can't believe she bedded him without putting up a fight. She sure as hell didn't like it when I—"

"Enough!" Calvin said, raising his hand for silence. "That's water under the bridge. It's pretty much been established that Jones is Logan Ralston. The whole town is talking about Jones and the fact that he's Ted Ralston's son. It appears that Jones is the new owner of the Ralston spread.

"I've already approached Jones about selling the ranch and he turned me down flat. He's going to be difficult to deal with. More difficult than Chloe Sommers."

"Maybe we can change his mind," Tate suggested.

Calvin stared over his steepled fingers. "It's not going to be that easy. We have no leverage. Nothing to bend him to our will. We have to work fast. I just received word that negotiations are to begin soon for the purchase of the right-of-way for the spur line. When negotiations begin, I intend to own all the land along the proposed route."

Tate grinned. "You got something up your sleeve, Pa? What is it? How can I help?"

"Leverage," Calvin mused. "It's all got to do with

leverage. Just how fond of Chloe Sommers is Jones?"

"Too damn fond for my liking," Tate said sourly. "I always considered Chloe mine. I figured she'd come around one day. Then that gunslinger came along and dazzled her with his reputation. I still want her, Pa. But I don't have a chance unless Jones leaves town or gets himself killed."

"Hmmm," Calvin said as the wheels in his mind began to turn. "I wonder just how much Jones values Chloe's life. How far would he go to keep her safe?"

A slow grin spread over Tate's features. "Am I thinking what you're thinking? Me and the boys can take Chloe someplace while you negotiate with Jones for the ranch."

"It won't be easy to snatch Chloe from under Desperado's nose. But having her in our clutches might just be the kind of leverage we need to convince him to sell out."

"Tuck Mapes told me he saw Chloe checking into the hotel today. I don't know why she left the ranch, but it's worth checking into. I'll find out what room she's in. It will make things a whole lot easier for us if she's left the ranch for good. There are too many men protecting her out there."

"Good. Meanwhile, I'll try to get some information from Thadeous Baker about Jones's plans for his newly acquired property. Jones doesn't strike me as a man anxious to buckle down to responsibility."

* * *

Desperado awoke before dawn the next morning with his arms full of soft, fragrant woman. He nuzzled Chloe's neck and smiled when she purred contentedly. He wished he could linger in bed but there wasn't time. He disentangled himself from Chloe's warm body and climbed out of bed. He lit the lamp, found his discarded clothing and dressed quickly. He stared down at the sleeping Chloe with aching tenderness as he buckled on his gunbelt; then he jostled her awake. All he received for his effort was a grunt of protest.

"Wake up, sleepyhead."

Chloe opened one eye, saw Desperado, and groaned. She recalled all those intimate things she'd done with Desperado last night and blushed. "Why should I wake up? It's still dark outside."

"I want to get you back to the ranch as soon as possible. The hands are probably getting jittery with no one out there to give orders."

All vestiges of sleep left Chloe. "I haven't changed my mind, Mr. Jones. I'm *not* going back to the ranch and pretend it's still mine. Issue your own orders."

"If all goes as I plan, you won't have to pretend."

"You're a stubborn man, Desperado Jones. Not only that, you're as dense as dirt. I don't want the ranch as a gift."

"What do you want?"

"If you don't know, then I'm not going to tell you. Just promise me you won't sell out to Talbot."

How much plainer could she get? Chloe wondered. She'd done everything but get down on her knees and beg him to marry her, but he was an expert at circumventing the issue. He must think her a besotted fool. He'd left her with nothing but her pride, and she wasn't going to give that up to the determined gunslinger. He could take his ranch and stuff it up his . . . Well, he could just go whistle if he thought she was going to live out there as his whore until he got itchy feet and left.

"I have no intention of selling the ranch to Talbot, now or ever," Desperado declared. "Now get dressed. I've got an appointment with the lawyer this morning."

"I'm not going anywhere with you, Mr. Jones," Chloe said, tilting her chin defiantly.

His determined smile did not bode well for her and Chloe knew it. She was far from prepared when Desperado rolled her up in the blanket and flung her over his shoulder.

"Put me down or I'll scream."

He swatted her butt playfully. "Think what finding me in your room would do to your reputation. Now be quiet. My horse is stabled out back. The fewer people who see us, the better it will be for you."

"Bastard!"

"I've been called worse." He opened the door, peeked out into the dark, deserted hall and headed for the rear exit. Fortunately, he didn't have to walk through the lobby and past the clerk, for the exit was just a few steps away from Chloe's room at the end of the hall.

No one was about when Desperado led his horse from the lean-to behind the hotel. "I'll come back for your clothes and check you out of the hotel later," he said as he tossed her aboard his mustang. "Quit squirming. It's going to be an uncomfortable ride if you insist on throwing a fit."

"You can't do this," Chloe hissed. "I was going out today to find a job."

"You've got a job. Running the ranch is no picnic."

"I can't go with you like this. I'm naked beneath the blanket."

He grinned down at her. "I'm quite aware of that. I did give you a choice, if you recall."

Her muffled curse was caught in the folds of the blanket as Desperado pulled it over her head, mounted behind her and rode hell for leather out of town.

Streaks of mauve and gray brightened the eastern sky as dawn broke over Texas. The cowboys were just stirring when Desperado drew rein before the ranch house, slid down from the saddle and reached for Chloe. Cory sprinted up to join them.

"You're back!" he said. "We were beginning to wonder if anyone was going to run the ranch after Miss Chloe left. Some of the hands wanted to leave, but I talked them into staying until someone showed up."

His gaze settled on the blanket-wrapped object in Desperado's arms. "That isn't . . . That's not Miss Chloe, is it?"

Suddenly Chloe's head popped up from the blanket. "Yes, it's me, Cory. I've been kidnapped from my hotel room."

Cory blanched, his disapproving gaze boring into Desperado. "Why did you go and do that?"

"The lady doesn't belong in town. This is her home."

"Miss Chloe said the ranch belongs to Logan Ralston. Are you Logan Ralston?" Cory asked point blank. "Rumor has it you are."

"Of course he's Logan Ralston," Chloe mumbled from within the folds of the blanket. "Put me down, Mr. Jones!"

"Stop fussing," Desperado warned.

"What should I tell the others?" Cory asked, returning his gaze to the squirming bundle in Desperado's arms.

"Tell them I'll come out to the bunkhouse and talk to them as soon as I get rid of the wildcat in my arms. See that my horse is taken care of, will you?"

Recognizing dismissal, Cory took up the mustang's reins and led him away. He looked back once and shook his head when he saw Desperado carrying Chloe into the house.

"That was embarrassing," Chloe fumed. "You can put me down now. I can find my own way to my room."

Desperado seemed to be taking a long time to reach the stairs and Chloe realized he was refamiliarizing himself with the home he'd been forced to leave years ago.

"Nothing much has changed," Desperado rasped. "It's a little more run-down, needs some work on both the inside and outside, but everything is as I remember it."

"Money was hard to come by after Ted died," Chloe said defensively. "I let the house slide in order to build our herd and hire on hands to work the ranch. Mama never was any good with money. Though Ted left money in the bank, it seemed to slip through her fingers."

Desperado tore his gaze away from the painfully familiar surroundings and mounted the stairs. "I assume you've taken Ted's old room," he said as he reached the landing.

"As a matter of fact, I haven't. I kept my old room. The last one on the right."

Desperado's arms stiffened around her. "That was my old room."

"I didn't know."

"Doesn't matter." He reached the door, found the knob with one hand and pushed it open.

"You can put me down now. I'd like to get dressed."

Desperado carried her to the bed, grasped an end of the blanket and deftly unrolled her onto the same quilt that had covered his bed many years ago.

"Damn you," Chloe hissed, trying to cover herself with the quilt. "Why do you insist on embarrassing me?"

"A few hours ago I explored every part of your body, just as you did mine. We were as intimate as a man and woman can be. Your body is no stranger to me, sweetheart."

Chloe knew he spoke the truth, but his high-handed method of bringing her back to the ranch rankled. Besides, his arrogance made her mad.

"Go ahead and get dressed," Desperado said. "I'm going out to the bunkhouse to talk to the hands. I could use some breakfast," he hinted as he left the room. "Could you fix us something to eat?"

He shut the door seconds before an object came flying at him. He chuckled to himself when he heard it hit the closed door and crash to the floor.

Chapter Twelve

Desperado walked into the bunkhouse to confront the Ralston hands. A few were openly hostile, some were willing to hear him out, others were merely watchful, waiting to find out which way the wind blew before pulling out or staying.

"I suppose you've heard the gossip floating around town," Desperado began. "I know you're wondering if it's true, and I don't blame you."

"You owe us the truth!" Rowdy charged. "I never did like you, and trusted you even less. Are you really Logan Ralston? Who are you? The new owner of the ranch or a no-good gunslinger?"

There was some muttering among the men and Desperado sought to calm them. "I am Logan Ralston," he admitted, "but I haven't used that name in more years than I care to count. I'm still Desperado Jones to all of you. A leopard doesn't change his spots overnight."

"Where does that leave us, Desperado?" Randy asked. "Are you gonna run the ranch now?"

"Nothing has changed," Desperado assured them. "Miss Sommers will still be boss around here. She'll give the orders."

"That ain't the way I heard it," Rowdy argued. "Miss Chloe said she no longer owned the Ralston spread. That we could leave, or stay and take orders from you."

"Miss Chloe was wrong," Desperado rasped. "If any of you want to leave and find work elsewhere, you're welcome to do so. Those of you who remain will be put to work building a new barn."

"How long do you intend to stick around?" Cory asked.

Desperado gazed toward the house, thinking that leaving Chloe was going to be damn difficult. "I don't know. Long enough to figure out why Talbot wants this land, I reckon."

"I don't understand how you can leave a woman in charge of your property and go off about your business without so much as a backward glance," Rowdy contended. "Isn't that a bit risky?"

"That's none of your business, Rowdy. Either you're staying on or you're not. But if you stay, I'll expect you to buckle down like the others."

"I'm staying on," Cory said. "Miss Chloe has been good to us. I ain't letting her down now."

"I'm staying, too," Sonny and Randy said in unison. One by one the others stood solidly behind

Cory, until only Rowdy had yet to decide.

"What's it going to be, Rowdy? Decide now or pack your things."

"I ain't no quitter," Rowdy muttered. "I'll stay on for a spell, but not because of you. Like Cory says, Miss Chloe has been good to us."

Desperado searched the face of each man in turn. They were hardly more than boys, he thought. Then he recalled how hard they had worked during the trail drive and how they had pulled together during hard times. Though they were young, he couldn't have asked for better drovers.

"You won't be sorry, and I know Chloe will be grateful. I'm going into town later to order wood for the new barn. Meanwhile, put the bull in with the cows we kept back for breeding. We need to build up a new herd if the ranch is to remain solvent. Now get to the chores, men, I'm going up to the house to have breakfast with the boss lady."

Behind his back, Rowdy muttered loud enough to be heard, "I'm betting he'll have more than breakfast with Miss Chloe."

Desperado pretended not to hear as he strode back to the house, his back stiff, his hands clenched at his sides.

He found Chloe in the kitchen, banging pots and pans around on the wood stove. "What are we having?" he asked. "I'm hungry enough to eat a whole hog."

"The hens are laying. I gathered eggs and whipped up some biscuits. There's bacon and fried potatoes, too. I could open a can of beans if that's not enough."

Desperado could tell by her clipped words that she was still angry at him. "Keep the beans for another time."

"I'm only cooking because I'm hungry, too," Chloe replied tartly.

Desperado took a seat at the table while Chloe dished up the food. When she set it before him, he dug in with gusto. "This is good. You're a tolerable cook." He flashed his dimple. "One of the things you do well. Another is—"

"I'm a tolerable shot, too, Mr. Jones," she injected before he could finish his sentence.

"I'm aware of that, sweetheart," he said as he shoveled food into his mouth and washed it down with hot, black coffee. When he finished, he shoved his chair back and patted his stomach. "That will keep me until I return for the evening meal."

"I won't be here to cook it for you," Chloe declared.

"You'd better be unless you want to be dragged back kicking and screaming. I told the boys you're still the boss. They're all going to stay on and help build the new barn."

Chloe's head shot up. "New barn?"

"I'm going to town to order wood and nails. As for the regular ranch work, you know better than I what needs to be done."

"What is all this going to gain you, Desperado?" Chloe asked softly. "Only a callous, irresponsible man would ignore his father's last wishes and walk away from responsibility."

Desperado uncoiled himself to his full, impressive height. "I never claimed to be anything other than what I am. That's what I've been trying to tell you. I'd be no good as a rancher, and even worse as a husband. Once I get everything settled with the lawyer, I'll be taking off for parts unknown, doing what I do best."

"Killing people."

"I only kill when I'm forced to. I'm not wanted by the law. I can bring people around without using excessive violence."

Chloe glared at him. "You probably scare them to death with that raspy voice and wicked look. You do that deliberately, don't you?"

He shrugged. "It seems to work."

"You're a fraud, Mr. Jones."

His dark eyes glittered dangerously. "A man would never get away with what you just said." He reached her in two long strides and pulled her into his arms. "But you, sweet wildcat, with your sharp tongue and even sharper claws, are much prettier than a man, and your body far more pleasing."

She gave a squawk of protest when his mouth came down hard on hers. His kiss wasn't gentle. It was hungry, voracious, filled with a need Desperado knew would remain with him forever. No matter where he went he would always remember the sultry heat of her mouth, soft and sweet and seductive. Fearing that he wouldn't be able to leave if he continued kissing her, Desperado broke off the kiss and pushed her gently away. Slightly off balance, she clung to him, panting, her eyes glazed.

"Wait for me," he rasped. "We'll finish what we began when I return tonight."

He was out the door before Chloe regained her breath and her anger.

Back in town, Tate Talbot glared menacingly at the frightened hotel clerk. "Are you sure Miss Sommers is in her room?"

"I haven't seen her leave and I've been here since dawn," the man answered as Tate slipped him a five-dollar gold piece.

"That's all I wanted to know," Tate said, smiling to himself as he went outside to inform his two cohorts of his findings.

"Chloe's room is near the first-floor exit," Tate told his friends. "Bring the horses around and keep them quiet while I slip into the room and get Chloe. We'll take her out to the old deserted mine at the end of Rogue Creek Road. We can take turns guarding her until Pa negotiates the sale of the Ralston spread with Jones."

The men led their horses around to the back of the hotel and waited while Tate slipped through the rear exit. His gold piece had earned him Chloe's room number and he found it without difficulty. To his delight he found the door unlocked and he barged inside.

The room was empty.

Tate's outraged bellow echoed through the deserted room and down the hallway. "Where in the hell are you, Chloe?"

"Looking for someone?"

Tate whirled, stunned to see Desperado lounging in the doorway, one brawny shoulder propped against the doorjamb, his arms crossed over his chest. "What are you doing here, Jones? Where's Chloe?"

"She checked out before dawn," Desperado drawled. "I've come for her belongings."

He pushed himself away from the door, found Chloe's carpetbag under the bed and began gathering her clothing. Then he opened the bureau drawers and emptied them into the bag. Tate stood by speechless as Desperado clasped the bag shut, grasped it with his left hand and made for the door. He stopped just short of the entrance and spun around to confront Tate.

"What are you doing here, Talbot?"

"That's my business," Tate said, finding his tongue.

"It's my business now. If you've come expecting to make trouble for Chloe, you're too late. She's back at the ranch where she belongs. Crawl back to your papa and tell him he'll never get his hands on the ranch."

Rage tinged Tate's face red and he forgot for a moment with whom he was dealing. His hand wavered toward his gun. He realized his mistake when he saw Desperado's face harden and his eyes turn flinty. Desperado's six-shooter was in his hand before Tate's weapon had even cleared his holster. Desperado's manner remained serene; he hadn't even dropped the bag he held in his left hand.

"Sonofabitch! How did you do that?" Tate asked, clearly in awe of Desperado's prowess.

"Don't ever draw on me again," Desperado rasped. "If you come within shouting distance of

Chloe, I'll shoot to kill. Now, are you going to tell me what you're doing here?"

"I . . . I just wanted to talk to Chloe. To apologize for . . . for the misunderstanding we had," Tate lied. "One of my friends saw her checking into the hotel yesterday."

"I don't believe you, but I don't have time to argue the point right now. I have an appointment with my lawyer. Heed my warning, Talbot, and you might yet live to a ripe old age."

Turning abruptly, Desperado left the room, slamming the door in Tate's face. A few minutes later he climbed the stairs to Thadeous Baker's office.

Mr. Baker motioned Desperado into a chair and drew out a sheaf of papers from beneath the clutter on his desk. "The appropriate documents are ready for you, Mr. Ralston," he said by way of greeting. "All that is required to make the Ralston spread legally yours is your signature on the proper line."

"Will you be able to proceed with transferring ownership after I sign?" Desperado asked.

"I had hoped you'd changed your mind," Baker said. "The Ralston place needs a man in charge. You've seen how it has deteriorated since Ted passed on."

"I haven't changed my mind," Desperado said. "Show me where to sign."

Baker dipped the pen in the inkwell, handed it to Desperado and shoved the papers across the desk. "Sign your name on the bottom line. Your legal name, that is," he said, peering at Desperado over his rimless glasses.

Desperado signed with a flourish and set the pen

down. "Now then, how soon can you draw up the papers deeding the property to Chloe Sommers?"

"Day after tomorrow, if that's what you really want."

"It's precisely what I want," Desperado rasped.

"May I make a suggestion?"

"Go ahead, but I won't promise anything."

"Why not simply add Chloe's name to the deed? Then you'd own it jointly. That way she can't be badgered into selling without your signature. I'm not unaware of Calvin Talbot's eagerness to purchase the Ralston spread. I've done legal work for Talbot on some of his acquisitions and know how he works. On her own, Chloe Sommers doesn't stand a chance against Talbot's machinations. This way, even if you leave, she'll be protected."

Desperado seriously considered the idea and could find no fault with it. In fact, it would solve a lot of problems.

"I lead a precarious life, Mr. Baker," Desperado said. "What would happen should something 'unforeseen' happen to me?"

"Miss Sommers will automatically inherit your share upon your death."

Desperado decided he liked the lawyer's suggestion. "Very well, your suggestion makes sense. I'll return day after tomorrow to sign the necessary papers."

"Bring Miss Sommers with you. I'll need her signature, also."

Neither Jones nor Baker were aware of the man pressed against the wall beside the open window, listening to the conversation. The moment he heard the final arrangements concerning Desperado's property, Tate Talbot crept down the stairs and hightailed it to his father's place of business.

Desperado rose and shook hands with Baker. "Much obliged, sir."

"Sit down, son, we're not through here," Baker said. "There's a little matter of the money deposited in the bank in your name."

Desperado sat down with a thump. "What! I don't have money here in the bank. I have a little put aside in Amarillo, but nothing here."

"You have more than you know, and you have your father to thank for his foresight," Baker said. "Before his death he put five thousand dollars aside in the bank in your name. That's how convinced he was that you were alive. I made all the arrangements myself. You see," Baker explained, "Ted knew his wife and her spendthrift ways well. He wanted to leave you money to run the ranch should you turn up one day."

Desperado felt the breath whoosh out of him. He couldn't believe his father had never given up on finding him alive. If only he'd known. He wouldn't have been so stubborn about returning home. Unfortunately, he couldn't go back and undo his mistakes.

"What if I had never returned?"

"Provisions were made for that possibility. Ted gave you ten years to show up after his death. If you failed to return at the end of ten years, the money was to go to Chloe. You made the cutoff date with time to spare. The money is all yours, son, waiting for you in the bank. Years of interest have increased the initial sum considerably."

For once Desperado was speechless. "I . . . I don't know what to say."

"Don't say anything. I'll close the office and walk over to the bank with you to explain things." He scraped back his chair, rose with some difficulty and ushered Desperado out the door.

"You know what that half-breed bastard has gone and done now, Pa?" Tate blasted as he burst into Calvin's office.

"No, but I have a notion you're going to tell me. Calm down, son, and tell me what's got you so riled. Did you get that little 'job' done? Where did you take the Sommers girl?"

"That's something else we gotta talk about. Chloe wasn't at the hotel. She snuck out without the clerk's knowledge. You can bet your ass Desperado had something to do with it."

"Can't you do anything right?" Calvin raged.

"It ain't my fault, Pa. But wait till you hear the rest. Desperado walked in on me while I was in Chloe's hotel room. He claimed she was out at the ranch. That he'd come for her belongings."

"What else can go wrong?" Calvin said tightly. "The railroad people will start negotiations soon for the right-of-way along the proposed route. Perhaps you'd better tell me the rest of your news."

"You ain't gonna like it, Pa. I followed Jones to Lawyer Baker's office. Jones signed the papers that gave him ownership of the Ralston spread. I nearly swallowed my teeth when I heard Jones tell Baker he wanted to return everything to Chloe."

"Excellent," Calvin said gleefully. "That means Jones doesn't intend to stick around. Once he's out of the way, I'm not going to let a woman stand in the way of progress. Soon all the land between here and Amarillo will belong to me. When the railroad people come to town, they're going to learn they're not dealing with yokels."

"There's more, Pa," Tate confided. "That sly old fart Baker talked Desperado into keeping the deed in his name and making Chloe co-owner. They'll own the land jointly. Chloe stands to inherit everything if and when Desperado dies. What are we gonna do now? I want Chloe as bad as you want the land."

"Kill him," Calvin hissed. "Arrange for an accident. Anything that will get Jones out of our hair. Reverend Tully owes me a favor. He'll marry you and Chloe with or without her consent. If we can't buy the land, we'll take it any way we can. And you'll have Chloe in your bed, though I don't envy you the task of taming the gun-toting little shrew."

"I'll tame her," Tate said with a braggart's confidence. "Just leave everything to me."

The telegram Desperado expected was waiting for him at the telegraph office. The clerk handed it to him and watched with interest as he read it.

"What made you suspect the railroad might be coming through Trouble Creek, Mr. Jones?" the man asked after Desperado had read the telegram and stuffed it into his vest pocket.

"Just a hunch," Desperado replied.

"The ranchers that sold out to Mr. Talbot should

have held on a little longer," the clerk said sadly. "They took the meager offer Talbot made for their land and left for greener pastures. Should have known something was up when that land speculator came to town and got himself elected mayor. He even put his own man in as town marshal. What are you gonna do about it, Mr. Jones?"

"Nothing I can do." Desperado shrugged. "What's done is done. Talbot owns all the land along the proposed new spur line except for the Ralston spread. It will be a cold day in hell when they get that."

He nodded good day and walked over to the lumber yard, where he arranged for wood, nails and paint to be delivered to the ranch the following day. A short time later Desperado headed back to the ranch to tell Chloe about his decision about the ranch.

Chloe had the chicken floured and ready to fry and biscuits in the oven baking when Desperado returned. She grunted a greeting and tried to ignore him as he washed up in the rain barrel beside the back door.

"Smells mighty good in here," Desperado said as he paused in the doorway to watch her move about the kitchen.

Chloe banged a frying pan on the stove and flung a dollop of lard into it from the lard can.

"I brought your belongings back from the hotel."

Still Chloe said nothing.

"I met a friend of yours skulking about in your room."

That caught Chloe's attention and she whirled to face him. "What are you talking about?"

"Tate Talbot paid you a visit. He was in your room when I got there. He was disappointed to find you gone."

"I . . . I don't understand. Did he say what he wanted?"

"The man had mischief on his mind, Chloe. What other reason would he have for being there? Now do you see why I wanted you out here where you'd be safe?"

Chloe bit the soft underside of her lip while she considered Desperado's words. "You think he would have done me harm?"

"I don't think, I know."

"Why? What could hurting me gain them?"

"I thought it through pretty thoroughly on the way home. The Talbots know who I am and that I now own the Ralston spread. I've already told them I wouldn't sell to them. They're not dumb, Chloe. They know there is only one way to convince me to sell."

"How could the Talbots make you do something you don't want to do?"

"Think about it, sweetheart," Desperado rasped as he joined her beside the stove. "They intend to use you to get to me. Had you been in your room, Tate would have carried you off and hidden you somewhere while his father pressured me to sell the ranch. I would have agreed to anything to keep you safe. That's why I wanted you where they couldn't easily get to you."

"My God," Chloe said shakily. "Are they that desperate to get the land? Why? Why would they break the law to get more land when they already have so much?"

Desperado plucked the crumpled telegram from his pocket and handed it to her. "Read this. Perhaps it will explain why the Talbots are land hungry."

Chloe perused the telegram with growing dismay. "I should have known there was a method behind their madness. What do you suppose they'll do now?"

Desperado shrugged. "Hard telling. The Ralston spread is the last piece of land along the proposed railroad route that Talbot doesn't own. He intended to ask an exorbitant price for the right-of-way and would have a good chance of getting it with all the land in his possession. I've known enough dishonest men in my life to know how his mind works."

Chloe remained thoughtful as she placed pieces of floured chicken into the sizzling fat in the frying pan. When the pan was full she covered it and turned back to Desperado. "There's no way Talbot can get the land now, is there? You're too strong a man to allow him to bully you into selling."

"Sit down, honey," Desperado said, pulling out a chair for her. "You need to know what I've decided about the ranch."

"Is everything in order? Is the ranch yours now?"

"Not exactly," Desperado said as he sat down beside her. "My original intention was to deed the land to you and ride away from Trouble Creek without a backward glance."

"I don't want your charity," Chloe bit out.

"Don't get your dander up," Desperado cajoled.

"Hear me out before you jump to conclusions."

Chloe spat out something indistinguishable and glared at him. "Very well, talk away, not that it will change anything."

"Mr. Baker is a savvy man. He knows you'd be vulnerable to the Talbots once I left you to handle the ranch on your own, and he didn't mince words when he said I'd not be doing you a favor by deeding the ranch to you."

"Smart man," Chloe muttered.

"He offered another suggestion. He said I should leave my name on the deed and add yours. We'd be co-owners. You couldn't sell without my signature and I couldn't sell without yours."

"Really, Desperado, I don't want—"

"Dammit, Chloe, listen to reason. It's the best I can do to protect you. This has been your home longer than it was mine. You belong here."

"So do you. Why do you think your father added the codicil to his will?"

"There are things I'll regret the rest of my life," Desperado said sadly. "I'll just have to live with them."

Chloe noted the hollow look in his eyes and felt pity for the young boy who had made unwise choices because he thought his father didn't love him. She also pitied the man who had to live with those choices.

"You'll inherit the ranch if I die first." He gave her an apologetic grin. "I don't expect to live a long life, given my profession."

"You don't have to leave, Desperado," she whispered huskily. "You can stay."

He reached out and caressed a velvety cheek with the back of a callused finger. "And do what?" he asked. "Practice my skill by shooting at bottles? Wait for someone to come along who's a faster draw than I am?"

"You won't be a gunslinger if you become a rancher," she said in a rush. "After a while people will forget Desperado Jones ever existed. Someone faster, younger, will come along to earn the title you abandoned."

She bowed her head so he couldn't read the desperation in her eyes. "Together we could make this ranch the way it was when Ted ran it." She inhaled slowly and plunged on. "If we're to be co-owners, why not be partners in the true sense of the word?"

Did he realize what she was suggesting? Chloe wondered. Would it take a knock on his head to make him aware that she loved him? God, the man was dense. She watched with bated breath as his expression softened and his eyes glowed with a strange light. Then he did something that totally confused her. He set the frying pan on the back of the stove, removed the biscuits from the oven and swept her up into his arms. Then he headed for the stairs.

"Desperado! What are you doing? Supper will be ruined."

"The hell with supper," he growled. "I'm going to carry you up to bed and make love to you."

"But it's not even dark!"

"It will be before we're done."

He took the stairs two at a time and didn't release her until he set her on her feet inside her room. She wasn't wearing a gunbelt but his hit the floor with a resounding thud. He attacked her clothing next, ripping off buttons in his haste to bare her to his hungry gaze. Then he tore off his own clothes and pulled her down onto the bed with him. When he kissed her, her mind shut down and her body took over.

His kisses fell like hot rain across her face, but it was her lips upon which he concentrated. He licked the tempting seam with the tip of his tongue, teased the moist corners, and thrust his tongue past her lips to explore the sweet inner surfaces. Chloe returned his kisses, sucking his tongue deeply into her mouth, then thrusting hers into his mouth to taste of him. It was heaven; it was hell; she wanted more.

Thrusting upward against the scalding heat of his body, she tried to convey without words what she wanted. Apparently he read her thoughts for he brought his hands into play, caressing her breasts, her thighs, that soft place between her legs.

She found his sex and tried to guide it inside her. She heard him groan, knew she was giving him pleasure, and caressed his length a moment or two before bringing him to her entrance. She was all but begging for release by the time he settled between her thighs and thrust upward and forward, burying his pulsating erection inside her hot passage.

She sobbed his name, rising up to meet his thrusts, her body on fire. Loving this special man was so easy, she thought in a moment of clarity. Why couldn't he return her love? Then her thoughts scattered as Desperado suddenly pulled out of her, turned her around, dragged her up onto her hands and knees and thrust into her from behind. She heard the air rasp harshly from his chest as he strained over her. She felt herself taking wing as his hands played with her breasts and his thighs slapped against her buttocks.

Then she was there. Soaring to the heavens, thrashing and crying and laughing, all at the same time. Nothing would ever compare to being loved by Desperado Jones. Then she heard Desperado call out her name, felt his hot seed filling her, and she died a little.

Some time later she heard Desperado's raspy voice whispering something in her ear. She tried to concentrate on his words but her passion-glazed mind refused to cooperate. She opened her eyes and found him smiling down at her. "Were you speaking to me?" She stretched languidly. "Did I shock you? You make me forget I'm a lady."

Desperado chuckled, flashing his dimple. "Lady, hell! You're all passionate woman. I wouldn't want you any other way." He continued to smile at her.

"Desperado, you're embarrassing me! Stop staring at me like that."

"Nothing we do should ever embarrass you, love. But if you must know, I was wondering how you'll look in fifty years. It's going to take at least that long to learn everything there is to know about you. I don't even know your favorite food, or color, or . . ." His grin widened. "Or which position you prefer during lovemaking."

Chloe's brow furrowed. "I haven't the foggiest notion what you're talking about. Fifty years. Have I missed something?"

"I don't know, honey, you tell me. Didn't you hear me ask you to marry me?"

For the first time in her life, Chloe was rendered speechless.

Chapter Thirteen

"Have you nothing to say?" Desperado asked worriedly.

"I don't understand," Chloe answered. "What brought on this sudden desire to marry me? I thought you were a loner, a man who shunned responsibility. Aren't you the same man who didn't want to be tied down to one place or to one woman?"

Chloe knew she should be ecstatic. Lord knows she'd given him enough hints about how she felt about him. But this sudden capitulation made her nervous and more than a little suspicious.

Desperado sat up in bed and stared off into the distance. "If you believe I can settle down, the least I can do is try to live up to your expectations. Besides," he said, his expression harsh with pent-up emotion, "as sure as shooting, that bastard Tate

Talbot will be back harassing you after I leave. The only way to keep him away is to give you my name legally. The idea of his hands on you puts me in a killing mood."

Disappointment shuddered through Chloe. "Is that the only reason you can think of for marrying me?"

"Isn't that enough?"

She jerked upright and leaned against the headboard of the bed, her arms crossed over her naked chest. "No. I want more from the man I marry, Desperado. I want . . . well, have you never heard of love?"

"Love is just an extension of passion," he said after a long pause.

"Passion is an extension of love," Chloe contended. "Do you feel nothing but lust for me? Please tell me 'cause I need to know."

"Can't you just give a simple yes or no to my marriage proposal?"

"I need more than protection from you, Desperado. My guns can provide that. The man I marry has to love me as much as I love him. There can be no simple yes or no until you tell me what's in your heart. I want you to describe exactly what you feel for me."

"You're asking for more than I'm capable of giving," Desperado growled. "I haven't looked deeply into my heart since I was a child and decided my father didn't love me. And look where that led me. I can't trust my heart, Chloe. I'm afraid to look too deeply into it for fear of what I'll find."

His frank admission startled her. It gave her insight into his soul, making her aware of the guilt and despair that had formed his life and made him what he was today. When he had sought to make amends with his father, it had been too late. Ted's premature death must have been a terrible blow.

"Forget the past," Chloe urged. "I know you hated my mother, but I am not my mother. You asked me to marry you and I'm saying no. Your proposal has to come from the heart, Desperado."

Desperado faced her squarely, his expression tortured. "Would you have me bare my soul, woman?"

Chloe scrambled to her knees and cradled his face in her palms so she could look into his eyes. She gasped in dismay at the anguish she saw in those expressive dark windows into his soul. "Why is it so difficult to express your emotions? Baring your soul is not a bad thing."

"I spent my formative years in an environment far different from yours. Indians do not express emotions, not even to their mates. How can I tell you how I feel when I can't explain it to myself?"

"Try. It's important."

Desperado let out a long, slow breath and fixed his beautiful black eyes on her. "I haven't felt for any woman what I feel for you. You make me happy in ways I never imagined. When I'm with you I think of things a man like me has no business thinking about. Home, family, stability. I want you in my bed every night. I want to wake up every morning with you in my arms. The thought of walking off and leaving you is painful. There, are you satisfied?"

Chloe gave a wrenching cry and threw herself

into his arms. "I love you, too! You fool! Don't you realize you just described love better than I've ever heard anyone describe it?"

Desperado seemed dazed. "I did?"

"Honestly, Desperado, men can be so dense sometimes. Now ask me again to marry you."

The corner of his mouth kicked up into a smile. "Maybe I've changed my mind. Will you take your guns to me and force me to the altar?"

"If I have to," Chloe declared tartly.

"Will you marry me, Chloe Sommers?"

"I thought you'd never ask," she said on a sigh. "Just name the day." Suddenly her expression turned wary. "You do intend to stay on here and become a rancher, don't you?"

"I'll give it a damn good try. You realize there are those who won't let me live down my reputation. If I settle in one place I'll have to have eyes in the back of my head."

"I'll guard your back," Chloe vowed. She gave him a quick kiss and scooted to the edge of the bed.

"Where are you going?"

"To see if I can salvage supper. Aren't you hungry?"

He reached for her. "Famished. But not for food."

"But we just—"

"And I want to again. Get used to it, love, I intend to exercise my marital rights often and with great zeal."

"We aren't married yet."

"You talk too much," he said, pulling her down on top of him. "I'm as ready for you as I'll ever be."

Chloe learned just how ready he was as he spread

her legs and thrust upward inside her. Soon they were lost in a world of their own making, where passion ruled and nothing mattered but mutual pleasure.

Needless to say, supper was late that evening. The biscuits were cold and somewhat soggy but the crispy fried chicken and mashed potatoes with chicken gravy more than made up for the mediocre biscuits.

"I'll tell the hands tomorrow," Desperado said, chewing on a biscuit. "They should be the first to know we're getting hitched."

"When is this big event to take place?" Chloe asked. "And where?"

"Lawyer Baker promised to have the deed ready for both our signatures day after tomorrow. As you know, Baker is also the Justice of the Peace. We can ask him to perform the ceremony after the deed is signed."

"There is no need to put my name on the deed if we marry," Chloe reminded him.

"I know, but that's how it's going to be. Let me do this my way, sweetheart."

"You always get your way."

"Not always. But if I can keep those six-shooters of yours away from me, life will be a helluva lot more peaceful. Come on," he said, placing an arm around her shoulders. "Let's go to bed. We've got a big day tomorrow."

Chloe remained in the house to prepare breakfast the following morning while Desperado walked to the bunkhouse to inform the hands about the latest development between him and Chloe.

"Morning," he drawled as he pushed through the door and strolled into the room. The hands were seated on benches on either side of a long table, eating the breakfast that Randy had prepared in the cookhouse. A dozen heads popped up to look at him.

" 'Morning, Desperado," Cory greeted. "Thought you left last night."

Desperado could tell by their expressions that the hands were speculating on where he had spent the night. He had no intention of satisfying their curiosity. He had come to tell them of his plans to marry Chloe, and that was all they were going to get.

"I wanted you boys to hear my news first," Desperado began. "Me and Chloe are getting hitched tomorrow."

Pandemonium broke loose. Some of the hands rushed over to pound Desperado on the back and offer congratulations. Others seemed startled by the announcement. Rowdy, however, sent Desperado a look of utter contempt.

"What kind of man are you? You have no business placing a nice woman like Miss Chloe in danger by dragging her into your violent life. Why don't you just leave? Miss Chloe will forget about you soon enough if you aren't around to pester her."

"Shut up, Rowdy," Cory warned. "Miss Chloe knows what she's doing."

"Thank you, Cory," Desperado said, "but I don't need anyone to defend me. I'm well aware of my shortcomings. I have indeed led a violent life. But Chloe has faith in my ability to change my wicked ways."

"You're a half-breed," Rowdy charged.

"I never claimed to be anything else."

"Miss Chloe is too good for you," Rowdy tossed back.

"You're absolutely right."

Suddenly Desperado knew exactly why Rowdy disliked him. He was surprised he hadn't realized it sooner. The young man was in love with Chloe and had probably felt threatened by Desperado from the start. Even though Rowdy realized his love was unrequited, jealousy had fueled his animosity. He pitied the young man and cast about for a way to diffuse Rowdy's hostility.

"I was hoping you and Cory would come to town with me and Chloe tomorrow and act as witnesses when we repeat our vows, Rowdy. I don't really know anyone in town, and it would please Chloe to have someone she knows and trusts to act as witnesses."

"You can count on me, Desperado," Cory said, beaming. "I'd be proud to be a part of your wedding."

"I'll have a feast waiting when you return," Randy announced. "Miss Chloe deserves something special for her wedding."

Desperado's dark gaze returned to Rowdy. "Well, what do you say, Rowdy?"

"Why me?" Rowdy asked suspiciously. "Why not Sonny, or Pete, or one of the others?"

"Because I asked you. And because Chloe would approve of my choice."

"I reckon I can do it for Miss Chloe," Rowdy muttered.

Desperado left the bunkhouse soon afterward. The buzz of conversation followed him out the door and he smiled to himself. He had doubtlessly shocked all the hands with his wedding plans. Desperado's reputation as a gunman and a loner was well known. The hands weren't the only ones who would be shocked by his marriage. Hell, he'd even shocked himself.

He had awoken this morning wondering how Chloe could love a man like him. He had nothing going for him except a lightning draw and the ability to frighten men into doing what he wanted without resorting to violence.

Desperado stepped into the kitchen and paused, his gaze tender as it settled on Chloe. He thought she looked radiant this morning. She wore the contented look of a woman who had been well loved. Her cheeks were flushed and her lips reddened from his kisses. Though he loved her taut little figure in trousers, he wondered what she would look like in a dress. Or without those infernal guns strapped to her slim hips.

"I hope you're hungry," Chloe said as she filled a plate with eggs, bacon and potatoes and set it down on the table. He sat down and waited for her to join him before digging in.

"Did you talk to the hands?" she asked as she filled his cup with coffee and settled down in a chair beside him.

"I did," he muttered around a mouthful of eggs. "I asked Cory and Rowdy to act as witnesses. I hope you don't mind."

"I don't mind, I'm just surprised at your choices. Rowdy has never warmed up to you like the others."

"He's in love with you," Desperado remarked dryly.

Chloe paused with the fork halfway to her mouth. "You're loco."

"I'm right. He sees me as a rival for your affections. Asking him to act as witness will jolt him back to reality faster than anything else I could have done."

Chloe hoped Desperado knew what he was doing.

The barn-raising got underway that morning. Desperado was grateful for the activity. It gave him little time to think about committing himself to one woman for the rest of his life.

Chloe was so excited she could barely swallow her supper that night. She could think of nothing but becoming Desperado's bride the next day. In the privacy of their bed that night, their loving seemed especially poignant as Desperado took her into his arms and pulled her naked body over him. He aroused her slowly, taking care to bring all of her senses into play as he used his hands and mouth to bring her to passion. He let her dangle on the brink of forever before joining their bodies in solemn promise. They strained together in silent communication until something inside Chloe uncoiled and broke loose. Then she cried out his name and shattered. Afterward she sprawled atop him, utterly spent and totally contented.

"Shouldn't I call you Logan?" Chloe asked sleepily.

"That's going to take some getting used to," he drawled. "I'll let you decide. Call me whatever makes you feel comfortable."

"My love," she whispered moments before she fell asleep. "I'll call you my love."

Chloe's wedding day dawned clear, bright and warm for early fall. It was close to nine o'clock before Desperado let her out of bed and after ten before they were ready to ride into town. Rowdy and Cory had saddled four horses and were waiting for them by the corral.

"Thought you had changed your mind," Cory teased, grinning.

"No way," Desperado growled. "We . . . I . . . overslept," he said somewhat sheepishly.

Rowdy maintained his silence, staring at Chloe as if he expected her to say something. Finally, he asked, "Are you okay, Miss Chloe? Are you sure this is what you want?"

Desperado sent her a speaking look, telling her without words that he'd been right about Rowdy. "Very sure, Rowdy," she replied. "Thank you for agreeing to be one of our witnesses. Shall we go?"

When they rode into town an hour later, Desperado asked the cowboys to wait with the horses as he and Chloe ascended the stairs to Lawyer Baker's office.

"Come in, come in," Baker said effusively. "It's been a coon's age since I've seen you, child," he said to Chloe. "You should have kept in touch."

Chloe offered an apologetic shrug. "I had little time for visiting. The ranch kept me busy."

"Have you convinced Logan to stick around and help run the place?" Baker asked. "Even a gunslinger has to settle down sometime."

"Let me answer that, sir," Desperado interjected. "I proposed to Chloe and she's agreed to marry me. Since you're the Justice of the Peace as well as a lawyer, we hoped you'd marry us today. We brought along a couple of witnesses."

Baker slapped his hand against his desk and gave a hearty chuckle. "About time someone took my advice. I'd be tickled pink to say the words over you."

"Let's get to the deed first," Desperado said. "Did you prepare it just the way I asked?"

"The deed is to be held jointly in both your names, but that is no longer necessary. Once you and Chloe are married, the ranch will automatically become Chloe's upon your death."

"That's not good enough," Desperado declared. "I still want Chloe's name on the deed. Show us where to sign."

"Very well," Baker said, whipping out a legal document with a fancy gold seal. "Both your signatures are required on the lines I have indicated with an X." He handed the pen to Chloe. "You first, my dear."

Chloe signed, then handed the pen to Desperado.

He signed his own name and handed the document back to Baker.

"Would you like me to hold onto this for safekeeping or would you prefer to keep it yourself?" Baker asked.

"I prefer to keep the deed in my possession," Desperado said. "There's a safe at the ranch; it should be secure there."

"I'll file a copy at City Hall," Baker said as he handed the deed to Desperado and watched as he folded it in half and placed it in his inside pocket. Then Baker pulled a second document from a drawer and placed it on his desk. "Call your witnesses. We can have that wedding now."

Desperado's reply was forestalled by the sound of footsteps pounding up the stairs. Moments later Cory burst into the office. "Desperado, Tate Talbot sent me up to get you. He wants to meet you out in the street in five minutes. You're not going to do it, are you?"

"Desperado! No!" Chloe cried, clinging to his arm. "This is our wedding day!"

Desperado gave her a look filled with desperate appeal.

"I should have known this would never work. Happiness is for other men, not me. I have to meet him, honey. And I'll probably kill him. I don't know how the town will react to that. Everyone knows the town marshal is in Calvin Talbot's pocket. I won't drag you down with me."

He shook free of her grasp. "Wait here with Cory and Mr. Baker. I don't want you getting hurt. Look on the bright side," he said with a grimness that belied his words. "Everything could turn out just fine and we'll still be married today."

Chloe didn't believe him for a minute. "If you walk out now, Desperado Jones, I'll never forgive you."

"If I don't, honey, I'll never forgive myself. This showdown between me and Tate Talbot has been a long time in the making. I can't forget what he did to you."

He pulled her against him, kissed her hard, then shoved her toward Cory. "See that she stays out of trouble, Cory." Then he was gone.

Chloe rushed out the door to the landing, but Cory, following Desperado's orders, wouldn't let her dash down the stairs after him.

The street was deserted except for Tate, who stood in the middle of the road. Desperado walked out into the street and stopped ten yards away from Tate. Desperado's gut roiled. He smelled a trap and wondered what Tate had planned for him. His cool gaze swept the length of the street, paying special attention to the storefronts and pillars. He found it difficult to believe Tate was foolish enough to challenge him when he knew he would lose. He had to have something diabolical up his sleeve.

Then Desperado saw sunshine reflect off an object on the roof across the street and suddenly everything became clear. A shootout wasn't what Tate intended. Tate's scheme was to distract Desperado while a second gunman drew a bead and cut him down from his vantage point on the roof. Desperado smiled grimly and planned his own strategy.

Desperado's raspy voice echoed ominously through the empty street. "What's the meaning of this, Talbot?"

"It's time we settled our differences once and for all, Jones. You've got something I want, and the only way I'm going to get it is if you're dead."

"You don't have a prayer, Talbot," Desperado sneered. "You can't outdraw me. You're writing your own death warrant."

"Let me be the judge of that."

Desperado watched through narrowed lids as Tate glanced up at the man stationed on the roof and nodded slightly. Years of experience ruled Desperado as he reacted with the kind of lightning precision that had earned him his name. From the corner of his eye he saw a head pop up on the roof across the street. Desperado didn't wait for the man to get a bead on him as he dropped into a crouch and cocked his gun at the same time he pulled it from his holster. He squeezed the trigger. He didn't need to look to know his bullet had found its mark.

Even as the gunman fell from the roof, Desperado rolled on the ground to escape Tate's bullet, which whizzed by the place where he had stood moments before. Quicker than the eye could follow, Desperado cocked his six-shooter, found Tate in his sights and fired. The bullet shattered Tate's collarbone, hitting exactly where Desperado had aimed.

Screaming, Tate fell to the ground, cradling his shattered shoulder. "Get him, Curly!" he yelled at the top of his lungs.

Desperado hadn't noticed the man peeking out

from an alley between the saloon and the barbershop, but Chloe saw him from her vantage point on the landing outside Thadeous Baker's office. She cried out a warning, but Desperado failed to hear as the gunman aimed his pistol. Chloe knew he wouldn't miss at such close range and reacted spontaneously. She drew her gun, fanned back the hammer and fired twice in rapid succession. The assailant's bullet went astray, missing Desperado by a full yard. Chloe's bullets were dead on target.

Desperado whirled around to face this new danger. He saw a man writhing on the ground near the alley; then he looked in the direction from which the shot originated and saw Chloe clutching her smoking pistol.

People were beginning to spill out into the street now. Calvin Talbot was one of the first to reach Tate. "Damn you, Desperado Jones!" he cried, punching his fist in the air for emphasis. "Look what you did to my son!"

"This one's dead," someone said, pointing to the gunman who had fallen from the roof.

"This one ain't going nowhere," another reported as he bent over the second gunman lying near the alley.

"You'll pay for this, Jones," Talbot promised. "You can't kill men in cold blood and expect to escape the law."

"I didn't ask for this," Desperado rasped. "Your son called me out. His cohorts were waiting to ambush me. That's not what I'd call a fair fight, or killing in cold blood."

"That's not how I saw it," Talbot snarled, "and

I'm sure the town marshal will agree. I'm not without friends in powerful places. I'm taking my son to the doctor now, but you can expect to hear from me soon."

"Suit yourself," Desperado drawled as he slapped his gun into his holster and turned away. The danger was over for the time being and he wanted desperately to be with Chloe.

"Good shooting, Desperado," Rowdy crowed as Desperado rushed up the stairs past him. "I saw it all. Those bastards were waiting to ambush you."

Desperado did not reply in his eagerness to reach Chloe. Questions and answers would come later. Chloe still stood where he had last seen her, on the landing with the gun dangling from her right hand. Her face was ashen and she appeared to be in shock.

"Thank you," he whispered as he gently pried the gun from her fingers.

"He was going to kill you. I had to shoot."

"Of course you did. You probably saved my life."

"I want to go home."

"I thought we were going to get married."

"I . . ." Her eyes held the glaze of shock, and Desperado knew better than to press her.

"Very well. We'll come back in a day or two, if that's all right with Mr. Baker."

"Any time you two decide to get married is all right with me," Baker said. "I saw what happened. Tate Talbot certainly intended to kill you."

"Come on, honey," Desperado said as he guided Chloe down the stairs. "I tried to tell you what to expect as my wife. Perhaps you should rethink your decision to marry me."

Desperado let out a long, sad sigh. Any woman fool enough to let herself love him was in for a rough time. He couldn't blame Chloe if she changed her mind.

Chloe's mind ran in a hundred directions. She recalled Desperado's expression when he faced down Tate. It was a mask of hard lines, taut cheek-bones, flattened lips and cold eyes more deadly than the gun he held. She didn't know that man.

They rode home in silence. Cory and Rowdy brought up the rear, whispering back and forth about what they had seen and commenting on Desperado's prowess with a gun. They had nothing but praise for Chloe, who had proven her worth by shooting the man who had threatened Desperado's life. They speculated on whether or not they would have had the guts to do the same had they seen the hidden danger. It was mutually agreed that Chloe's eyes were much sharper than theirs.

Before they reached the ranch, Desperado called the pair aside and told them to ride ahead and tell the others there would be no celebration. Not to-day, anyway. Maybe never, he thought grimly.

The hands were subdued when Desperado and Chloe rode into the yard. No questions were asked; obviously Cory and Rowdy had explained, embel-lishing the tale with grisly details. It was just as well. Desperado was in no mood for lengthy expla-nations. He helped Chloe from her horse, placed an arm around her shoulders and led her into the house. Once the door was closed behind them, he picked her up and carried her up the stairs.

"Where are you taking me?" Chloe asked, finally gaining her wits.

"Up to your room to rest. This couldn't have been pleasant for you."

She stared at him. "What about you? Did you enjoy killing a man?" She clutched his shirt with a desperation that shocked him. "I shot that man and didn't feel an ounce of remorse. I've pulled my gun on quite a few men since I learned to shoot, but I never knew if I actually could pull the trigger. Now I know. That man deserved to die."

Desperado perched on the edge of the bed with Chloe in his lap. He kissed the top of her head. "You saved my life."

"You saved mine more than once." She shuddered against him and his arms tightened around her. "That man would have killed you before you knew what had hit you. You were magnificent out there. I never realized how fast you were until I saw you in action. No wonder people are in awe of you."

"I don't blame you for not wanting to marry me," Desperado said. "It's the wisest decision you've ever made."

"Are you always so cynical?"

His laugh held no humor. "I find it helps to ease the disappointments in life."

"I never said I didn't want to marry you. I just felt it best to postpone it a day or two. Everything happened so fast I was in shock. When we marry I want to be fully aware of what's going on."

"Sweetheart, I think you should give our marriage serious thought. The Talbots want me dead and will stop at nothing to accomplish the deed. That ambush today is probably just the beginning. Lord only knows what will happen next. You are co-owner of the ranch now. I've given you all the protection I can, short of marrying you. Perhaps marriage wasn't a good idea. Better yet, perhaps I should leave."

Chloe leaped off his lap and glared at him, her face set in stubborn lines. "Just try to leave, Mr. Jones! You promised me a wedding and that's exactly what we're going to have."

"Chloe," Desperado began. "I don't want to see you hurt."

"Leaving me would hurt," Chloe contended. "Now, let's go down and tell the hands the wedding is merely postponed until tomorrow. With luck the feast Randy prepared will keep for another day."

"Will nothing I say change your mind?"

She gave him a saucy grin. "Nothing."

The following day dawned as fair and clear as the previous one, which boded well for their wedding plans, Chloe thought as she sat up in bed to study Desperado's handsome features. In sleep he looked younger. Less fierce, almost too handsome with his dark features, full lips and high cheekbones. Naked, he looked bigger, more muscular, even with his body in repose. His longish black hair curled damply against his nape, and his ridiculously long eyelashes looked like inky butterfly wings against his lean cheeks.

This was the man she was going to marry, Chloe

thought happily. She didn't care what he had been in the past; it was the future that mattered. She stretched contentedly and smiled, recalling their lovemaking the night before.

Thinking about their loving made her long for more and she bent down to tease him awake with kisses. But she never completed the kiss. Footsteps. Pounding up the stairs. Chloe pulled the sheet over both her and Desperado seconds before Sonny burst into the room.

"Miss Chloe! Desperado! You gotta wake up. I rode into town early this morning to get more nails from the lumber yard and saw the marshal with Calvin Tate. They were hiring drifters and no-accounts to ride with a posse they were forming. I rode off before they saw me. They're coming after Desperado. They claim he killed a man in cold blood and wounded two others. You gotta leave. They'll be here any minute. There was talk of a lynching."

Desperado was fully awake now as he leaped out of bed and began pulling on his clothing. "I'll be damned if I'm gonna run. I was the victim and have witnesses to prove it."

"They don't care about witnesses," Sonny said, gasping for breath. "They're gonna hang you from the nearest tree, before the townspeople can come to your defense."

"I'm not going to—"

"Go!" Chloe urged. "We can straighten this out later. Those men have little to lose by hanging you."

Desperado didn't want to go, but the odds were stacked against him. He was only one man. And he didn't want to endanger Chloe's life or the lives of the hands, who he knew were likely to do something rash if they thought it would help him.

"Very well. I'll ride north to Amarillo. There's a Ranger outpost there. Maybe they can straighten this out. Saddle my mustang," he told Sonny, "and throw some provisions in my saddlebags. I'll be down directly."

Desperado turned to Chloe, his expression softening. "I'll be back," he promised, taking her into his arms. He kissed her hard, then started to kiss her again, but Chloe pushed him away.

"Just go, we don't have time for this! I love you, Desperado."

Sonny's voice came to them from the foot of the stairs. "Hurry, Desperado. I can see the dust from the posse's horses."

Desperado spared one last glance at Chloe before bounding down the staircase.

Chapter Fourteen

Ominous dark thunderheads rolled in from the north, the direction in which Desperado rode. The morning that had started out with such promise had become a nightmare. Desperado had ridden from the yard scant minutes before the posse arrived. They had seen his dust and taken off after him, and now they were hard on his heels. Desperado guessed that Talbot wouldn't rest until the posse caught up with him. And once they did, his life wouldn't be worth a plugged nickel.

The rain came in torrents, a real gullywasher, but Desperado plunged on until he realized that continuing would endanger not only his life but that of his faithful mustang. He knew he had to hole up somewhere until the downpour abated, and he searched the barren landscape for a likely place. He rode on, through rock formations and towering buttes, finding little in the way of protection from the storm.

The lightning was fierce; jagged streaks of eerie light illuminated the sky and earth. One particularly bright flash revealed a crevice between two rocks, and Desperado turned the mustang in that direction, grateful for any protection, no matter how meager, from the storm. The rain was icy cold and he was chilled to the bone. He'd been riding all day; both he and his horse needed rest.

The crevice was large enough to ride his horse into, but not totally protected from the raging elements. Rain dripped onto him from where the rocks formed an inadequate roof, but at least it kept him out of the lashing rain and violent lightning.

Desperado unsaddled his horse and rubbed him down with his blanket, grateful that he'd had the foresight to roll it in his slicker to keep it dry. Then he dug in his saddlebags for something to eat. He sat down on the soggy ground and chewed on jerky and hardtack. Then he munched an apple, washing it down with water from his canteen. He'd have to thank Sonny for the provisions, if he ever saw the young hand again. Which at this point in time seemed highly unlikely.

Though Desperado couldn't see the posse, he knew they were still out there somewhere. Closer than he'd like, for he could practically smell the danger. His survival depended upon reaching the Ranger outpost before the posse caught up with him. After he had eaten, Desperado rolled up in the damp blanket and tried to sleep, an almost impossible task with the roar of thunder in his ears and lightning illuminating the night sky.

Before sleep claimed him, Desperado's thoughts were of Chloe. With Chloe at his side he could have brought the Ralston ranch back to its former splendor. He would have settled down nicely to a life of babies and rocking chairs. To waking up each morning with Chloe in his arms. He should have known better than to want things that were out of his reach. Such commonplace things as home and hearth had no place in the life of a gunslinger.

Rain was still falling when Desperado awakened the next morning. The blanket had provided scant protection against the torrential downpour, and he was wet to the skin and so cold his teeth were chattering. There was nothing available to make a fire and he wouldn't have made one even if there had been dry wood. Alerting the posse to his hiding place was the last thing he wanted to do.

Desperado chewed on another piece of jerky, drank some water and was ready to ride. He saddled his mustang and headed out into the rain. Amarillo was two days away and he still had a fork of the Red River to cross. That worried him some. After the gullywasher yesterday the usually placid stream could have dangerous currents seething beneath the surface. No matter, he had no choice but to cross the river when he came to it.

Desperado found shelter that night beneath a rocky overhang. It had rained intermittently throughout the day but nothing like the gullywasher of the previous day. He ate sparingly and slept fitfully in his damp clothing. The following day he came to the river.

Desperado viewed the raging river from a ridge with growing horror. He feared that forcing his mustang into the seething water was tantamount to suicide. He turned away to find another, less dangerous crossing, when he spied the posse coming up on him from the rear. Caught between the devil and the turbulent, rain-swollen river, he had but a moment to decide which he preferred. He chose the river.

A shot whizzed past his ear and Desperado realized he hadn't a moment to lose; the posse was within shooting range. He whispered a soft apology to his horse and urged him down the slope and into the water. He dared a brief glance over his shoulder and saw the posse skidding down the slope behind him.

Without a second to spare, he kneed his mustang forward. Bullets flew around him and he ducked low. But it wasn't good enough. His body jerked violently as a bullet tore through his back, but he managed to keep his seat. Then a second bullet ripped into his thigh. He hung on valiantly, but despite his best efforts, he slid from the saddle into the water. He must have blacked out then, for when he revived he was floating in the river. He suspected the icy bath had jolted him awake. Then all thought ceased as the current whipped him into the middle of the river and carried him away.

"I think we got him," Marshal Townsend said as he halted at the water's edge.

"Grab his horse," Calvin Tate ordered tersely.

One of the men broke away from the posse and grasped the mustang's trailing reins.

"There's blood on the saddle," the man reported.

"At least one of our bullets found their mark," Townsend said. "If the lead didn't finish him off, the river will. No man, not even Desperado Jones, can survive that raging current."

"I don't like it," Talbot muttered. "The man has more lives than a cat. I want to see his lifeless body before I'll believe he's dead."

"You wanna cross the river, then go ahead," Townsend said. "I ain't gonna do it, and neither are any of these men you hired off the streets. I'm just the town marshal. I don't get paid enough to risk my life."

Talbot scanned the river where he'd last seen Desperado. "Has anyone seen the bastard resurface?" he asked.

No one admitted to having seen Desperado since he'd fallen from the horse. "Any of our bullets could have killed him," Townsend said.

"We'll wait around a few hours," Talbot told the men. He sure as hell wasn't going to go into the river to look for a body. "Spread out along the bank and call out if his body washes up."

"Hell, he's probably miles downriver by now," Townsend grumbled. "I'm cold and wet and hungry, and so are the men. I say we go back now."

"I'm the one paying you," Talbot growled. "A few hours more isn't going to kill you. Now do as I say or no one gets paid. One thing more," he said while he still had the men's attention; "a bonus to the man who finds Desperado's body."

That night the posse camped on the riverbank. The next morning they saddled up and rode back to Trouble Creek. A disgruntled Talbot finally allowed that Desperado Jones was dead, and he had the gunslinger's bloodstained saddle to prove it.

Death wasn't so bad, Desperado decided as he gave up the fight to hold his breath. It was peaceful beneath the water, and the pain from his wounds was not so bad. Contrary to belief, his life didn't pass before his eyes during his final moments. He saw only Chloe. Chloe smiling at him. Chloe poking that damn six-shooter into his gut. Chloe stripping off her clothing for him and letting him love her. Chloe telling him she loved him.

Chloe . . . Chloe . . . Chloe . . .

He had to breathe. The pressure on his lungs was excruciating. He was still lucid enough to know that he need only take a couple of breaths of water into his lungs to end his life. Not that his life was so important. Before he'd met Chloe he'd had little to live for.

Suddenly something plowed into him, forcing him to take that fatal breath. Instinct prompted him to clutch the object and hold on with what little strength he had left.

He must have hit his head on the rock-strewn river bottom when he'd fallen from his horse, he thought, for blood was gushing from a cut above his eye, blinding him to his murky surroundings.

I can breathe under water, was Desperado's next thought as he dragged in a breath of what felt suspiciously like fresh, cool air. *I'm hallucinating*, Desperado decided as he dragged in another life-giving breath.

He wiped the blood from his eyes on his wet sleeve and forced them open, expecting to see the bottom of the river whirling past his eyes. Instead he saw dripping gray skies and the opposite riverbank. He closed his eyes and opened them again. The scene remained unchanged.

It took him a few minutes to realize he was being carried downstream by a pile of floating debris. He recalled being hit by something that had knocked the breath from him. The will to survive must have beat strongly within him, for he had held onto the debris by instinct alone.

Desperado rested against the debris, fighting to remain conscious as his body convulsed in agony. In control of his wits now, he knew with grim certainty that Talbot wasn't going to give up the chase until the river gave up his body. He had to get himself out of the water to safety.

Using the last of his meager strength, he hoisted himself atop the floating debris and let the rushing current carry him where it would. The devil and Talbot would have to fight for his soul.

Desperado was unconscious throughout the long night. He remained blissfully unaware that Talbot and the posse had left the area at daybreak to report his death. He didn't see the Indian tipis set up along the bank of the river, nor did he know that he had drifted miles downstream. He didn't hear the woman's cry that brought the inhabitants of the village to the river's edge. He didn't feel himself being lifted out of the water and carried to a brightly decorated tipi. Had he seen the elderly Indian couple bending over his body with tears in their dark eyes, he would have been rendered speechless. Indians did not show emotion.

Chloe's days were pure hell as she waited for word from Desperado. Mechanically she supervised the barn-raising and issued orders to have the cows brought closer to the ranch in anticipation of winter. When everything seemed to be progressing well, she decided to tackle the house. It needed a good cleaning. But she had no heart to begin the onerous chore, having little liking for housework.

While she was deciding what to tackle first in the house, a young Mexican woman approached the ranch, asking—no, begging—for work. She was barefoot and had walked a great distance. She also had dark purple bruises on her face and arms and walked as if she were in pain. Chloe hadn't the heart to turn away a woman so desperately in need, so she hired her on the spot. While Ted was alive he had employed a housekeeper/cook to run the household. But after Ted passed on and money became scarce, they had let the elderly woman go with a small pension.

Chloe gave Juanita the small room off the kitchen as living quarters. Though the woman was something of a mystery, and rather reticent about how she had sustained her injuries, Chloe was glad for another woman's company.

With the house in good hands, Chloe had more time to worry about Desperado. If he didn't return soon, or send some word that he had reached Amarillo safely, she was going to ride out and look for him. She prayed that he had survived the terrible thunderstorm that had ravaged the area shortly after he left.

The storm had been a harbinger of winter, ushering in colder temperatures. The hands were working feverishly to finish the barn and bring the animals in from the farthest pastures before the first snow arrived. Up until the rainstorm, the fall had been exceptional, with crisp, sunny days and cool nights. But even then Chloe knew it couldn't last. Where in the devil was Desperado?

Two weeks after Desperado rode away, unexpected guests arrived at the ranch. Calvin Talbot and Marshal Townsend. The hands paused in their labors to await the next development in the macabre game the Talbots were playing with Chloe and Desperado.

Chloe saw something that turned her blood to icewater as the pair rode through the gate. Calvin Talbot held the leading reins of a riderless horse.

Desperado's mustang.

The hands closed ranks around her to lend their support as the riders rode up to the porch and drew rein.

"Miss Sommers," Calvin Talbot said curtly, dispensing with formalities.

"What have you done to Desperado?" Chloe cried, unable to turn her gaze from the sweat-drenched mustang.

"Nothing more than the gunslinger deserved," Marshal Townsend answered. "The man was a menace to society."

"How would you know?" Chloe shot back. "All you've ever seen of society is whoever happens to be inside the saloon and whorehouse."

"Now wait just a damn minute," Townsend lashed out. "I was appointed by the town council to keep this city free of scum."

"Then why are *you* still here?" Chloe challenged.

"Did you hear what she just said, Mr. Talbot?" Townsend whined. "The bitch insulted me. Are ya gonna let her get away with calling me scum?"

"Calm down," Talbot hissed. "We're not here to exchange barbs."

Chloe's chin raised to a defiant angle. "Why *are* you here? What happened to the rest of your posse?" She was afraid to ask the question that was on the tip of her tongue. *What have you done to Desperado?* Never had she been so afraid to hear the truth in her life. There was only one way Talbot could have gotten Desperado's mustang. But she refused to believe what common sense told her had happened.

While Chloe and Talbot were talking, Sonny edged over to the mustang to examine his shiny coat. What he discovered must have shocked him for he suddenly cried out, "There's dried blood on the mustang's saddle! And more smeared on his withers."

"Damn you, Talbot!" Chloe shouted. "What have you done to Desperado!"

Talbot tossed the mustang's reins at Sonny. "I thought you might want to keep the horse to remind you how short the life of a gunslinger can be. Desperado Jones is dead."

"No! You're a liar. Where is his body? Even a scoundrel like you wouldn't leave him to the buzzards." She flew at him, grabbing his jacket and pulling him from his horse. They grappled on the ground a few minutes before Townsend dismounted and pulled her off of Talbot. Bruised but undaunted, Chloe did what came naturally for Chloe. She pulled her gun on Talbot.

"Say your prayers, Talbot," she spat. "I'm going to give you the same chance you gave Desperado. What did you do, shoot him in the back? That's the only way anyone could kill him."

"Desperado Jones was an outlaw, Chloe," Talbot argued. "There is only one way a man like him ends up. You saw how he attacked Tate and his friends in town. One dead and two wounded. He had to be brought down."

"You know as well as I what happened in town. Desperado was ambushed. He shot in self-defense."

"That's not the way the marshal saw it."

She speared Townsend with a scathing glance. "How could he see anything from inside the saloon? If Desperado is dead, where is his body?"

"He fell into the river and was carried away by the current," Talbot replied. "We stuck around the rest of the day but he never surfaced."

"Then he's not dead," Chloe said triumphantly.

"He was shot full of holes," Townsend said. "He was probably dead before he hit the water, that's why he didn't resurface."

Chloe's gun hand shook slightly but never wavered from her target. Her face hardened and her finger teased the trigger; she was as close to killing a man in cold blood as she'd ever been.

"Pull that trigger and Townsend will hang you from the nearest tree," Talbot warned.

Chloe could see beads of sweat popping out on Talbot's forehead. He was frightened, and he had every reason to be.

"Don't shoot, Miss Chloe," Cory pleaded. "Think of the ranch. Marshal Townsend will hang you for sure. It would just about kill the boys to see you hurt. They might do something foolish and get themselves killed. Is that what you want?"

"Talbot killed Desperado," Chloe charged, as if that condoned what she intended to do.

"Put your gun away, Chloe," Talbot warned. "It's over. Jones is dead and there is nothing you can do about it. The law is on my side."

Defeat was not easy to accept for a woman like Chloe Sommers. The weight of it beat her down and stomped her into the ground. But she recognized the voice of reason whispering in her ear and knew she couldn't risk the lives of the hands, who would surely come to her defense should Townsend try to hang her. They might ultimately succeed in their efforts. There were a dozen of them, after all, but one or more of them could be killed for coming to her defense. Did she want that on her conscience?

Slowly she lowered her gun and slipped it back into its holster. "You win this time, Talbot," Chloe gritted out. "Now get off my land. If either you or your rapacious son set foot on my property after today, I'll fill you both with so much lead you'll never be able to swim again. It will be legal, too.

According to the law, I'm entitled to protect my own property against intruders."

"You're not going to shoot anyone, Chloe," Talbot warned. "Step away where we won't be heard. I'd like a private word with you."

"You can say whatever you like in front of my hands," Chloe snapped.

"I insist," Talbot said in a menacing tone that caught her attention. "I don't think you'd like them to hear what I've got to say. It's about you and Tate."

Chloe turned ashen. She had no idea what Talbot intended to say, but he was right about one thing. She didn't want the hands to know the kind of humiliation and pain she had suffered at Tate's hands.

"Very well, but make it quick. I have little time to waste on the likes of you. I don't believe Desperado is dead. You can lie all you want, but my heart tells me he's still alive."

She stepped away from the hands, who had formed a protective ring around her, and followed Talbot to the newly raised barn, where they could talk in private. Townsend remained behind to keep an eye on the cowboys.

"Say your piece, Talbot," Chloe said, refusing to go any farther than the barn door.

"I'm not going to mince words, Chloe. Tate fancies you. I promised he could live out here on the ranch with you after you two got hitched. I'm not interested in anything but the parcel of land lying north of the creek."

Chloe had the audacity to laugh in his face.

"What makes you think I'd marry Tate? He's the last man in the world I want."

"I know you and Tate got off on the wrong foot," Talbot cajoled. "Tate admitted he made a mistake with you. But Tate is young and hot-blooded. He had too much to drink that night and couldn't control himself when you gave all the signs of being willing. Your own mother was promoting the match between you and Tate. If he hadn't gone off half-cocked that night, you probably would be married to him now."

"God forbid," Chloe said, rolling her eyes. "I'm just glad I found out what he's like before I consented to the marriage."

"Tate is planning to come out here soon to discuss plans for your marriage," Talbot confided. "He's still not fully recovered from his wound, but he's anxious to get hitched. Desperado's bullet shattered his collarbone, but he's not going to let that stop him, Chloe. Tate is determined to have you, and I'm just as determined to have this spread. When you and Tate marry, your property will become his and he can do what he wants with it."

"What's so special about this land?" Chloe asked. "You already own half the county." She already knew about the railroad but wanted to hear Talbot admit to his greed and ambition.

"I'm going to say just one word, Chloe, and let you figure out the rest. Railroad. Now do you understand?"

Chloe did indeed understand. "It's becoming clearer by the minute."

"I'm glad you see things my way. Cooperate and

everything will be just fine. Ultimately Tate and I will both get what we want."

"Maybe you didn't understand *me*, Mr. Talbot," Chloe said with emphasis. "I don't want any part of Tate."

"Then you're forcing me to get tough. You seem mighty fond of those young cowboys you hired on. You'd probably hate to see anything happen to them. If you don't let Tate court you, they are going to start disappearing, one by one, until none are left."

His words chilled her blood. "You wouldn't!"

He gave her an evil grin. "I got rid of Desperado, didn't I? Those untried boys will present little challenge after dealing with Jones."

"I'll sell you the land, Talbot," Chloe offered, desperate to keep the young men in her employ safe.

Talbot shook his head. "That's no longer enough. Tate was hopping mad when you climbed into bed with Jones. He always thought of you as his. I promised he could have you after I got rid of Jones, and I always keep my promises. I'd best be off now. The posse is waiting in town to be paid off."

He took two steps, then turned back, pinning Chloe with his malevolent glare. "I'm warning you. Either welcome Tate when he comes calling or suffer the consequences."

Rooted to the spot, Chloe watched grimly as Talbot and Townsend mounted up and rode away.

"Are you all right, Miss Chloe?" Cory asked when she found the strength to join them.

"Fine, Cory."

"What did that bastard say?" Rowdy wanted to

know. "If he insulted you, just say the word and the boys and I will take care of him."

One by one the hands gave verbal approval to Rowdy's violent solution to the problem. But Chloe knew these young men were no match for the wily Talbot. "Violence isn't going to solve anything," she said. "I need to be alone to think. Go back to work."

"Do you really believe Desperado is dead?" Sonny asked.

"Not for one minute," Chloe declared.

"Where do you think he is?" Randy wondered. "Those sure were blood stains on his mustang."

"I don't know," Chloe whispered. "I'd know in my heart if he were dead." She turned abruptly and strode toward the house. She didn't want the hands to see her with tears streaming down her cheeks.

Chloe sought the privacy of her room and finally gave in to the grief that had been building inside. She didn't want to believe Desperado was dead, but the evidence was too overwhelming to suggest otherwise. Still, what she'd told the hands had been true. Had Desperado been dead, something would have died inside her. But deep within her being she felt the spark of life that was Desperado. As long as she felt that steady beat she knew he still lived.

Common sense told her all wasn't well with Desperado, however. Had he been able, he would have returned to her. And there *was* the blood on his saddle, an ominous sign that didn't bode well for him. Talbot had said he'd been carried away by the current after he'd fallen into the river. The water must have been cold, for the days were no longer warm and the nights sometimes produced light frost. Could Desperado have survived the current, the bullet wounds, and the weather? He was a strong man, but no one was invincible.

The longer she thought about it, the more she realized she couldn't just sit there and wait and worry. As soon as she got things settled here, she intended to search for the man she loved. She would not rest until she discovered his body or found him alive. What she wasn't going to do was submit to the Talbots' plans for her future.

Tate Talbot came calling the following week. His shattered collarbone was still bandaged and he appeared to be in considerable pain, but Chloe soon learned he was the same bully she had grown to despise.

"Pa said you'd be expecting me," Tate said, walking into the house as if he owned it when she opened the door to him. She never considered not letting him in, at least not until she found a way to escape his plans for her without endangering her hired hands. As for his visit tonight, she figured she could handle a wounded man.

"He didn't give me a choice," Chloe returned.

"I come courting. Just like I did a couple years back, remember?"

"How could I forget?" Chloe said dryly.

"Pa said I couldn't bed you until after the wedding. He doesn't want anything to set you off or interfere with his plans before we're hitched." He sat down on the sofa and patted the place beside him. "That don't mean I can't kiss or touch you. Come here, honey, I want to see if your titties are still as soft and round as I remember."

"Go to hell, Tate Talbot," Chloe hissed.

Tate's expression turned ugly. "Now why did you go and say that? Here I was trying to be nice, just like Pa instructed. He wants us to set a date for the wedding. It can't be too soon for me," he said, leering at her. "You were the best piece I ever had. You had enough spunk in you to make it challenging for me."

Chloe clamped her mouth shut to keep from lashing out at him. "How can you ask me to set a date when I'm still mourning Desperado's death?"

"The hell with Desperado Jones!" Tate shouted. "I won't have my wife pining for another man. Not even a dead one."

"I'm not your wife."

"Next Saturday is as good a day as any," Tate continued as if she hadn't spoken. "I'll arrange it with Reverend Tully. He owes Pa a favor. No Justice of the Peace for us. We're gonna do it up all nice and legal, with the words spoken over us by a preacher. Yep, Saturday next," Tate repeated. "Pa will be pleased that I'm finally doing something right."

He rose abruptly and caught her wrist with his good hand, dragging her against him. "Shall we seal our engagement with a kiss?"

"No, thank you," she said coolly.

"I ain't gonna stand for your shenanigans after we're married. I'm gonna be the only one in the family wearing trousers. Go into town and buy yourself some fancy dresses like you used to wear.

Something that will show off those pretty titties I'm drooling to taste again."

Chloe struggled against him but he managed to bring her close enough to capture her mouth. Vomit rose in her throat when he thrust his thick tongue into her mouth. If he didn't release her quickly he was going to be damn sorry. She reached for her gun and remembered she'd left her gunbelt hanging on a hook beside the door. She might not be able to shoot him, but she sure as heck could hurt him without using a gun.

Suddenly Juanita appeared in the doorway, an old shotgun that had once belonged to Ted raised against her narrow shoulder. "Take your hands off of Senorita Chloe," Juanita ordered in a voice that meant business.

Tate's arms fell away and his eyes bugged out as he stared at Juanita. "Shit! How did you get here? I thought I told you to go back to your family."

"You know Juanita?" Chloe asked, stunned.

"Yeah, I know her. She's a whore I picked up in San Antone. I got tired of her and sent her packing."

"I wasn't a whore until you carried me away from my family and made me one," Juanita charged. "Now they will not have me back."

"And I don't want you here with my future wife. It ain't right."

"Put the shotgun down, Juanita," Chloe pleaded. "Shooting Tate can get you into a lot of trouble. Don't worry. I promise he'll get what's coming to him one day."

"I want that whore out of here, Chloe," Tate ordered.

"Are you the one who beat her?" Chloe asked. "She was a mess when she came here looking for work."

"She deserved it. She called me an animal and spat at me."

With a calmness she didn't feel, Chloe said, "Go home, Tate. I'm trying very hard not to get my gun and shoot you myself."

"But Pa said it was all right if we kissed and played around a little as long as I didn't poke you."

Chloe thought he sounded like a petulant child deprived of his favorite toy. "I'm not in the mood tonight."

"You'd better be in the mood Saturday next," he warned. "I want a willing wife in my bed." He moved reluctantly toward the door, then turned to glower at Juanita. "I mean it, Chloe. Get rid of that whore or I'll get rid of her in a way you won't like."

The moment the door closed behind him, Juanita ran into Chloe's outstretched arms.

"You're not going to marry that animal, are you, Senorita Chloe?"

"Not in a million years."

Chapter Fifteen

Chloe rode into town the next day to call on Thadeous Baker. He greeted her sadly, his expression conveying without words that he had heard about Desperado's death and commiserated with her.

"I'm sorry, Chloe," he said. "I was right fond of that boy."

Chloe couldn't help smiling. Mr. Baker was probably the only person in the world who dared to call Desperado a boy. "He's not dead, Mr. Baker," Chloe said with confidence.

Baker's relief was immediate. "You've heard from him? Thank God!"

Chloe shook her head. "No. I haven't heard a word, except for what Calvin Talbot told me. I suppose he's told the whole town that the posse killed Desperado."

"He couldn't wait to get the word out. Not everyone believes Mr. Jones was a killer, you know. Desperado wasn't a wanted man. Most considered him a good sort despite his reputation. I'm inclined to agree. I think Desperado Jones put on a good show, that he used his guns as a prop, though no one would dispute his ability to use them."

"You're a perceptive man, Mr. Baker," Chloe said. "Desperado told me he has never killed in cold blood and I believe him. I, on the other hand, could have killed Calvin Talbot without the slightest hesitation when he came out to the ranch yesterday. And it *would* have been in cold blood."

"Perhaps you should be made aware of the other bit of gossip Talbot has put out," Baker said. "It's all over town that you and his son Tate will marry next Saturday."

Chloe groaned. "I would never willingly marry Tate. I loathe him."

"Is there anything I can do to help?"

"I wish there were. Talbot threatened my hired hands if I refused to marry Tate. He wants my land because the railroad is considering building a spur line to Amarillo. They're going to start buying land for the right-of-way and Talbot wants to own it all. There's been talk for a long time about the Fort Worth and Denver City Railroad and the Atchison, Topeka and Santa Fe meeting up in Amarillo and then continuing on to Dodge City. A spur line through Trouble Creek would make taking cattle to market a whole lot simpler.

"Somehow Talbot got wind of the proposed spur and bought up land along the route at bargain prices. I'm the only holdout. The other landowners caved in to his pressure, and those who didn't soon found their homes and loved ones threatened. Talbot needs my land to become sole owner of all the land lying within the proposed route. With all the land in his pocket, he would be in a good position to dicker with the railroad for more money than they would have paid individual owners. Talbot stands to make a fortune."

"There is more to it than that," Baker revealed. "As the only lawyer in town, I'm privy to many of his legal transactions, though I have no liking for it. During the course of business I've learned the man has political aspirations. He wants to amass enough money to become a force in the state of Texas. He plans to run for political office in a year or two."

Chloe groaned. "There are enough dishonest politicians without Talbot joining their ranks."

"What are you going to do about Tate?" Baker asked.

"I'm going to be gone long before Saturday," Chloe confided. "I wanted you to know my plans in case . . . in case . . . well, someone should know."

"I don't like the sound of that," Baker said. "Where will you go? Who will run the ranch?"

"Winter is closing in. Things are at a standstill right now. The hands are capable of running the ranch in my absence."

"Where will you go?"

"To look for Desperado. He's still alive. I can feel it here," she said, placing a hand over her heart. "I came to town to buy provisions and warm clothing, and to see you, of course. I want to sign a paper giving Cory authority to act in my stead during my absence. Buying supplies, paying the hands from my funds, that sort of thing. Can you do that?"

"I'll draw something up immediately," Baker said. "But should you be going alone? Inclement weather isn't the only danger out there."

"I don't want anyone to risk his life on my account. Write up the paper and I'll return to sign it after I've finished shopping."

Tate Talbot was looking out the window of his father's office when he saw Chloe leaving Baker's office. "Wonder why Chloe was visiting the lawyer," Tate muttered to himself.

"What did you say?" Calvin asked, distracted by his son's muttering. "Speak up."

"I just saw Chloe leaving Lawyer Baker's office. What do you suppose she has up her sleeve now?"

"Nothing good," Calvin replied sourly. "Can you see where she's headed?"

Tate craned his neck to see where Chloe was going. "The general store."

"Hmmm, why don't you go see what she's up to?"

"I ain't feeling good, Pa. This damn shoulder is giving me fits. I don't think that old horse doctor knows what he's doing."

"Quit whining and go see what Chloe is about. Old Doc Hockmeyer has been treating animals and people in this town many years before we came and he'll still be here after we're gone."

Tate moved stiffly toward the door. "I don't know what you're worried about, Pa. Chloe knows she has no choice. Come Saturday we'll be married.

Reverend Tully knows what to do in case Chloe turns obstinate, doesn't he?"

"Leave the good reverend to me," Calvin growled. "He knows what he has to do. I have information that could ruin him, should I choose to reveal it. He has a wife and children to protect. He'll do as I say."

Confident of his father's ability to handle the situation, Tate left the office and walked over to the general store. Chloe didn't see him enter and neither did the clerk. Both were engaged in lively conversation. Tate scooted down a side aisle and crouched behind upright bolts of material, listening to what Chloe was saying.

"Is this the warmest jacket you have, Mr. Dudley?"

"That one is lined with sheep's wool," Dudley explained. "You won't find anything warmer."

"I'll take it. And those heavy stockings and boots I already picked out. What about corduroy trousers? Do you have something in my size?"

Dudley eyed her critically, then went to a shelf where boys' trousers were folded neatly into a pile. "These should work," he said, pulling out a pair of tan corduroys in an appropriate size. "Anything else?"

"Trail food," Chloe said. "Something nourishing but easy to pack. Oh, and a canteen. Mine has seen better days."

"It's a bad time of the year to go on a trip, Miss Sommers," Dudley advised.

"There's no help for it," Chloe said. "Please wrap everything and tally the bill."

Tate slipped out the door while money was exchanging hands and hightailed it back to his father's office.

"She's gonna leave, Pa," Tate exclaimed, bursting into the office. "She's buying trail food and warm clothes. We gotta stop her."

"I warned her what would happen if she didn't submit to my wishes," Calvin hissed. "Go round up some of those drifters who stayed in town after the posse disbanded. Tell them I have another job for them. Make sure they know they'll be well paid for following orders with no questions asked. Hurry. I want this taken care of before Chloe returns home today."

Chloe left Baker's office for the second time that day, having signed the paper giving Cory authority to run the ranch in her absence. Her last stop before returning home with her packages was the bank, where she withdrew fifty dollars to take with her.

The supper hour had come and gone by the time Chloe rode into the yard. She was weary but satisfied with her day's work. Her sense of well-being was shattered when Cory hailed her from the bunkhouse. She noted his grim expression, and her heart constricted in fear. What had gone wrong?

"Bad news, Miss Chloe," Cory informed her. "Rowdy is missing, and no one has seen him since he rode out to mend a fence in the north pasture."

The color leached from Chloe's face. "Did anyone look for him?"

"Sonny and Randy rode out after he failed to show up for supper but found no trace of him. I'm worried, Miss Chloe. He wouldn't take off without telling us."

A terrible premonition shook Chloe. Had the Talbots somehow gotten wind of her plans to skip out before the wedding? Was this their retaliation? Calvin had promised dire repercussions if she didn't submit to their plans for her. Oh, God, let Rowdy be all right, she silently prayed.

"We have to go out there and search again," Chloe said. "He might be lying injured somewhere. Choose two men to remain behind, Cory. The rest of you, follow me."

Cory quickly picked two men to remain behind while the others saddled up. Chloe rode at their head, but they never reached the gate. She pulled hard on the reins when she saw a horse plodding toward them, its reins dangling on the ground. Though dusk had darkened into night, Chloe could see a figure slumped over the saddle.

She leaped from the saddle and ran, knowing what she'd find.

"That's Rowdy's horse!" one of the men exclaimed.

Chloe reached Rowdy first. She raised his head and felt something sticky on her hands. Blood. "Help me lift him," she said when the others reached her.

"Is he dead?" Sonny asked.

"I don't know. Carry him into the house where I can get a good look at him."

"He's still breathing," Cory said triumphantly.

Grim-faced, Chloe bent over Rowdy after he'd been carried into the house and laid out on a bed in one of the spare rooms. Juanita had brought in a basin of water and some clean rags while the hands crowded the doorway.

Chloe found a scalp wound that bled profusely but didn't look particularly serious, and a chest wound, where the bullet had entered in the front and exited through the back.

"He's alive," Chloe said, feeling for the pulse in his neck. "His chest wound needs immediate attention."

"Let me," Juanita said, moving Chloe gently aside. "I have some experience with gunshot wounds. I used to help the padre at the mission with wounds before I was . . . taken from my home. I will need antiseptics. I saw some in a cupboard in the kitchen."

Chloe stepped aside and let Juanita take her place beside Rowdy. "The previous housekeeper kept a supply of antiseptics to treat minor wounds," she said. "I'll get them."

Suddenly Rowdy opened his eyes. They were unfocused but lucid. "Miss Chloe. I have to tell you—"

"Don't talk, Rowdy. You can tell me later."

"No . . . now. Ambushed," he gasped in a voice that didn't carry beyond Chloe. "Talbot's men. I was to tell you . . . the wedding . . ." His voice faded away as he lost consciousness, but Chloe didn't need to be told what he was going to say.

"What wedding, Miss Chloe?" Cory asked, having moved close enough to catch Rowdy's last words. "Are the Talbots forcing you to do something you don't want to do?"

Talbot's warning was clear. Chloe had no idea

how the Talbots had learned she planned to skip out on the wedding, but she should have known they'd find out. There was no question now of leaving. The Talbots meant business. She valued the lives of her men too much to leave them to Talbot's mercy.

"I'm going to marry Tate Talbot next Saturday," Chloe replied. "I'm not being forced. It's my choice. It's what I want to do," she insisted. She decided it was better to let the hands think this was what she wanted rather than have them do something foolish.

"Don't worry about us, Miss Chloe," Randy ventured. "We can take care of ourselves. If you don't want to marry Tate Talbot, let us know and we'll take care of it."

Chloe's lips thinned. That was exactly what she didn't want. She'd bargain with the devil to save the lives of the boys she'd watched grow into men. "I *want* to marry Tate."

Rowdy hung on to life by a slim thread. He had a stout heart, a healthy body and a strong will to live. By Saturday he was taking liquids and remaining lucid for longer periods of time, thanks to Juanita, who cared for him with tender concern. During one of his more rational moments, Chloe advised Rowdy not to tell the others what he had told her about Talbot. The reason, she explained, was to keep the hands safe.

Time had passed so swiftly that Chloe didn't realize it was her wedding day until she heard riders enter the yard and stomp up to the porch. The visitors didn't bother knocking as they burst into the house. Chloe had started down the stairs when she heard the racket and she paused on the bottom landing when she saw the Talbots and a man she recognized as Reverend Tully. Two men she didn't know accompanied them.

"Where's the dress I told you to wear for our wedding?" Tate growled.

Chloe was stunned by Tate's appearance. He was pale and thinner than she had ever seen him. He was holding his shoulder as if it pained him, as indeed it must, for suffering was etched across his drawn features.

"I didn't have time to shop for clothes," Chloe shot back. "I had a wounded man to nurse back to health. Of course, you'd know nothing about that, would you?"

"Enough of this chitchat," Calvin said, taking charge of the volatile situation. "It doesn't matter what Chloe wears for her wedding. You can make her do your bidding after she's legally yours. A beating might be in order."

Chloe smiled grimly. The day didn't exist when Tate would beat her.

"Both of you stand over by the reverend," Calvin ordered impatiently. "This should only take a few minutes. I've even brought along witnesses. Go ahead, Reverend, begin."

"I won't repeat the wedding vows," Chloe said stubbornly.

Calvin smiled. "Is that young man you're nursing back to health going to make it? Life is so precarious."

"Bastard!" Chloe hissed. She turned to appeal to the reverend, to make him aware of her reluctance. "How can you condone this, Reverend Tully? You can't force someone to repeat vows. I don't want to marry Tate Talbot."

"Miss Sommers has a point, Mr. Talbot," Reverend Tully observed. "This isn't right. I'm a man of God. Marriage is a holy state. Both participants must be willing."

"Believe me, Reverend, Miss Sommers is willing," Calvin said. "Either you marry them or your family suffers the consequences. You have a wife, young children and a congregation to think about. Imagine how they would feel should they learn that you sinned with a whore. You'd be defrocked and thrown out of your church."

Tully winced as if in pain. "That was a long time ago, Mr. Talbot. I've suffered for my mistake and have come to grips with my failing. It would destroy my wife to learn of my indiscretion. Have you no conscience? I beg you to reconsider and leave this young woman alone."

"I have no conscience," Talbot sneered. "But I have ambition to go far in this world. Open your book and get on with it."

Tully sent Chloe an apologetic look and began to read the words of the marriage ceremony. When he asked Tate to repeat the vows, he did so with alacrity. When Chloe's turn came to say I do, she balked, sending Tate a venomous look.

"Say it," Calvin commanded, "unless you wish harm to one of those youngsters working for you.

I have men stationed right outside the door. A word from me and—"

"I do," Chloe hissed, "but not without protest."

Tully nodded his understanding and continued. "I now pronounce you man and wife."

"It's done!" Calvin crowed. "The license. Sign the the marriage license."

Tully offered the document to the two witnesses for their signature. "Sign your X if you can't write. I'll witness it."

The two men did as they were told, since neither of them could read or write. Then Tully showed Tate where to sign. The young man barely glanced at the document as he took the pen in hand and scribbled his signature.

"Now your turn, young lady," Tully said, sending her an enigmatic look.

Chloe held back. "Do it!" Calvin barked. When Chloe remained motionless, Calvin said, "Which of those young cowboys outside do you like least?"

"No! Don't hurt anyone else. I'll sign."

Something caught her eye and she spared a moment to scan the document. Her expression remained blank as she glanced at the reverend. Something reassuring in his steady gaze convinced her to pick up the pen and inscribe her name. Reverend Tully whisked the paper away, waved the document to dry the ink, folded it in half and handed it to Chloe. He let out an audible sigh that could have been relief when neither Tate nor Calvin looked at it.

"Put it in a safe place," Tate said as Chloe folded it yet another time and stuffed it into her pocket.

"See that the marriage is entered in the church records," Calvin told Reverend Tully.

"I will take care of everything," the reverend assured him.

"Let's go," Calvin said, herding the reverend and the two witnesses out of the house. "The lovebirds need privacy. Tate has waited a long time for this day."

After a few lewd remarks and some obscene suggestions for Tate, everyone trooped out the door, including the preacher.

"Hot damn, you're finally mine," Tate said, salivating with excitement. "Go upstairs and take off those damn trousers, and everything else. I want you naked."

Chloe took one look at Tate and laughed. "Look at you. You're so damn weak you're lucky if you can climb the stairs."

"I'm well enough to make you holler with pleasure. By the time I'm through with you, you'll forget you ever bedded that half-breed gunslinger. Go on now, I'll be up directly. I need a drink."

"The liquor is in the chest by the door," Chloe said, hoping he'd drink himself into a stupor. "Help yourself." Then she hurried up the stairs. She wanted to warn Juanita to remain out of sight for a few days, until she decided how best to handle Tate. She ducked into Rowdy's bedroom, explained the situation to Juanita and told her to take Rowdy to the bunkhouse when the coast was clear.

Chloe had just entered her room when Tate burst in without knocking. "You're not naked," he blasted in a show of authority. "Pa said you have to obey me now."

"Your father isn't here, Tate," Chloe said. "You're on your own, and we both know you're not strong enough right now to force yourself on me."

"You're my wife," Tate contended. "I can do what I please with you and you can't say no."

He approached her boldly, as if he expected her to submit meekly to his authority. Chloe had other ideas. "There's only one thing I have to say to you, Tate, and I won't repeat it, so listen carefully. Touch me and I'll kill you. Maybe not now. Or even today. But rest assured I'll find the perfect time and place to end your miserable life. Maybe I'll wait until you're sleeping and put a bullet in your heart. Or perhaps I'll wait until you're awake and aware of what I'm doing."

Tate clutched his injured shoulder, his face devoid of all color. "You little bitch! You're just ornery enough to do it. Have it your way for now. But as soon as I'm healed properly, I'm gonna make you sorry you defied me."

Before her false bravado failed her, Chloe strode from the room, carefully skirting Tate.

"Where are you going?"

"I've got a ranch to run."

"We're not through," Tate warned. "You can have your way for now, but one way or another I'm gonna have what's mine. Remember this, Chloe Talbot. My shoulder is gonna be healed soon and I'll be as good as new."

*　　*　　*

The fires of hades burned within Desperado. The only respite from the consuming fire within him was the welcome coolness that bathed his heated brow. He tried to move and wondered vaguely if his punishment for the life he'd led included torture, for his muscles screamed at the unrelenting agony of a thousand needles puncturing his flesh.

He heard voices and was surprised when he recognized the guttural tongue he hadn't spoken in many years. The language of his mother's people, the Apache. Forcing himself up from the bottomless depths of pain and despair, Desperado managed to get his eyes open. A red haze hampered his vision, confirming his belief that he'd died and received his just reward. He was in hell. The devil had finally won out.

Then the haze began to clear, replaced by dim images of human figures. He blinked and his vision returned, revealing more of his surroundings. A fire burned in a pit nearby. He stared into the leaping flames and licked his dry lips. To his surprise, someone lifted his head and held a gourd filled with sweet, cool water to his mouth. He drank greedily, then lay back down and closed his drooping eyelids.

Was he truly in hell? he wondered. Perhaps not, for he seriously doubted that anyone in hell would offer him a cool drink. Then someone spoke and he tried to focus on the words and language.

"You are safe, Fast Hand. Rest and get well."

Fast Hand. His Indian name, given to him by his adoptive parents when his skill with a gun became apparent. The kind of peace he hadn't felt in many years washed over him, and he slept.

The next time Desperado awakened he saw Prairie Moon, his adoptive mother, bending over him, a tender smile wreathing her dark, care-worn features. He shifted his gaze and saw Black Bear, his stalwart Indian father, squatting beside him.

"The spirits have answered our prayers, my son," Black Bear said reverently. "You will live."

"I thought . . ." The words stuck in Desperado's throat, rusty from disuse. He tried again. "I thought . . . I had died and gone to hell. How did you find me?"

"Our small band left the reservation several years ago to roam and hunt where we will. We had camped beside the river on our journey south to our winter hunting grounds. The Spirit of the River brought you to us. We found you in the water, more dead than alive. We thought you were lost to us forever, but then you came back to us."

"How long have I been like this?"

"We found you fourteen suns ago," Prairie Moon said. "You had two bullets in you. One in your back and another in your thigh. Who did this to you, my son?"

"Someone who wanted me out of the way permanently." He tried to rise. "I have to leave. Chloe—" His words ended in a gurgle of pain as he fell back upon the pallet.

"You are too weak, my son," Prairie Moon scolded. "You must rest and regain your strength. Who is Chloe?"

"The woman I love. She convinced me to abandon my dangerous life and become a rancher. But she was wrong. Even when I'm not looking for trouble, it comes looking for me. As soon as I finish what I started out to do I'll be moving on. Chloe deserves better than I can offer her."

"You won't be doing anything soon, my son," Black Bear said. "You will rest here with us and heal."

Desperado's strength returned slowly. He worried about Chloe constantly, and was impatient to complete his journey to Amarillo to inform the Rangers of the problems at Trouble Creek, so he pushed himself to the limits. He allowed himself another week to recover, then he rose from his pallet and began a regimen of exercise to regain his strength.

Randy spent several days searching the riverbank for anything that would either prove or disprove that Desperado had drowned. He had left the ranch in the dead of the night. The others knew of his mission and together they had made up a story to explain his absence to Chloe.

The hands weren't happy about Chloe's marriage to Tate Talbot and they unanimously agreed that Chloe had been forced to wed Tate, even though she had denied it. They wanted to help her but had no idea how to go about it, except to find Desperado. Chloe had been so adamantly convinced that Desperado still lived that she had made believers of them. So they had conspired together to learn the truth for themselves and drew straws to see which of them would look for Desperado. Randy had won.

Randy guided his horse along the riverbank. The water was calm now, nothing, he supposed, like the turbulent force it had been the day Desperado had been carried away by the current. He followed the river downstream for many miles, scanning both banks for something, anything pertinent to Desperado's disappearance. He was ready to admit defeat when he spotted an object caught amid debris on the opposite shore.

Randy kneed his mount into the water, crossed the river and retrieved the object. It was a hat. Desperado's hat. He'd recognize it anywhere. Randy had no idea if finding the hat was a good sign or a bad one, but it was enough to make him continue the search.

Randy knew he was probably in Indian territory, and that Indian raiders had been active since the war ended, but he pushed on. He came upon the Indian village unexpectedly. The dozen or so tipis were pitched on a grassy plain that stretched along the riverbank. Before he could turn tail and ride away, he was surrounded by a group of braves. One grabbed his reins and led his horse into the village.

Randy was no coward, but he'd heard about Indian atrocities and expected the worst. Being scalped and stripped of his skin were two things that came to mind.

Suddenly he was pulled from the saddle. He fell heavily but quickly regained his feet, determined not to show fright. A tall, imposing man of indeterminate age approached, and Randy rightly assumed he was the chief.

"I am Black Bear," the chief said in barely understandable English. "Why have you come to my village?"

"I—" Randy gulped, searching for courage. "I'm looking for a man. Mr. Desperado Jones. Have you seen him?"

A dangerous glint turned Black Bear's dark eyes to polished ebony. "Why are you looking for Desperado Jones?"

"He's my friend; I work for him. We were told he was dead, but my friends and I refused to believe it. I . . . we need his help. That's why I'm looking for him. We need to know what happened to him."

Black Bear stared at Randy for what seemed like an eternity before he appeared to come to a decision. "Come with me," he said as he strode briskly away.

Randy followed, wondering what was in store for him now. Black Bear stopped abruptly and pointed to two braves who were engaged in a game of wrestling. Without a word of explanation, Black Bear left Randy to figure out what he was supposed to do next.

The wrestlers broke apart, laughing and patting each other on the back. Then they separated and went in opposite directions.

Randy observed the taller of the two. He looked vaguely familiar. Though somewhat thin, the Indian gave every indication of being strong and virile. He was dressed in buckskins and looked at home in his surroundings.

*   *   *

Desperado was satisfied with his recovery. He was able to hold his own with Yellow Dog during a wrestling match and was eager to return to civilization. He was on his way now to tell Prairie Moon and Black Bear that the time had come for him to leave. He hadn't regained his full strength yet, but he was reasonably certain he could hold his own against his enemies. During shooting practice yesterday he'd learned that his illness had had no effect on his aim or speed. Desperado Jones's reputation wouldn't suffer because of his wounds.

Desperado stopped in mid-stride, his carefully honed instincts alerting him to a stranger's presence. He rested his hand lightly on his weapon and whirled to confront the danger. His eyes widened in disbelief when he saw Randy staring at him as if he'd seen a ghost. Several rapid strides brought him to Randy's side.

"What in the hell are you doing here?" he asked the stunned young man.

Chapter Sixteen

"Desperado, thank God I found you," Randy said with such heartfelt relief that Desperado feared something horrible had happened back at the ranch during his prolonged absence. Was Chloe in trouble?

"How did you know to look for me here?" Desperado asked the young cowboy.

"I didn't. Calvin Talbot told us you were dead, that you had drowned in the river. We all believed it except Miss Chloe. Then the boys and I decided to take matters into our own hands and look for you ourselves. We all hoped you'd merely been wounded and were holed up somewhere to heal. I won the draw and here I am. Only I never expected to find you with Indians. Do you know these people?"

"These are my people," Desperado said, making

a wide sweep with his arm to encompass the small village. "You probably met Black Bear, my foster father, when you were brought into camp. But for them I *would* be dead."

Randy shuddered. "Then it's true. You *were* wounded by the posse."

Desperado nodded slowly. "I cheated the devil once again. The current was wicked that day. You'd have to see it to believe it. To this day I don't know why I'm still alive. But enough of me. There has to be another reason why you came looking for me. Something has happened at the ranch." He motioned toward a nearby tipi. "Come inside, out of the wind. Then you can tell me everything."

Sitting cross-legged before a small fire, Desperado leaned back against an ornate backrest and stared at Randy, a frown marring his handsome features.

"I planned to leave the village tomorrow. It's good that you found me before I left. Tell me, what has happened in my absence?"

Randy cleared his throat as he cast about for the words to tell Desperado that Chloe had married Tate Talbot. "You're not going to like this," he finally said. "I don't know how it happened or why. I think it has something to do with Rowdy being shot."

Desperado's attention sharpened. "Rowdy was shot? Is he all right?"

"It was touch and go for a while, but Juanita is taking good care of him. She won't let none of us upset him with talk about his shooting, so we don't know much about it."

Desperado cursed. He had a damn good idea who was responsible for Rowdy's shooting, but he let it go until he learned more. "Who is Juanita?"

"Miss Chloe hired her right after you left. She'd been beat up pretty good by some man and Miss Chloe felt sorry for her."

"Is that what sent you off searching for me? Rowdy's shooting?"

"Not exactly," Randy hedged. "Oh, hell, I don't know no other way to say it. Miss Chloe married Tate Talbot a couple of weeks ago. Maybe longer than that, I lost track of time."

Desperado shot to his feet. "She what?"

"It's true. When Cory questioned her about it, she said it was what she wanted. Don't none of us believe her, but there wasn't a thing we could do about it."

"Chloe would never willingly marry Talbot," Desperado said, as if trying to convince himself.

"He's living with her at the ranch," Randy blurted out. "Calvin Talbot's been nosing around the place, riding over the land as if he owned it. Talk in town is that the railroad is coming through Trouble Creek. That's why Talbot has been buying up land. He knew about it and bought all the land along the right of way. The Ralston spread was the last holdout. Do you reckon that's true?"

"I'm sure of it," Desperado rasped. "They've forgotten one thing, though. I own half the ranch and I'm still alive. They can't do a thing without my permission, and I'm not giving it. I've got to leave right away, Randy, but I'd like you to do something for me."

"Name it, Desperado."

Desperado confided in a low voice exactly what he wanted Randy to do.

"I won't fail you, Desperado. I don't believe Miss Chloe is happy and I'll do anything to make things right."

An hour later Desperado and Randy rode off in opposite directions. Desperado was sickened at the thought of Chloe lying in Tate Talbot's arms, responding to him in the same wanton way she had to him. Then the sickness inside him turned to rage. How dare she marry Tate! Not only had she married Tate but she'd told the boys she had done so willingly. What did Tate offer her that he could not? Desperado asked himself. *Respectability*, a voice within him whispered. She'd married Tate before he was cold in his grave, had he really been dead. She hadn't even taken time to mourn him. Spurring the sturdy mustang that Black Bear had given him, he rode like a man possessed toward Trouble Creek.

Chloe strode out to the bunkhouse to see Rowdy. She hadn't dared let him and Juanita return to the house while Tate was living there. Following Chloe's advice, Juanita had made herself scarce whenever Tate was anywhere near.

Rowdy was sitting up in his bunk, accepting broth from the spoon Juanita held to his lips. The pair were so engrossed in one another that they hadn't heard Chloe enter. She cleared her throat and approached the bunk.

"How are you, Rowdy?"

"Oh, he's doing just fine, Senorita Chloe," Juanita answered. "But he's too weak to get out of bed yet."

Rowdy gave Juanita a weak smile. "I can speak for myself, Juanita. I'll be up and around in a day or two, Miss Chloe. Juanita tends to baby me."

"Take all the time you need, Rowdy. There's not all that much to do right now."

"Is Juanita safe here?" Rowdy asked worriedly. "She told me what Tate did to her. I'd kill the bastard if he wasn't your . . . husband," he ground out. He gave Chloe a sheepish smile. "I'm sorry, Miss Chloe, but I don't think much of a man who'd beat a woman. Not to mention the . . . other things he did to her."

Chloe felt her cheeks redden. Rowdy didn't know half of what Tate was capable of. "Tate's shattered shoulder isn't mending properly. He's in a lot of pain and unlikely to take much of an interest in running the ranch right now. If the boys don't mind her staying here, I think she's safe enough."

"I'll take care of her," Rowdy said. "I'll be up and around soon."

As if speaking of the devil had conjured him up, Tate appeared in the doorway. He saw Juanita at Rowdy's bedside and flew into a rage.

"What's that whore doing here? I thought I told you to get rid of her. It's a good thing I followed you out here or I'd never know she was still here. Is she servicing your hands? Is that why you've let her stay against my wishes?"

Rowdy started to rise from his sickbed but Juanita pushed him back down. "I'll leave," she said.

"No, you won't!" Chloe argued. "You'll stay. Furthermore, you can move back into the house. I hired you, and Tate has no say over my employees."

When Juanita started to protest, Chloe said, "Rowdy is well on the way to recovery. One of the hands can see to his needs during the night, and you can still come out here and care for him during the day."

"Like hell!" Tate ranted. "I'm your husband. You'll damn well do as I say. You know what Pa said about submitting to me, don't you?"

"Your father has what he wants," Chloe said evenly. "He couldn't care less about our problems."

"Oh, yeah, well, I'm in charge here now and I'm tired of having green boys trying to do a man's job. They're fired. All of them."

Just then Cory and the others walked into the bunkhouse. "What's this about being fired?" Cory asked.

"You heard me. You're all fired. I'm hiring on men I can trust. Pack your gear and get out of here."

When none of the men moved, Tate said, "You heard me. Get! And don't look to Chloe for help this time. She has no say in this. She knows what will happen if she interferes."

"What do you want us to do, Miss Chloe?" Cory asked.

Chloe didn't dare contradict Tate. She could handle him without difficulty, but she couldn't protect the hands should Tate go whining to his father. Calvin was fully capable of carrying out his threat to hurt the boys. The attack on Rowdy had been a warning, and she didn't want another shooting on her conscience.

Chloe looked into the faces of the boys she'd come to depend upon and felt a crushing sadness. If only Desperado were here, she thought. Suddenly she realized there was a face missing.

"Where's Randy?"

The hands glanced at one another in silent communication, waiting for Cory, their spokesman, to explain.

"Randy didn't like what was going on here and decided to leave. He asked me to tell you that he enjoyed working for you, Miss Chloe, but he didn't want to continue with Talbot in charge."

Chloe nodded. "He was free to go where he wanted." She couldn't blame Randy and realized the best way to protect the boys was to let them all go. She knew they were waiting for an answer to Cory's question and gave the only one possible.

"I think you should all leave. If Tate wants to hire his own men, then I have no choice but to let him." She sent Tate a belligerent look, daring him to contradict her as she said, "With the exception of Rowdy, who is unable to travel, and Juanita, whom I refuse to send away."

Tate decided to take exception. "I told you, I don't want the Mex—"

"And I told you, Juanita stays to nurse Rowdy."

Her hand hovered over her gun. She wasn't going to let Tate have his way on this. She'd do whatever was necessary to keep Rowdy and Juanita here. With no means of support, Juanita would end up in a whorehouse, servicing the needs of men like Tate Talbot.

Obviously influenced by Chloe's gun, Tate backed down. "Just keep her out of my sight," he snarled. "And as soon as her patient is recovered, they both go."

Chloe didn't argue. As soon as Rowdy recovered enough to leave, she intended to leave herself. She hadn't given up on finding Desperado alive. So much time had passed, however, her hopes were dimming. Were he alive, she knew he would have come back to her.

"Have it your way, Tate," Chloe said, sending him a scathing glance as she whirled and strode back to the house. Tate was hard on her heels.

"I've been thinking," he said as he closed the kitchen door behind them. "Maybe I spoke too quick. Juanita can stay." He leered at her. "I need a woman in my bed, and since you refuse to be a wife to me, she can take your place."

"Touch her and you're a dead man," Chloe hissed from between clenched teeth.

"Now see here, Chloe. I've been damn patient with you these past few weeks. I want you in my bed. Our marriage is legal, so why are you acting like we ain't married?"

Chloe knew for a fact that she and Tate weren't really married. She had read the marriage license before she'd put it in the safe and had had a good laugh over it. Reverend Tully was a good man. She'd had no idea he was capable of that kind of deception. But she couldn't confront the Talbots with her knowledge until she spoke with the reverend. She knew Calvin Talbot had it within his power to ruin the reverend. She hoped there was some way they could prevent such a thing from happening.

"I never wanted to marry you, Tate," Chloe said.

"Well, we are married. Read the damn marriage license if you don't believe me. Tonight you're not going to lock the door against me, do you hear? I have rights. Lock me out and you're going to be sorry. Unless," he added slyly, "you want me to take that fiery little Mex in your stead. I won't be as gentle with her as I would with you."

Without giving her time to answer, Tate strode toward the door. "I'm going to make sure those cowboys clear out like I told them," he threw over his shoulder.

Chloe felt the walls closing in on her. She couldn't allow Tate to mistreat Juanita. She'd already seen the result of his heavy hand. But she would die if Tate touched her. Once had been enough. What to do? Then it came to her. She would ride into town and ask Reverend Tully's advice. Only he could tell her if he was ready to face the consequences should her bogus marriage to Tate be made public.

Though the weather was turning ugly, Chloe hitched the wagon to a team of horses and drove into town, saying she had to buy supplies. The hands had already left, and Tate had gone off to tell his father of this latest development and to recruit new hands. Chloe drove directly to the white clapboard parsonage beside the First Baptist Church of

Trouble Creek. A small, plump woman with a warm smile answered her knock.

"Is the reverend in?" Chloe asked.

"He's in his study, dear." If Chloe's trouser-clad figure and guns shocked her, she gave no hint of it. "You're Miss Sommers, Ted Ralston's stepdaughter. Come in, I'm sure Reverend Tully will be happy to see you." She ushered Chloe into the tidy parlor. "Make yourself comfortable while I tell him you're here."

Chloe sat down on an overstuffed chair, fidgeting with the fringe on her jacket. A few minutes later the reverend strode into the parlor.

"I've been expecting you, Miss Sommers. I regret putting you through that ceremony, but I tried to make amends in my own way. I shouldn't have buckled under Mr. Talbot's threats and I won't do so again. Did you read the marriage license?"

"Indeed I did, Reverend. What everyone signed is an application to join the First Baptist Church of Trouble Creek. I'm not really married, am I?"

The reverend smiled. "No, indeed. I was hoping you'd read it and understand what I did. I took a chance that neither of the Talbots would inspect it after the ceremony. I had to do something. I couldn't marry an unwilling bride. I went through with the ceremony because he threatened the lives of my loved ones if I didn't."

"That's why I'm here," Chloe confided. "I can't continue with this farce. I've held off Tate thus far but I don't know how much longer I can keep him away from me. I need to tell the Talbots that no legal marriage took place, but I'm afraid of what they will do to you. I know they threatened you. Do you think Calvin Talbot will . . . well, I heard what they said about your error in judgment and I want you to know I don't hold that against you. But others might not be so forgiving. You could lose your position in the church."

"I've already taken care of that, Miss Sommers. I fully expected you to repudiate your 'marriage' and took steps to prevent Mr. Talbot from harming me any further than I've already harmed myself.

"I confessed to my wife and she has forgiven me. Molly is a special woman, I love her and our children dearly. I'm the one who has to live with my sin. As for my congregation," Tully continued, "I plan to disclose my sin from the pulpit Sunday and ask for forgiveness."

Chloe hoped Reverend Tully's congregation was as forgiving as his wife had been, for the reverend was a good man. He had made a mistake and would carry it upon his conscience forever. That ought to be punishment enough. Besides, all humans were flesh and blood, with the same inclination to sin. Only God had the power to judge and condemn.

Chloe rose to leave. "Good luck, Reverend."

"Good luck to you, Miss Sommers. Something tells me you're going to need it. If you ever decide to marry for real, I'll be happy to perform the ceremony."

Chloe's expression grew pensive. The only man she wanted to marry was Desperado, and though she refused to accept it, he might no longer be listed among the living. She wouldn't believe he was dead until she saw his bones.

Chloe buttoned her coat to the neck as she left

the parsonage. The weather had turned nasty and she didn't linger in town any longer than it took to buy supplies and have them loaded in the buckboard. A light dusting of snow covered the ground by the time she rolled into the yard. Juanita came out of the house to help her unload the provisions.

"How is Rowdy?" Chloe asked as they carried groceries into the house.

"He's doing very well," Juanita said. Her dreamy smile told Chloe that Rowdy was special to Juanita.

"You seem mighty fond of that rascal," Chloe said wryly.

Juanita blushed prettily. "He's very nice. Nothing like—" Her words ended in a gurgle of surprise when Tate stomped into the kitchen.

"About time you came back," Tate complained. "I'm hungry. What's for supper?"

"Fried potatoes and ham," Chloe said.

"I will fix supper, Senorita Chloe," Juanita said, scooting out of Tate's way.

" 'Bout time you made yourself useful," Tate grumbled. "Me and Chloe got business upstairs in the bedroom, don't we, honey?"

Chloe blanched. "I don't think—"

"Juanita looks mighty fetching today," Tate drawled. "Remember what I said? I'm so hard-up right now it don't make much difference which of you I take." He rubbed his crotch suggestively.

"Leave Juanita alone," Chloe hissed when she saw Juanita pale and back away. "Go back to the bunkhouse," she told Juanita. "I'll manage here."

"But . . . you don't know what he's like," Juanita cried on a note of panic.

"I'm married to him," Chloe said to allay Juanita's fears. "Of course I know what he's like. I'll be fine. Why don't you put Rowdy in the wagon and take him to town." She reached into her jacket pocket and pulled out all the money she had on her. "Get a hotel room."

Juanita gave Chloe a long, considering look before nodding her understanding and scooting out the door.

"That was wise," Tate said. "But you shouldn't have given her money. She's capable of earning her keep. Whores know how to survive. Go upstairs and take off your clothes. It's really you I wanted anyway."

"I thought you were hungry."

He reached out to touch her breast but she neatly evaded him. He scowled. "I'm starved. I want to see if you taste as good as I remember. We're finally gonna have our wedding night. Pa said I was a fool to let you have your way. I ain't afraid of you."

In a surprisingly swift move he drew his gun with his uninjured left hand and pointed it at Chloe.

"I've been practicing with my left hand while my busted shoulder is healing," he said when he noted Chloe's astonishment. "I ain't taking no chances this time. Leave those damn guns down here."

Chloe had no choice but to unbuckle her gun belt and let it fall to the floor. "Don't think disarming me changes anything," Chloe warned. After imparting those chilling words, she left the room.

Chloe made a short detour to the study. Minutes later she had removed the "marriage license" from the safe and was ascending the stairs to her room.

Now that she knew Reverend Tully couldn't be hurt by Calvin Talbot, she'd decided to confront Tate with the bogus license tonight. She didn't want him to think they were married a moment longer than necessary. She had looked for the rifle her stepfather had always kept on a wall bracket, but it wasn't there. Tate must have gotten to it before her.

Damn him, she thought. But just because he had disarmed her didn't mean she wasn't dangerous.

Desperado spurred his mustang, fighting snow and wind in his eagerness to reach the ranch. Fear rode him. What had the Talbots done to Chloe to make her marry Tate? Or had she married Tate because she wanted to? The more he thought about Chloe and Tate together, the angrier he became. What kind of woman would hop into bed with another man scant days after being told that her fiancé was dead?

He should just ride off into the sunset and forget Chloe, Desperado thought angrily. She'd made her bed, let her lie in it. The only problem with that line of thinking was that Chloe's bed included Tate Talbot. If Chloe preferred Tate to him, so be it, Desperado reflected. But he damn well was going to let her know exactly what he thought of her.

Darkness came quickly this time of year. It was already pitch black when Desperado met the buckboard on the road. The woman driving the team was wrapped from head to toe in a woolen shawl and seemed frightened when Desperado appeared in the road. Unable to drive around him, she drew rein and reached for the shotgun she'd placed beneath the seat.

"I mean you no harm," Desperado said as he approached the buckboard. "Have you come from the Ralston spread? I recognize the horses."

The young woman appeared frightened of him, and Desperado decided to go on his way without troubling her further. Suddenly a head popped up from the wagon bed. "Desperado, is that you? Is Randy with you?"

Though the voice was shaky and weak, Desperado knew immediately that it belonged to Rowdy. "It's me, Rowdy. Randy and I crossed paths and I sent him off on an errand. What are you doing out on a night like this? Randy told me you'd been wounded."

"Tate Talbot ordered us all off the ranch," Rowdy explained. "He wanted to hire his own men. This is Juanita. She works for Miss Chloe."

Desperado was shocked. "You mean to tell me Chloe let Tate fire the lot of you without a fight? That doesn't sound like the Chloe I know."

"They're married now," Rowdy said bitterly. "I just don't understand why she did it."

"Senor Tate is a very bad man," Juanita injected. "I do not think Senorita Chloe likes him."

Desperado gave a snort of laughter. "She married him, didn't she?"

"*Sí*, but—"

"You'd best be on your way," Desperado said, glancing at the inky sky and thickening snowflakes. "Rowdy could catch pneumonia in his weakened state."

"Oh, *si*," Juanita said, sending Rowdy a worried glance as she picked up the reins and swatted them against the team's hindquarters.

"Where are you going?" Rowdy called as the buckboard pitched forward.

"Polecat hunting," he called back.

Chloe carefully locked the bedroom door and waited for Tate to make the first move. She didn't have long to wait. She saw the knob jiggle, and when it wouldn't turn, Tate began pounding on the door with the butt of his gun.

"Open up, Chloe!" Tate yelled.

No answer.

"Stand back, I'm gonna shoot the lock."

Chloe moved aside just in time as Tate's shot shattered the lock. Then he pushed the door open and strode into the room. He had removed everything except his longjohns.

"You ain't naked," he charged.

"You'll never see me naked, Tate Talbot!"

His grin said otherwise as he pointed his gun at her and said, "Strip. Now."

Desperado rode his horse into the barn, removed his saddle and gave him a quick rubdown. He glanced at the house and saw light spilling from an upstairs window. Chloe's window. The bunkhouse appeared deserted, confirming Rowdy's words that everyone had left.

Desperado tried the back door first, found it locked, and walked around to the front entrance, certain he'd find that door locked also. It was. He spit out a curse and stared thoughtfully at the door. Then he calmly raised his booted foot and kicked the door, gratified when he heard wood splintering as the bolt ripped through the doorjamb.

Chloe had removed her shirt and her trousers and stood before Tate now in her drawers and camisole. She glanced at the nightstand, where the false marriage license rested in a drawer. She wondered what would happen if she were to show it to Tate now. Then her practical side took over and she realized it would serve only to enrage him. In the mood Tate was in, and with his gun aimed at her, her only option was to get Tate into bed with her. And when lust made him incautious, she'd disarm him. She'd shoot him if she had to, though she'd prefer not to. Then she'd show him the fake marriage license and order him off her property. But she couldn't do that until she had the upper hand.

"I told you to take everything off," Tate repeated, waving the gun threateningly.

"I thought you might like to remove the final layer yourself," Chloe said archly. She sidled toward the bed. "I'll lie down and you can—"

Her words skidded to a halt when a loud crash shattered the night.

Tate whirled on his heel, startled and more than a little angry at the untimely interruption. "What the hell—" He walked to the door; a blast of frigid air rushed through the open panel. "Someone's broken into the house." Gripping his pistol in his left hand and picking up the lamp with his right, he started for the stairs. He paused halfway down and held the lamp high, gasping when he looked into the face of death.

"Desperado." His voice held a note of disbelief, and a healthy amount of fear. "You're dead. Pa said he killed you."

Desperado walked into the circle of light, a sneer curving his full lips. "As you can see, I'm far from dead." His cool gaze slid insultingly over Tate, frowning when he noted Tate's state of undress. "Did I interrupt something?"

"Damn right you did! My wife and I were—"

"Desperado! My God, you're alive!"

Desperado glanced upward and saw Chloe standing on the top landing, staring at him with a mixture of joy and disbelief. She was in the same state of undress as Tate, wearing only camisole and drawers. It was obvious to Desperado that he had interrupted an intimate moment between husband and wife.

"I'm very much alive, Chloe," Desperado rasped. "Does that disappoint you?"

Chloe frowned. "Disappoint me? Dear God! I'm thrilled. Ecstatic. I never once believed you were dead."

"Tell that to someone who will believe you," Desperado drawled sarcastically. "If you were so distressed over my death, why did you marry Tate almost immediately?"

"I'm not . . . We're not—"

"Shut up, Chloe," Tate warned.

"Do as he says, Chloe. I'll deal with you later."

"Deal with me? You don't understand."

"I understand only too well." He returned his attention to Tate. "Are you aware that I own half this ranch, Talbot? As part owner I'm telling you to get the hell off my property. Tell your father no part of this spread is his or yours to sell."

"You're a wanted man," Tate charged. "When Pa hears you're still alive, he'll get the marshal to run you down again. It's not too late for a hanging."

"You're dead wrong, Talbot. There's not going to be a hanging. There are too many witnesses who saw what really happened that day you challenged me. I'm not running this time. Tell Calvin that," Desperado spat.

"Go away, Jones. Chloe married me and I'm entitled to live here with her. We're newlyweds. We want to be alone."

"No, I—" Chloe tried to explain but Desperado's scathing glance told her he wasn't in the mood to listen right now. She clamped her lips together and fought to control her growing anger. How dare he assume she'd willingly married Tate!

"You're the one who's leaving, Talbot," Desperado rasped in that mean-as-hell voice that usually got the result he wanted.

Tate set the lamp down on the stair and used his right hand to keep his left hand from shaking. "I'm the one holding the gun," Tate reminded him.

Desperado's mirthless laugh sent chills down Chloe's spine.

In one flawless move, Desperado drew his weapon and shot the gun from Tate's hand. It flew into the air and landed on the floor at Desperado's feet. He kicked it aside while keeping his fathomless black eyes riveted on Tate, who was nursing his stinging hand.

"Are you still here?" Desperado drawled.

"You're not gonna send me out in the cold and snow without my boots or clothes, are you?"

Desperado appeared to be thinking. "Let him get dressed, Desperado," Chloe urged. "You don't want his death on your conscience."

Desperado gave her a contemptuous look but decided to follow her advice. "Get his duds," he ordered.

Chloe scurried into the spare bedroom where Tate had been sleeping and gathered up his boots and clothing, adding his sheepskin coat to the bundle. Then she walked down the stairs and handed them to Tate. His movements were awkward, favoring his shattered collarbone as he pulled on his clothing.

"You ain't gonna get away with this," he snarled as he sidled around Desperado to reach the door. "Wait till Pa hears what you done."

Chloe waited until he was outside, then she launched herself at Desperado, expecting him to welcome her with open arms. Instead, he caught her and held her at arm's length. Puzzled, she stared at him. His face was rigid, his expression devoid of all emotion.

His contemptuous glance slid down her thinly clad body; then he hefted her over his shoulder and ascended the stairs.

Chapter Seventeen

"Put me down!" Chloe screamed, pounding on Desperado's back. "What do you think you're doing?"

No answer was forthcoming.

"Why are you angry with me?"

He stormed into the bedroom and tossed her down on the bed. She bounced once, then settled onto the feather tick. It was so dark she could see nothing but yawning blackness. Then she heard his retreating footsteps. She scooted to the edge of the bed, swung her legs over the side and would have risen if Desperado hadn't returned carrying the lamp. He set it on the nightstand and stood over her, his expression rigid with accusation.

"Did Tate please you in bed?" he ground out as he removed his jacket and unbuckled his gunbelt.

Oh God, of course Desperado would think the worst. Chloe watched in trepidation as he tossed both his jacket and gunbelt across the room and began unbuttoning his shirt. She swallowed convulsively, aware that she had to defuse Desperado's anger before he did something she couldn't forgive.

"You don't understand. Let me explain."

"What's to explain? I have perfect vision, I know what I saw. Wasn't a half-breed good enough for you?"

His hands went to his waistband, fumbling with the buttons on the flap of his trousers.

"You're crazy! What are you doing?"

"Crazy enough to believe you when you said you loved me. Now I'm going to let you make the comparison. When I'm finished, tell me who has the better technique, me or Tate. I'm interested to know what he has that I don't."

He sat on the bed and removed his boots; then he pulled off his trousers.

"What have you heard about Tate and me?"

"Enough."

"Desperado, don't do this to me. I was devastated when Calvin Talbot told me you were dead. I refused to believe him, but when you didn't return, I feared the worst. Nevertheless, I never gave up on you."

"You married Tate," he charged.

"Who told you?"

"Does it matter?"

He rose to his full height and loomed over her, his face half hidden in the shadows. The breath slammed from Chloe's chest as her gaze slid over his hard body. He was somewhat thinner than she remembered, but still magnificent. Her gaze lingered a moment on his massive erection and she blanched. She'd forgotten how quick his passion was to kindle. Then she noticed the puckered red wound on his chest and another on his thigh and cried out in dismay.

"You're hurt!"

"The wounds are healing."

"Did the posse do that?"

He nodded. "They left me for dead but I cheated them."

"Tell me about it."

"Not now."

He reached for her and pulled her to the edge of the bed. Then he quickly and efficiently removed her camisole and drawers. His expression did not change as his gaze roamed freely over her naked form, but Chloe saw his eyes kindle with appreciation. Fire leaped into the dark centers, and she felt her own blood heat and thicken.

"Does Tate do this to you?" Desperado rasped as he dropped to his knees, spread her legs and touched her heat with the tip of his tongue.

"Tate never did anything to me," Chloe claimed on a rising note of passion. She had no control over her body where Desperado was concerned.

Suddenly he pushed her backward on the bed, leaving her legs hanging over the sides. Then he placed her legs over his shoulders, lowered his head and explored her thoroughly with his tongue.

"Desperado! Please."

Desperado gave her a heart-stopping smile, then positioned her in the center of the bed. She cried out when he found a new way to torment her.

"Does Tate know how sensitive your nipples are?"

"I told you . . . Ohhh . . ." Her denial ended in a strangled sigh when his mouth closed over the tip of one breast. Her nipples had become so sensitive lately, the merest touch of his tongue sent waves of ecstasy shuddering through her.

Lifting his head, he stared at her, clearly puzzled. "By your response, I'd say Tate ignored your breasts. Pity. You should have told him what you liked."

"Damn you! If you don't listen to me, you're going to live to regret it."

"I listened to you once," he bit out. "You said you loved me. You lied." He stared at her mouth. "Are your kisses as sweet as I remember?"

He kissed her then, and Chloe wandered helplessly in a sensual fog of surrender. His lips were soft against hers, not hard and censuring as she expected them to be. Though the kiss was not gentle, neither was it punishing. It held a combination of hunger for her and disappointment in her. She recognized the hurting inside him and knew she had to find a way to tell him the truth about herself and Tate before the wedge of distrust separated them beyond repair.

The opportunity came when Desperado released her mouth and returned to her breasts. "Your breasts are larger than I recall," he said as he took a dark red bud into his mouth and suckled her.

Finding her mouth free, Chloe wound her fingers in his dark hair and lifted his head so she could look into his eyes. His frown told her she had interrupted his feast far too soon, but she refused to be intimidated by his dark scowl.

"You listen to me, Desperado Jones," she said in a voice that captured his attention. "I am not now nor was I ever married to Tate Talbot. Oh, there was a ceremony, all right, but it wasn't legal. Tate thinks we're married, but he never touched me. I wouldn't let him."

"You expect me to believe that?" he asked incredulously. "I know what I interrupted tonight."

"You don't know a damn thing. I didn't have my guns on me when Tate broke into my room, but I planned to disarm him and tell him we aren't really married. I've kept him away from me ever since our bogus ceremony. I would have found a way to discourage him tonight, too."

Desperado stared at her, his expression one of wary hope. "What makes you think the ceremony wasn't legal?"

Chloe pulled the blanket up to her chin. The fire in the stove needed rekindling and it was growing cold in the room.

"I was unwilling, and Reverend Tully knew it. He performed the ceremony because somehow Calvin obtained damaging information that could have ended his marriage as well as his career.

"But Reverend Tully was smarter than the Talbots thought," she continued. "The marriage license that he prepared and all parties signed wasn't a marriage license at all. It was an application to join the First Baptist Church of Trouble Creek. I was the only one who thought to read the document before I signed. I waited to confront Tate with the bogus license because Calvin threatened to harm my hired hands. He's responsible for Rowdy being shot. It was meant as a warning."

"That story is pretty farfetched even for you, Chloe," Desperado charged. "How did you keep Tate from consummating the marriage? He's always been hot for you."

"I threatened him," Chloe said. "Old Doc Hockmeyer did a poor job of treating Tate, and his shattered collarbone isn't healing properly. He was never a threat to me, Desperado. I can handle him with one hand tied behind my back."

"You were both in your underwear," Desperado accused.

Exasperation sharpened her voice. "He caught me unaware and disarmed me. Then he ordered me upstairs to bed. I played along with him until I could find the right moment to disarm him. Then I was going to inform him we weren't really married. I no longer had to worry about the ranch hands being hurt because Tate chased them off the land.

"I spoke with Reverend Tully earlier today and he told me he had taken steps to defuse Calvin's threats, so there was nothing preventing me from confronting Tate with the truth about our sham marriage."

"If all this is true, I owe you an apology," Desperado offered.

Chloe propped herself against the headboard and reached into the nightstand drawer. "Read this," she said, handing Desperado a document that looked suspiciously like a marriage license.

Desperado held it to the light and perused the document. Chloe watched him closely. When she saw the dimple flash in his right cheek she knew he finally understood. Then he read it again, more slowly this time, and the corners of his mouth kicked up into a smile. Then a rumble started in his chest and he tipped back his head and roared with laughter.

"Remind me to thank Reverend Tully," he said, dashing mirthful tears from his eyes. Suddenly he sobered. "God, sweetheart, I was so frightened for you, but there was nothing I could do about it. I was more dead than alive when I was fished from the river. Prairie Moon nursed me back to health."

"Prairie Moon?"

"My foster mother. The tribe had camped on the riverbank to rest before continuing their trek to their winter hunting grounds in the south. I hadn't seen Prairie Moon or Black Bear in years, but they hadn't forgotten me."

She reached out to touch the healing wound that marred his chest. "Someday I hope to be able to thank Prairie Moon for saving your life."

"I'm sorry," Desperado rasped as he leaned over to kiss her ear.

"For what?"

"For almost doing something I'd regret the rest of my life. When I make love to you it will be because we both want it."

"I want what you want, Desperado," Chloe whispered against his lips.

"Oh God, sweetheart, I nearly lost my mind when I learned you had married Tate. I should have known there were circumstances I wasn't aware of. I was so damn jealous I allowed my temper to rule me. You do forgive me, don't you?"

"I forgive you. I'm just glad you're alive. I need you, Desperado, don't ever leave me."

"Never, sweetheart, not as long as I have a breath left in my body.

"Don't move, I'll be right back," he said as he rose from the bed and pulled on his trousers.

"Where are you going?"

"To see if I can close the front door. I was so anxious to get you upstairs I left it hanging open on its hinges. I can hear the wind whistling through the house from up here."

"Don't be long."

Desperado took up the lamp and descended the stairs. A rush of cold air hit him and he shivered. He had indeed left the door gaping open, and a fine dusting of snow covered the foyer. He set the lamp down and pushed the door shut. The wood had shattered and the lock no longer worked, so he did the next best thing until it could be properly repaired tomorrow. He brought a chair from the kitchen and propped it beneath the knob.

Then, recalling the shattered lock on the bedroom door, he dragged a chair up the stairs and into the bedroom, positioning it beneath the knob. There was only one more thing left to be done before he could return to the warm bed and Chloe. He selected pieces of kindling from the wood box beside the stove and fed them into the dying fire.

"The room should be warm in a few minutes," he

said as he peeled off his trousers and slid beneath the quilt. He turned to Chloe and drew her into his arms.

"I feared I'd never have you in my arms like this again," he rasped against her lips. "When I fell into the river and was carried away by the current, I was convinced the devil was about to claim me. In addition to my wounds, which I knew were life-threatening, I was very close to drowning. I have no idea how I ended up in Black Bear's village. Perhaps the devil didn't want me and he spit me back."

Chloe shuddered. "Don't talk like that. You survived for a reason. I needed you. Never more than I do right now. Kiss me, Desperado. Love me again, I've missed you so."

Desperado's answer was lost in a groaning sigh as his arms tightened around her. He kissed her with all the pent-up love and longing in his heart. A heart Chloe had brought to life with her abiding faith in him. He couldn't get enough of her sweet lips as he kissed her again and again, drawing her tongue into his mouth, then plunging inside hers to taste her more fully.

After an eon of kissing and tasting, it was no longer enough to satisfy him. His dark eyes glinted with purpose as he pressed a path of kisses to her breasts, where he paused to flick her hard nipples with wet strokes of his tongue, relishing her soft moans of encouragement. But that still wasn't enough to satisfy Desperado as he trailed his mouth down her body, stopping briefly to worship her navel before continuing to the moist nest between her legs.

He inhaled her heady fragrance, sweet and tangy and so arousing, his rigid staff gave an involuntary jerk. Ignoring his raging need, he spread her with his fingers and lapped delicately at her tender, pink flesh.

He raised his head and whispered, "I love the way you weep for me."

"Only for you," Chloe gasped as he returned to his succulent feast.

Chloe felt the beginning of her climax deep within her core. It spread to every part of her body and exploded violently where he plied his mouth and tongue with remarkable diligence. She convulsed once, twice, then cried out, the pleasure so intense she feared she would die of it. She came back to herself when she felt Desperado slide up her body, spread her thighs and thrust deep within her center.

"I'm home, sweetheart," he groaned against her mouth as he buried himself deeply within her tight passage.

"Welcome back," Chloe gasped. Her arms went around him, holding him snugly as he began the slow, arousing rhythm of love.

"Are you with me?" he rasped.

"All the way," Chloe replied. And she was, though she was more than a little astounded that she could respond to his loving after the volatile climax he had wrested from her only moments before.

Chloe had never felt him so hard, or seen him so intensely focused. Despite the coolness of the room, he had thrown off the quilt and beads of sweat dotted his forehead. His face was starkly outlined in the light cast by the lamp. Then all thought ceased as he grasped her hips and pierced her so deeply she felt as if he'd touched her soul.

"I . . . can't . . . wait," he bit out through clenched teeth. "Come . . . with me, love. I'm going to . . . ahhh . . ."

"I'm with you!" Chloe cried as she arched up against him and dug her fingers into his back. Pleasure burst through her at the same moment that Desperado cried out her name and spent himself.

"Did you draw blood?" Desperado asked a short time later as he lifted himself off of her and flopped down beside her.

Dazed, Chloe hadn't the slightest idea what he was talking about. "What?"

"My back, love. I think you scarred me with your nails."

"Oh. I'm sorry."

"I'm not. I love your passion. I recall a time when being with a man frightened you."

"That's before I knew that making love needn't be painful or degrading. Before I knew you," she added.

"God, Chloe, I love you. Are you tired?"

"Not really. Why?"

"Because I want to love you again. And maybe again after that."

"Only if you let me love you," Chloe said.

"You don't have to, love. I'd not ask that of you."

Her eyes glittered. "Try to stop me."

Desperado made no attempt to stop her. He let her love him and enjoyed every delicious, agonizing moment. Toward morning he loved her again, and afterward they slept.

Chloe awakened first. Only embers burned in the stove, and she eased out of bed to rekindle the flame. She was shivering when she climbed back into bed, and she warmed herself against Desperado's solid form.

"Your feet are like ice," he said, startling her.

"I thought you were sleeping."

"I was until you put your cold feet on me. You should have awakened me. I would have stoked the fire for you."

"You were sleeping so peacefully I didn't want to awaken you."

He yawned and stretched. "I'm so hungry I could eat a bear."

"You're too thin," Chloe observed.

"I was able to take little except broth while I was recovering from my wounds. All I need is a couple weeks of solid food."

"I can fix that," Chloe said as she started to rise.

"No, stay in bed. It's probably freezing down there. I'll go down first and light the stove. Wait a half hour, then join me in the kitchen."

Chloe lingered in the warm bed a few minutes after Desperado left. Then she got up, washed thoroughly in cold water from the pitcher, and got dressed. The delicious aroma of coffee wafted through the air and she hurried down to the kitchen.

"I'll fix flapjacks," Chloe said as she got out the

ingredients. "That ought to fill the hollow in your belly."

"Bacon would taste good."

"There's plenty of bacon. You slice it while I mix the batter."

Soon the kitchen was filled with the delicious aroma of cooking food. When everything was prepared, they sat down and proceeded to devour nearly every crumb Chloe had cooked.

"A few more meals like that and I'll surpass my previous weight," Desperado said, patting his stomach.

Chloe smiled and poured him more coffee. "I wouldn't want you to get too fat."

He returned her smile, then grew pensive. "I suppose we should discuss our next move where the Talbots are concerned."

Chloe blanched. "You expect trouble?"

"I always expect trouble. Have you looked outside? There's a few inches of snow and it's blowing pretty good out there. It's unlikely the Talbots will attempt anything until the weather moderates, but they'll probably come out here with blood in their eyes."

"What are we going to do? Oh, God, I can't lose you again."

"First they have to be told that your marriage to Tate isn't legal. They have to know they have no claim on our land."

"What if they show up with another posse?"

"I hope Randy arrives before it comes to that."

"Randy? What's Randy got to do with this? He left the ranch without even a good-bye."

"Randy came looking for me. You'd convinced the hands that I wasn't dead and they decided that one of them should set out to find me. Randy stumbled into the Indian village the day before I planned to leave. He told me everything that had been going on with you, and I sent him to Amarillo on an errand. I would have gone myself, but after I heard about your marriage to Tate I rode straight here."

"I wondered how you knew. Why did Randy go to Amarillo?"

"There's a Texas Ranger outpost at Amarillo. I instructed Randy to bring a Ranger to Trouble Creek. I'm not going to let Marshal Townsend hang me because the Talbots want me out of the way. The Rangers have legal authority and can settle this business with the Talbots and their dirty dealings once and for all."

"So what are we going to do until Randy returns with the Ranger?"

"No one can do anything until the weather breaks. Meanwhile, we're all cozy and warm here. There is enough food on hand to keep us from starving, and plenty of wood chopped and stacked outside the door. We'll take care of the chores first, then spend the idle hours making love."

"Desperado, be serious," Chloe chided.

He flashed his dimple at her. "I am serious, though I find it difficult to believe you'd agree to share your life with a half-breed who has made countless mistakes. All I want to do is clear up this mess with the Talbots and start over again with the woman I love. Who knows, maybe one day we'll have a child and be a real family."

Sooner than you think, Chloe thought, smiling to herself. She'd had her suspicions for a few weeks now, but she no longer doubted her condition.

While Chloe and Desperado discussed their future, Tate and Calvin Talbot sat at the breakfast table, arguing.

"Jones would have shot me if I hadn't left, Pa," Tate whined. "Chloe and I were in our underwear when he busted into the house. He was fit to be tied when he saw us together like that."

"That bastard doesn't know when to stay dead," Calvin bit out. "He's a dangerous enemy. He and Chloe share ownership of the ranch. There's no way in hell Jones will let us sell part of the land to the railroad. How could he still be alive? No man is invincible. He should be lying on the bottom of the river, or decaying along the bank somewhere." Calvin shivered. "It's almost as if he's unstoppable."

"Chloe is still my wife," Tate contended. "Nothing can change that. I'm going back to the ranch and claim what's mine."

Calvin glanced out the window. "Not in this weather, you're not. Early blizzards never last long. Meanwhile, I'll speak to Marshal Townsend. There are probably enough drifters in town to hire another posse and do the job right this time."

"You want me to sit back and do nothing while Jones screws my wife?" Tate spat.

"Don't worry. I'm sure you'll find a way to punish her once Jones is taken care of." He rose, checked his watch, glanced out the window again and sighed. "I suppose I'll have to go out in this if I'm going to enlist Townsend's help. I suggest you keep your temper in check until I decide what's to be done."

Calvin left the house, braving wind and snow to reach the marshal's office. The distance wasn't great, but by the time he reached his destination he was out of breath and chilled to the bone.

"Mr. Talbot," Townsend greeted as Calvin entered the office and shook the snow off his greatcoat. "What brings you out in this weather?"

"Desperado Jones," Calvin said curtly as he walked to the stove to warm himself. "The bastard is alive and at the ranch with my son's wife. He returned last night and forced Tate out of the house."

Townsend turned ashen. "Alive? My God! The man can't be killed. No wonder he's a living legend." He leaped from his chair. "I gotta get out of town. He's gonna come after me, mark my words. There ain't a man alive who can outdraw him."

"Coward!" Calvin spat. "You'll do nothing of the kind. I got you appointed marshal and you'll do as I say. First we've got to hire another posse. As soon as the weather breaks, we'll ride out to the ranch and have us a hanging."

"Count me out," Townsend asserted. "I ain't going anywhere near that ranch."

"You will if you want to keep your job."

"I don't care about the job. No siree, Mr. Talbot. I value my life, even if you don't. Find yourself another town marshal."

He pulled off his badge and tossed it down on the scarred desk. "I've been thinking of taking a wife.

My brother over in El Paso has a woman all picked out for me. Reckon I'll mosey over that way when the weather breaks and have a look. Marty says she's a widow woman with money. I gotta act fast before someone else beats me to her."

Talbot couldn't believe his ears. "Has everyone in this town gone mad? Not even my own son will stand up to Jones. He's scared, just like you. Well, go ahead and run away with your tail between your legs. There are others in this town eager to take my money if you're not."

Talbot slammed out of the office. He didn't need the law to do what needed to be done. Bucking the wind, he walked over to the Devil's Den and barged through the door. The saloon was overheated and stank of sweat and stale beer. Because of the nasty weather, the room was crowded with men who had nothing better to do than drink and gamble.

Wasting little time on formalities, Talbot banged his fist on the bar until he gained the attention he sought. Men turned away from their card games and drinking to stare at Talbot.

"I'm looking to hire men willing to ride in a posse. As the mayor of this town, I'm authorized to deputize those of you who volunteer."

"Did someone rob the bank?" a scruffy cowboy asked.

"No, nothing like that," Talbot answered.

"Who's the unlucky bastard you're chasing?" another man called from the back of the room.

"Desperado Jones," Talbot sneered. "This time he won't get away. I'm offering a decent day's wage for all who volunteer. I know exactly where to find

Jones. I intend to hang him from the nearest tree."

"What's his crime?" a drifter asked.

"Murder and attempted murder," Talbot answered.

"That ain't the way I heard it," a witness to the shootout challenged. "I heard it was more like an ambush."

Talbot sent the man a menacing look. "I doubt you'll find a single witness to testify against me in a court of law. Now then," he said, returning to the subject at hand, "how many here can I count on to join the posse?"

"Where's the marshal?" someone asked.

"He had business out of town. Forget the marshal. Call out if you're willing to work for me."

Silence.

"Are you all afraid of Desperado Jones?"

"I'm afraid of any man who can outdraw me," a man muttered to his companions.

"And I don't fancy chasing ghosts," another added. "I heard tell Jones was shot dead, fell into the river and drowned. Count me out."

A chorus of "Me too" followed, enraging Talbot.

"The lot of you are cowards," Talbot charged.

Suddenly a man pushed through the crowd. "Count me in, Mr. Talbot. Hell, what have I got to lose? I need the money powerful bad and I ain't afeared of ghosts or legends."

"Anyone else?" Talbot asked, ráking the men with a contemptuous glance. Two more men stepped forward.

"You'll do," Talbot said. "I'll send word when

you're needed." Then he took his leave, chagrined that only three men had offered to ride with the posse. Still, that made five men, counting himself and Tate. Enough to send Desperado Jones to hell.

Chapter Eighteen

Snow had stopped falling and the sun peeked out from behind a bank of gray clouds. Nearly a week of pure bliss had followed Desperado's return. Between bouts of loving, the animals were fed, the doors repaired and meals cooked and eaten. The day the weather broke, Desperado tried to prepare Chloe for the inevitable visit from the Talbots.

"You know they won't let us live in peace," Desperado contended after he'd broached the subject.

Chloe turned slowly from the stove, where she was making their breakfast. "Do you suppose they'll bring a posse?"

"I'd be willing to bet on it."

"What are you going to do?"

"Sit tight and wait for Randy to return with the Ranger."

"What if the Rangers can't spare a man? Or they refuse Randy's request outright?"

"I'm not running, honey," Desperado said. "I've had my fill of running."

"They'll hang you."

"Not if I can help it."

Chloe wiped her palms on her denims and started to walk away.

"Where are you going?"

"To get my guns and make sure there's enough ammunition on hand. The only way they'll take you is over my dead body."

Desperado stared at her. "God, I love you. Does nothing frighten you?"

"Only the thought of life without you."

"Sit down, honey, and eat your breakfast. If they come, it won't be for a while yet."

Desperado wasn't about to let Chloe place herself in danger. He'd lock her in her room if he had to. Calvin Talbot was ruthless. Desperado knew this vendetta was no longer a matter of land or railroad rights; it went far deeper than that now. Calvin Talbot had taken a simple desire for land to a more personal level. Talbot couldn't tolerate defeat. Nothing short of Desperado's death would satisfy him now. Talbot would go to any lengths, attempt anything to see the deed done.

"What are you thinking?" Chloe asked when Desperado fell into an uneasy silence.

"About many things. If I hadn't taken it into my head to visit Trouble Creek, I would have never met you."

"Are you sorry?"

"God, no! If not for you I would have gone through my entire life without knowing love. I've come to a difficult conclusion concerning my father. I now realize he really did care for me. He kept me alive in his heart all those years when everyone else gave me up for dead. I no longer blame him for sending me away to please your mother. I've even tried to put aside my hatred for the woman who separated me from my father."

"I know my mother wronged you, Desperado. She told me once that she'd never liked you, but I never realized the depth of her hatred, or what she had done to you. She'd always feared Indians and must have felt threatened by your Indian blood. I'm not apologizing for my mother. She was a complex woman not even I fully understood."

"I don't expect you to apologize for your mother. She brought you into the world, and I'm grateful to her for that. Forget Norie, honey. Now there's just you and me and the love we share."

"And the Talbots," Chloe reminded him.

"We'll cross that bridge when we come to it. Meanwhile, let's take care of the animals and wait for the next development. Maybe we're anticipating something that will never happen."

"Ha! Maybe I have black hair and weigh two hundred pounds."

Two rapid strides brought him to her side. His eyes sparkled with mischief as he eyed her critically. "Two hundred pounds? Hmmm, I don't know. I'm not sure my arms would reach around you." He made a circle with his arms, placing the fingertips of both hands together and visually comparing the circumference inside his arms to her trim figure. "That's a whole lot of woman."

"Fool," Chloe chided, walking into his arms. "I don't intend to get that fat, not even when I'm carrying your child."

"Now that's a thought," Desperado mused. "You could be carrying my child now."

Chloe buried her head against his shoulder. She thought about telling him she was already carrying his child, but the time wasn't right. He didn't need someone else to worry about with the Talbots stalking him.

Apparently he wasn't expecting an answer, for he kissed her hard. Then he reluctantly removed his arms from around her. "I'd best get the chores done before unexpected company shows up. Don't worry, love. Everything is going to be just fine."

Chloe wished she felt as confident as Desperado.

"One more thing," he said, pausing at the back door. "Desperado Jones is a man with a violent past. I'm putting all that behind me. It's time you called me Logan."

"I'd like that, too . . . Logan," Chloe whispered. She said his name again, loving the way it rolled off her tongue.

Toward mid-afternoon Chloe glanced out the kitchen window and saw a group of riders approaching the house. She ran for her guns first, then grabbed her jacket from the hook by the door and rushed outside to find Desper . . . Logan. She

Connie Mason

found him inside the new barn, forking hay into the horse stalls.

"They're coming!" Chloe said, skidding to a halt beside him. "Too many for us to handle. You saddle the horses and I'll pack provisions."

"No!" He grabbed her arm, stopping her in mid-flight. "I told you, I'm not running. I've done nothing wrong." He stepped out of the barn and spotted the riders immediately. His brow furrowed as he squinted into the distance. Suddenly his lips curved into a smile.

"What's so funny?" Chloe asked, growing angry at his stubbornness. "Do you have some kind of death wish?"

"Look at the riders, honey. Go ahead, take a good look."

Chloe focused her gaze on the group of men riding through the front gate and gave a whoop of gladness. "The Ralston cowboys! They've come back."

"Come on, let's welcome them home."

Placing an arm around her shoulders, he led her into the yard to await them.

"Desperado!" Cory cried as he slid off his dancing horse and thumped Logan on the back. "None of us believed you were dead. We came back as soon as we heard the news."

"How's Rowdy?" Chloe asked.

"He's mending. Juanita is taking good care of him. I told him we'd let him know when it was safe to return."

"The whole town is talking about the new posse Mr. Talbot has hired," Sonny revealed. "Only three men agreed to ride with him and Tate. We figured it was time to come back. Together we can whup their asses."

"Sonny, mind your language," Cory chided.

"Sorry, Miss Chloe."

"Forget it, Sonny," Chloe said, smiling. Except for Logan, she'd never been so glad to see anyone in her life. "Have you heard when the posse intends to ride?"

Cory shrugged. "Soon, I reckon." He looked to Logan for direction. "What do you want us to do, Desperado?"

"For starters," Logan said, "you can call me Logan. That goes for the rest of the hands, too. Logan is my name. Desperado Jones is a legend. I think it's time to let the legend die."

"If that's what you want, Desper . . . Logan," Cory said, grinning boyishly.

"Now that that's taken care of, I want you boys to remain in the bunkhouse when the posse arrives. There are only five men, I can handle that number without help. The fewer men involved, the less chance of one of you getting hurt. I'll signal if I need you."

"Logan, is that wise?" Chloe asked worriedly.

"It's the way it's got to be, honey. I don't want you out here, either. You're to remain in the house while I confront the posse."

"No!"

"No arguments, Chloe. I'm not taking chances with your life."

Chloe said nothing. Rather than argue with Logan she would do as she pleased. She wasn't taking any chances with *his* life, either.

The hands went to the barn to tend to their horses, then they drifted to the bunkhouse to await further orders from Logan. Chloe and Logan returned to the house. If Logan was nervous, he didn't show it as he checked his guns and positioned them in his holster. Then he sat down and nursed a cup of coffee, moving his chair to where he had an unobstructed view of the road. Chloe sat beside him, sharing the silence.

Logan spotted them first. Chloe saw him stiffen and knew the moment she dreaded had arrived. She glanced out the window and saw five riders. They thundered through the gate and skidded to a halt in front of the house. Calvin Talbot dismounted and bellowed for Desperado to come out peacefully. Logan rose and walked through the house to the front door. Chloe was close on his heels.

Logan hissed a final warning. "Stay out of this, Chloe."

Ignoring him, Chloe darted in front of him and yelled a warning through the closed door. "Shoot him in cold blood, Calvin Talbot, and I'll kill you. I'm a crack shot and you know it."

Abruptly Logan shoved her aside and opened the door. He stepped out onto the porch, his right hand poised at his side. "You're making a mistake, Talbot. You don't have enough men with you to take me."

"There are five guns trained on you, Desperado. You don't stand a chance," Tate said pugnaciously.

"I could kill you right now for bedding my wife. Don't try to deny it. I know what went on here after you chased me from my own home."

"I'm not your wife and this has never been your home," Chloe called from the doorway.

"You know better than that," Tate guffawed. "Reverend Tully married us before witnesses. We both signed the marriage papers. Pa was there, too, he can verify it."

"Bring me the document Tate signed," Logan told Chloe.

Chloe raced upstairs and removed the document from a drawer. Then she raced back down and gave it to Logan.

"Get back in the house," he ordered her as he handed the document to Calvin. "Read what Chloe, Tate and the witnesses signed, Talbot. Then tell me if Chloe is married to Tate."

"Let me see, Pa," Tate said as he dismounted and joined his father.

"Sonofabitch!" Calvin cursed as he scanned the document. When he finished, he passed it to Tate. "Here. Read for yourself. You were an idiot to sign something without reading it first. We've been had. I'll drag that preacher's name through the mud for this."

"What the hell!" Tate cursed, unable to comprehend what he was reading. "This is an application to join the First Baptist Church of Trouble Creek. This ain't a marriage license."

"No, it isn't," Chloe gloated. "Reverend Tully outsmarted both of you. He knew it would be morally wrong to force a woman to marry against her will, so he did what he could to help me. He substituted what you're reading for the marriage license and prayed that you wouldn't inspect it too closely."

"You mean we ain't married?" Tate asked, clearly bewildered.

"That's exactly what it means," Logan answered. "Chloe is going to marry, all right, but she's going to marry me. Neither you nor your father has a legal hold on this land. Now I suggest you get the hell out of here before I lose my temper," he rasped.

"You said this was going to be easy, Mr. Talbot," one of the men riding with the posse complained. "I ain't gonna trade shots with Desperado Jones."

The other two men shifted uncomfortably, eyeing Logan with misgivings. "Ain't a man alive can outdraw Desperado Jones," the second man said. "I don't need money that bad. I'm getting the hell outta here while I still can."

"Stay where you are," Calvin snarled. "The first man to turn tail and run gets a bullet in his back."

"If either of the Talbots even look like they're going to shoot at you, they'll leave here in a casket," Logan said in a voice that would have frightened a ghost from his grave. "This is between the Talbots and me. They've been trying to get rid of me ever since I refused to do their dirty work for them. If I were you, I'd ride back to town while you still can."

That was all the three men had to hear. None of them had anything against Desperado Jones. Hell, they admired the man. They just happened to be hard up for money. Without a backward glance, they spurred their mounts and rode away.

When Calvin raised his gun as if to shoot, Logan said, "Shoot and you're a dead man."

"Damn you!" Calvin ranted. "Why did you have to come along and ruin everything? If not for you, Tate would be married to Chloe and this land would be his. The land no longer matters, now. This is a personal vendetta between you and me, Jones."

"He's mine, Pa," Tate claimed. "He took my woman."

"I was never yours, Tate!" Chloe exclaimed as she joined Logan on the porch. "You took me by force and taught me to loathe all men. Thank God for Logan. He showed me what love could be like between a man and a woman. You're nothing but an animal."

Tate charged at Chloe, forgetting Logan in his eagerness to punish her. "You bitch! You liked it and you know it. I gave you exactly what you wanted."

All of a sudden Tate was looking down the barrel of a six-shooter that was loaded, cocked and ready to fire. He skidded to a halt, his eyes bulging in fear. "You ain't gonna shoot me, are you?"

"I'm tempted," Logan said. "If I ever hear you say anything bad about Chloe again, I'll come gunning for you. Do I make myself clear?"

"You can't threaten me," Tate said with false bravado.

"I just did."

"Do something, Pa. You're the mayor."

"What happened to your brave town marshal?"

Logan asked. "My guess is that he was afraid to come out here to face me."

"He's a coward," Calvin spat. "Just like my son and all the other men in this town. You haven't heard the last from me, Desperado Jones."

"You're talking to the wrong man," Logan said. "My name is Logan Ralston, and don't you forget it. Now get on your horses and ride. If you know what's good for you, you won't come back."

"Company," Chloe announced, pointing to a pair of riders cantering down the road. It wasn't until they reached the gate that she recognized one of the men. "It's Randy!"

Suddenly men began spilling out from the bunkhouse. "It's Randy," Cory cried, waving his hand in greeting. "We saw him from the window. Who's that with him?"

Logan grinned. Randy couldn't have picked a better time to arrive. Not that he needed help. He had the situation well in hand. From the corner of his eye he saw Calvin and Tate edge toward their horses.

"Oh, no, you don't. You're not going anywhere until Randy gets here with the Ranger."

"Ranger?" Tate said. "Texas Ranger? The Rangers have no cause to interfere in our business. Everything Pa did was legal."

"Shut up!" Calvin bit out. "You don't know a damn thing."

Randy and the Ranger reined in beside the Talbots. Randy slid from the saddle and gave his report to Logan. "Sorry we're late. We were delayed by the weather. And Captain Danson was waiting for an answer to a telegram he sent. I told him everything that you told me to say, Desperado."

"You arrived in plenty of time, Randy. I'm glad you're here, Captain Danson," Logan said, offering his hand to the Ranger.

Captain Danson shook Logan's hand. The ranger was a man of around forty with a sun-baked, weather-beaten complexion. "So you're Desperado Jones. I've wanted to meet the fastest gun in the West for a long time. What's going on here, Mr. Jones?"

"The name is Logan, Captain. Logan Ralston. Desperado Jones no longer exists. How much did Randy tell you?"

"Enough to bring me to Trouble Creek." He directed his gaze at the Talbots, singling out Calvin. "You must be Calvin Talbot. Our office has received numerous complaints about your land dealings. Several ranchers reported that they were cheated out of their land, that you used underhanded methods to force them to sell to you at rock-bottom prices."

"I've done nothing illegal," Calvin protested.

"Maybe, maybe not," Danson said as he studied Calvin through keenly intelligent brown eyes. "That's why I'm here. I've been authorized to investigate your transactions with area ranchers."

"All my land dealings have been aboveboard," Calvin claimed.

"There's been talk about the railroad building a spur line clear to Dodge City," Danson revealed. "Rumor had it that the spur would pass through Trouble Creek. It's no coincidence that the land you purchased lay in the railroad's proposed path, is it?" Danson charged. "I think you might be interested in a telegram I received before I left Amarillo."

He removed the telegram from his pocket and handed it to Calvin. Calvin briefly scanned the telegram, glanced at Danson as if he wanted to say something, then reread it.

"No! This can't be true," he cried after the second reading. "I've put all my cash into those properties. The railroad *has* to come through Trouble Creek."

"What's it say, Pa?" Tate asked.

"Here, read it for yourself." He handed the telegram to Tate, his scowl deepening.

"The railroad ain't coming through Trouble Creek!" Tate exclaimed. "They're gonna bypass the town and hook up with the Denver City Railroad in Amarillo. That means we're left with land we can't use. We're land poor."

"I'm not even sure you'll keep the land after my investigation is concluded," Danson revealed. "The ranchers claim you used illegal means to force them to sell out to you. Complaints have been building for some time against you, Mr. Talbot. Even if Randy hadn't arrived when he did, I would have showed up here sooner or later to look into the claims."

Logan sent Calvin a mocking grin. "Seems to me that all your machinations have brought you nothing but trouble with the law, Talbot. Your son is going to be in even bigger trouble when Captain Danson investigates the ambush Tate planned for me a few weeks ago."

"Randy told me about that," Danson said. "I'd like to talk to Marshal Townsend before I begin the investigation. Randy said you were shot and left for dead, Desper . . . Mr. Ralston."

"Townsend!" Tate spat, throwing caution to the wind. "He skipped town the same day he learned Desperado was alive, the yellow-bellied polecat."

"You've said enough, Tate," Calvin hissed. "You never did know when to keep your mouth shut."

"Sorry, Pa," Tate apologized.

"I'm Chloe Sommers," Chloe said when no one saw fit to introduce her. "Would you like to come inside, Captain? There's coffee on the stove. You and Randy must be cold and hungry. It won't take long to rustle up something to eat."

"Thank you, Miss Sommers, coffee and a bite to eat sounds mighty good. There are questions I'd like to ask you and Mr. Ralston about that shoot-out in the street, and now is as good a time as any."

"Desperado killed a man in cold blood," Tate blurted out. "That wasn't a shoot-out, that was plain murder."

"I suppose you have witnesses to prove that, Mr. Talbot," Danson said.

"I said shut up, Tate," Calvin warned. "Sometimes my son talks too much, Captain," Calvin said more reasonably. "Of course there were witnesses."

"As soon as I finish here, I'll want to meet them," Danson advised.

"We'll just mosey on back to town," Calvin said, edging toward his horse. "I'll be in my office if you want me, Captain."

"Just wait a damn minute," Tate said. "I ain't going nowhere without my wife."

Chloe faced Tate squarely, hands on hips, her lips a belligerent scowl. "I'm not your wife and never have been, Tate Talbot. If you don't get off my land, you're going to be mighty sorry."

Calvin pushed Tate none too gently toward his horse. "Mount up, Tate. You never were too bright. Must have taken after your mother."

"Don't leave town," Danson warned.

No answer was forthcoming as they mounted and rode away.

Chloe ushered Danson through the house and invited him into the kitchen. Randy was also invited inside but he opted to return to the bunkhouse with the hands. "They'll be anxious to hear about my adventures," he explained. "Especially the part about my stumbling into an Indian village."

Logan and Danson sat at the kitchen table and conversed quietly while Chloe prepared food for the Ranger. She set a plate of ham and potatoes in front of Danson, pulled up a chair and joined them.

"Did you tell Captain Danson about the ambush Tate planned for you, Logan? And why it had been arranged in the first place?" she asked.

"I explained that the only way Talbot could get his hands on the Ralston spread was to kill me and have Tate marry you. So he challenged me. But Tate never intended to draw against me, for he knew he would lose. Instead, he resorted to trickery. I saw the man on the roof and suspected foul play. Actually, there were two men hidden from view, both with their sights on me. They would have killed me before I had a chance to draw on Tate if I hadn't spotted them first."

He said nothing about Chloe shooting one of the men, and the guarded look he gave Chloe warned her not to reveal her part in the shoot-out.

"I assume you have witnesses," Danson said around a mouthful of ham.

"Chloe and two hands from the Ralston spread saw the whole thing. If that's not good enough, ask Mr. Baker, the lawyer. He was a witness to the shooting. They were all standing on the landing outside the lawyer's office and had an unrestricted view. There might even be some townspeople willing to speak out against the Talbots now that you're here to protect them."

"What about the town marshal? Didn't he try to stop the shoot-out?"

"Ha!" Chloe snorted. "Townsend is Calvin Talbot's man. Calvin got Townsend appointed marshal even though he had little experience for the job. He spent his days drinking in the Devil's Den saloon and his nights carousing with whores. He was a coward and Calvin's lackey."

Danson's eyes crinkled with amusement. "You don't mince words, Miss Sommers."

"That's one of the things I find so endearing about my fiancée, Captain," Logan said. "By the way, you're invited to the wedding if you're still in town."

"Logan Ralston," Chloe chided, "if you're planning a wedding any time soon, I should be the first to know about it."

"Oh, didn't I tell you?" he said with a grin.

"I want to personally thank Reverend Tully for what he did for you," he went on. "Since he was so helpful, I was going to ask him to perform the ceremony at his earliest convenience. Perhaps Mr. Baker will consent to give the bride away, if that's agreeable to you."

"When is all this going to take place?" Chloe wanted to know.

"I think the weather is going to hold for a while. How does next week sound? I want to invite the whole town to the church. Afterward they can all come out to the house for food and drink. We can get Juanita back and hire a woman from town to help with the preparations."

"You've got everything all planned, haven't you?"

"Sounds like it to me," Danson said, suppressing a chuckle.

"I have but one request, and only you can grant it."

Chloe's brows rose. "Name it and I'll think about it."

"Can you please wear a dress when we stand up in church? I don't care for myself, I love you in trousers, but you might shock the preacher, not to mention the congregation."

Danson rose abruptly, his lips curved in amusement. "I think that's my cue to leave. If I need to question you further, I'll ride out. And about the wedding. I'd be proud to attend."

Danson took his leave. Chloe started to clean up the kitchen. She let out a startled gasp when Logan came up behind her, grasped her around the waist and pressed a kiss on her nape. Then he turned her to face him, and her gaze flew up to meet his when she felt his erection pressing against the softness between her legs. She brought her hand between them and touched him.

"What brought that on?" she asked coyly.

"Thinking about our wedding. I pictured you without your trousers and gunbelt. The thought of you in a dress was so arousing I couldn't help myself. You didn't answer my question, honey. Will you honor my request?"

"A dress," Chloe whispered wistfully. "I can't remember when I wore a dress last." Suddenly she frowned, finally recalling when she'd last worn a dress.

"What is it? Did you remember something?"

Chloe buried her head against his shoulder. "I remembered when I last wore a dress. It was the night I went to the dance with Tate. The night he—" She shuddered, the memory still vividly painful. That night she'd removed her ripped and soiled dress and vowed never to let a man take advantage of her again. The following day she'd ridden into town and bought a supply of boys' trousers and silk shirts. And a pair of six-shooters.

"Forget about that night, honey. Think about your future with Logan Ralston. I promise that no man will ever hurt you again."

He lifted her face so he could look into her eyes. They were misty with tears. He touched her lips with his and tasted her tears.

"Are those tears of joy or sorrow?"

"I have nothing to be unhappy about," she said, giving him a watery smile. Her arms tightened around him. "I have everything I want right here in my arms. Make love to me, Logan. I want to put the past behind me."

He swept her into his arms and took the steps two at a time. "I don't know what I ever did to deserve you, love."

"I'll remind you every day for the rest of our lives."

Logan closed the bedroom door behind them and turned the key in the newly repaired lock. Then he undressed her, worshiping her with his eyes and mouth as each piece of her clothing fell away.

"Let me undress you," Chloe whispered as she carefully removed his coat and vest and undid the buttons on his shirt.

When she didn't move fast enough to suit him, he aided her by removing his gunbelt and peeling his trousers down to the tops of his boots. Then he sat on the edge of the bed and finished the task. Chloe had already joined him on the bed, touching him intimately while he struggled with his clothing.

"If you don't stop that, this will end before it gets started."

"I love touching you," Chloe said with a hint of mischief. "Your body is so different from mine."

"Thank God," Logan said, rolling his eyes heavenward.

"Will our loving change after we're married?"

"It's bound to," Logan teased.

Chloe reared up on her elbows and glared at him. "Explain yourself, Mr. Ralston."

He flashed his dimple at her and said in that sexy-as-hell voice, "Our loving can only get better. You know what they say. Practice makes perfect."

Chloe flopped back down on the mattress. "If it gets any better I'm likely to die from pleasure."

Logan laughed. "You'll only die a little. Each time we make love will be like a glimpse of heaven. Now shut up and let me love you."

Their loving was slow and sweet at first. Logan took his time to arouse her, paying special attention to her sensitive breasts. But when he finally slid inside her wet center, his gentleness gave way to fierce need as he penetrated her with strong, deep strokes, wringing a cry from her and sending hot blood singing through her veins. His loins pumped against hers, giving her everything he was capable of giving, accepting her passionate homage in return.

Sweat drenched their bodies, love filled their souls, and then the end came in a firestorm of heat that fused them together, body and soul.

"If that didn't make a baby, then I don't know what will," Logan gasped against her mouth.

"Baby?" Chloe asked. She was still dazed, her body vibrating with the aftermath of passion.

Logan rolled to his side. "You want children, don't you? We've never talked about it."

"Do you?"

Chloe let her breath out in a long, slow sigh. He was silent so long, she feared his answer would be negative. Whatever was she going to do if he didn't want children?

"I'd love to have children with you," he said after a long pause.

Chloe knew he'd given her the perfect opening to tell him about the baby, but she was too tired. There was plenty of time to give him the happy news, she decided as she slid effortlessly into sleep.

Chapter Nineteen

The next day dawned cold and clear, with no sign of snow on the horizon. After breakfast Logan announced that he was going to town to call on Reverend Tully. Chloe decided to remain at the ranch since there was much to be done now that the hands had returned. Logan kissed her lingeringly and rode off.

Chloe decided not to accompany the hands when they rode out to repair fences and round up strays. She busied herself with chores in and around the barn, thinking about her baby and imagining Logan's pleasure when she told him she was expecting.

Around midday she heard wagon wheels and walked out into the yard to greet Juanita as she drove the buckboard through the gate. Rowdy sat beside her, looking pale but much better than the last time Chloe had seen him. She hurried up to greet them.

"Mr. Ralston stopped at the hotel and told us it was safe to return," Juanita explained as she jumped from the seat and went around to help Rowdy.

"I'm glad," Chloe said, genuinely happy to see the pair. "I've missed you. I'll help you bring Rowdy into the house."

"No need for that, Miss Chloe," Rowdy said. "I'm well enough to bunk in with the boys now." He gave Juanita a shy smile. "Maybe Juanita can check up on me once in a while."

"If that's all right with Senorita Chloe," Juanita said.

Chloe recognized a budding romance when she saw one. "Of course Juanita can continue to supervise your recovery. She can help you settle in now, if she'd like."

"Oh, *sí*," Juanita said, glowing happily.

Chloe watched them walk off together to the bunkhouse, then returned to the house to fix herself some lunch. Logan returned just as she was about to sit down to a cold lunch of leftover roast beef.

"I'll set a plate for you," Chloe said, greeting Logan with a lusty kiss.

"Ummm, if that's the kind of welcome I can look forward to, I'll make a practice of leaving more often. Did Juanita and Rowdy return?"

"They arrived a short time ago. Rowdy seems to be recovering well."

"Juanita takes good care of him. Did you see the reverend?"

"I did. How does Saturday sound? Reverend Tully is free to perform the ceremony on Saturday, and I told him that would be fine. I also took the liberty of posting invitations to the townspeople in various locations around town. The post office, telegraph office, bank and barbershop."

"Saturday. That's only four days away."

"Too soon?" Logan asked.

She shook her head. "No, I'm more than ready. I'll need to make a trip to town, however, to purchase provisions for the reception and to ask Mr. Baker to give me away. Then I'll need to find someone to help Juanita prepare food for the reception."

"We'll take the buckboard into town tomorrow," Logan said. "I don't want you going alone. Not while the Talbots are still around. I spoke with Captain Danson today. He's been interviewing witnesses to the shoot-out. He said everyone who had seen it corroborated my version of what happened. He told me I have nothing to worry about from the law."

"Thank God," Chloe said with a sigh. "What about Marshal Townsend?"

"Gone. He lit out of town, just like Tate said."

"And the Talbots?"

"They're still around, but I wonder for how long. Captain Danson is investigating their dealings with ranchers who sold land to him. He's going to ask Thadeous Baker to relinquish those documents pertaining to Talbot's transactions. Talbot could go to jail if Danson proves he had anything to do with the cattle rustlings and strong-arm methods used to frighten ranchers."

"The Talbots deserve everything that's coming to them," Chloe said with asperity.

They finished their lunch and Logan rose to leave. "Where are the hands working?"

"In the south pasture, repairing fences."

"I reckon I'll ride out to help. But first I'll stop by to see Rowdy."

"Send Juanita back to the house," Chloe said. "I want to tell her about the reception and the extra work it will entail. Maybe she knows of someone in town willing to help." Suddenly she looked thoughtful. "Can we afford it? There isn't much money left in the bank."

"There is plenty of money," he said cryptically. "I'll tell you about it later."

"I have something to tell you, too," she called after him.

Logan entered the bunkhouse, gave Juanita Chloe's message, and approached Rowdy's bunk.

"How are you feeling?" he asked, searching Rowdy's face. He thought Rowdy lacked his usual color but seemed to be well on his way to recovery.

"Much better. I'll be pulling my weight around here in a day or two."

"Don't rush it. Things are slow right now. I plan to buy cattle to fill out our herd soon. That's when you'll be needed."

"Desperado . . . I—"

"Call me Logan, that's my name now. Spit it out, boy. What's on your mind?"

"I owe you an apology. I didn't like you at first. I thought you were out to hurt Miss Chloe and didn't trust you. Truth is, I wanted to be like you and knew I never could be. I envied your . . . relationship with Miss Chloe. We all knew what was going on between you two. There was a time I wanted to kill you."

"What changed your mind?" Logan asked curiously.

"I guess it was getting to know you, and realizing you really cared for Miss Chloe. I was jealous, if you want to know the truth. But since meeting Juanita I realize that what I felt for Miss Chloe was infatuation. It was all wishful thinking with no substance. I'll leave if you say you no longer want me here."

"I guessed what your problem was long before you realized it yourself," Logan said. "I don't hold grudges, Rowdy. You're welcome to stay. Taking that bullet was rough on you. I'm sorry it happened."

"Much obliged, Desper . . . Logan. You won't be sorry."

"By the way," Logan said in parting, "Chloe and I are getting married Saturday. I hope you're well enough to attend."

"Depend on it," Rowdy said.

Logan smiled all the way to the south pasture.

The next day Logan hitched the horses to the buckboard for their trip to town. With Juanita's help, Chloe had prepared a list of provisions needed for the reception. Juanita had given her the name of a poor Mexican family with daughters in need of work, and Chloe hoped to hire them to help with the reception.

They set out shortly after breakfast, turning down the muddy main street of Trouble Creek two hours later. Chloe had been so intent upon her list and wedding plans that she had not told Logan about the baby. But Logan hadn't forgotten to explain about the money his father had left for him in the bank. By the time he finished telling her how he intended to fix up the house and restock their herd, they were pulling into town.

Logan parked the buckboard in front of the general store. "I have some business at the bank," he said as he lifted her to the ground. "Buy whatever you need and have it loaded in the buckboard. Tell Mr. Potter I'll pay for the purchases when I'm finished at the bank. Buy yourself something pretty to wear," he added in parting.

Chloe made her purchases with time to spare. Logan returned to pay for them and they went together to the lawyer's office. Mr. Baker didn't seem surprised to see them.

"I wondered when you two would come back to be married," he said jovially. "I couldn't believe Chloe had married that no-good Tate Talbot. It's all over town how Chloe and Reverend Tully outfoxed the Talbots." He shook his head. "It makes me hopping mad when I think how that unholy pair tried to force Chloe into marriage. This isn't the first time they defied the law to gain their own ends.

"That Texas Ranger fellow was here yesterday to question me about their dealings. I gave him plenty of information and the documentation he requested. I hope that pair gets what they so richly deserve."

"We all feel that way, Mr. Baker," Chloe said. "Their illegal dealings have gone on too long."

"Right. But enough of that. Let's get down to important matters. I reckon you're eager to get hitched."

"I hope you won't mind, Mr. Baker," Logan explained. "But we owe Reverend Tully a great deal and I've asked him to marry us in the church. Our wedding will take place on Saturday. We're here because, well, Chloe has something to ask you."

Chloe took up where Logan left off. "I don't have a father, Mr. Baker. Ted was the closest thing to a father I had and he's dead. I wonder . . . that is, will you give me away?"

A wide grin split the old man's craggy features. "Why, that's the nicest thing anyone has ever asked me to do. I'd be right proud to give you away. Tell me the time and I'll be there with bells on."

"Ten o'clock Saturday morning," Logan said. "Don't be late. Nothing is going to stop us this time."

"You can count on me."

They took their leave and walked to the cafe for lunch. Then they returned to the buckboard. The supplies had been loaded inside and covered with a tarp they had brought along for that purpose. Logan lifted Chloe onto the unsprung seat and leaped up beside her. "Didn't Juanita give you the name of a family who might be willing to help with the preparations for our reception?"

371

"She did. The Lopez family lives in a small house on the street behind the Devil's Den."

Logan grasped the reins and set the team into motion. They located the house with little difficulty. Senora Lopez answered Chloe's knock. Chloe stated her business, explaining that Juanita had sent her. Senora Lopez called her two daughters, Lolita and Maria, and Chloe explained again what she wanted. Both girls promptly agreed to help Juanita prepare the wedding feast. The senora thanked Chloe profusely when Chloe mentioned the pay each girl would receive for two days' work. They promised to be at the ranch bright and early the following morning.

Their business concluded, Logan drove the buckboard out of town. The weather still held. The sun was dipping low in the sky, but to Chloe the day was still bright with promise. Never had she been so happy. Logan must have been of the same mind, for he put his arm around her and hugged her. Then he smiled, and kept smiling.

Chloe smiled back. This was the man she'd always known existed beneath the rough exterior of Desperado Jones. This was the man she'd fallen in love with, not the man with the violent reputation. The legend of Desperado Jones was a sham, invented in part by Desperado himself to instill fear in his enemies. No man in his right mind wanted to tangle with the legendary gunman with a lightning draw. The fear he had inspired had probably saved Desperado's life on more than one occasion. That plus his skill to draw faster and shoot more accurately than any other man.

"What are you thinking, love?" Logan asked when she remained silent for a long time.

Her green eyes sparkled. "I'm wondering—" Her sentence ended in a surprised gurgle when she felt cold steel pressing against her neck.

"What's the matter?" Logan asked when he felt her stiffen.

"I . . . we're not alone," Chloe managed to say.

"Who—"

"Stop the wagon," a voice from behind them ordered. "Don't try anything if you want your whore to live."

"Tate Talbot!" Logan rasped. "Where in the hell did you come from?"

"I hid beneath the canvas. What took you so long? I was about to suffocate under there."

"What do you want?"

Ignoring Logan, he sent Chloe a purely evil grin. "I want *her*. Just once before I leave. Pa is already packed and ready to light out before that blasted Texas Ranger arrests him. Pa just learned that the railroad intends to buy land in the Oklahoma panhandle. The Oklahoma spur will complete the line from Amarillo to Dodge City. Pa intends to head up there and buy up land. There's still money to be made, and the Texas Rangers can't touch us there."

"Shouldn't you be with your father now?" Chloe asked in an effort to distract him.

"This won't take long," Tate said. "Empty your gunbelts, both of you. Toss your guns back here."

When Logan's right hand inched toward his gun butt, Tate cocked his own gun and warned, "I swear I'll shoot if you try anything funny. Chloe owes me a wedding night, but if I have to kill her I will. Neither of us will have her then. It's your choice."

"Don't shoot," Logan rasped as he removed his guns and tossed them behind him into the wagon bed.

"You next, Chloe," Tate ordered.

Chloe hesitated but a moment before tossing her guns to join Logan's.

"Now what?" Logan asked.

"Get down. Real easy like. My gun is still pressed against Chloe's neck and my finger is mighty itchy."

Logan climbed down from the buckboard, casting about for a way to take Tate without endangering Chloe's life.

Tate pulled a rope from beneath the canvas and tied Chloe's hands behind her with his free hand. Then he pulled her down into the wagon bed and rolled her up in the tarp.

"Don't hurt her," Logan warned. "There's nowhere you can run, no place you can hide if you harm her."

"Shut up, Jones," Tate growled as he climbed down from the buckboard. Obviously he had come well prepared, for he held another rope in his free hand. "Walk over to that tree," he ordered, pointing to a sturdy tree a dozen yards from the buckboard. "Don't try to be a hero. I'd just as soon shoot you as look at you. The only thing holding me back is the thought that I could be hanged for murder."

Logan did as he was told, casting furtive glances over his shoulder at Chloe, who was struggling in vain to escape from beneath the canvas. He would have jumped Tate and taken a chance at getting himself killed if it wasn't for Chloe. His death wouldn't help her. He needed to live for her sake.

"Hug the tree," Tate said. When Logan complied, Tate began twisting the rope around Logan's wrists, securing him to the tree. Then, for good measure he wound the rope around Logan's body.

Logan couldn't move, could scarcely breathe. Never had he felt such overwhelming fear for another human being. He loved Chloe completely, and the thought of Tate hurting her made his blood run cold. He knew what Tate intended. He wouldn't kill Chloe, but he'd make her wish she were dead. Rape was a horrible thing for any woman to endure, and Chloe had already suffered Tate's brutality once.

"Don't worry, Jones," Tate gloated. "You can have her after I'm through with her. If you still want her, that is. Just remember this while I'm rutting with your woman; I had her first. My leavings are all you've ever had of her."

"Bastard!" Logan hissed, struggling to free himself. "I'll follow you to hell and back if I have to."

The color drained from Tate's face. Logan's threat might have frightened him but it didn't deter him. "Be grateful that you don't have to watch," he said in parting. "By the time I'm through with Chloe and she works free of the ropes, I'll be long gone. I had a friend follow the buckboard with my horse. When the buckboard stopped, he tied my horse out of sight and skedaddled, like I instructed."

Logan cursed violently as Tate returned to the buckboard, but Tate was so intent upon having his way with Chloe that he paid Logan little heed. He climbed into the wagon bed and unrolled the canvas imprisoning Chloe. She came out kicking and yelling.

"Damn you! What have you done to Logan?"

"Your lover is fine, just don't expect any help from him. I didn't kill him, if that's what's worrying you. I don't want the law on my tail." He placed his gun down where he could reach it in a hurry and pulled off her boots. Then he began unfastening her trousers. "This was a lot easier when you wore skirts," he complained. "Hold still. You're hurting my shoulder with all your squirming and lurching. This ain't gonna hurt you. I just want that wedding night we never had."

"I'm warning you, Tate," Chloe hissed. "I'm not going to let you do this to me."

He gave a vicious snarl and slapped her, hard. "How are you going to stop me?"

Chloe reeled from the blow. While she lay stunned and in pain, Tate managed to work her trousers and drawers down her hips. Chloe cried out a protest when she felt him jerk her trousers and drawers the rest of the way down her legs and over her feet.

Apparently Logan heard her cry for he called out her name.

Chloe watched in trepidation as Tate sat back on his haunches and stared at her, his eyes glittering lasciviously. He licked his lips and grinned at her. "I didn't get to see you the last time. It was too dark. You're one fine-looking woman, Chloe. All over." Squatting at her feet, he reached over to unbutton her blouse. "Now let me see your titties. They look bigger than they were the last time I had my hands on them."

Rage built inside Chloe. She wasn't going to let Tate do this to her again. The moment he bent over her to remove her blouse, she pulled her legs back and kicked him in the chest. Tate grunted and went flying over the side of the buckboard. He landed hard, and she heard him scream. She scooted to the side of the buckboard and gazed down at Tate, her face filled with loathing.

"My shoulder, I'm dying," he hollered, rolling on the ground and grasping the shoulder that had never mended properly.

"Chloe, what's going on?" Logan yelled. "Talk to me. What did the bastard do to you?"

"I'm fine, Logan, really," Chloe called back. "I'll free you as soon as I get rid of these dang ropes."

"Where is Tate?"

"On the ground. I think he re-injured his collarbone when I kicked him out of the wagon." She gave Tate a contemptuous look. "He's no longer a threat."

"You kicked him out of the wagon?" Logan repeated incredulously.

She heard Logan laughing, and suddenly the tension drained from her. She knew intuitively that Tate Talbot would never be a threat to her again. The fear and terror of that night he had raped her would no longer invade her dreams. She had vanquished them along with the man himself.

It took five minutes for Chloe to work her wrists free. Tate's one-handed knot hadn't been strong enough to hold and she was able to slip her hands free. Then she donned her clothing and boots and leaped down from the wagon bed. Tate was still lying on the ground, sobbing like a baby. She wasted little sympathy on him as she deftly removed his knife from the sheath at his waist.

"Help me," he cried as she stepped over him.

Chloe didn't bother to answer as she raced to Logan's side.

Logan searched Chloe's face; then he let his troubled gaze wander over her body as she sawed at the ropes binding him. "Are you all right?"

"I'm fine," Chloe assured him as the last rope fell away from him.

He was literally shaking when he finally held her in his arms. The knowledge that the legendary Desperado Jones had been helpless to save the woman he loved tormented him. He thanked a God he had abandoned years ago for giving Chloe the strength and courage to singlehandedly save herself. Then he kissed her. He tasted salt from her tears and his own eyes misted.

"Don't cry, sweetheart. It's over," Logan soothed. "I'm going to kill the bastard so he'll never hurt you again."

"Your cheeks are wet," Chloe said in wonder as she brushed away moisture from the corners of his eyes. It seemed inconceivable that a strong man like Logan would cry.

"Something must have gotten in my eyes," Logan said gruffly as he blinked away the telltale moisture. His arm hugged her shoulders as he led her back to the buckboard and lifted her onto the seat. "Stay here," he advised.

"Where are you going?"

He located his gun in the bed of the buckboard and walked over to Tate.

"Logan, what are you going to do?" Chloe asked, alarmed by the look of cold fury on Logan's face.

"I'm going to put a wounded animal out of his misery," he said as he aimed his weapon at Tate.

"Go ahead," Tate groaned. "You'd be doing me a favor. The pain will kill me if you don't."

"Noooo!" Chloe cried, scrambling down from the buckboard. "You can't kill him. That would make you a cold-blooded murderer. Do you want that on your conscience the rest of your life?"

Logan cocked his gun. "I'd be doing the world a favor."

His voice was hard, cold, emotionless. This wasn't the man Chloe knew and loved. This was Desperado Jones, a man without a conscience. A hired gunman. She couldn't let him turn back into the legend. "You once told me you never killed in cold blood. You said you rarely killed at all, only when your life was threatened."

"This scum threatened *your* life," Logan said through gritted teeth. He aimed for Tate's heart; a clean shot that would end his suffering as well as his miserable life.

"Desperado!" Chloe screamed, hoping her use of his professional name would break through his icy veneer. "Desperado Jones! Is that the name you want to carry the rest of your life? Logan Ralston wouldn't kill; he'd hand his enemy over to the law."

The hollow look in Logan's eyes slowly faded and his fierce expression melted away as he released the hammer and shoved his pistol into his gunbelt. "Desperado Jones has been laid to rest," he vowed. "I promise he'll never surface again. Thank you for preventing me from doing something I'd regret the rest of my life."

"I know how much you hate Tate, but you can't hate him more than I do. You know what we have to do, don't you?"

Logan nodded and walked over to the buckboard.

"You're not leaving him here, are you?"

"No. I'm going to put Tate in the buckboard and take him back to Trouble Creek. I'm sure Captain Danson will know what to do with him."

"I'll get the rest of the guns from the wagon bed," Chloe said.

When Logan lifted Tate to place him in the buckboard, he screamed and passed out.

"It's just as well," Logan said. "The trip back to town won't be pleasant for him."

Tate remained mercifully unconscious. He revived shortly before Logan drove the buckboard down the muddy main street. "Wait here," Logan said to Chloe as he drew rein in front of the now vacant town marshal's office and climbed down from the seat. "I'm going to look for Captain Danson. Keep an eye on Tate. If he looks like he's going to run, shoot him."

"I ain't going nowhere," Tate gasped. "Get me to a doctor. Find Pa. Tell him I'm in a bad way."

"First things first," Logan said as he walked away.

Logan found Captain Danson in the cafe, eating supper.

"What brings you back to town?" Danson asked, surprised to see Logan again so soon.

"I've got Tate Talbot in the back of my wagon," Logan explained. "He hid beneath the canvas covering our supplies and got the drop on us. He's as obsessed with Chloe as his father is with me." His voice lowered as he explained what Tate had done and how Chloe had saved herself.

"That's one spunky woman you've got, Ralston," Danson chuckled. "I've got Tate's old man in jail. Caught him leaving town. I've found enough evidence against him to send him to prison for a long time. After what you've just told me, Tate will be joining him."

"You'd better send for old Doc Hockmeyer," Logan suggested. "Talbot is in a great deal of pain. An old wound he sustained never healed properly, and when Chloe kicked him out of the buckboard he must have landed on his bad shoulder and aggravated the injury. He's been screaming like a stuck pig."

"I'll see what I can do," Danson said, rising. "You and your woman no longer need to worry about the Talbots. I'll be taking them both to Amarillo to stand trial."

Chloe and Logan watched dispassionately as Danson and a volunteer carried Tate to the veterinarian's office. Then they climbed back into the buckboard and headed home.

"I've had about all the excitement I can take for

one day," Chloe sighed as she leaned her head against Logan's broad shoulder.

"Can I interest you in a different kind of excitement tonight?"

"I'm always interested in *that* kind of excitement," Chloe said, smiling up at him.

"Maybe we should wait until we're married," Logan suggested.

Chloe sent him a startled look. "Is that what you want?"

"No. I just thought you might."

Chloe settled more comfortably against Logan's shoulder, growing drowsy as the moon came up to guide them home. She must have slept for a time; when she awakened she remembered there was something she needed to tell Logan.

"Logan . . ."

"I thought you were sleeping."

"There's something I need to tell you."

"It can wait until tomorrow."

"No, it can't. You see—"

"Riders coming," Logan said, removing his arm from around her and reaching for his weapon.

He didn't relax until he heard someone call out, "Is that you, Logan?"

A half dozen riders approached the buckboard and drew rein. "Yeah, Cory, it's me. Something wrong at the ranch?"

"No. We thought something had happened to you and Miss Chloe. When you didn't return from town before dark, me and some of the boys thought we'd ride out to see if you'd encountered trouble."

"We're fine, Cory," Chloe assured him. "We had

a run-in with Tate Talbot, but I'll let Logan tell you about it later."

The buckboard and its escort reached the ranch a short time later. Juanita had supper waiting for Chloe and Logan. They washed up in the bucket of clean water beside the back door and sat down to eat.

"I reckon the boys are anxious to hear about our delay," Logan said after he'd eaten his fill of Juanita's excellent meal. He scraped back his chair and rose. "I'll be back in a little while."

While he was gone, Chloe heated water on the stove and filled the brass tub with Juanita's help. Juanita stood guard at the kitchen door while Chloe had a good long soak. After she washed her hair and rinsed the soap off her body, she dried herself with a soft cloth and went up to bed, sliding naked between the sheets. She was dozing when Logan slipped into the room.

"Are you awake, honey?"

"Almost. What took you so long?"

"I took a bath in the bunkhouse. Randy heated water for me in the cookhouse."

Lamplight highlighted the glistening drops of water clinging to his dark hair as he quickly undressed and slid into bed beside her.

"Ummm, you smell good enough to eat." To prove his words, he gnawed delicately at her ear-lobe.

"So do you."

"You're not too tired, are you?"

"For you? Never."

"I was so proud of you today," Logan said. "Most

women would have fainted dead away had they found themselves in your situation. But not my brave Chloe."

"I wasn't going to let Tate ravish me again," Chloe murmured. "Tate Talbot is an abomination; I don't want to talk about him."

"Neither do I. I just wanted you to know how much I love you. It wouldn't have mattered if Tate had . . . well, you know. It wouldn't make me love you any less. What scared the hell out of me was the possibility that he would do you serious harm, or kill you."

"Thank you for that, Logan. You're one man in a million, the only man I want to make love to me."

She snuggled against him, smiling when she felt his erection prodding against her stomach. She ground her loins against his, savoring his hardness, his need for her, and felt blessed.

He aroused her slowly, taking his time to taste and touch her in all the places that gave her the most pleasure. Then she loved him, using her mouth and hands to rouse him to a fever pitch. When he finally eased into her, they were both so wildly excited they climaxed too quickly. After they had rested, there was nothing for it but to begin again.

"Was that the kind of excitement you had in mind?" Logan teased much later as they rested quietly in each other's arms.

"That's exactly what I had in mind. Now can I tell you what I've been meaning to tell you for the past few days?"

"Ummm."

Chloe took that for a yes. "I'm going to have a baby. Are you happy?"

No answer except for his slow, even breathing.

"You're sleeping!" Chloe charged, exasperated. "Oh, well, I reckon it will keep." She yawned as she fit herself into the curve of his body and joined him in slumber.

Chapter Twenty

The church was packed. People had swarmed in from surrounding ranches to attend the wedding of the notorious Desperado Jones and Miss Chloe Sommers, the gun-toting young lady from the Ralston spread. A group of drifters had read the open invitation Logan had posted and had spruced up to attend the wedding. The word among the drifters was that they were attending not only a wedding but a funeral. In years to come they could brag about witnessing the death of Desperado Jones at the same time they attended the wedding of Logan Ralston.

It was widely circulated about town that Desperado Jones was abandoning his life as a gunslinger and turning respectable. By now most everyone knew that he was the long-lost son of Ted Ralston and owner of the Ralston spread. Though many doubted that a restless spirit like Desperado Jones could settle down to ranching, there were those who predicted that Chloe Sommers was the one woman who could tame the legendary gunslinger. They made one helluva pair. Together they had defeated the land-grabbing Talbots. The pair of crooks were in jail waiting to be transported to Amarillo for trial.

A murmur arose from the crowd when Logan entered the church with Cory, his best man, and strode down the aisle to where Reverend Tully was waiting to perform the ceremony. Logan looked dashing and more than a little dangerous in his newly purchased Sunday best, making more than one woman's heart flutter. He was dressed all in black, down to his black silk shirt, neckcloth and superfine jacket. His trousers hugged his muscular thighs like a second skin and his boots were polished to a splendid luster. His ebony hair was slicked back from his forehead and tied at his nape with a black cord.

Logan fidgeted nervously as he waited for Chloe to walk down the aisle. She hadn't allowed him to see beforehand what she was wearing, but it didn't matter. She could wear sackcloth and she'd still be breathtakingly beautiful. He had caught her rummaging in a trunk in the attic yesterday, but she'd chased him away before he caught a glimpse of what she was digging for.

Beside him Cory appeared as nervous as he. Unaccustomed to wearing fancy duds, he constantly ran his finger around the constricting neckline of his white shirt.

Suddenly the church grew quiet and Logan glanced toward the entrance. His gasp of admiration combined with those of the spectators to produce a hum of approval. Logan had never seen Chloe like this. Couldn't even picture her in such finery. She was a vision in blue velvet trimmed with antique lace. The gown must have come from the trunk, Logan decided, for a town like Trouble Creek couldn't possibly provide so elaborate a dress on such short notice.

Juanita, wearing typical Mexican wedding finery, preceded Chloe down the aisle. Chloe followed, clinging tightly to Thadeous Baker's arm, her wide skirts swaying provocatively, her smile directed at Logan, as if no one existed but him.

Since no flowers were available in winter, Chloe carried the Ralston family Bible, decorated with white ribbon and a bow. As she floated down the aisle, Logan wondered how he had lived to be nearly thirty without her.

Logan glanced at the front pews, noting that all the ranch hands were present. Even Rowdy was there, pale but looking better than he had yesterday. Suddenly Chloe was standing beside him. Thadeous kissed her cheek and placed her arm on Logan's. Smiling into each other's eyes, Logan and Chloe turned to face the preacher.

The ceremony began.

Chloe repeated her vows loud and clear. Logan's voice wobbled slightly but never faltered as he spoke his vow. Then Reverend Tully pronounced them husband and wife, and Logan pulled her into his arms and kissed her amid enthusiastic cheers.

Afterward Chloe couldn't recall how they had arrived outside, or what she'd said to the well-wishers who congratulated them. Her husband was so handsome her heart pounded with pride. She hoped her baby would look just like him if it turned out to be a boy. Her silent musings halted when Logan lifted her into the buckboard for the ride home. They left town in a flurry of dust. They had scant time to prepare for the guests that would begin arriving at the ranch to partake of food and drink.

"I'm never going to forget today," Chloe sighed as she leaned against her husband's broad shoulder.

"As soon as it's dark I'm chasing every one home," Logan vowed. "I've never seen you look so beautiful. There's a special sparkle in your eyes I hadn't noticed before. Did getting hitched put it there?"

"It's the dress," Chloe teased. "Ted bought it for me on his last trip to San Antonio before he died. But don't get used to it, Logan Ralston. Trousers are too comfortable to give up forever. I'm going right back to wearing them after the ba—" Her mouth snapped shut.

"What were you going to say?"

"Nothing that can't wait."

His dark enigmatic gaze rested disconcertingly on her. "Tell me, Chloe. I think it might be important."

She flushed. "Why would you think that?"

"Let me guess. You're going to have a child." Her mouth dropped open. "I've noticed changes in your body lately and it just dawned on me what you almost said. Why didn't you tell me?"

She gave him a wobbly smile. "I did try to tell you on more than one occasion, but something kept interfering."

He flashed his dimples, momentarily distracting her. "Are you happy?" she asked.

"I couldn't ask for anyone more perfect for the mother of my children. How long have you known?"

"A month or so. I'm well into my third month."

Logan sawed on the reins and the team came to a halt. His face drained of all color as he stared at her. "You knew before you were attacked by Tate Talbot?"

"Yes. Why?"

He spit out a curse. "You should have let me kill Tate," he rasped in a voice reminiscent of Desperado Jones, a man Chloe thought had been laid to rest forever.

"You did the right thing, Logan. Tate didn't hurt me."

"You could have been hurt badly. And the baby . . ." She saw his hands shaking and realized just how upset he really was.

"We're both fine, Logan," she said soothingly. "As soon as we get rid of all our guests tonight, I'll show you how well I am."

"Is that a promise, sweetheart?"

She gave him a teasing smile. "You can depend on it."

"Damn," Logan rasped, "let's get this party over with. I want to see if what I told you is true."

Puzzled, Chloe asked, "What was that?"

"I told you sex would be better after we married and I can't wait to test my theory. But I'm warning you now, it will probably take years of steady love-making to prove my theory."

"I've always been good at tests," she said with a twinkle. "Let's go home and celebrate the beginning of the rest of our lives."

Logan picked up the reins and the team jerked forward, carrying them home.

The last of the wedding guests had left. Chloe and Logan walked arm in arm up the stairs. In the cozy confines of their bed they loved, then loved again, and yet again.

The rest of their lives had begun.

AUTHOR'S NOTE

I hope you enjoyed *Gunslinger*. I thought Desperado and Chloe were a match made in heaven. No one but Desperado Jones could have tamed Chloe. Then again, it took a woman with Chloe's spunk and determination to tame Desperado Jones. I love to create strong, virile heroes and give them spirited, independent women like Chloe Sommers to help them mend their wicked ways. Though sometimes flawed, my heroes always come around to my heroine's way of thinking in the end.

Writing *Gunslinger* was great fun. I tried to show the goodness in Desperado while at the same time giving him qualities that frightened men and made women tremble. I hope I succeeded.

My next book, *The Black Knight*, a medieval romance, will be a November 1999 release.

I enjoy hearing from readers and reply personally to all my mail. Sometimes it takes a while, so be patient. For a bookmark and current newsletter, please send a legal-sized, *stamped,* self-addressed envelope in care of Dorchester at the address on the copyright page of this book, and include your name and address on your letter in case the envelope goes astray. Visit my website at:

http://members.aol.com/conmason/index.html/

All My Romantic Best,
Connie Mason

Pirate

Connie Mason

Determined to ruin those who kept him from his heart's only desire, handsome Guy DeYoung becomes a reckless marauder who rampages the isles intent on revenge. But when he finds his lost love, and takes her as his captive, he will not let her go until she freely gives him her body and soul.

__4456-0 $5.99 US/$6.99 CAN

BEYOND THE HORIZON
CONNIE MASON

As the sheltered daughter of the once prosperous Branigan family, beautiful Shannon is ill-prepared for the rigors of the Oregon Trail, but she is still less prepared for half-breed scout Swift Blade. His dark eyes seem to pierce her very soul, stripping away layers of civilization and baring her hidden longing to his savage gaze. His bronzed arms are forbidden to her, his searing kisses just a tantalizing fantasy; but as the countless miles pass beneath the wagon wheels, taking them to the heart of Indian territory, Shannon senses that this untamed land will give her new strength and the freedom to love the one man who can fulfill her wild desire.

___52306-X $5.50 US/$6.50 CAN

BRAVE LAND, BRAVE LOVE

CONNIE MASON

Brave, bold and brash are the traits of the men bred in the land down under, and there is none braver than Ben Penrod. Though Ben is heir to the vast Australian holdings of Penrod station, he has no intention of saddling himself with a wife ...until he meets his match in the most alluring and contrary creature he's ever beheld. With hair like moonbeams and eyes like aquamarines, Tia is only as big as a child, yet her lush curves proclaim her as all woman. And instead of being pursued, Ben finds himself being refused by the one woman who captured his heart for all time!

___52282-9 $5.50 US/$6.50 CAN

Dorchester Publishing Co., Inc.
P.O. Box 6640
Wayne, PA 19087-8640

Please add $1.75 for shipping and handling for the first book and $.50 for each book thereafter. NY, NYC, and PA residents, please add appropriate sales tax. No cash, stamps, or C.O.D.s. All orders shipped within 6 weeks via postal service book rate. Canadian orders require $2.00 extra postage and must be paid in U.S. dollars through a U.S. banking facility.

Name_____
Address_____
City_____State_____Zip_____
I have enclosed $_____ in payment for the checked book(s).
Payment <u>must</u> accompany all orders. ❑ Please send a free catalog.
    CHECK OUT OUR WEBSITE! www.dorchesterpub.com

WILD LAND, WILD LOVE

CONNIE MASON

Australia in 1812 is a virgin land waiting to be explored, a wild frontier peopled by even wilder men, a place where a defenseless woman risks both her virtue and her life. But hot-tempered, high-spirited Kate McKenzie is sure she can survive in Australia on her own ... until she meets her match in Robin Fletcher. In the brawny arms of the former convict she discovers that a defenseless woman can have the time of her life losing her virtue to the right man.

___52278-0 $5.50 US/$6.50 CAN

Dorchester Publishing Co., Inc.
P.O. Box 6640
Wayne, PA 19087-8640

Please add $1.75 for shipping and handling for the first book and $.50 for each book thereafter. NY, NYC, and PA residents, please add appropriate sales tax. No cash, stamps, or C.O.D.s. All orders shipped within 6 weeks via postal service book rate. Canadian orders require $2.00 extra postage and must be paid in U.S. dollars through a U.S. banking facility.

Name_____
Address_____
City_____State_____Zip_____
I have enclosed $_____ in payment for the checked book(s).
Payment <u>must</u> accompany all orders. ☐ Please send a free catalog.
  CHECK OUT OUR WEBSITE! www.dorchesterpub.com

CONNIE MASON

BOLD LAND BOLD LOVE

New South Wales in 1807 is a vast land of wild beauty and wilder passions: a frontier as yet untamed by man; a place where women have few rights and fewer pleasures. For a female convict like flame-haired Casey O'Cain, it is a living nightmare. And from the first, arrogant, handsome Dare Penrod makes it clear what he wants of her. Casey knows she should fight him with every breath in her body, but her heart tells her he can make a paradise of this wilderness for her.

___52274-8 $5.99 US/$6.99 CAN

SIERRA
Connie Mason
Bestselling Author Of *Wind Rider*

Fresh from finishing school, Sierra Alden is the toast of the Barbary Coast. And everybody knows a proper lady doesn't go traipsing through untamed lands with a perfect stranger, especially one as devilishly handsome as Ramsey Hunter. But Sierra believes the rumors that say that her long-lost brother and sister are living in Denver, and she will imperil her reputation and her heart to find them.

Ram isn't the type of man to let a woman boss him around. Yet from the instant he spies Sierra on the muddy streets of San Francisco, she turns his life upside down. Before long, he is her unwilling guide across the wilderness and her more-than-willing tutor in the ways of love. But sweet words and gentle kisses aren't enough to claim the love of the delicious temptation called Sierra.

__3815-3 $5.99 US/$6.99 CAN